# PRIMROSE HILL

G J BELLAMY

ISBN: 9798871078761

This publication is a work of fiction. All names, characters and events in this publication, other than those clearly in the public domain, are fictitious and any resemblance to real persons, living or dead, or actual events is purely coincidental.

Copyright © 2023 by G J Bellamy. All rights reserved.

The moral right of the author has been asserted.

No part of this publication may be reproduced, stored in a retrieval system, or transmitted in any form or by any means, without the prior express written permission of the publisher.

G J Bellamy

gjbellamy.com

For
Barry and Edna

# Contents

| | |
|---|---:|
| Introduction | VII |
| Cast of Characters, Maps | IX |
| 1. An ordinary day at the agency | 1 |
| 2. Touring the scene | 13 |
| 3. Settling in | 28 |
| 4. Biscuit | 43 |
| 5. Visitors | 56 |
| 6. Meeting the gang | 68 |
| 7. Sightings | 81 |
| 8. Chasing 'round the shops | 93 |
| 9. A walk in the park | 108 |
| 10. Many, many biscuits | 122 |
| 11. A stranger in the garden | 133 |
| 12. Embarrassment | 150 |
| 13. Sunday spies | 167 |
| 14. Among the animals | 180 |
| 15. Who is watching whom? | 191 |

| | | |
|---|---|---|
| 16. | Shouting the odds | 201 |
| 17. | Brittany in Britain | 215 |
| 18. | A whiff of something | 227 |
| 19. | Awkwardness | 242 |
| 20. | The Old Country | 253 |
| 21. | Shockwaves | 267 |
| 22. | Visiting hour | 284 |
| 23. | What are the odds now? | 299 |
| 24. | Gossip | 313 |
| 25. | St. George's Square | 325 |
| 26. | Indian Extravaganza | 336 |
| 27. | Disappearing act | 348 |
| 28. | Another disappearance | 358 |
| 29. | All change | 371 |
| 30. | Going for a walk | 384 |
| 31. | The fog clears | 392 |
| 32. | Camden Lock | 399 |
| Epilogue | | 416 |
| Also By G J Bellamy | | 430 |

# Introduction

If you're new to the series, or it has been a while since you read an installment, here's a little (re-) introduction to the background and setting of Burgoyne's and the secret agency hidden within it.

Sophie started her domestic service and typing firm within the last twelve months. During that time, she and her staff have been involved in a number of 'special' cases. These operations have usually divided into two parts.

Penrose, Superintendent of Special Duties, acts as the co-ordinator for Scotland Yard in the case, and usually employs Burgoyne's staff members to work as domestic servants while they are spying for the police. In the field, Sophie reports to Detective Inspector Morton and Detective Sergeant Gowers.

Often, Archie Drysdale of the Foreign Office — Sophie's cousin — has Burgoyne's investigating foreign spies.

Penrose and Drysdale work together in a small, loose network of agents that can react quickly to foreign or domestic threats. Drysdale is a spymaster. Sophie reports to him, keeping him informed on their foreign spy intelligence-gathering efforts. The police and spy cases often overlap.

Sometimes, the Home Office is also involved because its jurisdiction differs from that of the FO. Purely concerned with threats within the British Isles, the HO does, however, possess more assets and personnel than the FO, and so takes the lead in any operation. Lord Laneford of the Home Office is Archie Drydale's counterpart within the network.

Sophie's core spy team comprises herself, Ada — a trained servant, and Flora — an actress and Sophie's school-friend. Frequently assisting are Lady Shelling (Sophie's Aunt) with whom Sophie lives when in London, and Elizabeth, a researcher, who works in the agency's offices.

While the cases are ongoing, Sophie still has the headache of running her typing and domestic service business, while trying to keep her secret work hidden.

# Cast of Characters, Maps

**Family & Friends**
Sophie Burgoyne / Phoebe King
Henry Burgoyne, vicar - Sophie's father
Lady Shelling (Elizabeth Burgoyne) - Auntie Bessie
Ada McMahon / Nancy Carmichael - Sophie's friend
Flora Dane / Gladys Walton - Sophie's long-time friend
Archie Drysdale - Sophie's second cousin

**The Agency**
Miss Jones, typist and office manageress
Elizabeth Banks, researcher and office helper
Nick, errand boy

**White Lyon Yard**
Hawkins, butler
Marsden, footman

**Alexandra Gardens**
David Saunders, banker, 31. Number 12. Dog: Ginnie, English setter.

Colleen Saunders, 25, David's wife and is expecting her first born.

Captain Bristow, 43, Royal Navy retired. Number 14. Dog: Bo'sun, Newfoundland.

Alan Mellish, 32, chemist. Number 19. Dog: Topper, Jack Russell.

Mrs Cynthia Fitch, widow, 46. Number 24. Dog: Titus, Labrador retriever.
Major Neville Cummings, 64. Number 9. Dog: Vindaloo, Irish terrier.
Grigory Kuritsyn, 34, communist. Number 15. Dog: Vova, Bloodhound.
Dulcie Villard, 28, coiffeuse. Number 2. Dog: Lulu, Poodle.
Mrs Sandra Pringle, 33, widow. Number 20. Dog: Nankin, Pekinese.
Charles Clark, 40, composer and musician. Number 1. Dog: Bertie, Basset hound.

**St. George's Square**
Mrs Murray. Dog: Cherry.
Miss Boddington. Dog: Imp.
Matthew Hamilton, 34, the victim. Dog: Georgie, Shetland sheepdog (Sheltie).

**Scotland Yard and Government Departments**
Superintendent of Special Duties (Inspector) Penrose
Inspector Morton, CID
Sergeant Gowers, CID
Ralph 'Sinjin' Yardley, Foreign Office agent
Len Feather, Yardley's chauffeur, Foreign Office agent
Lord Sidney Laneford, Home Office

PRIMROSE HILL    xi

## Map of Alexandra Gardens

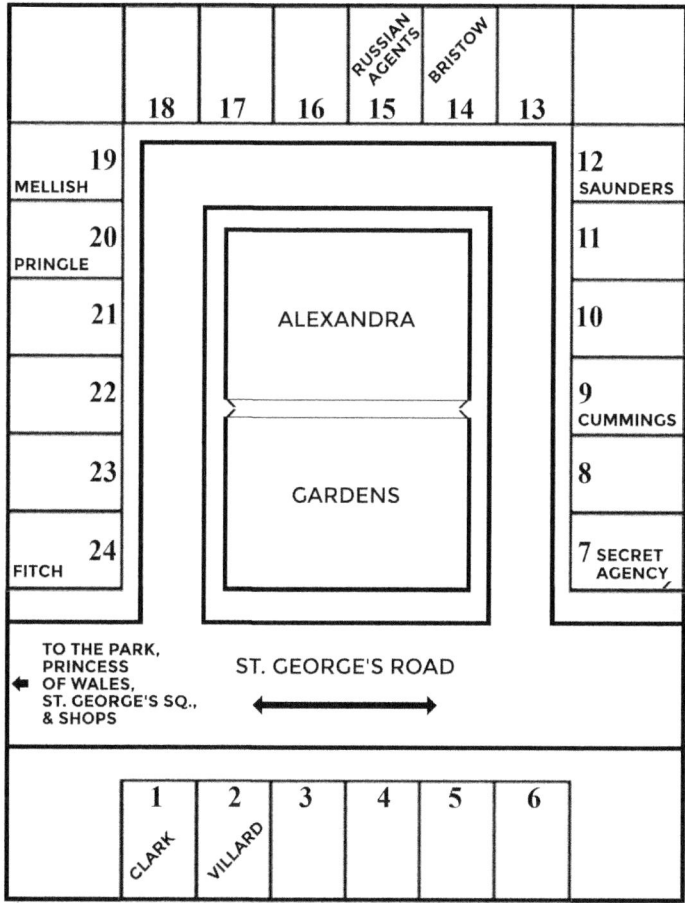

## Map of Primrose Hill

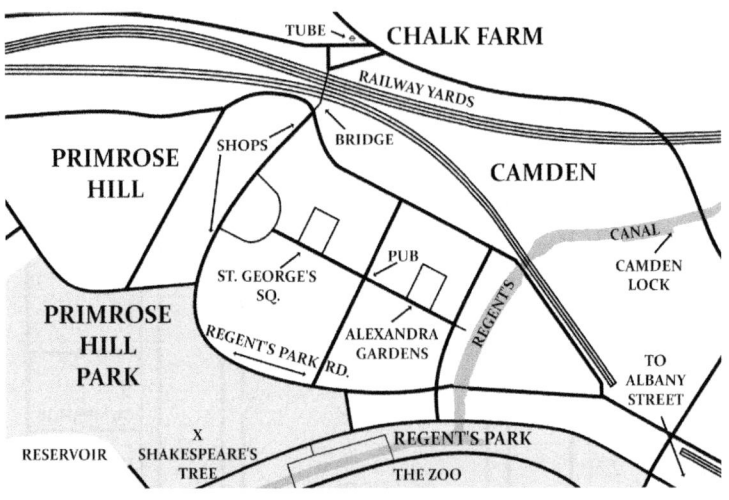

# Chapter 1

# An Ordinary Day at the Agency

Looking south from the rounded top of Primrose Hill Park, only the parts of London which extend above the trees can be seen. It is a sweeping vista of spires, St. Paul's dome, factory chimneys, Nelson's Column, and, hiding the rooftops, a hazy smoke that thickens with distance. The big sky overhead imbues one with an on-top-of-the-world feeling.

On Monday night, the 28$^{th}$ of February, 1921, an enveloping fog hid the glow of the city. It was white, therefore recently formed, and yet to mix fully with the smoke from a million chimneys. Down by the distant river Thames, where the densest fog lay, it would soon turn to a breath-stealing pea-souper. However, up on airy Primrose Hill, where the advance of the polluting effect was slower to take hold and would be weaker in effect, the fog might even lift before becoming noticeably tainted. Despite that, it appeared to be a good solid 'London Particular' in the making, and it played havoc with pedestrians and traffic alike.

Cinder paths criss-crossed the park. At just after seven, Mr Saunders, about thirty-years-old, was walking his dog, an English setter. They kept close to the boundary fence where there were more street lamps. His usual habit was to make for the top of the hill, but there was no point tonight — there would be nothing to see. The dog needed exercise, therefore the man had to go out, but it was no night for making a long excursion out of the necessity.

The intervals between lamps were longer inside the park. The only way the dog-walker could save himself from becoming disorientated was by ensuring the path was always underfoot. Light from the lamps did nothing, as it only radiated a yard before failing. However, he knew the area like the back of his hand, which he could still see, and his dog knew where she was by her own methods. Although they were not lost in the dark mist, it was far from enjoyable for either of them to be out.

"Colleen was right about the fog being worse in the park," said Saunders to his dog. "It's no good, Ginnie, old girl. We'll have to turn back."

Their walk abandoned, they retraced their steps in a north-east direction. On the other side of the nearby fence lay Primrose Hill Road. This curved boundary road was one of a matched pair with Regent's Park Road. Where the roads met at a crossroads, they formed a point, and here, in a corner, lay a park entrance for which Saunders was now heading. Very few people were out, and the enveloping mist made such stray sounds as there were seem distant, often issuing from unexpected directions.

An unseen car crawled through the crossroads to the accompaniment of a man giving a stream of instructions. "Turn the wheel a touch to the left… That's it… Straighten up, or you'll be in the park." The speaker was outside the vehicle, and guiding it by following the kerb. Saunders waited by the park gate to allow the car to pass, wondering who it was driving, having assumed they must be local men trying to get home. The car passed, and its noise soon diminished. He tentatively stepped off the pavement.

It was easier for man and dog to walk along the pavement because of the line of iron railings that protected pedestrians from the drop to the basement areas where were found the entrances for servants and tradesmen. After less than a hundred yards, the street terminated by intersecting with short and twisting Chalcot Crescent. The unbroken terraces of three-story houses shrouded in mist were relieved only by the occasional soft glow of interior lamps — some lower, some higher. This suggested to Saunders that he walked in a narrow defile or gorge wherein the towering cliffs to his side were occupied by cave-dwellers. When he passed one of the infrequent gaps between the houses, he stared into a nothingness that was neither fog nor night.

Saunders well knew the next intersection where a curved street and the open side of a square lay adjacent to each another and so formed a stretch of road of very surprising width because it bore no relation to the volume of local traffic that used it. This feature, obvious by day or lamp-lit night, had now disappeared so completely that Saunders, although certain of where he stood, was sufficiently disorientated that he had to search for the street sign. He found it on the iron fence outside the first house in the square.

"Fog's getting worse." He stooped to peer. "Of *course*, this is St George's Square... We're in the home stretch, Ginnie."

They passed by a dozen tall houses and left the square. Ten more houses brought them to the crossroads of St. George's Road and Fitzroy. Diagonally opposite, yet hidden, lay The Princess of Wales public house. It was quiet, with no traffic about. They began crossing. The instant they were in the road, the dog started acting up by whining and pulling.

"What's the matter, Ginnie? Can you hear another dog, eh...? I wonder who that would be, out in this weather?"

Saunders then heard a dog's bark from somewhere close to the public house. A man's yell of pain followed.

"Hello! I say, is everything all right!?" Startled and feeling apprehensive, Saunders called, but received no answer while crossing the road to the Princess. A Sheltie suddenly appeared out of the fog, stopped a moment at Saunders' feet, and then scampered away to bark nearby. Saunders followed.

He found a prostrate man. The light from a house outlined his hatless form, but revealed few details. Saunders knew who it was, though — knew him by his overcoat and thick head of hair. He knew the dog, too. Now Saunders could add to his knowledge that the man was dead. Ten or twenty yards away, it was difficult for Saunders to say because of the fog, there sounded the deep clang of some heavy metal item striking the railings. He thought someone began running, but was not entirely sure. Within a few seconds, he gathered his wits and entered the public house to telephone the police.

"Good Morning, Miss Burgoyne," said the fruiterer, standing by his stall near the crossroads in covered Leadenhall Market. He displayed his wares on a wide, raised and slanting stand, which made it look as if a giant cornucopia had spilled all its contents in an orderly fashion. The cascade of colour and the variety of forms attracted the gaze while the complicated scent of all the differing fruit combined to whisper the word 'fresh'.

"Good morning, Bob," she answered. The early morning sun streamed through the glass roof high overhead, illuminating the tops of the two-story buildings on the western side of the avenue.

"What'll you 'ave today? Fancy some nice tangerines? They're very sweet and very juicy. Come off the boat from Morocco yesterday."

"Just think of that," said Sophie, impressed and smiling. "I'll take a dozen." She often stopped to get fruit for the office and to take home to White Lyon Yard.

"Very good, miss." A stream of city workers on their way to work entered from Gracechurch Street, then passed through the market to reach Lime Street — the hub of Britain's insurance industry.

"And two pounds of grapes and some bananas, please."

"I 'ave to say, your ladies at the office do like their bananas... How about this nice-looking bunch?" He picked some up.

"Yes, perfect, and the bunch that was next to it." She looked over the fruit. "Bob? What is this?" Sophie had picked up a large green and red fruit that filled her gloved hand.

"You are 'olding a mango from Trinidad, and it's in perfect condition. I don't carry 'em often, 'cause demand's tepid at best. But give yourself a treat, Miss Burgoyne, because they are truly *de-licious*. They're good for you. Messy and 'ard to cut on account of the big stone inside, but well worth the trouble taken. You'll come back and thank me. Of that, I'm sure."

"Sold!" Sophie laughed. She selected two more mangoes, then handed them to Bob to be put in a paper bag. A queue formed behind her, so she quickly finished her transaction. Mindful of her heavy shopping bag full of fruit, she left the market via Lime Street Passage. This passage was no length at all. When it connected with narrow Lime Street, Sophie knew she must face 'The Onslaught.' That was how she thought of the fifty yards of Lime Street, packed with rapidly walking insurance clerks, brokers, and underwriters, all heading in the same direction. Usually, one dared not go against the flow but, two or three mornings every week, Sophie did just that.

The flow of commuters made it impossible for her to contest the right of way on Lime Street's narrow pavements. Instead, she could walk in the road because vehicles shunned the street in rush hours. There the pedestrian traffic was lighter, but there, also to be found, was that most dangerous and unpredictable of insurance workers — the runner. Perhaps he was late, or he suffered from claustrophobia and sprinted to escape the seething street. Perhaps he just did it for the exercise. Sophie had been in several collisions already. She found that the only way to avoid a scene and the ridiculous hat-lifted apology that followed, was to hold to the centre of the street, proceed slowly, and glare at each runner and potential accident-causer as he approached. Now that walking in the middle of Lime Street and glaring was her established habit, and running erratically was theirs, they learned to avoid her. The runners understood that the well-dressed young woman carrying the bag of fruit must be given a wide berth. Those with whom she had previously collided did not wish to hear again Sophie's stinging delivery of 'You should look where you're going!' which also had given them the distinct impression that they were about to be walloped with a bag of fruit.

Sophie proceeded fearlessly, but with caution. Crossing Fenchurch Street during the morning rush was another arduous task fraught with danger. Without incident, she made it over to the relative calm of Philpot Lane and began enjoying her walk again. Spring had arrived in London, and the air was noticeably sweeter. The weather had produced several false starts but, by Tuesday, 22nd March, 1921, it could be said that spring was here to stay — if one kept one's fingers crossed.

Soon she was walking south on St Martin's Lane, and could see ahead the agency's offices at the corner of Sack Lane. The glow of morning light was kind to the old buildings in the area and made them look their best. Sophie entered and ascended the staircase. In the agency, she immediately encountered Miss Jones.

"Good morning, Miss Burgoyne," said the rather severe-looking lady.

"Good morning, Miss Jones. And a beautiful morning it is, too."

"Very much so, Miss Burgoyne. The better weather makes *all* the difference."

"Doesn't it? I've got something new. Have you ever tried a mango?"

"No. I can't say I've ever even seen one."

"*That* can be immediately rectified." Sophie rummaged in her bag. "I'd never seen one before, either." She produced a mango. "There."

"Oh, fancy that. It's a funny-looking thing. Do you think it's sweet?"

"I sincerely hope so. If not, I'll be having a word with Bob, who convinced me they're worth trying. He's usually very reliable." Sophie put the fruit away. "We shall conduct our taste-testing experiment later. Is everything all right?"

"Everything is just fine, Miss Burgoyne."

The telephone rang. Sophie almost jumped. As she was nearest to the instrument, she answered the call.

"Hello, Archie... Yes, I'm in the office all day... I'll see you later, then... Goodbye." Sophie replaced the receiver and said to Miss Jones. "That was Mr Drysdale."

"I thought it was," replied Miss Jones. "I must get on with my work. My girls will be here soon." She turned and left.

While putting the fruit in a bowl and then going to her office, Sophie wondered how much Miss Jones knew of the agency's secret operations. An unobservant person must have noticed something in the recent months, and the office manageress was far from being unobservant. Sophie supposed there was a serious conversation pending, one she would rather put off from having altogether, but which would inevitably come to pass.

Archie arrived at ten. Elizabeth showed him to Sophie's office and shut the door once he was inside.

"It takes a lot to winkle you out of your shell," said Sophie. "Why the unexpected honour?"

"I consider it to be spring now, and it is the season for me to find or fabricate excuses to get out of the office as often as possible. London is so much the better when the weather's pleasant."

"I'd say it is. But you're here for a reason, aren't you?"

"Of course. As a captain of the typing and domestic service industries, your time is undoubtedly valuable, so I shan't waste it. I'm here in the capacity of spokesman on behalf of the FO, HO, and Yard. A little jointly run scheme we had popping along blew up in our faces last Friday. We had a man on the spot at a certain place. He was keeping watch upon several individuals. By a sheer fluke, he was unmasked and made known to the very parties we are interested in."

"How annoying."

"Yes, very. So we took to kicking the matter about between us, when Penrose mentioned that perhaps someone from your agency might be brought in. We all decided that was a good idea, in part because we couldn't really think of anything else to do."

"Is that a compliment or an insult?"

"Neither. It is more a testimony to our dull imaginations than anything else. When Penrose mentioned Burgoyne's, it seemed to all the perfect solution."

"That's more like it. I prefer the agency being seen as the perfect solution."

Archie smiled. "There are two operations combined into one... Sorry to be vague, Soap, but, because so many departments are involved, you must agree to the undertaking before I can tell you what it is."

"Not more absurdity?"

"There must always be some. With three governmental bodies involved, you can hardly expect anything less."

"What if I retract my agreement should I not care for the proposition once it's explained to me?"

"That's hardly sporting, old thing. Permit me to champion my cause, so to speak. There is *no* danger involved. The job is static in nature. All costs except food and travel are covered and the operation will run for approximately ten days. Plus, I have an idea you will enjoy the work, certain elements anyway. The pay is eight pounds per day. Three people are needed because it involves around the clock surveillance."

"Am I correct in thinking that there is no domestic service required in this operation?"

"You are correct."

"Hmm... Two operations... Ten days is much too long for me to be away from the office."

"The place is only a twenty-minute tube ride and a half-hour walk from here."

"Ah... What intrigues me are these supposedly *enjoyable* elements you mentioned."

"Soap, you must accept the work first."

"You're just like Superintendent Penrose. He does this 'say yes, first' business to me, too, and I think it's so unfair. Very well, I accept."

"Excellent. I knew you would."

"I'm glad I'm so predictable. Honestly, I feel as though I'm being treated like a trained dog."

"Interesting you should choose such an expression. In Primrose Hill, there is a charming little garden square..."

"Where is Primrose Hill? I've seen the name."

"North of Regent's Park, you will find Primrose Hill Park. In a sort of semi-circle on the northern and eastern sides is the suburb of Primrose Hill."

"I'm much obliged. Please continue."

"Yes, the particular place is called Alexandra Gardens. Twenty-four houses face it. Burgoyne's shall be stationed at number seven. You will possess the whole of the rather pretty three-story house with a basement area below. It is in good repair, comes fully furnished, and is tastefully decorated."

"*Ooh*," said Sophie, "that sounds rather nice."

"It is. The area was once quite fashionable but, at present, it is in somewhat of a decline. Several houses in the square are quite dilapidated — a result of war-time economies and the slump in house prices. It may pull back up, or it might sink further. We shall see. I'll tell you this much — in the strictest of confidence, mind you. I have half a mind to buy a place in the area."

"Ah...! Don't say it's for you and Victoria?"

"Shh. You mustn't repeat it to Bessie *or* Flora."

"I won't. But how *lovely*. Have you found a particular house?"

"Yes. You'll be staying in it. So take good care in case I eventually buy the place. Victoria has to see it first, of course."

"Oh, absolutely. We shall take the greatest care."

"Right. So, at number fifteen, which is in a state of *dis*-repair, there lives a snug little nest of six foreign communists. They are relatively harmless, except their propaganda is occasionally treasonous. These fellows often supply British communist sympathizers with vetted news stories from Russia and glowing reports about Comrade Lenin's revolutionary pontifications. We know their names, where they go, and what they get up to. This operation is not so much about them. We are, instead, expecting the arrival of a senior Russian agent. The house is being watched for his advent, and your agency will take over the watch. This gentleman is coming to Britain to establish a spy network. At the moment, we don't know who he is, or what he looks like. Our information indicates his stay at number fifteen Alexandra Gardens will be a brief one. However, on this point we *are* certain — he will arrive between the first and seventh of April. We expect him to find his own place to live shortly afterwards."

"Hold on a second. Wasn't the Anglo-Soviet Trade Agreement signed just the other day? Aren't Russia and Britain the best of friends now? Although I don't quite see how it's possible."

"Yes, Lloyd George got the blockade on Russia dropped, and the agreement was signed, but we're still not friends, despite the hearty handshakes all round. That agreement is really based upon a deeply profound and mutually held distrust. Hence, we shall now both employ agents to find out what we really think of one another. Our job, now your job, is to identify the Russian agent. We must do this as early as possible, before he begins recruiting and gets everyone running off with our secrets. Naturally, we must know who he is first. Then we can turn him into a double agent, if he is indeed open to being turned."

"Will the people at number fifteen know this agent is a spy?"

"I doubt it, although they might speculate he is."

"Hmm... How was the FO agent discovered?"

"I didn't say he was an FO agent."

"Very well, then. How was the HO agent discovered?"

"I didn't say he was an HO agent."

"You're making things unnecessarily difficult, Archie. How was the man discovered?"

"He accidentally dropped his notebook in front of number fifteen, and a Polish communist picked it up."

"Oh, *la*, that would do it."

"As it most decidedly did. Although, the agent assures us his notebook only documented the comings and goings of the current occupants. The hapless fellow and his assistant will stay in place for another couple of days, and leave before the end of March. Your agency shall take up residence on the first of April, as though you are the new tenants arriving at the beginning of the month."

"This all sounds very interesting," said Sophie. "What, exactly, do we do?"

"There is no access to number fifteen from the back, so only the front door needs to be monitored."

"By using binoculars?"

"Yes. Number seven doesn't have a working telephone line, so we'll use couriers. The idea is this. Starting April the first, someone will follow every new visitor who leaves number fifteen, having been alerted by you. We need not bother with previously identified visitors, only the new faces."

"Supposing the Russian agent comes and goes at night? We might not get a description of him."

"Then there will be some rather fruitless chasing about by the four men stationed in a house around the corner. They are already familiar with the inhabitants and the regular visitors."

"Ah, I see. All this effort being expended means it's terribly important."

"Quite so. If the Russian agent escapes us here, we might not find him again. We could detain and question the inhabitants of number fifteen in an effort to locate him, but that would tip off senior Cheka officials in Moscow."

"Cheka?"

"A brutal bunch of fellows who are the Russian secret police. They manage a wide range of security matters. The man who is coming is likely to be a trusted Cheka officer. Alternatively, he may be a Russian citizen who has established connections in Britain. We just don't know."

"And, I suppose," mused Sophie, "in not knowing who he is, you can't follow him from the port."

"True, and he may even be in the country already. All we know is that he will arrive at Alexandra Gardens in the first week of April."

"Have you any thoughts about what our cover story should be?" asked Sophie.

"Yes, we have a few ideas. However, your question brings me to the other purpose of this operation. Scotland Yard is investigating a murder on St George's Road, Primrose Hill.

It occurred in February, and the case has since run into difficulties. The Yard believes the murderer lives in Alexandra Gardens."

"Good Heavens!" exclaimed Sophie. "And you're thinking of buying a house there?"

"Conditional upon the murderer being caught, and Victoria's heartfelt approval. Properties in Primrose Hill are reasonably cheap, at present."

## Chapter 2

## Touring the scene

In the afternoon, Sophie went to see Superintendent Penrose at Scotland Yard. There, she was to be briefed on the police operation in Alexandra Gardens.

"Let me get a chair for you," said Penrose. He stood up quickly to remove a substantial pile of case files from one of the visitors' chairs.

"Are you having a spring clean?" asked Sophie.

"I wish I were," he answered. "Sorry about this mess, but we're chasing a fella who's escaped from prison. As you can see, he's led a busy life." Penrose put the files down on top of another pile. "The man's desperate, and it's likely he's had help from family, friends, or associates. We went through the files to draw up a list o' the same. Hasn't helped. He's still missing, and nobody's seen him. I'll tell you summat. His mother's lying, but I wouldn't expect her to do otherwise."

Sophie and Penrose seated themselves.

"Now, Miss Burgoyne. Thank you for coming about this Alexandra Gardens business."

"I'm finding it intriguing — doubly so. May I ask if you are aware of the *other* operation?"

"Number fifteen is full of Soviet sympathisers, and we're waiting on a Russian chap to start a spying operation against the government."

"That's good. Clears the air, doesn't it? One thing that has been bothering me is where does the Home Office fit in?"

"They're paying the lease on number seven because of their interest in the residents at number fifteen. They also want to be kept up to date on what happens."

"And the Foreign Office is only interested in the Russian spy?"

"That's it. Until he takes up permanent residency, anyway. Then the HO will take over. The Yard's interest is confined to the murder investigation only."

"I must have missed seeing the story in the newspapers."

"Not surprising, because it only came out piecemeal. We weren't sure if it was an accident or murder at first, so the newspapers only gave a brief report of an accident. The autopsy ruled that out, but the papers didn't pay attention to the case again until after the inquest, which determined it was murder."

"That's why I missed it. Well, Inspector, what can you tell me?" Sophie sounded bright, and her eager look showed she was ready to get started.

"Matthew Hamilton is the deceased's name. Aged 34, worked in an advertising agency as a copywriter, and his employer said he did his job well. For the last eighteen months, he lived in a flat in St. George's Square, which is very close to Alexandra Gardens. Six, no, seven months ago now, he ended a long-standing relationship. The lady in question moved to Scotland, so we don't consider her to be a suspect. Truth is, we *have* no suspects, but let's press on."

Penrose shifted in his chair. "Do you remember a foggy night on Monday, twenty-eighth of February?"

"Ah... I missed it. I was in Havering-under-Lyme until the Wednesday. It was my father's birthday, you see, so we had a little celebration."

"That sounds very nice." Penrose smiled. "So the fog was quite bad overnight, but it cleared out the next day. Mr Hamilton went out with his Shetland sheepdog — some call them a Sheltie — at ten to seven on Monday evening. Two other tenants in the building heard him leave. One tenant said she expected him back within a quarter hour — because he was only walking the dog, you understand. Out he went, and despite our extensive enquiries, no one saw him again until twenty-five past seven, by which time he was dead."

"Then he was outside for thirty-five minutes," said Sophie.

"And he was discovered a minute's walk away from his home, although it would have taken longer on account of the fog."

"Then either he was lost, or had visited someone."

"That's what we thought. I doubt he was lost, because he was familiar with the area. A man named Saunders discovered his body only a hundred yards from Hamilton's flat."

"What about Mr Saunders?"

Penrose smiled again. "David Saunders lives in Alexandra Gardens with his wife, Colleen. They have a nice English setter. I recall that you quite like dogs, Miss Burgoyne."

"Oh, yes. We always had one until three years ago."

"That's helpful, and I'll explain why in a moment. Saunders has no motive. Although he knew Hamilton slightly, being fellow dog owners, he knew him no further than that. Mr Saunders is happily married and a senior clerk at Coutts & Co. The bank informed us that, when it opens its next branch, Saunders will be the manager. Only, he doesn't know yet. Besides that, he has some savings, a mortgage on the house, and a baby on the way."

"He doesn't sound like a murderer to me."

"We try to keep an open mind, but no, he seems all wrong for the part. Now, Miss Burgoyne, would you mind my explaining *how* Hamilton was killed? It wasn't particularly grisly, but all murders are upsetting to some extent."

"I think I can bear it."

"Hamilton was struck once and it broke his neck. One vertebra was completely crushed. Death wasn't instantaneous, but occurred while he was unconscious by means of internal bleeding. At first, the detective in charge of the case thought he may have fallen awkwardly, allowing his neck to hit the edge of the kerb. But that doesn't tally with where Hamilton ended up, which was against some railings. When the pathologist gave evidence at the inquest, he stated Hamilton was struck forcibly with a heavy, metallic object possessing a continuous, unsharpened edge of at least five inches, and that he would have immediately collapsed. He wouldn't commit to anything more than that. Privately, he said the weapon used must be something like the rear face of an axe, but probably with a convex curve to it. He suggested that, if the murderer stood further back, he might have used a steel rod. He also explained that the blow landed horizontally, so there's no telling if the assailant was directly behind or to one side, or shorter or taller than Hamilton, who was five feet ten inches tall."

"How ghastly... What about mechanics' tools?"

"It may be — the shaft of a large spanner would be about right for the wound, but seeing as no weapon was recovered, we're only guessing."

"So there's no point in conjecture."

"Not until we have a suspect. Now here's what we do know. Hamilton was wearing a heavy, well-worn overcoat. In the pockets were a socialist tract, a list of very strange homeopathic medicines, the stub of a cinema ticket, a program for Cruft's dog show, which has taken place since the murder, and a business card for a coiffeuse who does house calls. That's only a fancy name for a hairdresser, but there you go. Among all this rubbish accumulated in his pockets are things that point to several people in the area. After going through all the statements we've taken, how I see it is like this. When Hamilton used to take his dog for walks, he got chatting to various other parties, who also have dogs. While a party is explaining something they're interested in, they hand Hamilton a bit of paper, and he puts it in his pocket, but leaves it there. We can trace each of those articles back to a specific person in Alexandra Gardens, although the Cruft's program could also be from someone in St. George's Square. It's like there's an unofficial dog-walking club. Anyone who wants to be numbered among them must have a dog. Therefore, you'll need to have a dog."

"But I don't have one."

"Don't you worry about that, Miss Burgoyne. We'll find you a nice quiet police dog."

"Oh. Are police dogs nice and quiet, then?"

"The one we'll lend you will be. The dog will be your excuse to get close to and be friendly with the others in the Gardens."

"That's novel."

"I'm quite pleased with the notion, because it's my idea." Penrose laughed. "You don't mind, then?"

"I don't see why I should... You seem to be fixed upon dog owners."

"I am. What do you think a CereBone might be?"

"Um... A dog biscuit?"

"Exactly that. They're bone-shaped and about three inches long. There's a fella named Mellish in Alexandra Gardens who makes 'em. He says they're in the testing stage and, to that purpose, he handed out a bagful to every dog owner living nearby. So Hamilton had a bag in his coat. He'd broken the biscuits to make them easier for his Sheltie to chew. There were seven pieces remaining. Saunders, the witness, had his bag with two biscuits left in it. A constable saw him give one to his dog in the pub. Next to Hamilton's body lay a third bag, but it was empty. Now, with one bag distributed to each dog owner, the empty crumpled bag, which was not soaked through or otherwise damaged when recovered, probably belongs to the murderer who therefore must be a dog owner." He picked up his pipe. "Mellish made up ten bags from his test batch — two for himself and he distributed eight bags in Alexandra Gardens. Also, Saunders having a bag lets him off the hook."

"How fascinating... Ah, Inspector. Did anyone enquire about the quantity of remaining biscuits among the other dog owners?"

"They did. It appears the canines of Primrose Hill are partial to their CereBones. They ate them all. By the time we questioned them, every owner had thrown away their empty bag. Now there's one more part to tell. Saunders was coming back from the park when he heard a dog bark followed by a man's yell. Hamilton's Sheltie appeared out of the mist by the Princess of Wales public house and then disappeared into it again. Saunders found Hamilton's body a moment later. Then he heard someone moving away in the fog. Next, he heard the clang of a metal object striking the railings about twenty feet from where he was standing. He believes the person was running, but can't be sure. The point he is certain about is that the murderer was moving towards Alexandra Gardens in the fog. He then telephoned the police."

"Dear me, what a dreadful business… What happened to the dog?"

"They're looking after it at the pub. The locals have taken it to their hearts, in a manner of speaking, so it won't want for a home. Apparently, Hamilton's family doesn't care for dogs."

"Then if no one else appears to have a compelling motive," said Sophie, "the murderer, it seems, lives in Alexandra Gardens. So our job is to become dog owners to gain their confidence and, hopefully, gather information to narrow the list of suspects."

"If you could whittle it down to just the one, I'd be much obliged."

Sophie laughed. "We shall certainly try, Inspector."

"Before we go over the details, a word of caution. The Communists at number fifteen have a dog, and they also received a bag of biscuits. So you'll be meeting the very people whom you are also to watch for the spy operation."

"Then we shall be extraordinarily careful in how we conduct ourselves."

"I'm sure you will. They're a suspicious lot — they believe they're being persecuted or summat. That's why we reckoned two or three ladies from Burgoyne's would be unlikely to make them jumpy."

"We'll try not to frighten them," said Sophie with a smile.

"I don't suppose you will. Right, shall we get down to brass tacks, then?"

"Nick. A moment, please." Sophie called the fourteen-year-old messenger to her office. She shut the door when he was inside. "Take these notes to Flora and Ada."

"Yes, miss." He took the notes. "Another *special* is it?"

"You are correct."

"Do you think you could fit me in somewhere, miss? I mean, everyone else gets to go, and it's hard on a fella to be left out of things."

"I can appreciate your feeling that way. It so happens there may be something for you to do this time. Where we're going, there will be no domestic service involved. Have you ever been to Primrose Hill before?"

"That's that park, isn't it? No, the nearest I've been is Camden. I delivered some typing to this right funny place. A round warehouse that used to be a railway shed, and the bloke there looked shifty to me."

"One of our clients looks shifty? Which one?"

"No, it wasn't a client. It was a job for old Plunkett, and he asked me to take it to Camden for him. He gave me a tanner, so I did… I was on me lunch, miss, so I wasn't diddling you or nothing."

"I'm relieved to hear it. Where we're going is close to the park. I've yet to see the place, but it's possible I *may* need you to deliver messages. Don't get too excited; it's only a possibility."

"I hope it comes off." Nick looked at the envelopes. "I see from this envelope that Miss Flora's at her house, rather than at the theatre. Has she really taken up with Lord Laneford?"

"Nicholas, you shall not pass comment on Miss Dane, or anyone else, for that matter… How on earth did you find that out?"

"I don't remember," said Nick, looking particularly innocent at that moment. "But I have eyes and ears, miss, and I can hardly help what I *see*."

Sophie narrowed her gaze. "Have you been listening at doors?"

"Yes, miss. Nobody tells me nothing. So how am I to find out? Shows you how good I am at sneaking about."

"You mustn't do that. This is grounds for me to dismiss you."

"I know, miss. I ain't stupid, and I wouldn't do it normally. You see, I'd like to be a spy an' all. So how am I to get the job without practising first?"

"I employ you as a messenger, not as an eavesdropper."

"Well, miss. *You* get employed as a maid *and* as an eavesdropper, so I'm only copying you."

"That is an entirely different matter, as you well know. You're getting cheekier by the day."

"My mother says the same. I don't mean to be rude, miss... I dunno, I won't be a messenger all me life, so I've got to make a start on something. What I'd really like to be is a spy."

"I thought you were going to work at the docks like your dad?"

"Not now. How could I, knowing what you ladies get up to?"

Sophie smiled. "How much do you know?"

"I pick up bits here and there and put 'em together. As soon as Miss Flora's involved, I know you have a special on the go."

"Good grief! Is it as obvious as that?" Sophie looked irritated. "Do you think Miss Jones knows what we do?"

"She don't talk to me much, except about the deliveries and that... I'd say she knows something's going on, but ain't interested in finding out more."

"I can imagine her adopting such an attitude.... This is all rather disturbing, Nick. In future, you shall not listen at doors nor attempt to acquire information by any other means while at this office! Do I make myself clear?"

"Yes, miss."

"That you were forthright in your answers counts for a great deal. I understand how being a spy must seem attractive to you, but it is a career that cannot be chosen. My understanding is that they recruit most spies from the army, navy, or diplomatic circles. Even then, they are usually selected because of their useful connections or specific skills."

"Oh," said Nick, his disappointment becoming apparent. "I suppose I'd have to be a gentleman like Mr Drysdale."

"We shall not discuss him, either. You are very bright, and I'm sure you'll get on well in your eventual occupation. At the moment, your occupation is to deliver those messages, your usual office duties, and helping Miss Jones without upsetting her in the slightest." She raised her eyebrows.

Nick grinned. "Bob's your uncle, miss."

Early Tuesday afternoon, on the 28th of March, Sophie, in her chauffeur's uniform, drove her car named Rabbit; Ada was with her in the front passenger seat, while Flora and Lady Shelling sat in the back. Aunt Bessie had insisted on joining the scouting party, having decided that a murder investigation might be an interesting diversion. They were going to Primrose Hill.

"There are many socialists, anarchists, and meddling would-be reformers in Hampstead, so I presume there are also some to be found in Primrose Hill." Aunt Bessie delivered her pronouncement as Sophie changed gears while slowing the car at a policeman's signal to halt. They waited to be waved through Euston Road.

"What makes you say that?" asked Sophie.

"Because Karl Marx is buried in Highgate Cemetery, and the Webbs live in Hampstead."

"You mean Sidney and Beatrice Webb?" asked Flora.

"My dear," said Aunt Bessie, "I had the great misfortune of attending a dinner where they were also present. I spoke to both of 'em, and, let me tell you, I shall never repeat *that* mistake."

"What happened?" asked Sophie. The car began moving again.

"He is, perhaps, the longest-winded man I have ever met. Webb wants to interfere with everyone and is at pains to explain how he'll do it. I can forgive much, but for goodness' sake, it must be brief. However, I reluctantly learned this.

He hates Marx and wants the Russian Revolution to fail. I could only tolerate five minutes of the man's meandering dissertation before I shoved off. Blow me down if I didn't turn and immediately bump into his confounded wife. She was standing there quietly, hanging on his every word. Naturally, I assumed she was feeble-minded, because she *must* have heard it all before. However, even though she proved to be otherwise, she is also an arch-meddler. At least she was mercifully succinct. Beatrice Webb hates Lenin because he's a Marxist. I find it remarkable how intellectuals can be so positively dim-witted about everything outside of their cause, and so vicious about their competitors within it."

"That's interesting — the idea of competing socialist thought," said Sophie. "I suppose the Communists at number fifteen might have differences of opinion."

"I'm sure they do. Communists living in Primrose Hill — proves me point, eh?"

"Yes, but they are émigrés and, therefore, bound to be in a minority," said Sophie.

"Good. Although I can't understand why they haven't been deported. I'm all for freedom of speech, but they are a foreign group that wants to control our country and *abolish* free speech, so out they should go." Aunt Bessie paused for a moment. "Miss McMahon, have you ever encountered Communists?"

"Yes, Lady Shelling. In Poplar, they hand out leaflets every Friday, while avoiding the coppers. We take 'em for lighting the fire. The leaflets say 'ow we should have a workers' government, and go on strike, an' all that, and that the revolution is wonderful. But in the newspapers, all you read about is the fighting in Russia. Why would we want that?"

"The answer is, we don't," said Aunt Bessie. "What do they say about jobs and wages?"

"That there'll be jobs for everyone, and the wicked capitalists won't get their profits no more, and all that money will go to the workers."

"It's beyond me how they expect their system to work... Where are we now?"

"By the side of Euston Station."

"I like Euston Station," said Aunt Bessie. "It has such a grand entrance."

"Oh, I agree," said Flora. "Going under the arch has never failed to impress me since I was a little girl."

"I'm the same," said Sophie. "The entrance represents the gateway to exciting adventures, particularly in Scotland… How is Uncle Raymond, by the way?"

"As barmy as ever," said Aunt Bessie. "I saw them last year. Helen, his wife, you know, is sixty. She has the clearest skin and eyes — it's quite remarkable. Although her hair is silver now, she still wears it in a long braid. Helen has somehow managed to retain a graceful and quite youthful air. Drinking water from the mountain stream has served her very well."

"Mrs Burgoyne should bottle it, and say she's discovered the fountain of youth," said Flora.

"If only she had discovered such a thing!" said Aunt Bessie wistfully.

Ada, who had never been through Euston, studied her Bartholomew's map. "We gotta go through Millbrook something or other. That's short. Then comes Camden 'igh Street where we turn right." Staring at the map, she held up her right hand and turned the map with her left. "Yes, it's right we want." She smiled to herself, enjoying being the navigator.

They passed by the Camden Theatre.

"Miss," said Ada, staring at the impressive cinema with its Italian Renaissance-style front, "What is an 'ippodrome?"

"Um, hippos is Greek for horse… I don't know what drome means."

"Like in aerodrome," said Flora. "Perhaps it means field."

"Ask your father," said Aunt Bessie to Sophie. "He knows at least ten Greek dialects… But why would they call a cinema a horse something or other?"

"'Cause it smells like a stable, my Lady," declared Ada.

In the back, Lady Shelling broke out with laughter.

"The Hippodrome Theatre used to have circus acts twenty years ago," explained Flora.

"So they've all copied the name," said Sophie, "but show moving pictures instead. That doesn't make any sense."

"They're calling them films now," said Flora.

"Are they? Saved from committing a dreadful future faux pas! Thank you."

"I know what a faux pas is," said Ada to Sophie, "because I had to look it up in the dictionary. Does that mean I know French?"

"Yes, it does."

Ada looked pleased, but shook her head. "I don't know French. But I tried out that phrase on one of me brothers. He didn't 'alf look stupid after I said it, 'cause he 'ad no idea what it meant. Then he got annoyed when I explained it. Said I was giving meself airs. You can't help some people. They're doomed, and that's all there is to it... Miss, we're looking for Delancey Street. It's coming up on the left. Once we've turned there, keep going straight. The road changes into Gloucester Avenue, and we're finally in Primrose 'ill. Then they change their minds again and call it Regent's Park Road, while Gloucester goes off in a different direction."

"How far to Regent's Park Road?" asked Sophie.

"Um... A quarter mile, more or less."

As they travelled along Gloucester Avenue, the character of the architecture changed. Aunt Bessie remarked,

"These houses are rather elegant."

They drove further, and then they all began exclaiming.

"It's such a lovely area, and right on the park, too," said Sophie.

"Very grand," said Flora. "I wonder if the houses in Alexandra Gardens are like these."

"We can 'ope," said Ada. "We're getting the whole 'ouse, aren't we, miss?"

"Yes, although I can't imagine the place being quite as big."

They crossed a bridge over a canal, passed a church, and then Primrose Park appeared on their left. Sophie brought the car to a halt.

"Why are we stopping?" asked Aunt Bessie. "Have we arrived?"

"No, Auntie. I only want to look at the big house on the corner. Because while driving, I'm missing everything."

"Oh... Are we *buying* a property, then?" asked Aunt Bessie.

"No chance of that."

"Miss? How much would an 'ouse like that cost?"

"It has to be thousands," answered Sophie. "Are you conversant with property prices, Auntie?"

"Not particularly. If you're referring to that corner house, I would say twenty thousand."

"Good grief," said Sophie. "How can anyone afford it?" She put the car in gear and they set off again.

"Somebody can. While we're only permitted the pleasant and very economical luxury of dreaming," said Flora.

Auntie Bessie smiled. "I think you could find yourself such a house, Flora. It would mean your marrying, though."

"Actually... Well, we are all friends here, so please don't let this go any further. I'm seeing Sidney. He's Baron Laneford, Lady Shelling."

"I *knew* it!" said Sophie. The car screeched to a halt.

"Are you really, Miss Flora?" asked Ada in an incredulous voice.

"Laneford. Laneford... No, I don't believe I've met him," said Auntie Bessie.

"He's *ever* such a nice gentleman, my Lady," said Ada. "One of the best."

"Is he?"

"How on earth did you meet again?" asked Sophie.

"We bumped into each other in Selfridges. I shan't bore you with the details, but we are now seeing each other regularly."

"I'm so happy for you," said Sophie. The car became quiet. "We'd better continue on."

She turned the car west into Fitzroy Road. Here, the attractive houses were smaller and, although some were well kept, several were looking dilapidated. After a hundred yards, Sophie pulled up at the kerb before the crossroads. The Princess of Wales lay on the other side of the road.

"Mr Hamilton was killed in front of the second house along. He fell against the railings. I'm sure you can imagine everything hidden by a dense fog. It was bad enough that Mr Saunders, who had been walking his dog in the park, could not see across the street. He arrived on the corner nearest to us at approximately seven twenty-five." The attention of the car's occupants was fastened upon what was otherwise a mundane and peaceful scene, but one which they were rapidly imbuing with fear and horror. "Mr Saunders' dog made a fuss, undoubtedly sensing another dog nearby. The unseen dog, a Sheltie, had barked. Then a man yelled, and Saunders called out, but received no reply. He crossed the road and found Hamilton's body and the Sheltie close by. Saunders entered the Princess of Wales to ring the police. He later stated that there was another person leaving the scene in the fog, and that he was carrying something metal which clanged against the railings. It's believed that object is the murder weapon."

"I don't think Mr Saunders killed Mr Hamilton," said Flora. "If he had, he just wouldn't raise the alarm."

"But s'posin' he did that just to give himself an alibi," said Ada. "If he knew there was another person out in the fog, he might think he'd been found out, so he popped into the pub, and that makes him look innocent."

"It's possible," said Sophie. "What do you think, Auntie?"

"I think I require some tea. But to answer your question, if Saunders killed Hamilton, it is inconceivable for him to have raised the alarm *unless* he feared discovery, as Miss McMahon just pointed out. Therefore, he did not fabricate the story of another person being on the scene. It certainly means there *was* someone else present. Has any such person spoken to the police?"

"No one has come forward," answered Sophie. "Perhaps whoever it was is reluctant to get involved."

"Quite possibly, although unlikely, I should think. If you follow through with that line of reasoning, it would mean there must be a witness who is now convinced that *Saunders* is the murderer. If that is correct, there may even be an element of self-preservation involved."

"Meaning that if this person believes Saunders killed Hamilton, then he might also have no scruples about killing a witness?"

"I've no wish to overdramatize this abominable act of violence, but, yes, it is a possibility... Really, I should consider the other contenders first but, if I were opening a book, I'd put Saunders at 50 to 1, and expect the odds to lengthen."

"You are *not* going to bet on this, Auntie."

"Did I say I was...? No, I did not. I simply framed the possibility of Saunders being the murderer in betting *terms*. That's all I did. Nothing more than that."

"I'm sorry if I was short with you, Auntie."

"So you should be, but I accept your apology."

"Actually, that's rather a useful idea — rating the suspects as if in a horse race."

"So my little idea — that's *all* it was — might be useful?"

Sophie smiled to herself. "I'm sure it will be *very* useful. Let's view the house."

## Chapter 3

## Settling in

### 28 March, 1921

The car entered Alexandra Gardens. Sophie wore her chauffeur's peaked cap pulled down low and her leather coat buttoned up high. Strictly staring at the road ahead, she drove at a funereal speed. The rest of the band of agents pretended they were interested in houses or the daffodils and the last of the catkins on the hazel trees in the pretty gardens. None of them, they had agreed, were to stare directly at any person in the square.

"Oh, I say. Number seven looks very nice," said Flora. "I shan't mind staying there."

The house had three upper floors, attics in a mansard roof, and a basement area. It possessed, as did all the others in the square, an Italian style of English interpretation. The restrained ornamentation of corbels and pediments gave the stuccoed building a clean, uncluttered appearance, while the comfortable symmetry conveyed all that was necessary to impress upon the onlooker that they beheld a house of substance, which also made for a pleasant home.

"They've kept it in good repair," said Aunt Bessie. "The same, however, cannot be said of several other houses. Some are very dirty — particularly number fifteen."

"That must be soot from the railways, my Lady," Ada explained, while studying the map she held. "It sort of curves all the way round from north to east... Makes the area look like an island, what with the park on the other side and the canal we crossed."

"Show me what you mean," said Aunt Bessie.

Ada held the map for her and pointed out Primrose Hill.

"So it does," said Aunt Bessie. "Thank you."

"Someone is coming out of number fifteen," said Flora.

A tall man, accompanied by a bloodhound, gave the slow-moving car only a cursory glance before setting off towards the park with his dog.

"Blimey. He really looks like a Russian," said Ada.

"Absolutely," said Flora. "It's the full beard and moustache that does it."

"Yes," agreed Aunt Bessie, "and the long overcoat with the astrakhan collar. Also, his workman's boots look foreign."

Sophie, briefly glimpsing the man, said, "The shape of his homburg is quite different from that of British hats."

"What type of dog is it, miss?"

"That's a bloodhound."

"The dog certainly looks British," said Aunt Bessie. "I know a gentleman who looks remarkably like a bloodhound — not the ears and nose, of course. Obviously, I shan't be so unkind as to name him."

"Have I met this gentleman?" asked Sophie.

"I'm not telling you any more. Sophie, if we have finished our survey, I would like some tea."

"There are many shops nearby," said Sophie, "so there's bound to be a tea room amongst them. Everyone, please remember to be careful. The murderer *might* be sitting at a nearby table."

---

The end of March was rainy and mild, and the tulips were on the point of blooming. Late on the last day of March, two detectives left number seven, Alexandra Gardens for the last time. Stationed overnight, two other detectives kept watch in the square from a strategically parked and therefore unobtrusive car. The only thing of note that happened before dawn was that the sky cleared.

The axis of Alexandra Gardens is roughly north-east to south-west. On three sides of the small gardens, the houses face directly onto it, with only two narrow pavements and a carriage drive intervening. The fourth is opposite the thoroughfare of St. George's Road. It is on this fourth side that the numbering begins, because these were the first townhouses to be built, in 1852. The fact of greatest importance to be remembered is that in Primrose Hill the preferred term used by the builders and sellers of such properties is *villa*. What are the differences between a townhouse, a semi-detached, or a detached house on the one hand, and a villa on the other? Absolutely none. The simplest way to understand the word *villa* is to think of it in the negative. When is a house not a villa? The answer is, of course, when the area is unfashionable. Primrose Hill abounds in villas, although, to the absolute horror of many freeholders, some of them are being converted to flats.

The townhouse, or villa, that the secret agency was to occupy — number seven — lay in the south-east corner of the square. Its side was on St George's Road. The house, being the last one in a row and therefore technically a semi-detached, was consequently of greater distinction and value in the world of villas. Useful for spies in occupancy, it also had a door in the high brick side wall of the back garden.

On Friday, April the first, at a quarter to eight, a taxi stopped outside number seven. Three young women got out, and the unloading of suitcases began. Several curtains stirred in adjacent houses during this process. Excitedly, and with the front door key in one hand and a suitcase in the other, Sophie mounted the front steps to the elevated ground floor. The flagstone basement area lay below. She had decided that a tub full of geraniums would look very nice in that quaint little nook — if it were her house. Under the stone-columned portico, with its pretty balcony on top, she unlocked and opened the front door. They all entered, laden and chattering.

"Oh, it's right beautiful," said Ada.

"And it's fully furnished with lovely things," said Flora, staring into the reception rooms.

"Yes, it is lovely. The furniture's a bit dated, but it's all good solid stuff," said Sophie.

Forgetful of their mission, they instead explored the house for many minutes. During this time, Sophie wanted to tell her friends that Archie was thinking of buying the house, but could not, because she had given her word. Their tour revealed there was work to be done.

"They tidied it," said Ada, referring to the detectives, "but they didn't clean it up proper. I'll wash all the sheets first."

"No. You're the housekeeper, so send them out to the laundry. I saw other sheets in a cupboard."

"One's got holes, and the other has a nasty stain."

"Oh," said Sophie.

"If we're discussing deficiencies," said Flora, "there's nothing in the larder."

"I'd better write out a shopping list," said Sophie, picking up her notebook. "You take first watch, Flora, while Ada and I put things in order."

"Should we use our other names?"

"You're right, we should. Here's the list of Communists, Gladys, and you'll need these binoculars and notebook." She handed the items to her.

Flora climbed the stairs to the attics. There, the detectives had set up a comfortable and well-hidden observation post behind one of the three attic windows. From the comfortable chair, Flora had an unobstructed view of the front door of number fifteen. Almost as soon as she had settled, a man left the house. By consulting the photographs and sketches contained in a file, she identified him and wrote an entry in the new log book.

Sophie and Ada conferred over the long list they were creating. While they were busy, Flora shouted down from the top of the stairs in the attic,

"Milkman!"

"Thank you!" called back Sophie.

Ada rushed to the window.

"Good, he comes nice and early, and he starts on the other side of the square. I must catch him, though. He has bottles, not churns. What do we want?"

"Um…" Sophie consulted the list. "A pint of milk, a pound of butter, a dozen eggs, and a loaf."

"Do you like 'Ovis?"

"Only if there's nothing else."

"I'm the same. I don't reckon the bread off the milk cart, miss. There must be a baker's nearby, but I won't ask the milkman where, 'cause he'll take it personal."

"You can ask him about laundries, though… Nancy, do you like the cream off the top of the milk?"

Ada paused before answering. "Yes, miss."

"Both Gladys and I do as well."

"Oh."

"It would be ridiculous for us to get three pints, so just get the one pint of milk and a small double cream instead."

"All right, miss."

"We could have cream on fruit or… Do you like Force cereal, you know, the wheat flakes?"

"Ooh, yes. I *love* 'em, miss."

"Good," Sophie smiled. "Of course, cream on a fruit pie would be nice." Sophie paused a moment. "I've just had a marvellous idea! I'll ask Mrs Barker to come in and cook for us. Do you think she might?"

"I 'ope she does. I'm not very good at cooking."

"Nick will arrive at eleven to collect and deliver messages, so I'll send a note to her then."

"I've got to go, miss, or he'll be gone."

"Yes! We can't miss the milkman on the first day."

The United Dairies milk cart's first stop in the square was at number twenty-four. The milkman got down from his bench on top, opened a hatch in the side of the covered cart to take out a wire basket. With three full bottles in it, he climbed the steps to the front door to leave the milk and take away the empties. He knocked on the door and a woman answered immediately. They talked while he gave her the weekly bill and she paid him with exactly the right amount of money. He put the money in his satchel, then handed her a pint of milk. The horse moved on to stand outside number twenty-three. After delivering two pints, being paid, and chatting with the maid at the next house, he returned the empties to the cart. Some houses had no milk delivery and several used a rival dairy. Ada caught up with him and his horse outside number twenty.

"Good morning," said Ada.

"Good morning, miss." He saluted by touching his peaked cap. A short man with a lively face, he wore a long, striped apron under his jacket. He also carried on a strap over his shoulder a leather satchel to hold coins. While they spoke, birdsong from the gardens floated on the cool, brightness of the morning.

"I'm from number seven. I'd like a pint of best milk, a small double cream, a pound of butter, and a dozen eggs, if you please. Tomorrow, we'd like two pints. Next week, a pint a day and we'll see 'ow that goes."

"Certainly, miss. Are you staying long term?"

The horse shook his head, making the harness rattle.

"No, we're not."

"Ah. Then it'll have to be cash. If you was staying long term, then you'd pay for the week every Friday."

"Oh, I see. I've got money with me."

"Er, well, don't worry about that for now. I'll bring it over in about ten minutes. That'll save you carrying the milk back. Don't want to drop it, eh?"

"No, I don't... I'm Miss Carmichael. What's your name?"

"I'm Jack, and I'll tell you this now, because everyone asks eventually: that's Old Tom." He nodded towards the horse. "He knows the round better than I do myself."

Ada smiled. "I'll see you in a minute, then."

She returned to the house, leaving Jack recording number seven's order with a pencil stub. He licked the point first before writing the order in his large, leather notebook. By himself, Old Tom slowly clip-clopped to the next house.

Sophie was cleaning and dusting in the parlour with the dining room next on her list of things to do when Flora bellowed down from the attics. "Dog! Number 20!"

"Thank you!" replied Sophie.

She put down the duster to peer through the lace curtains. Sophie noticed they were old, but very good ones. Through this screening barrier, she hazily observed, on the other side of the square, a woman carrying a Pekinese. This woman crossed over the road to the pavement surrounding the park. There, she put down the dog, and began a slow promenade around the outside of the garden.

Sophie consulted a list of suspects provided by the police, then called up the stairs,

"That's Mrs Pringle!"

"Who!?"

"*Mrs Pringle!*"

"I can't understand what you're saying!"

"I'll tell you later!"

"All right... Dog! Number 14!"

Sophie hurried back to the window. Realizing there was no point to her shouting, 'Captain Bristow', she observed the man and his Newfoundland dog making a bee-line for Mrs Pringle.

"Dogs! And I'm loathe to report this! Numbers one and two!"

Sophie smiled. She saw the people for herself now — Mr Charles Clark with a basset hound, and Dulcie Villard from number two, accompanied by a well-trimmed poodle. All four dog owners now formed a loose conversational group. The time was 8:33.

"Communists! Three of them going to work! I'm not yelling *those* names!"

"Oh, go on!"

"No! They're too difficult! Shouting is very wearing!"

Ada returned from talking to the milkman.

"Did you hear any shouting?" asked Sophie from the window.

"No, miss. Has something 'appened?"

"No. Gladys and I were bellowing. I just wondered if you heard us outside and am relieved you didn't."

"Oh... I'd better go up and tell her not to shout for a while. Jack, the milkman, wants paying daily, so he'll be knocking on the door any minute."

"Good grief. Gladys mustn't startle the fellow on our first day. Let me bring you up to date, Nancy. It's twenty to nine. Those Communists are going to work. The dog-walkers have met either by prearrangement or it's their habit."

"When's our dog coming?" asked Ada.

"Ten o'clock. I'd better get back to work."

"I'll see Glad. Oh, yes, miss. A woman was watching me while I was talking to the milkman. She was behind the curtains, ground floor, number twenty-one. The sun caught her just right, and she was standing there like a blinking statue."

"Twenty-one isn't on our list. I'll ask about her when the police come to collect the report."

"Very good, miss." Ada went upstairs.

Some minutes later, the milkman knocked on the door. Ada answered. Nearby, and hidden from view, Sophie listened. Ada received the items, placing them on the hall table, and then paid.

"Jack, do you know of a good laundry round 'ere?"

"Yes, Watson's in Erskine Road. No more than a hundred-yard walk." He indicated the direction by pointing his finger. "By Regent's Park Road."

"Thank you. Now tell me something, Jack. Is it true there was a murder round the corner?"

"There was." He suddenly looked solemn. "Dreadful business. A man struck down right there on St. George's."

"And the police ain't caught him?"

"No, nor never will, if you ask me. It all happened in a fog, so who's to see the murderer...? Nobody!"

"I 'ope it wasn't anyone living in the square."

"Perish the thought. No, it just couldn't be."

"That's good to 'ear. I do for two young ladies, and I won't 'ave them getting nervous when we've just moved in. You know what will happen otherwise? I'll have to spend all me time calming them down."

"Don't be disturbed. Take it from me. This is a nice, quiet neighbourhood and there's never been any trouble here, and likely won't be ever again."

"Thank you for saying that, I'm sure. So the people here are all right, are they?"

"Oh, yes. It's like anywhere, though. There are always one or two oddities," he unconsciously glanced towards number fifteen, "but I reckon they're harmless."

"I mustn't keep you. Just the pint tomorrow."

"I've got a note of it in my book, Miss Carmichael. Good day." He touched the peak of his cap.

"Good day."

Ada closed the door.

"He don't know nothin', miss, 'cept I think the Communists might 'ave given him trouble."

"An unpaid milk bill, perhaps?"

"Must be something like that. I ought to go, miss. I've to take the sheets round to the laundry."

"Very good. However, I don't want you doing housework all the time, so we'll get a maid in to do the cleaning."

"Then I really am an 'ousekeeper?"

"That's right. I'll give you the week's money, and you'll keep the receipts and tally them. You're responsible for the supplies as well as getting information from the surrounding domestic servants."

"Oh, that's lovely, miss. Who are you thinking of bringing in as maid?"

"Myrtle."

"She's all right, and she can keep her gob shut... I suppose I shouldn't speak like that if I'm the 'ousekeeper. It won't look good on my employer. I'll watch what I say, I will an' all."

"I'm sure you'll be fine. I was thinking you might visit our neighbours on either side to find out the best places to shop. By introducing yourself, you may learn something."

"I'll do that, Miss King."
"Have you become formal already?"
"Indeed, I 'ave, Miss King."
They both laughed.

---

Nick arrived at eleven and rapped a fast tattoo on the door. Sophie answered the summons.

"Good morning, Nicholas."

"Good morning, miss. Have I done something wrong?"

"Is that how you knock on people's doors?"

"Always, miss. I think it's cheerful."

"You may think it cheerful, but others may find it irritating. Come in."

"I always get an answer. Some people hide, you know, miss. They think it's a bill collector come round. So my knocking like that lets them know they're safe to open the door."

"Who behaves like that?"

"Mr Rodgers, Maggie the typist at Fortesque & Co., and the lot who run the travel agency that's always changing its name. They're Baker's Tours at the moment."

"So they're all in financial difficulties, are they?"

"I s'pose. Although if Mr Rodgers stopped drinking, he'd have a lot of money. But I think he's afflicted." Nick tapped the side of his head.

"Oh, dear... You may as well continue knocking on doors like that, but never do it at private houses."

"I'll have to break meself of the habit, then." He shrugged. "Caught anyone, miss?"

"No. They haven't brought the dog yet, so we've not got our excuse to meet any of the suspects."

"That's a shame. I wanted to see the dog... This is a nice house. Who does it belong to?"

"I haven't been told, so I can't give you an answer. Come and have a look, though."

Sophie gave him a quick tour of the downstairs.

"It's right respectable, and it's got everything in it. I'd like a house like this... Where's Ada?"

"You must refer to her as Miss Carmichael. She is the housekeeper."

"Ow. Gone up in the world, has she?"

"You shall refrain from making that type of personal remark. At the moment, she is either at the laundry or the shops. There's nothing in the house, so I can't even offer you a cup of tea."

"Never mind, miss. What about Miss... It's Miss Walton, ain't it?"

"I don't know how you come to know that. She's up in the attics, keeping watch."

"That sounds like a cushy job."

"I have some messages for you to deliver. Myrtle is to come in and clean, starting tomorrow."

"I don't know where she lives."

"Mile End, but get the exact address from Elizabeth."

"Right-o."

"This note is for Mrs Barker. She's to come when convenient and cook a few meals for us in advance."

"I know where she lives."

"How do you know that?"

"I just know."

"You've been snooping."

"No, miss, I wouldn't call it that. But if there's a paper on a desk, well, I'm training myself to read it upside down for when I *am* a spy. It so happened I read something you were sending to Mrs Barker. I won't do it again."

"No, you won't. I'm finding your 'honesty is the best policy' approach very annoying. Stop spying immediately."

"I said I would."

"What else do you do?"

"Nothing."

"I don't believe you."

"No, it's true, miss."

Sophie frowned. "It had better be." She stared hard at him, but his youthful, angelic features remained untroubled. "Come with me. We'll examine the side gate together. I think in future it would be better if you used it instead of the front door. There seems to be a lot of nosey parkers in the square — including us!" She laughed.

They descended the stairs into the narrow, neglected garden that promised to be overgrown with weeds by the summer.

"What's in the shed at the back, miss?"

"I haven't had time to look."

They approached the full wooden door in the wall that served as a gate.

"There's only a bolt," said Sophie.

She pulled on the rusty bolt, which suddenly and noisily came unstuck. The door opened haltingly — evidence the entrance was rarely used.

"I can oil all that for you," said Nick. "Do you have any?"

"No. Perhaps there's some in the shed."

They approached the small wooden structure, stepping on stones that were sinking into the lawn. The boards appeared sound, while the creosote had faded to where the grain pattern attractively stood out, but the wood looked thirsty. They found the door unlocked.

"No one's been in here for a while," said Sophie. "Ugh, spider webs." She recoiled from a large one at face height.

"I don't mind spiders," said Nick, who entered, brushing the web aside. "There's a tin of oil on the windowsill."

"That's good. Please see to the gate. I have to go, because I'm expecting the dog to arrive imminently."

By the time Nick had left with the messages, there was still no dog and Ada had yet to return. Sophie decided to go for a walk. She fully intended examining the surrounding streets, including the scene of the murder but, as it was so pleasant, she changed her mind. Entering by the nearer of the two latched iron gates, she went over to a bench in the empty gardens and sat down.

The warm sunshine was lovely, so she unbuttoned her coat. It had been so long since she had found time just to sit in the sun and do nothing. Winter was truly past, and warm days were to be expected for the foreseeable future. She felt the relief as if shedding a burdensome weight. Leisurely, she began examining her surroundings. Overall, it was a pretty square of elegant, yet practical houses. Some were scruffy, but most were well-maintained. She noticed one that had been sub-divided into flats. From where she sat, Sophie could not see number fifteen very well because a tree coming into leaf was in the way. There were several mature, medium-tall trees in the gardens — one of them a pear tree. Around the perimeter was an iron railing and, immediately within the fence, there was a quickset hedge of hawthorn and hazel which reached to shoulder height. The leaves were quite advanced already, and a wall of green replaced what would otherwise have been a view of traffic and pedestrians. This gave the garden a cloistered feel, even though overlooked by every house. Sophie removed her hat. Then, shutting her eyes, she turned her face to the sun for a few moments.

When she opened them again, she noticed a woman standing on the steps of number twenty-four staring in her direction. The woman began walking towards her and, from her manner, Sophie instantly knew that trouble of some type was approaching. Remembering the list, Sophie believed the woman might be Mrs Fitch. She avoided looking at the approaching menace in her effort to remain calm. After the gate shut, it was a matter of seconds before the woman could no longer be ignored. The instant Sophie turned her head, the newcomer spoke.

"Excuse me, but these are *private* gardens." She had a well-to-do, commanding voice.

"I thought they were, too," replied Sophie.

"No, you misunderstand. You have no right to be here, unless you own a house that faces on to the gardens."

"Ah... What about a lease?"

"Long-term lessees may use the gardens; short-term lessees and renters may not."

"That seems unfair."

"It is not unfair. The unanimous decision was arrived at by the approved method in a property owners' council meeting. The rule is designed to keep out *those* tenants who live in *those* houses which have been converted to flats. It is because the owners pay for the upkeep of the gardens, while the tenants do not."

"Which council is this?" asked Sophie.

"The Alexandra Gardens Maintenance and Improvement Association Council, of which I have the honour of being the chairwoman." She managed to convey equal parts of pride and humility in her answer.

Sophie could see that there were faults to be found in this reasoning but, as the concept had been so suddenly sprung upon her, and as she was not in Alexandra Gardens to bicker with her neighbours, she decided it was best she left.

"None of this was explained to me when I took on the house. Neither is this rule posted anywhere that I could see. However, I shall leave now, at your suggestion." Sophie stood up. "I am Miss King. My cousin, Miss Walton, and I have taken number seven for a few months. We shall use Primrose Park, instead."

"Have you taken the whole house?"

"Yes."

"Then there's no problem, after all. You may stay, and I apologize for disturbing you. Good Lord! What must you think of me?" The woman laughed. "I'm Mrs Fitch, by the way." She offered to shake hands. Sophie politely responded and then had hers heartily and excessively shaken.

"Are dogs permitted in the garden?"

"Yes, but only from the first of November to the thirty-first of March... Do you have a dog?"

"I do."

"Then why didn't you say so!? That makes all the difference. I'll leave you in your seclusion, but we're *bound* to meet later when I'm out with my boy, Titus. It's been a pleasure meeting you, Miss King. Goodbye!" As abruptly as she had arrived, thus, also, she left.

Under her breath, Sophie muttered, "How extraordinary."

## Chapter 4

## Biscuit

Ada returned from her shopping expedition. She had taken the sheets to the laundry and they would be ready at four. As it was nearly one, she and Sophie were getting lunch ready in the practical kitchen, which was lined with sturdy cupboards, counters, and many drawers.

"We'll have hot potato salad," said Sophie, as she cut up spring onions at an enamel-topped table. "I'm too hungry to wait for it to cool down."

"I like it like that," said Ada, straining the potatoes over the massive porcelain sink.

Someone knocked on the front door.

"Don't tell me the police have finally arrived with the dog," said Sophie.

"We're about to eat, so it's bound to be them... Are you at 'ome if it ain't, miss?"

"I have to be."

Ada opened the door to find Detective Sergeant Gowers holding a leash with a good-sized dog wagging its tail on the other end.

"Oh, 'ello, it's you, Sergeant Gowers."

"Yes, hello. I'm ever so sorry I'm late. Er, may we come in?"

"Yes, of course."

They entered, and the dog sat down to wait in the tiled hall.

"This is a smashing place. It's in a good area, too."

"Not so good when there's been a murder just round the corner," said Ada.

"Murder aside, of course."

Sophie came from the kitchen.

"Good afternoon, Sergeant Gowers. Will you stay for lunch?"

"Good afternoon, Miss King. Thank you. I'd like to take you up on your offer, but I should have been somewhere else an hour ago. We've got a couple of things on the go, and it's just been one of those days where you can't get anything done."

"I fully understand. I presume this is the dog?"

"Yes. The officer in charge of it, well, he's busy with another matter at present. As I'm your liaison officer — that's a fancy way of saying I come round for a chat now and again — he gave me the dog to give to you."

"Oh. He's... It's a he, is it?"

"Yes, that's correct."

"He looks very clean... Actually, he looks remarkably friendly. Do you think he is?"

"I couldn't say. All I can tell you is that he behaved himself in the car. I parked on another street. You know, the neighbours might notice the car outside and we don't want them thinking too deeply."

"No, we don't" said Sophie, laughing.

"He's a Belgian Shepherd. I've got a list of commands here. Could you?" He offered the leash to Ada, who tentatively took charge of the dog. Gowers took out a paper from his jacket pocket and unfolded it. "Apparently, just say the word, and he'll obey it." He gave Sophie the list.

"Good grief, there are a lot of commands." She quickly counted them. "Thirty?"

"He must be a right smart dog," said Gowers.

"What is his name?"

"I don't know. His handler was in such a hurry when he dropped him off, he left without saying."

"Oh." Sophie looked at the back of the list. "What does he eat?"

"I'm very sorry, but he didn't tell me that either. The officer had to leave immediately, you understand. "

"We'll work it all out. Hello, boy." Sophie bent forward and smiled. "Are you friendly?"

Sophie put the list in her pocket and approached the dog with her hand extended. He certainly seemed friendly, almost as if he were smiling at her. Of a medium-size, with a curly and woolly light-tan coat, he had an intelligent look. He stared back at her expectantly. The dog sniffed her hand. She patted his head, and he wagged his tail.

"Would you like some water?" she asked. "Come along." Sophie took the leash and turned towards the kitchen

"I must be going," said Gowers. "I'll come round later this afternoon, if I may."

"Thank you very much for bringing the dog when you're so busy. Oh, Sergeant Gowers," said Sophie, "would you use the side entrance when you come? We don't want the neighbours wondering who you are."

"I certainly shall, Miss King."

After eating lunch together, the three women gathered in the hall to give the new dog their full attention.

"Sit," said Sophie. The dog remained standing.

"Come," said Ada from a short distance. The dog did not move. Instead, it wagged its tail.

"He looks lovely and cuddly," said Flora, "but he's perfectly useless as a police dog. He hasn't obeyed a single command."

"Perhaps he's used to a man's voice," said Sophie.

They tried again, each giving commands in the deepest voices they could achieve.

"'Ow'd you get your voice so low, Miss Flora?" asked Ada.

"You sort of have to let it come from your lungs. I can't explain it any better than that."

"Reminds me of when we played the trick on that rotten butler. Your special voice is not working on the dog, though."

"This is ridiculous," said Sophie. "The handler should have been present to explain matters to us."

"That would have been a help. Although he follows us about nicely," said Flora. "Don't you, boy?" The dog wagged his tail. "What shall we call him?"

"We'll have to come up with a name. The other dog owners are *bound* to ask... How totally unnecessary. Blast it!"

The dog woofed.

"That's never his name," said Ada in disbelief. "Say it again."

"Blast-it, lie down."

The dog *did* lie down.

"Oh, *surely* not," said Sophie.

"Blast-it, roll over," said Flora, and the dog obeyed.

"What an absurd name to give a dog," said Sophie. "Oh well, at least that's sorted out. I should be on watch while you're having a break, so I'd better go." Sophie left for the attics.

Afterwards, Flora and Ada continued testing the dog with some of the easier commands. They discovered that, having once spoken his name, the dog would obey that person without the name having to be repeated each time.

"I wonder what this command is for," said Flora. "Up." After a moment's hesitation, the dog effortlessly leapt onto the hall table.

"Good godfathers!" exclaimed Ada. "He's like a kangaroo."

"Down!" said Flora, pointing to the floor.

Ada examined the tabletop and in relief said, "Thank goodness he didn't scratch it."

"We'll have to be careful what we say in front of him."

"Yes, we will an' all. What do you reckon he eats?"

Flora looked at the list of commands. "There's a note at the bottom — the writing's appalling. It says we should reward him. That's not very helpful, but I remember we gave Old Calabar biscuits to *our* dogs," said Flora.

The dog barked twice.

"Biscuit?" asked Ada.

The dog barked again.

"Biscuit must be his name," said Flora.

Biscuit could not have been happier at this development.

"Oh. Miss King thinks his name's Blast-it."

"Yes! But we shan't rush to tell her otherwise." Flora raised her eyebrows.

Ada giggled.

---

At two-thirty, after Flora had resumed her surveillance, Sophie took Biscuit for his first walk around the square and noticed a curious thing. Whereas the square had been empty, within a few minutes of her appearance, three dog owners and their charges came out. Then, and leaving no doubt in Sophie's mind, they all began converging upon her. From the attic window, it seemed to Flora that they had ambushed Sophie and Biscuit.

"Good afternoon," said the first and fastest interceptor, raising his hat. "Beautiful weather we're having, wouldn't you say?" He was of average height, an active and muscular man in his early forties. One might guess he had been in the navy and one would have been correct.

"Good afternoon," replied Sophie, "and it most certainly is fine weather."

"The name's Bristow, and this here's Bo'sun." He patted the shoulder of the bear-like Newfoundland dog. Just then, the dog was far more interested in Biscuit than in humans, and pulled his owner in that direction. Biscuit maintained a reserved attitude.

"He's a lovely-looking dog. I'm Miss King, and to complete the round of introductions, this is Blast-it."

"Oh, really...? Hello, Blast-it... May I enquire what sort of dog it is? It looks like a definite breed."

"He's a Belgian Shepherd."

"I see...? Are you sure? I thought those were black dogs with a shaggy coat and pointed ears."

"I'm positive he's a Belgian Shepherd."

"Ah... Probably a variety with which I'm unfamiliar."

"That must be the case."

"Here's Miss Villard with Lulu. Perhaps she can settle the matter for us."

Sophie did not believe there was a matter to be settled but, with the sense of a slight, although definitely rising, irritation, could not prevent the man from waving to the woman in her late twenties, who immediately came over escorting a smart poodle.

"I say, Dulcie. Have you and Miss King been introduced?"

As they had not, the introduction was made — dogs included — friendly Biscuit meeting the oh-so-refined Lulu. As soon as that was out of the way, Bristow took up his theme and addressed Miss Villard, who was thin, dark, and fashionably dressed.

"Are you familiar with Belgian Shepherds? If so, would you mind telling us how you would describe one?"

"I have seen them." She had a pleasant voice, and the abrupt question did not seem to trouble her in the least. "A medium-sized dog with long brown hair. Something like an Alsatian."

"There you are!" said Bristow, as though he had discovered an immense secret. "Belgian Shepherd and German Shepherd! But I think you'll find they're black, Dulcie."

"No. The one I saw had pale brown legs and a dark brown back."

"You must have seen a different variety. Here's the problem. Miss King says her dog is a Belgian Shepherd."

"Then it must be so."

"I'm sure it is, but it doesn't help us, really, because Blast-it doesn't *look* like one. Here's old Cummings. Let's get his opinion." Bristow waved again.

Sophie's annoyance increased as the tall man walked towards to the group.

The introductions were complete after Sophie had had no choice but to reply, yet again, that her dog's name was Blast-it. Cummings, at sixty-four, had been in the army in India. His dog was an Irish terrier named Vindaloo because, as Cummings was quick to point out to Sophie, he was the same colour as a good spicy curry.

"So what do you think, Cummings? Is Miss King's dog typical of Belgian Shepherds?"

"I'm not in a position to say. I understood them to have a very short, mid-brown coat and a dark muzzle."

"That must be yet another variety," said Bristow.

Cummings scrutinized Biscuit. "He looks like a good fellow," he said to Sophie while smiling.

"He's absolutely the best," she replied.

"I wasn't inferring that he's a mongrel, or anything like that, Miss King," said Bristow. "It's just I've never seen your variety entered at Cruft's." He uttered the word as if that settled the matter.

"The dog show? Oh, of course." Sophie nodded. "Perhaps I should enter him. Then you'll see for yourself and will believe me when I say he's a Belgian Shepherd. Good day. Walk, Blast-it!"

Biscuit obeyed, much to Sophie's relief.

"That's a well-behaved dog," said Cummings, while watching Sophie walk away. "I think you might have upset her."

"I didn't mean to, but then people can be so touchy about their dogs. I've never seen that type before, and I simply thought she had made a mistake."

"Your naval officer's way of speaking is much too blunt, Captain," said Dulcie.

"Everyone has to take me as they find me. I suppose I'll have to apologize — yet again. What I'd like to know is what sort of person calls their dog Blast-it? Rather unseemly for a young woman who obviously comes from a good family."

"But does she?" asked Dulcie. "We have yet to find that out. What have you learnt?"

"Not much," said Bristow. "Cynthia Fitch says it's two young women leasing number seven for a short-term. That's all I know."

"I believe they have a maid," said Cummings. "I saw her talking to Jack, the milkman."

"A maid?" said Dulcie. "I'll say goodbye, darlings. There are a few things I must do before tomorrow. I have an important appointment with the Duchess of Rutland in the morning."

"Again?" asked Bristow.

"When someone of her rank can do nothing with her hair," explained Dulcie, "she must have a sympathetic coiffeuse help her look her best for all engagements." She smiled and left them.

"Dulcie makes a fortune off the Duchess' head," said Bristow. "It's all absolutely beyond me how much has been invested in it."

"Quite," said Cummings. "I'm going in, Bristow."

"I'm off to the park, so I'll see you later."

When Dulcie entered the lower half of number two — she had lodgers in the upper half — she immediately sought her maid, and found her in the kitchen.

"Mildred. Two women have taken number seven. They have a maid. Find out what you can."

"Oh... What does this maid look like?"

"I don't know, yet. She will have to pass our window to go to the better shops. If you were to go after her..."

"I will do that, madam."

At number seven, Sophie gave vent to her feelings.

"What an insufferable man!"

"Who is, miss?" asked Ada.

"A boor named Bristow."

"I saw you with those three people, but what did he do?"

"He impugned Blast-it's ancestry and did so while completely ignoring what I was saying. He went on and on like a demented thing, and got everyone else involved."

"Oh, would you like some tea?" asked Ada sympathetically.

"No, thank you. I'll wait until tea-time." Sophie visibly relaxed, then smiled. "That's very kind of you. I'm making more of it all than it was. Although, having two contretemps on the day we move in is pushing it a bit. I hope not all the neighbours prove to be so difficult."

"They won't, miss. I know it's early days, but did anyone look like they could be a murderer?"

"No. They all seemed normal, and I learned nothing."

"Oh, well. We don't want to crack the case too soon, or they'll 'ave us out of 'ere before you can blink."

Sophie smiled. "I had better go up to see how Gladys is getting on. Come along, Blast-it."

To stifle a laugh, Ada said,

"I'll go to the shops now and be back in plenty of time for tea. I have to get dog food."

Someone knocking on the door interrupted them.

"Who can that be?" whispered Sophie.

"Are you at 'ome, Miss King?"

"Yes, Mrs Carmichael."

They both started laughing.

"Oh, miss. Please don't call me that until I get proper used to the idea of housekeeper."

While Ada answered the front door, Sophie darted into the parlour. There, she read the list of dog commands to look busy.

"Hello, Ada. Remember me?"

"Mrs Barker! What a sight for sore eyes you are. Come in, come in."

"Is that how you answer the door?" Mrs Barker was serious as she entered, but then laughed.

"Only for you." Ada closed the door. "You must call me Nancy, though. 'Cause of the case."

"Oh-*er*. Whatever's going on?"

Just then, Sophie entered the hall and greeted the visitor.

"Thank you for coming so promptly. I didn't expect you until tomorrow at the earliest."

"When Nick said it was an emergency, I dropped everything and came at once."

"But I never told him to say that. You were to come if and when convenient."

"He as good as said it was a matter of life or death." Mrs Barker's face darkened.

"That boy is incorrigible. I don't know what's got into him of late. Mrs Barker, I assure you, I shall have a very stern word with Nicholas. He will *not* get away with it."

"I'm glad to hear it. He put me in a tizzy, but there. I'm here now. What can I do to help?"

"We were hoping you could cook some dinners in advance. It's possible the work might demand all our attention simultaneously, and we don't want to go hungry." Sophie smiled.

"Something like a beef pie would be nice," said Ada.

Mrs Barker smiled. "I'll see what I can manage. For how many and for how long is it?"

"There are three of us staying for at least ten days, but we're likely to have visits from the neighbours."

"And don't forget, Sergeant Gowers will be comin' round daily for reports," added Ada.

"Then a couple of cakes and some pastries will hold you for a few days. I won't get it all ready today, so I'll come again tomorrow. Will you be entertaining?"

"I don't think so," said Sophie. "Although that situation might change."

"Understood. First, I'll inspect the kitchen and see what's on hand. Then I'll make up a list for your approval, Miss Burgoyne."

"Thank you. While here, you must call me Miss King."

"Like I did before?"

"Yes, so that our true identities remain hidden. Miss Dane is Gladys Walton, Ada is Nancy Carmichael, and I'm Phoebe King."

"What a funny thing, but it's quite exciting, isn't it? Do I change my name as well?"

"Do you want to?"

"I'll have to think about it and let you know, but I'd like to get started, if you please."

"The kitchen's this way," said Ada.

All three of them entered the kitchen. Mrs Barker wore an expression as if there had yet to be a kitchen built that could satisfy her exacting requirements.

"What is that?" She pointed to Biscuit, who had been lying on the mat next to the back door but now sat upright.

"Blast-it is a police dog on loan to us," said Sophie. "They believe there's a murderer, a dog owner, living in Alexandra

Gardens. Blast-it provides us with the reason to mix with all the other people round about who own dogs. That makes him like a Trojan dog."

"I can see why he's here, then. Why would they call a dog Blast-it?" asked Mrs Barker in disbelief.

"You'd have to ask the police that question. However, just watch what he can do. Blast-it. Heel… Sit."

"He's well-trained, I'll give him that," said Mrs Barker. "But, Miss King, he can't be in the kitchen while I'm cooking. It seems unhealthy, and he'll get underfoot."

"You're quite right. We'll put a blanket down for him in the hall upstairs."

"I'll do that, Miss King," said Ada.

"Thank you, Miss Carmichael."

"Housekeeper, are you now, Miss Carmichael?" asked Mrs Barker. "Well done."

Mrs Barker began her close inspection of the kitchen by opening cupboards and drawers to examine the pots and utensils. She finished by saying, "They'll do." The gas stove, she said, was, "Not bad." What drove her into raptures was the thick marble cold shelf in the larder. "I've *never* seen a prettier-patterned shelf," she declared. "And it's a good size, too." Shortly after that, she busied herself with making a list of meals, pies, and pastries for Sophie and started a shopping list for Ada.

There came a knock at the front door. As Ada was upstairs, Sophie answered the summons. She was shocked to find Hawkins, Lady Shelling's butler at White Lyon Yard, standing on the doorstep. He wore a light raincoat over his cutaway coat. A taxi was waiting at the kerb.

"Gracious me!" exclaimed Sophie. "Has anything happened to Auntie?"

"Miss Burgoyne…"

"Shh! Keep it down and come inside."

He entered, and she closed the door.

"Well?"

"Miss Burgoyne, I am glad to say that Lady Shelling is enjoying the best of health…"

"Thank *goodness!*"

"She sent me to deliver this note to you. I am to await your reply."

He handed her an envelope. The note indicated — more or less demanded and certainly expected — that Lady Shelling should be invited to luncheon or tea or both this coming Sunday.

"What!? She can't just waltz in here during a mission."

Hawkins cleared his throat.

"Yes?"

"Lady Shelling realizes that her arrival at the front door might cause some speculation among the nearby residents. Her ladyship is prepared, in the interests of justice, to preserve the integrity of the mission by using the back door. Lady Shelling was most particular that you should understand the great sacrifices she is making on your behalf."

"I've *never* heard such... No matter. Obviously, her ladyship wishes to come. Excuse me a moment, Hawkins."

"Of course, Miss Burgoyne." The butler assumed a tactfully patient attitude while waiting in the hall.

Sophie went to the kitchen. While she was gone, there came yet another knock on the door. As no one else was about, Hawkins answered the knock. He discovered a youthful and rather shifty looking salesman on the doorstep.

"Good afternoon, sir. I'm from The Breezy Vacuum Company..."

"No, thank you." Hawkins began shutting the door, but the salesman stopped it with his foot.

"Remove your foot," said Hawkins quietly, "or I will hurl you and your contraption onto the pavement and then summon the police to press charges to the fullest extent possible."

The salesman removed his foot. "People like you..." He did not get to have his say because Hawkins shut the door in his face.

Sophie returned after having a hurried and very tense consultation with Mrs Barker, who had consented to cook on Sunday.

"Who was that?" asked Sophie.

"A salesman, Miss Burgoyne. I explained to him that the household does not require a vacuum cleaner. I presumed that was the case."

"You presumed correctly, thank you. I understand salesmen can be rather persistent."

"Occasionally, Miss Burgoyne."

"Please inform Lady Shelling that we will be delighted to have her join us on Sunday for luncheon at twelve-thirty. And, yes, she must use the back door for safety's sake."

"I will communicate, at once, the extension of this most gracious invitation to her ladyship. Good day, Miss Burgoyne."

"Good day, Hawkins."

He bowed silently and left.

Sophie returned to the kitchen and there consulted with Mrs Barker about the dramatic changes required to the coming Sunday menu. Then someone else knocked on the door.

"I can't believe how busy it is here. Where is Ada?" asked Sophie.

"Upstairs, sorting out some bed linens in case I stayed overnight. I think I must now."

"If you could, that would be most kind. Excuse me."

Sophie opened the front door.

"Good afternoon and welcome to beautiful Alexandra Gardens! Allow me to introduce myself. I am Comrade Grigory Petrov Kuritsyn at your service. May I come in?"

The large Russian gentleman raised his hat to reveal a mass of wavy hair. He was in his mid-thirties and physically filled the doorway. Accompanying him was a mournful-looking bloodhound.

# Chapter 5

# Visitors

With a large Russian Communist and his bloodhound on her doorstep, Sophie was unsure what manner to adopt. He was a neighbour after all, although one upon whom she was spying. He also seemed cheerful and had been friendly. After a moment's hesitation, she said,

"Thank you for your kind welcome. Please, come in. But would you first tie your dog to the railing, though? We have a dog, you see, and they've yet to be introduced."

"Eminently sensible." Kuritsyn clicked his heels and gave a slight bow. "Come, Vova. You shall guard against subversives while I speak to the lady comrade of the house." He quickly descended the steps to secure the dog, who laid himself down at once.

Sophie could not imagine what he meant by subversives, but it seemed inappropriate to ask at that moment. She held the door open. As soon as he entered, he began.

"I am from number fifteen. To whom do I have the honour of addressing myself?"

"I am Miss King."

"Excellent! I see you have a Belgian Shepherd. That is also excellent." Biscuit had quietly taken a place next to Sophie to study the newcomer. "But I have not presented myself to you to speak about dogs. No. I am here because Comrade Lenin wishes the people of Britain all the best, and hopes to assist them on their glorious path towards destroying the class structure and redistributing all wealth. He believes that you, our British friends, have the resilience to rise up and throw off your shackles of slavery, seize power, and then put all the money which the filthy capitalists have stolen from you into your *own* pockets."

"Oh," said Sophie.

"Yes. To learn more about the coming British revolution and hear the latest pronouncements from our most illustrious leader, Comrade Lenin, you must attend our meeting this Thursday. But be aware that they do not serve tea and no dogs are allowed. Once, I took Vova, and he howled when we sang the Internationale. From then on, the committee banned all dogs forever."

"Really?" She was at a loss how to reply. "That's unfortunate... Your dog is a *he*? I would have thought Vova was a feminine name."

"No. It is the familiar name for Vladimir — Lenin's first name, but no one dares call him Vova. The changes in Russia have forced my dog, Vova, to undergo several name changes in the last few years. Before the revolution he was Czar, which is obviously far too dangerous these days. So I changed it to Julius, in honour of the leader of the Mensheviks, but he had the misfortune of falling out of favour. Next, I got into serious trouble when I called him Lenin. The authorities said my shouting *Lenin* in the streets and have a dog come running was counter-revolutionary. They threatened to shoot both of us unless I changed the name to Vladimir. But I am talking about my dog again, when I intend talking about the glorious revolution."

He reached into a pocket and produced a wad of small leaflets.

"How many inhabitants are in the house? Please include the exploited toilers."

"There are four," answered Sophie, stifling a laugh.

"Good!" He counted out four leaflets and handed them to her. "I have a quota of fifty to distribute each day. Would you like extras for your friends and family?"

"No, thank you."

"That's a pity. I urge you to come to the meeting. All the details are in the leaflet. There will be many rousing speeches made, and the sense of brotherhood and, er, sisterhood, is most uplifting."

"I'm rather busy at present..." It was the last place she wanted to go.

"We will have a new speaker straight from Russia this week, or perhaps next. He will bring the latest pronouncements from the Kremlin. It promises to be most illuminating and an evening *not* to be missed by those who desire class warfare."

Sophie, hoping the visiting speaker might prove to be the mysterious spy, said,

"I *am* busy, but I can probably find the time to attend. I wouldn't want to miss something as exciting as that."

"You'll go?" Kuritsyn looked shocked. "You mean you will actually go? Then permit me to say on behalf of the liberated masses, the Politburo, and all Soviets everywhere, etc., etc., that this is indeed a great honour. I shall leave, now, Comrade Miss King. Good afternoon."

"Good afternoon, Mr Kuritsyn."

He bowed and left. Sophie shut the door and exhaled a large breath. Ada came downstairs.

"I 'eard you talking to the Russian gentleman, miss. I didn't dare make a sound or come down. Why'd he come in 'ere?"

"On the surface to deliver these." She waved the leaflets. "This one's for you."

Ada took it and read the title out loud. "'Britain's Fate 'Angs In The Balance.' Why would I want this?"

"To interest you enough so that you attend their meeting. That's where they will convert you into a sympathizer or an ardent believer, Comrade Carmichael."

"I don't want to go, miss."

"I'm going. I'm told there will be a new speaker shortly to arrive from Russia. Perhaps he's the spymaster we want to identify."

"Blimey, that'd be useful if he was."

Mrs Barker entered the hall. "I heard every word that man said. Is he mad, do you think?"

"I don't know," replied Sophie. "He did sound rather potty, but I thought he was putting it on."

Flora descended from the attic and stopped on the landing.

"I say. Did a Communist just enter the house?"

"Yes, Comrade Glad. Comrade Kuritsyn has invited us to listen to riveting speeches about the coming revolution."

"Not blooming likely, Comrade King. But — to give him credit — he just showed up on our doorstep, and that's tremendously sporting of him."

Someone knocked on the back door. They all looked at each other.

"That must be Nick or Sergeant Gowers," said Sophie. "It's too soon for it to be Auntie. She's coming to luncheon on Sunday, by the way. Hawkins delivered her demand for an invitation."

"*That's* who it was getting out of the taxi," said Flora.

"Her ladyship's coming?" asked Ada in astonishment.

"I'm afraid so," said Sophie. "She's even going to use the back door as though she were a spy." Sophie went to answer the knock.

Flora laughed. "If it's the police, it's a good job they didn't arrive earlier and bump into our friendly Communist." She returned to the attics.

"I have a shopping list," said Mrs Barker to Ada. "It's long, so get the shops to deliver if you can."

"I'll do that. And I've still to go to the laundry."

"It never stops, does it? I have a lot of cooking to do and, of course, the policeman will want a mug of tea." Mrs Barker turned to go, but looked back towards Ada. "This place is like Bedlam."

"It is an' all," replied Ada.

---

Not one, but two detectives graced the parlour with their presence.

"What an unexpected surprise," said Sophie, as she poured tea from the household's third best teapot into a third best china teacup. Sitting across from her at the pleasantly decorated tea table, which Ada had set up in record time, were Sergeant Gowers, whom Sophie had expected to call, and Inspector Morton, whom she had not.

Shock was nearer to the word she had in mind regarding Inspector Morton. Sophie liked the detective — there was no question of that. But, from recent events, she now knew that a proposal was in the offing. Not that he had said anything on the subject, or even so much as hinted at it.

They had gone to a football match together, where she had exuberantly cheered and sung with the crowd until flushed in the face. They had both had a marvellous time, especially as the home team, Chelsea, won the match. Afterwards, they enjoyed their tea together while chatting cheerfully about past cases, and became quite forgetful of the time.

Since then, they had met several times, but these had been hurried, unsatisfactory meetings during the day and when work permitted. One such meeting occurred when Inspector Morton arrived unannounced at Burgoyne's Agency. At first, Sophie assumed he had come concerning a new case, but when it became apparent that this was not the reason for his visit, an awkwardness descended first upon her and then upon him. Morton, invariably a decisive man, seemed at this meeting to be grasping for things to say. He soon departed, claiming that a pressing matter required his attention. When he had left her office, and Sophie was clearing away the tea things, she considered their meeting and could discover no discernible reason for his visit. About to pick up the tea tray, she asked herself why he had come. It was only when she put the tray down again in the office kitchenette that a possible answer occurred to her. He was going to ask her to marry him. "Surely not," she had said quietly, yet thoroughly astounded by the thought. From then on, her certainty grew that Morton would pop the question when the opportunity and his nerve permitted. She felt awful for her friend, because that was how she considered him, anticipating his disappointment and embarrassment once she had reluctantly replied with a negative. If things were awkward now, she could not imagine how difficult they would become later at times when they would inevitably be thrown together on a case. Sophie disliked unpleasantness, and she believed the atmosphere between them in the future might verge on the horrific. However, while pouring tea in the parlour of number seven, she was in command of herself and the tea ceremony.

Inspector Morton, perched on the edge of the settee, his hat still in hand, marvelled at the graceful authority with which Sophie caused the amber stream of liquid to issue from the teapot and to land, without a splashed drop, into the pretty floral-patterned cup. He did not know that Sophie and Ada had decided that they should use the third best tea set in case the policemen smashed the daintier cups in their large hands. Neither was Morton aware that the only reason he and Gowers were in the parlour at all was because Mrs Barker refused to have them cluttering up the kitchen when she had such a mountain of cooking to do.

"Help yourself to sugar, Inspector," said Sophie.

"Thank you very much. I will." He sounded extraordinarily grateful.

"Sergeant Gowers." Sophie passed the next filled cup to him.

At that moment, Gowers felt like a prize prune — one, he firmly believed, that was about to be translated into another type of fruit — that most unwanted of people when a couple who wish to be alone are present: the gooseberry. His foreboding began when Morton insisted upon accompanying him to Alexandra Gardens, supplying the thinnest of excuses for his totally unnecessary presence. Gowers' foreboding increased when, upon entering number seven, Morton adopted an almost perpetual smile. His alarm broke all bounds when they settled in the parlour.

"Thank you, Miss King." Gowers took the cup and saucer. "So this Russian fellow, Kuritsyn, just knocked on the door and got straight down to business?"

"Yes, Comrade Gowers. Forgive me, I must stop speaking like that, but I am finding the situation incredibly humorous."

"Well, of course, one would," said Morton.

Gowers picked up the leaflet on the table and scanned it quickly. "It beats me why people continue to go to these meetings. I went to one a couple of years ago and came away thoroughly depressed."

"Oh? Why was that?" asked Sophie.

"First off, everyone was so serious, as if they had been born with scowls on their faces." Gowers wrinkled his nose. "They weren't glum because of the war, as it was finally turning in our favour. No, it was that everything they were saying was all about struggling against oppressors, and overthrowing this, that, and the other. Made me feel tired just listening to them. But then, I thought to myself, that, should this stuff of theirs actually catch on, they'd be no end of trouble for the police. That's my self-interest, of course. But what I really didn't like was that they completely failed to mention who it was who would run things in this one-party system of theirs. I studied the fellas on the podium and thought there wasn't one of them fit to organize a church bazaar, let alone a country."

"Perhaps that would be a fitting test for all future politicians," said Sophie. "If they can run a church bazaar, then they can enter their name on the ballot."

"That's an excellent idea," said Morton.

Sophie's eyebrows rose a fraction of an inch.

Gowers produced a notebook and asked,

"Have you collected any information about the inhabitants of Alexandra Gardens?"

"I have nothing much worth recording at the moment," said Sophie.

"Well, you wouldn't," said Morton. "But I'm sure you'll get information soon enough, Miss King. You always do." He beamed at her.

"I hope so."

Gowers decided to plough on, despite his superior officer's unhelpful interruptions. "Who have you met so far?"

"I've met Mrs Cynthia Fitch, who is in charge of the committee that looks after the gardens. She told me off for sitting in the park, but then we sorted things out after a fashion. She's a very abrupt and awkward person."

"Yes," said Gowers. "She's also an expert on dogs and has a private income. Now *she's* the type who could organize a church bazaar with her eyes shut. I reckon she'd offend half the volunteers, but she'd get the job done, nonetheless."

"Mrs Fitch is *exactly* that type of person."

"She told you off?" asked Morton.

"She was rather officious, but I doubt she can help herself."

Morton looked annoyed on Sophie's behalf.

"Talking of rude people," continued Sophie, "Mr Bristow has a very blunt manner. He doubted that Blast-it was a Belgian Shepherd. I was most put out by his attitude."

Morton, functioning as a Greek chorus of one, said, "Who does he think he is?"

Gowers gave him a despairing look before asking Sophie, "You're calling the dog Blast-it?"

"That's the name he responds to."

"Somehow, I don't think that can be right. You see, the chap who looks after the dog... Well, I don't know how to explain this other than he's a big softie. He'd call a dog Buttercup or Bingo, but not Blast-it. How'd you find out the name?"

"I'm not sure, other than by trial and error," replied Sophie, wishing to gloss over the matter.

"Oh," said Gowers, who was none the wiser.

"Do you think Bristow might be the murderer?" asked Morton.

"No, he's just rude."

"We'll keep an eye on him, though," said Morton significantly.

"Have you met anyone else, Miss King?"

"Miss Villard and Major Cummings. Both of them seemed pleasant, but the meeting was brief."

"She's a hairdresser who has some upper-class clients."

"Ah… Have you seen her poodle? She must cut its hair, too. Surely she wouldn't go to a client's house to attend the lady *and* her dog?"

"If she does, let's hope she uses different scissors."

Sophie laughed.

Gowers continued. "The major served in the Royal Army Service Corps in India. Watch him, though, or he'll have you eating curry before you know it. He's mad about Indian cooking."

"Is he? How interesting. I've never tried authentic Indian food before."

"It's too hot for me. Eating it is like lighting a fire in your mouth that water can't put out. All you can do is sit and wait until the pain goes away."

"It can't be *that* bad, Sergeant."

"You try it and see."

"I don't think you should get too friendly with the neighbours," said Morton. "One of them is a murderer."

"I haven't forgotten, Inspector… But I *would* like to try a proper curry just once."

"Would you, really?" Morton appeared to be hatching an idea.

"Thank you for the tea but, if you'll excuse me, I'll go now and talk to Miss Dane," said Gowers, more or less disgusted by his superior officer's behaviour.

"What, you're going *now*?" asked Morton.

"Yes, sir. Also, there's a lot of work waiting for us back at the Yard."

Morton did not respond to this prompt, so Gowers left.

"Lovely weather we're having," said Morton to Sophie. They both looked uncomfortable.

---

Some people briskly walk their dogs in Primrose Hill Park before dinner, while others prefer a more leisurely stroll afterwards. This Friday, before dinner, the paths were much busier with pedestrian traffic than usual on account of the fine weather. Primroses and the first cowslips were showing. The leaves on the trees were filling in, but the carpet of bluebells under them was yet to show any colour. It was a lovely evening, and the day's warmth had brought out the scents of spring.

A thin woman wearing an old, winter-weight overcoat was walking her mixed-breed dog, which was not too dissimilar to a border collie. The woman walked quickly, at a speed that should have outdistanced everyone else on the path, except she took short steps and kept stopping suddenly. Then, bending forward, she appeared to speak to her dog while looking all around.

Flora, released from the thralldom of observing number fifteen's front door, was now standing at one end of a grass section in the park. This lay behind the observation point from which the centre of London could be seen. With her back to the view and also to the other people in the park, she hurled a ball so as not to disturb anyone who might have been admiring the scenery. Biscuit either raced across the grass to retrieve the ball or made a massive leap in trying to seize the ball mid-air. Often he succeeded, much to Flora's delight and to the amusement of newly arrived passersby.

"Good *boy!*" Biscuit had returned the ball to her. "That's enough for today. Time to go home and eat our dinners." Biscuit woofed.

She attached the leash, and they walked towards Regent's Park Road. Coming towards them was the thin lady. Flora could not help but notice her erratic behaviour. Several times, as they neared each other, she saw the woman stop. When passing, the woman darted a suspicious look at Flora, almost as if fearing an attack, and then she said "Quick!" to the dog before hurrying on even faster.

It was a minor incident, but a puzzling one for Flora. Next, a gentleman with an English setter walked towards her. He bid her good evening. From the description of him and his dog in the file the agency had received, she believed the man to be David Saunders, the witness to the murder.

Not a minute later, there appeared a formidable-looking woman in tweeds and very sensible shoes. It was Mrs Fitch, and she was exercising her black Labrador retriever, Titus. Without any ado, she accosted Flora.

"Hello. You've just moved into number seven, haven't you? That must be right, because I saw your dog about earlier. Also, I spoke to Miss King. I'm Cynthia Fitch." She took off her glove and extended a very square and capable-looking hand.

"I'm Gladys Walton. What number do you live at?"

"Number twenty-four. Directly opposite your house."

"Yes, I suppose it is."

"I must have a look at this young fellow."

Without regard for the dog's personality nor seeming to require permission from Flora, Mrs Fitch examined Biscuit. Being long accustomed to the handling of dogs, she examined his eyes, ears, teeth, throat, paws, and nether regions. The compliant dog yielded all its rights to this masterful being. Then Mrs Fitch stood back and looked him over.

"Yes," she said slowly. Then she stood at another angle to complete her assessment. "Come," she ordered, and Biscuit obeyed. Mrs Fitch patted him on the head as if he were *her* dog. Her own dog, Titus, waited for her to finish the examination of the newcomer. Mrs Fitch suddenly glanced at Flora. "He's a perfect Laekenois. Have you entered him in any shows?"

"Um, not yet," replied Flora, puzzled over the term, but unable to reveal her ignorance concerning the dog by asking what she meant.

"Well, you've missed Cruft's." Mrs Fitch managed to imply that Flora had, out of sheer perversity, done so deliberately. "But you'd be better off entering him in a few smaller shows first, anyway. Get your name down right away. *Right* away, Miss Walton. That's my advice." She looked again at Flora, suddenly smiled broadly, and said, "Good night... Titus!"

"Good night."

Flora watched as the woman stomped off at a smart pace and felt a powerful urge to obey Mrs Fitch's command immediately.

# Chapter 6

## Meeting the Gang

After five, Nick had brought a routine message from the agency. Sophie answered it, and also sent a note to Archie Drysdale, informing him they were installed in the house, and asking him where the Home Office agents were to be found? These were the ones who would take up the chase in the event of the Russian spymaster being identified. She asked Archie the question because, so far, no Home Office agent had made himself known, and she did not know whom to contact.

The log book maintained in the attic, wherein the activities of their dog-owning neighbours were recorded by time of day, was quickly becoming a mess of useless detail. Sophie set about reorganizing the collection of information by number, setting aside several pages for each house. Even this was less than ideal because houses eight to twelve were on the same side of the square as number seven, and their entrances could not be seen from the attics. This was inconvenient because the Saunders lived at number twelve, and Major Cummings at number nine.

In contrast, the separate log book for number fifteen was in perfect order. Sophie studied the day's entries and accompanying notes, trying to see the pattern of the residents' lives. Three men went to work at the docks — this fact she knew from the file notes issued to her. They usually left together but at varying times, Monday to Saturday, and returned separately just before dinner, except on Saturday, which was a half-day for each of the three, and they sometimes spent the afternoon distributing leaflets. Of the other three, one worked late shifts at a printing company. Another, a man who wore glasses and was known to be a doctor, rarely stepped out of the house, and then only on Fridays, Sundays and, even more rarely, some evenings. Kuritsyn appeared to devote his time to loafing about Primrose Hill, Camden, and Swiss Cottage, handing out leaflets and receiving cautions from the police. He also did the shopping for the house. Whenever there was a meeting, several of the men from number fifteen attended it, and Kuritsyn sometimes gave a speech. According to the notes, the Communists held their meetings in different places in north-west London. So far, only the doctor had yet to be sighted by the secret agents.

Sophie trained the binoculars on a hatless man walking his Jack Russell terrier. She consulted her list and identified Alan Mellish, aged 32, a chemist, and the manufacturer and purveyor of patent nostrums. This, then, was the dog biscuit man. Not that she had ever thought about how a dog biscuit manufacturer should look, Sophie was completely unprepared for the gentleman upon whom she now levelled her field glasses. His hair was long and, if she was not mistaken, he had it tied back with a red ribbon. He wore a green summer blazer, a blue shirt open at the neck with a red silk scarf around his throat, while hung across his shoulders was a long orange and white woollen scarf which was painful to see. His bare feet were encased in open sandals and his legs were engulfed in a pair of extremely stained and baggy brown corduroy trousers that could only be described as revolting. She stared, wondering what possessed him to appear in public dressed in such a way.

Ada climbed the stairs to the attics carrying Sophie's dinner tray.

"I've brought your dinner, Miss King. It's a pity we can't all eat together."

"A disadvantage of the job. Thank you for bringing it. I've been thinking of nothing but food for some time. But take these and have a look at Mr Mellish. You can't miss him."

Sophie vacated her seat and held out the binoculars. Ada settled in her place and looked through them.

"Blimey. How can his mother let him go out looking like that?"

"He's thirty-two and is a chemist who formulates dog biscuits."

"Then he should know better... Perhaps he'll give us some biscuits for our dog. Glad came back from the park and said Biscuit went mad chasing after the ball. She said he can jump really 'igh."

"Is that so? Why did you call him Biscuit?"

"We don't think his name's Blast-it, 'cause he only woofed once when you said it. When we said Biscuit, he woofed twice. So we don't *really* know, but we believe that's his name, and he *is* biscuit-coloured."

"Then you were keeping it a secret from me?" Sophie sounded rather offended. "I've been telling *everyone* his name's Blast-it."

Ada turned to face her.

"I'm very sorry, Miss King. I won't do it again. It seemed much funnier when we were planning it, but it wasn't fair to do that to you."

"Please, do nothing like this again. I am sure... No..., I'm *certain* Gladys was the instigator. However, she shall not get away with it. Two can play at that game."

---

The evensong of Alexandra Gardens descended upon the square with the low sun blessing it with a golden light which made the buildings glow. The air trapped among the tall houses and only moved by the gentlest of breezes had achieved a balmy, summer-like warmth. To many of those who had eaten and were not going anywhere special, it was really too nice of an evening to stay indoors.

Sophie, watching from her eyrie, saw the numbers of people out and about, and the rich field of opportunity which presented itself. She bellowed from the top of the stairs.

"Gladys!"

"Anything the matter!"

"Take Blast-it for a walk!"

"What!? He's *been* for a walk?"

"I'll come down!"

"I'll come up! I don't understand what you mean!"

They met on the stairs and arranged things between them — deciding they would both go out while Ada took over of the watch.

"Ready?" asked Sophie as she put on her grey gloves.

"Almost." Flora was using the pier glass in the hall to adjust her wide-brimmed hat to a rakish angle. "That'll slay them," she said at last.

Biscuit patiently waited, holding the leash in his mouth.

"Shall I take Blast-it, or shall you take Biscuit?" asked Sophie.

"You found out. Sorry, but I couldn't resist. The thought of you bawling for Blast-it in the square was too delicious to pass up."

"We are not amused."

"I am, but, once again, I'm sorry, it was bad behaviour."

"I shan't lecture, because we're on a mission."

"Certainly, we are. Do we have our story straight?"

"Yes, we do. Come along, Blast-it. Look at him. He doesn't need us. He could take himself for a walk." Sophie took charge of him.

"You should see him jump," said Flora. "My goodness, it's as if he's on springs."

Together, they had worked out their cover story, and parts of it were almost true. They were pretending to be cousins from Winchester, who each had inherited a half share in a large property that was far too big, inconvenient, and expensive for them to keep. So, by selling the property, they intended to buy a house in London — in Primrose Hill — *if* they found the area suitable. The property motif was important, because all the dog owners they were investigating were also house owners or had bought long leases. It was doubly important because Sophie and Flora would be the youngest members of this society. To fit in they must not only have a dog but also must be of the propertied class. The house that they fictionally owned and were selling was loosely based on the house Flora's parents occupied. Having lost his ancestral home, Mr Dane had received from a deceased relative, an archdeacon, a six-bedroomed country home, in need of repair, and which stood on two pretty acres. In the proposed fiction, the house gained the name Plumtrees, and grew in size to fourteen bedrooms and thirty acres.

As birds of a feather, the propertied dog owners flocked together in the square. There were five of them present.

"So, you see, it is much too inconvenient for us." Flora had been holding forth to an interested audience on the expensive trials of owning a country home. "It's miles from anywhere and, while we will both always love dear old Plumtrees, it has to go. That's why we're here, of course. To see if Primrose Hill suits us, and if *we* suit Primrose Hill." She ended with a laugh and touched her hat in a winsome way.

"Let me be the first to say," said Mr Bristow, "that I trust you'll find the area to your liking. I, for one, certainly hope you do."

"We definitely need more people of the right sort in Primrose Hill," said Miss Villard.

"That's very kind of you to say," said Flora, who disliked snobbery.

"A disturbing piece of news came to our attention," said Sophie. "That there was a recent murder somewhere nearby."

"Yes, sad to say, there was," said Major Cummings.

"We all knew the gentleman who was killed," said Miss Villard.

"You knew him?" said Sophie. "Oh, how awful for you. I'm so sorry... We both are."

"Yes," added Flora, "I can't imagine how dreadful it must have been. What was his name?"

"Matthew Hamilton," said Major Cummings. "He was a decent fellow, and one just can't imagine why he, of all people, should be murdered."

"It was a passing vagabond, intent upon robbery," said Bristow. "Must have been!"

"No, impossible," said Miss Villard. "Nothing was taken."

"Ah! Because he was disturbed, you see, by Saunders coming along at the right moment."

"Not quite the right moment. I doubt Hamilton would say it was!" said Cummings.

"That's true enough. Isn't that the way of it, though?" Bristow started stabbing the air with a finger. "If Saunders had been just two minutes earlier, why, then we wouldn't be standing here discussing the matter."

"Do the police not have any leads?" asked Sophie.

"Useless bunch," said Bristow. "All they do is drink tea and polish their buttons. The detective that interviewed me, my word, if I had him under my command, he'd soon learn the meaning of the word discipline."

"If you hadn't already realized," explained Cummings to Sophie and Flora, "Bristow here used to be a captain in the Royal Navy."

"They were the best days of my life. Some say it's your schooldays. Well, for me, it was my time spent in the senior service."

"That must have been fascinating," said Flora.

"It certainly was."

"Coming back to the police," she said, "they probably have difficulties. We understood it to have been a foggy night, didn't we, Phoebe?"

"Yes. We wondered what Mr Hamilton was doing out on a night like that."

"Yes, it is curious," said Cummings. "I've also considered the fog, and concluded that, as it was such an awful night, he would not have gone out unless he had a pressing engagement or an emergency had arisen."

"No one's come forward to say it was one or the other," said Bristow. "Clearly, he was off his chump."

"Don't be so unkind," said Miss Villard.

"Shouldn't have said that with him dead and all that sort of thing. He was nice enough in his way, but I never really took to him. We were not close."

"But a woman would take to him," said Miss Villard.

"What? Are you inferring he was out in the fog meeting a girl? Nobody does that sort of nonsense."

"A couple in love might." Miss Villard turned to Sophie and Flora. "He was quite handsome, and there were several hearts, not a mile away, which beat a little faster when he walked past."

"Oh, you do like your romance," said Bristow.

Addressing Sophie and Flora, Cummings said,

"Miss Villard prefers considering it as a crime of passion."

"And why not? That means it is safe for all of us, instead of our fearing a wandering vagabond who might return and do the same again."

"I hope our deliberations aren't putting you off Primrose Hill," said Cummings.

"Far from it," said Sophie eagerly. "We're finding it fascinating."

"Speculation shall positively run rampant tonight at number seven," said Flora.

"Relieved you're taking it so well," said Bristow. "By the way, Miss King, apologies for questioning your Belgian Shepherd the way I did earlier. I've been put straight by the Supreme Authority on all things dog related. It's a Laekonois, of course. SA says you should enter him in Cruft's."

"I know of Cruft's," replied Sophie, "but who or what is SA?"

"Mrs Fitch." The three residents answered practically in unison.

"She lives at number 24," said Miss Villard.

"I met her in the park," said Flora.

"Earlier, she told me off for sitting in the gardens," said Sophie. "Then she said it was all right."

"Then you got off lightly," said Bristow. "Mrs Fitch can make a tremendous fuss sometimes. She's more of a stickler for the rules than I am, and that's saying a lot."

"She's truly excellent with dogs, but rather the reverse with people," said Cummings.

"Unless they obey her," said Miss Villard.

"Here comes another of our number." Bristow nodded to the newcomer. "You'll like her. Sandra Pringle is a charming woman."

Sophie, whose back was towards Mrs Pringle, did not like to turn and stare. Instead, she found that she did not need to learn for herself *one* thing about the newcomer, because Miss Villard deliberately caught her eye. By privately signalling with significantly raised eyebrows, she allowed by her look only a single meaning: Mr Bristow admired Mrs Pringle. During the introductions, Sophie now observed this fact for herself, as evidenced by a significant change in Mr Bristow's manner, which was instantly transfigured from brusque to gallant.

Sandra Pringle's Pekinese was apt to be a troublemaker with the other dogs, so it was simpler for her to scoop up the hairy, creamy-coloured bundle.

"And how is Nankin today?" Bristow was ostensibly referring to the dog.

"As demanding as ever. He looked such a fright this morning. It took simply ages to brush his hair and make him presentable."

"Well, he looks fabulous now, so it was well worth the effort, Sandra."

Mr Bristow was beamed upon by Mrs Pringle. An attractive and fashionably dressed widow in her early thirties, she clearly enjoyed his attentions.

Cummings changed the subject.

"We were just discussing the murder. Miss Dane and Miss King are thinking of buying a house in Primrose Hill, but are sensibly cautious because of what occurred."

"Quite worrying," said Mrs Pringle, addressing the agents. "It happened just around the corner. It gave me such a turn, I couldn't sleep for a week afterwards."

"Oh, I can sympathize with you there," said Flora, who possessed the ability to sleep through an earthquake and a hurricane, should they ever coincide. "I have such extraordinary trouble sleeping. Don't I, Phoebe?"

"You most certainly do, Gladys." Sophie struggled to reply in case she laughed. "Excuse me. We'll be back in a moment." She took Biscuit for a quick walk so that she could compose herself.

"In the past, I've had tremendous difficulty getting to sleep," said Mrs Pringle. "That was until I started taking Slumbertina. It's an absolute wonder, and the only reason I couldn't sleep after the murder was because my supply had run out."

"You poor thing," said Flora.

"I *know*. It couldn't have happened at a worse moment. But there, events often coincide like that, when you least want them to."

"I don't think I've ever heard of Slumbertina," said Flora.

"Probably not," said Bristow. "Our resident inventor cooks it up in his workshop, and there's frequently a gap between batches."

"That sounds interesting. I don't believe I've met the gentleman," said Flora.

"Once seen, never forgotten, is our Mr Alan Mellish. Has a perky Jack Russell named Topper."

"I look forward to meeting him, then. And you say he makes batches of Slumbertina?"

"He makes a lot more besides that," said Cummings. "A word of warning. He'll talk to you for hours on end about his supplements and remedies, in the hopes you'll buy something from him."

"That's true enough," said Miss Villard, "but a few of them are extremely good."

"But who knows what he puts in them?" said Cummings.

Sophie returned to the group

"Now, now, Major," said Mrs Pringle. "Alan assures us he only uses the finest ingredients."

"I don't doubt he does but, on the other hand, he's unlikely to say he uses the cheapest ones. I'm sure everything is wholesome, but not knowing what the ingredients *are* causes me some concern."

"I always think if it smells all right and tastes all right, then it won't do you any harm."

"Yes, Bristow, that's good as far as it goes," said Cummings, "but what if a poisonous substance has no taste or smell?"

Mrs Pringle laughed pleasantly. "He doesn't use *poison*. I'm still alive and I've used several of his preparations besides Slumbertina. I've suffered no ill effects."

Sophie hoped to guide the conversation around to dog biscuits and their relation to the night of the murder, but the dogs, who had been well behaved up until now, suddenly started to act as if the talking had gone on far too long. In particular, Bo'sun pulled hard, and the strength of the Newfoundland set Bristow in motion.

"Time's up for me," said Bristow, straining hard on the leash. "He pulls like a tugboat when he wants to be off somewhere. Good night, ladies, Cummings."

With his departure, the group soon broke up and the dogs of Alexandra Gardens actually got the walks to which they had been looking forward.

While walking Biscuit around the square and back to the house, Sophie and Flora discussed their neighbours.

"Good grief, we'll have to be careful what we say," observed Flora.

"Miss Villard has to be the worst gossip of the lot."

"Their tongues wag more than their dogs' tails do. I agree with you about Miss Villard, and I see what you mean about Mr Bristow. He's a bull in a china shop if ever there was one."

"You won't believe this. I mean, I don't even *know* Miss Villard, and yet she signalled to me that Mr Bristow is enamoured with Mrs Pringle. I could see it for myself, after she did. But I'm a total stranger to her. Why," said Sophie, "would she take me into her confidence?"

"Who can say? What signal did she use?"

"Her eyebrows disappeared into her hair. Next, without moving her head, she turned her eyes towards Bristow, and then, with *great* significance, towards La Pringle."

Flora was quiet for some seconds. "That sort of signal requires practise, which means she is an adept, a scandal-monger of the highest order."

Sophie smiled. "All the more reason for us to tread carefully."

"Yes, indeed. None of *them* looked like a murderer to me. They all looked quite ordinary."

"Well, they would."

"I meant nobody looked ill at ease."

"No, they didn't. Mind you, whoever it was would be doing their absolute best to look normal. They might even ask innocuous questions to reinforce the impression of complete normalcy. Like Mrs Pringle saying she couldn't sleep after the murder. It establishes in the minds of her audience the idea that the murder frightened her and therefore infers she could not possibly have slain Mr Hamilton."

"This same modus operandi could go for them all, really. One thing we did find out. Handsome Mr Hamilton attracted the attention of several ladies."

"The police put nothing like that in the report they gave us... Bristow annoyed me," Sophie continued, "talking about the police in the way he did. He has no clue what he's talking about half the time, yet speaks as though he does."

"More than half, I'd say."

They stopped, because Biscuit wanted to use a tree.

"This is the most embarrassing part of having a dog."

"Female dogs are far more discreet in their habits."

"Blast-it is very well-behaved, though."

"You're continuing to call him that?"

"Oh, yes. I'm committed to the name now. It might also cure me of my rather dreadful outbursts."

Flora smiled.

The shadows had lengthened across the square and were advancing up the fronts of the more easterly buildings. The air was turning chill. They arrived on the pavement outside number seven and looked up.

"I like this house," said Flora.

"It has elegant proportions, and the square's lovely... Come on, let's go in."

---

Sophie had already resumed her turn in the attic. Nothing was happening now in the square, nor had there been any activity for a while. Earlier, she had watched people going out for the evening. A man and woman, whom she assumed were walking to the nearby underground station, looked absorbed in each other and happy together. Two private cars arrived at different houses to whisk away some passengers. Sophie had idly wondered where these and others were going. After that flurry of minor interest, Sophie settled in for the long haul — her shift finished at four a.m. She was determined to stay awake. The worst aspect of this surveillance was not being able to use a light, which made the chance of her falling asleep more likely. Sitting comfortably in the dark, Sophie imagined that the agents previously stationed in the attic must have had iron wills, forbidding themselves to sleep, and remaining alert by determination alone. Although it was only a few minutes past nine, she was already losing track of the time, as she could not see her watch. She also wondered what the others were doing and why they had not come to see her.

The night swallowed the gardens which lay within the hedge. There were four street lamps, one more or less at each corner, but these were barely adequate to illuminate the road outside the hedge. The lamps' saving grace was that they revealed anyone approaching or leaving number fifteen. And so they did now.

Four men grouped closely together quickly entered the house. Sophie recognized one as an inhabitant and was certain there were at least two strangers among them, but the dim light hid details and they moved too fast, which gave her no time to note any distinguishing characteristics. Out of habit, she uselessly looked at her watch.

Ten minutes later, the door of number fifteen opened again. She recognized Kuritsyn by his size and shape as he stood on the doorstep, silhouetted by the hall light. He scanned the square. She noticed he did not look towards number seven's attic.

He switched off the hall light but left the door open. Having descended the stairs with Vova on a leash, Kuritsyn stopped on the pavement. From there, he looked around once more, and then briefly put his free hand up to his ear. At this signal, a man, muffled up and with his hat pulled down, shut the door and descended to join Kuritsyn on the pavement. This unknown man was carrying a suitcase. The two of them and the dog set off at a brisk pace in the direction of number seven, evidently to exit the square and turn south.

Sophie jumped up. Not recognizing the second man, she believed he might be the spy they were looking for. She ran downstairs.

## Chapter 7

## Sightings

Sophie burst into the parlour to find Flora sitting comfortably, shoes off, and sipping cocoa.

"Try not to make so much noise," said the cocoa-drinker. "Mrs Barker's gone to bed."

"You don't understand. It's *him*."

"Who?"

"The Russian spy. You must follow him."

"He's here already!? Well, I *would* follow him, but *I'm* not dressed to go out while *you* are."

Just then, Ada entered the room wearing her dressing gown and carrying two small mugs on a tray.

"What's going on, miss? I was bringing you up some cocoa."

"I believe the spy is leaving the square, and someone has to follow him."

"But I 'ave to be up at four," said Ada in dismay.

"I'll go, then. You take over the watch, Flora."

Sophie hurriedly put on her hat, coat and gloves, and checked to see if she had her cosh, torch, and police whistle, which she did.

"Take Biscuit with you," said Flora.

Upon sensing the excitement and that a walk might be imminent, the dog presented himself with his leash in his mouth.

"Very well."

Barely making a noise, she opened the back door and was about to descend the steps when Biscuit stopped and emitted a low growl. Sophie froze, realizing there had to be someone nearby and, judging by the direction of Biscuit's stare, that person was on the other side of the garden wall.

The wait seemed interminable in the silence. It crossed Sophie's mind that the dog had made a mistake. She said to herself she would wait another minute and then go in, because any chance of finding the two men in the dimly lit streets was now gone.

Within a few seconds, she heard a murmur of low voices nearby, but could not distinguish what was being said. It sounded like two men. After a minute, she heard a tone of finality in the words, as if the conversation had come to an end. Then she heard the phrase, "Come, Vova," and immediately understood that the Russians had set a trap to see if number seven contained police spies — a trap she would have walked into had Biscuit not been so well-trained. She went back inside and said good night to Ada, who retired to her room. Sophie went to the attics to see Flora. Biscuit followed her.

"Hello? What are you doing back so soon?"

"Because any moment you should see Comrade Kuritsyn appear below us. The stranger with the suitcase has gone off somewhere. I think there's another stranger still inside number fifteen."

Within a few seconds, Flora and Sophie could see Kuritsyn ambling along at the speed of his dog, who was sniffing everything that came within nose reach.

"He and another man, one of the strangers, set a trap by the side door. If Blast-it hadn't alerted me, I would have blundered into them, and then they'd know we were spying for the authorities."

"How devious of them. And what a good boy you are." Flora patted Biscuit's head.

"Isn't he? The trap means they think we would use the side entrance."

"Do you think Kuritsyn suspects us?"

"Obviously, he did, but perhaps less so now. Of course, he came earlier to find out what we're up to, and if we're with the police. I don't think I gave anything away, though."

"Well, let's say you didn't. The others at number fifteen would still want to confirm they were no longer under observation, whatever he reported back to them."

"I suppose you're right... Well, then, because they set a trap, it must mean the spymaster has yet to arrive. They're making sure it's safe before he comes, which further means they know he's important... Good grief! Then Kuritsyn was testing me with that twaddle about a Russian speaker who would arrive this week or next." In the dark, she frowned. "I'm a complete imbecile sometimes."

"I would have answered the same as you, so don't worry about that. Tell him you're no longer interested in going to the meeting. That will make him reconsider."

"I hope it does. I'll see if it's necessary tomorrow."

Sophie returned downstairs to take off her coat. She heard a tap on the back door, which proved to be Nick.

"Hello, miss."

"Hello. Did you see anyone about in the street?"

"No one acting suspicious, if that's what you mean. Although a few blokes went into the pub."

"Did you see a man carrying a small suitcase?"

"No."

"I see. In future, should you see anyone loitering near the side of this house, continue on and avoid them completely."

"All right. Was it the Russians or the murderer? If it's the murderer, I'd better stay and look after things."

Sophie smiled. "No, it was only the Russians. Have you any messages?"

"The final report from the office is that everything is fine, and Miss Elizabeth says she'll buy more ink if you give her the say so."

"Yes, she may buy more ink and anything else she thinks the office needs."

"She always likes to ask first, don't she, miss?"

"Elizabeth does." Sophie looked at her watch. "Nine forty-five. It's rather late for you to be out, so go *straight* home and be careful. Tomorrow, first thing, mind you, take this note to Mr Drysdale. Have Elizabeth telephone him first to see if he's in the office or at his flat."

"Right you are."

"You're vital to this operation, Nick. I don't know why, but the Home Office agents we were expecting never turned up! Also, there were supposed to be couriers arriving at regular intervals, but we haven't seen a single one all day. I can't imagine what's happened to them."

"They must be busy with something else." Nick straightened himself up, as if preparing for a speech. "That being the case, miss, and my work being so important, like, I could really do with a motorbike."

"A motorbike! I presume you are joking. The thought of you hurtling around London on such a machine fills me with horror."

"I knew you'd say something like that."

"They're also very expensive and you're *far* too young."

"I could deliver a ton more stuff for the office, and a good second-hand one is twenty nicker... Sorry, miss, that's quid, er, pounds. I meant to say pounds. And they're safe if you know what you're doing. My mate's brother has a motorcycle and I've been on the back of it. I didn't feel scared, and it was great. You should try a motorcycle, miss. They're a lot of fun."

"No, thank you. They look too unsafe."

"So, are you saying no?"

"Yes."

"What, never? Not even in a million years?"

"Not even in a million years."

"Then, how about this? Could you teach me how to drive, please?"

"Why the sudden rush?"

"I want to get ahead, I do. So I should start when I'm young. You said no to the motorcycle, and that's fair enough, miss, but if I know how to drive, I could help you out on your missions."

"Missions, indeed." Sophie studied the fourteen-year-old for a moment. "Oh, very well. I'll teach you, but don't you dare rush me, or I'll change my mind."

"Oh, miss! You're the best, you really are. I was sure you'd say no."

"I nearly did, so remember that."

"I won't bring it up again until after this job's over. Is that all right, miss?"

"Thank you for your consideration, but I'll let *you* know when it is convenient for *me*. Is that understood, Nick?"

"I've got it straight. But it won't stop me from thinking about it."

"I imagine not."

Sophie was about to say something else when a cry filtered in from the St George's Street side of the square.

"That's a woman's scream," she said.

"Shall I see what it's about?" asked Nick.

"We'll both go."

They used the side entrance to access the street so as not to be observed from the square.

Outside, the road was empty. The only movement to be seen was a woman with a dog walking beyond the Princess of Wales and heading towards St. George's Square. Twice they saw her stop abruptly and speak to the dog.

"It must have been she who screamed," said Sophie.

"Well, she's not running away, but she's acting funny," said Nick. "Do you think she's off her head, miss?"

"It's uncharitable to pass a remark like that. The lady is obviously upset and has troubles. As she's not in any danger, we may not intrude, so let's return to the house."

When they were inside, Flora called down from the top floor, asking what had happened.

"I'll say good night, because I must go upstairs," said Sophie to Nick.

"Good night, miss. I'll get those messages delivered first thing."

As he left, Sophie noticed the hems of his trousers no longer met the tops of his shoes. Nick was growing, and she realized his uniform would soon need alteration or replacement.

In the attics, Sophie and Flora discussed the woman who had screamed. Flora, sitting in the chair, said,

"She must be the same woman I saw earlier in the park. She was acting oddly then, and she gave me a dreadful glare, as if thinking I might attack her."

"How strange," said Sophie. "I wonder what's wrong with her to behave so."

"I'd say she's just plain frightened. Yet I don't see why — when in a park full of people. It was light, and her dog was with her. No one was threatening in any sense. Now she's screaming. I couldn't see her, but she must have been close to the square."

"Perhaps her condition's war-related."

"It could easily be that. A lot of people have been detrimentally affected by losing loved ones or their income. Really, everything's changed, hasn't it? I think it's worse in some ways now than it was before, and there's still so much discontent in the world."

"Unfortunately, that's true. I felt that, even though it came as a massive relief, the war ended too abruptly. But everything that went before, all my life and the way the world was, seems so distant now, as though I view it through a telescope. It's as though it's become unreal and, personally, has nothing to do with me."

"I feel exactly the same, but you must remember, we were growing up, too. It might be our natural transition to maturity."

"Good heavens," Sophie laughed. "I don't *feel* very mature. In fact, I still feel like a schoolgirl. Do you know I have dreams in which Miss Dilling is lurking somewhere, and ready to pounce?"

"The Dilling was always an excellent pouncer. A dream about school with her in it qualifies as a nightmare."

"It's never about school, exactly. I'm upstairs on a tram, smoking a cigarette."

"You don't smoke!"

"I *know*. Anyway, that's what I'm doing, and my stop is approaching and I'm too scared to go down in case the Dilling catches me. What do you think it all means?"

"You had pickled onions and cheese before bed."

"Pshaw. Absolutely not."

"Then, there's something preying on your mind. Is there?"

"Um... Nothing in particular that I can identify. Except everything, I suppose. The business requires constant attention, plus there's the type of work we're doing now."

"I can't interpret dreams, but I think you might need a holiday."

"Perhaps you're right. It happens occasionally that I feel rather stretched. Mind you, being here is just like a holiday of sorts. It's different from anywhere else I've stayed, *and* we're keeping our own house, which I find a delightful idea." At that moment, Sophie wanted to mention Archie's interest in the property.

"They say a change is as good as a rest, and I know what you mean about the house. Should I ever make my fortune, a house exactly like this would be perfect. However, access to sudden wealth is a long way off and rather unlikely." Flora got out of the chair. "I've done my duty and kept your seat warm for you. Now I'm off to bed, so I'll say good night and God bless. Let me tell you this, first. Binoculars are highly dangerous. Be careful where you point them and avoid the top floor of number twenty-one. The man there did not close his curtains when retiring for the night. It was almost shocking."

The house settled down to rest. Flora, Ada, and Mrs Barker were asleep in their different bedrooms. In the attic, Sophie had rigged up an old curtain on some rope. Behind this effective screen was a small table where she could write notes by candlelight if need be. At eleven on the dot, the need arose because number two entered his house. Sophie got up and went behind the screen to consult the notes on him. Charles Clark, 40, musician with the London Symphony Orchestra, no known attachments, with a long lease on the house. She thought she had seen the last of him for the night, but the demands of housebound dogs had Clark, with his basset hound, back in the square within the minute.

Clark walked slowly because his dog walked slowly, and there was little for Sophie to see. However, before long, Mrs Pringle, carrying her Pekinese under an arm, hurried down the steps of number twenty to join Clark. Sophie, now much more interested, picked up the binoculars to study them.

Down at pavement level, Mrs Pringle spoke to Clark.

"How was it tonight?"

"Uh, I can barely bring myself to speak of it." The thin, forty-year-old man watched his dog sniffing a railing as he answered. "I used to find Charlie Chaplin amusing, but playing piano accompaniment to The Kid twenty-seven times in a row has made me loathe him."

"It can't be as bad as all that." Mrs Pringle laughed as she spoke. "You improvise and interpret as you play. I thought that's what you liked?"

"It is, and, in its way, it's more liberating than playing for the London Symphony Orchestra. However, playing the same improvised performance, night after night, certainly has its own set of very confining limits."

"You're just difficult to please."

"There is that," said Clark. "Anyway, the LSO is making changes." He sighed. "It appears I'll have to turn up in person for all rehearsals and performances from now on. They're cracking down on the hiring of substitutes, and I'm sure they'll soon ban the practise entirely."

"I'm sorry to hear that."

"Artistically and professionally, I suppose I can see their point. The LSO is quite second rate, really, and needs to improve. Economically, however, they are damaging my livelihood, and I'd wish they would leave everything as it is."

"Wasn't that why the LSO formed in the first place, so that the musicians *could* continue to use substitutes?" asked Mrs Pringle.

"Precisely so. Still, at least it's taken a few years for the same hypocrisy to creep into LSO's management... Enough of my woes. How was your day, Sandra?"

"Tolerable, but uneventful, as usual, Charles. The exciting news is that some new people have moved into number seven."

"Oh, really?"

"They are two young women, cousins, in their early twenties, and from a good family. They obviously have money, because they're thinking of buying a house in the area."

"Very interesting."

"Yes, and they have a maid. Dulcie Villard thinks they also have a cook. And you'll never believe this. Kuritsyn has already paid them a visit."

"Has he, indeed? I hope he hasn't driven them away."

"Do you think he might? I hate to think what he said to them, and they must be quite provincial. Coming from Winchester, they're not likely to be socialists. So I wonder what they made of our Communist?"

"They were probably shocked. Although, Kuritsyn is rather tame for a Bolshevik. He *says* all the right phrases, but I don't think he believes half of them."

"He has to be careful what he says, or they'll deport him."

"Yes... Cynthia was on about Cruft's again yesterday. She firmly believes Titus has the chance to win a first place next year."

"He is the quintessential Labrador retriever. A perfect example of the breed... For what it's worth, I think she's right."

"But what if she did enter him, and Mrs Murray adjudicated?"

"This time there'd be murder."

The flat word momentarily froze the conversation as each pursued private thoughts.

Clark broke the ice first. "Will you enter Nankin again?"

"No. Being passed over twice by addle-brained judges is quite enough for one little dog. Isn't that so, Nanky?" Mrs Pringle stroked her Pekinese, then set him down to walk.

"Addle-brained," repeated Clark. "They come off like that, but they aren't, you know. I firmly follow Cynthia's lead in this matter. Mrs Murray is against anyone from Alexandra Gardens entering Cruft's — it's as simple as that."

"So you think Mrs Murray deliberately destroyed Cynthia's application form? She doesn't seem to be the type of person to do that."

"Are you going over to the enemy's camp?" asked Clark with some heat.

"No, I'm not. I'm simply expressing a reasonable view. Mrs Murray said she'd never received the application. Cynthia swears she gave it to Matthew."

"Yet Hamilton swore he gave it to Mrs Murray."

"Yes, but Mrs Murray insists she never received it..."

"So the deed was done between Murray and Hamilton." He paused a moment. "Naturally, I do not wish to speak ill of the dead, but Hamilton was always her creature."

"Oh, Charles, don't. And I can't imagine he would ever lie so blatantly. He wasn't that kind of man. An opportunist, yes, but not out and out wicked."

"In one sense, I believe he lied to women all the time. Hamilton was ever the prince charming and, believe me, he was well aware of the effect he produced. Why, how many times have I heard *Matthew says this* or *Matthew thinks that*? It was as though he had hypnotized them. If you recall, even *you* were not immune to his influence."

"You're being very rude and quite churlish, while he was *always* pleasant. You could do with borrowing a leaf from his book. It wouldn't harm you in the slightest."

"I'm sorry, Sandra. That *was* rather bad of me."

"I know you disliked him, but surely now that he's gone, you can forget the past; forgive him, even. I had to do it with Cynthia after she inexplicably turned nasty towards me last year. Now we're on reasonable terms again."

"She's become very touchy of late. Lonely, you see. But with Hamilton, I heard him laughing at me while I was playing at the cinema. He was a dozen feet away, and I knew it was him. He passed it off as having been caused by a jocular remark he made about the film to his friend, and that their mirth was entirely unconnected with me. But I don't believe it. He laughed at me, while I was playing... and made me make a mistake... Argh!" Clark's rage made him inarticulate.

"That was months ago," said Mrs Pringle. "It's over, and you must let it go. If he did slight you, it was surely unintentional."

"I don't think so... I wish I *could* let it go, but the wretched memory of his smirking face in the stalls, lit by the reflection from the screen, haunts me still."

Sandra Pringle tried to picture the features of the handsome, wavy-haired and laughing man, picked out in the low light, but she found she could not recall what he looked like very well.

"He's a fading memory," she said. "It's only you who remembers or cares about what happened."

"Are you saying that you *don't* care?"

"I'm saying that it's time for you to set it aside, because you're the only one being hurt by the memory. How you might accomplish that, I'm not sure."

"You're right. I need to do something. Sorry for being such poor company. Money worries, don't you know? This business with the LSO has put me in a foul mood."

"We all have money worries. My income has dropped considerably, and who knows whether it has stopped dropping. I'll have to start a business or get a job. I have no ideas about the one, and few qualifications for the other. I should learn to type, I suppose. I wonder where one does that?"

"Oh, Sandra. Don't tell me it's come down to that."

"Near enough. If you had a fortune, I'd take you up on your marriage proposal and endure your moods."

"Do you mean that?"

"Yes. Why not? We're both lonely and we get along well."

"And you're truly over Hamilton?"

"As I said before, there was never anything much between us. He was only after my house, silly. I spotted his motive soon enough."

"Ah. I didn't know that."

"Well, it's also the reason he was so friendly with Cynthia, despite the application incident. It wasn't that he wanted her; it was her house he wanted. You should talk to Dulcie. She can tell you a thing or two about Matthew."

"I might do that... But coming back to what you just said. Would you only marry me if I had money?"

"You're wasting your talents. Find some ambition and stop fooling about between the Picture Palace and the LSO. So you sleep on that, because I'm finding it rather chilly."

"You're right. I'll finish working on the score for that blessed musical. Good night, Sandra."

Sophie watched them part and go to their separate houses. She wondered what they could have been talking about so animatedly.

# Chapter 8

# Chasing 'round the Shops

At 8:30 Saturday morning, Jack the milkman was studying the note left by Ada before her early morning watch, which read, *Five pints best milk. Three large pots double cream. Two pounds of butter. Two doz. Eggs. - Knock for money. Thank you.* He knocked, and Mrs Barker answered.

"Good morning," said Jack.

"Morning," said Mrs Barker, her face already flushed from the heat of the stove. She held an envelope in her hand.

"Give me a moment to add up the total." Jack began writing in his notebook. "This is a big order."

"We have company coming tomorrow."

Mrs Barker waited. He gave her the total, and she handed him a ten-shilling note from the envelope. Jack shook his satchel to find the coins for the change. Then he handed her the items, and she put them on the hall table.

Mrs Barker, taking the eggs from him, asked, "Before you go — do you know who owns this house?"

"Oh, um. Let me see. It's been let for some years. A family by the name of Radcliffe owned it from when it was built. I suppose they still do, although she died in sixteen, and he must be easily pushing eighty by now. He might not be alive, either. I don't think they had any children."

"Ah, I see. Thanks for telling me. I have to get back to the kitchen."

"I'm sure you do. I hope your dinner tomorrow goes all right."

"Let's hope so."

Ada was out shopping. After visiting the third shop, she concluded she was being followed. She was in two minds. Should she have it out with the young woman, who looked like a well-dressed maid, or should she keep quiet? Her inclination was for the former, but she thought better of it. There was no telling how the case might be harmed if she had a row in the middle of Primrose Hill. As Ada finished her shopping, she wondered if being followed had to do with the Communists, which she thought unlikely, or was it connected to the murder? — which possibility she did not like to contemplate.

Mrs Barker had been joined by Myrtle, a maid-of-all-work. She had immediately taken to the quiet, willing girl, and so she gave her pointers on how to accomplish more expediently the preparation of vegetables and explained how to cook certain things. They were working steadily when there came an unexpected tap at the back door. They both jumped.

"Bloody Nora!" exclaimed Myrtle.

"You will *not* say that again in my kitchen, no matter how much you're provoked."

"I'm very sorry, Mrs Barker. I shan't do it again."

"See that you don't. Go on, answer the door."

Myrtle did so. She opened the door upon a man in his early thirties, casually dressed in old clothes of good quality, and wearing a flat cap.

"I'm terribly sorry to disturb you," he said. "I wonder if I might see Miss King or Miss Walton. If they are not available, may I speak to Miss Carmichael?"

"I don't know, I'm sure, sir." The visitor puzzled Myrtle. He was obviously a gentleman, but she could not understand why he was at the back door. Also, she did not recognize a single name he had mentioned.

"Who is it?" called Mrs Barker, who left her work to come over.

"The name's Laneford," said the man to her.

"Lord Laneford?" asked Mrs Barker, now arrived at the door.

"Ah, yes."

"Oh, I'm ever so sorry, my Lord. Please, do come in."

"Thank you."

Sidney Laneford entered and removed his cap. He quickly surveyed the kitchen before turning to Mrs Barker. She signalled with her eyes for Myrtle to resume what she was doing.

"I know I'm interrupting you, but it's rather important I speak to one of the ladies immediately."

"Well, you see," Mrs Barker became wary, "Miss King's asleep at present, and Miss Carmichael's out at the shops. I would call Miss Walton, but she's busy at the moment."

"Up in the attics, is she?"

"You know about that, do you, my Lord?"

"I'll just pop up and see her."

"No, no, my Lord. You can't possibly do that."

"Oh?"

"If you could wait just a moment. Myrtle, go upstairs and tell Miss Walton that Lord Laneford wishes to speak to her."

"Yes, Mrs Barker," said Myrtle, realizing that 'Miss Walton' must be Flora.

After she had gone, Laneford said,

"Please, don't let me hold you up. I'm sure you're fully occupied."

"Well, if you don't mind, my Lord. I do have a lot to do. Can I make you some tea?" she asked brightly.

"Ordinarily, that would be most welcome, but I'm sure I'll be seeing Miss Walton at any moment."

Mrs Barker smiled, then continued working.

In the attic, Flora was whole-heartedly lounging. She was comfortably attired in an old dress suitable in which to do nothing and see no one. Her feet were propped up on the arm of the chair, her slippers kicked off, and her head resting on a soft cushion while she lazily held the binoculars in a comfortable position to scan the square below. Her long dark hair was spread untamed across the russet coloured fabric.

Minus the binoculars and the notebook lying on her stomach, any artist of merit would have said, "Don't move. I must capture this moment," beginning to sketch immediately.

Myrtle knocked on the doorpost.

"A human being!" said Flora. "What a relief to talk to someone, and I've only been here an hour. Come in, Myrtle, and tell me your life's history."

"Oh, I can't, Miss Walton," replied Myrtle in a sepulchral voice. "There's a gentleman here to see you."

"What!?" Flora sat bolt upright and then got up.

"Yes. And he's Lord Laneford."

"Sidney? He can't see me like this. Send him away."

"I don't think I can do that," awkwardly replied the kitchen maid, all the while marvelling that Flora had used the baron's first name.

"No, I suppose you can't." Flora stood pensively. "I've got it. Run downstairs and tell him to have a cup of tea or something. Then come right back here. Understood?"

"Yes, miss."

Myrtle hurried from the room. When she got downstairs, she gave Lord Laneford a worried look.

"Yes?" he asked.

"Please, my Lord. Can you have a cup of tea or something? I have to go back upstairs quick."

"Ah," said Laneford. He turned towards Mrs Barker. "May I take you up on your kind offer?"

"Yes, of course, my Lord."

Myrtle returned to the attic. Without a moment's pause, Flora gave the bewildered maid a crash course on how to observe the inhabitants of the square and which ones required particular attention. Flora then flew to her room to change her dress as only an actress habituated to quick changes can do.

At the bottom of the stairs, she found Biscuit sitting outside the open hall door to the kitchen, obviously interested in the visitor, but forbidden to set a paw inside Mrs Barker's domain. Even though he had visited Flora in the attics earlier, his tail wagged. She stroked his head and entered. Laneford rose when he saw her. Whenever they met, he was always surprised by how lovely she looked.

"Good morning, my Lord," said Flora.

"Good morning, Miss Walton. I'm sorry for the intrusion, but I'm here on urgent business."

"I see. Perhaps we can adjourn to the parlour, where discussion will be more convenient."

Laneford smiled at Flora's unusual formality. "As you wish."

In the parlour, Flora said,

"Sidney, what are you doing here so early? It's not even nine, and you'll throw us all into an uproar."

"Again, I apologize for arriving unannounced, but it was out of necessity. The Home Office has blundered, I'm sad to say. Agents were supposed to be on hand and couriers were to come to the house every four hours. A chap, and I've a pretty good idea who it is, in recalling the two agents from the house, effectively cancelled the complete operation, despite being given explicit instructions to the contrary. I'll get to the bottom of *that* matter. Because I only learned of this error an hour ago, I could find no one available to step in at a moment's notice. I'm here as a temporary, stop-gap measure. That's a pretty dress, if I may say."

"Thank you. I rather like it, too. How did you find out?"

"Drysdale rang me up. Apparently, an office boy arrived at his flat at eight with messages from Miss King. Among them was one asking, 'Where is the Home Office?' He got on to me immediately. I got on to someone else who will put the machinery back in place, but that won't be until this afternoon. In the meantime, you'll have to suffer my presence as best you can. Unless, of course, you have an urgent message that needs delivering."

Flora smiled. "The only thing noted was that Miss Phoebe King, at about two o'clock, saw a fox walk past a cat and they more or less ignored each other. All the humans are behaving normally. According to Nancy's notes, Mrs Fitch took out her dog named Titus at 6:00 a.m. The Russians who work for a living went out at a quarter to seven, and Mr Saunders, banker and eyewitness, no, actually earwitness to the murder, took his dog, Ginnie, presumably to the park at seven-twenty before returning and then setting off to work. At eight, when I took over, a whole horde of dog owners emerged or re-emerged. Mrs Saunders is looking quite advanced in, um, her condition. Major Cummings has an Indian servant. Mr Clark and Mrs Pringle have yet to appear, but then they were in deep conversation late last night. They stood in the shadows so as not to be seen from the other houses. That's about it, unless Myrtle has spotted the Russian agent who arrived last evening. Sophie thinks he was one of the two strangers among the group and, as far as we know, one of those strangers is still in the house."

"Drysdale mentioned that. He also said they tried a ruse to see if there were any agents left in this house."

"Yes, they did. Kuritsyn, accompanied by one of the two unidentified strangers, waited around the corner by the side door to see if anyone followed them. If Biscuit hadn't alerted Phoebe, she would have blundered into them."

"Ah. Yes, that is very fortunate. You see, the observers are not supposed to leave the house. Instead, they are to signal to someone in another house on St George's Road. I believe it's done from a back window. Upon receiving the signal, agents will then follow the target."

"Why wasn't a telephone installed?"

"We can't. The terms of the lease specifically exclude alterations without written approval. We applied and were refused in very rude terms."

"Pardon? But you're the Home Office. I thought you just ordered people about."

"That's very seldom, but we're bound by a contract in any event."

"What about radios?"

"They're all in use, and the departments that have them… You've not worked for the HO, so you may not understand this. Every department, and every sub-department, is like its own principality. Radios are a scarce commodity, and everyone guards them jealously."

"Doesn't your department have any?"

"No. Technically, I'm not even an employee. I occasionally advise on financial issues, and now I'm involved in our secret network, which is not even officially recognized."

"You get paid for this work?"

"Oh, yes. Rather well, actually."

"I'm glad to hear it, Sidney. But who has the radios?"

"Kell of the Secret Service and Thomson of Special Branch. Neither are particularly interested in this project because they're strapped for money. They won't lend their radios to it, but they did lend a few of their agents. I think that's more to keep an eye on us than to assist in the mission itself. There's a fair amount of departmental rivalry. Then there's a chap named C. Believe me, my dear, we don't want him involved in anything we do. He'd either take over in a heavy-handed way or neglect the mission entirely, considering it inconsequential. He's obsessed with getting back into Ireland. And, personally, the further he is from Primrose Hill, the better I like it."

"You've crossed swords with him."

"He is intractable and overbearing. Good at his job, but he believes everyone else is an idiot."

"Don't you worry about him, Sidney. He is beneath you."

Laneford smiled. "Let's not talk of them. Instead, how are you, my dear?"

They spoke quietly together for some minutes. During that time, Sophie awoke. She had slept for some hours, but the day looking nice, the excitement of the mission, and voices in the hall downstairs all combined to get her up, washed, and dressed. The first person to meet her upon her descent was Biscuit, carrying his lead in his mouth.

"You'll have to wait a moment," she told the dog.

On her way to the kitchen, Sophie passed the parlour and heard voices.

"Good morning, Mrs Barker."

"Good morning, Miss King."

"Who is in the parlour?"

"Lord Laneford and Miss Walton," replied Mrs Barker.

"Lord Laneford? What on earth is he doing here? And at this hour?"

"I couldn't say, I'm sure."

"Then, Ada's in the attics?"

"No, she's out shopping. Myrtle's up there."

"Ah, good. She must have arrived early! But Myrtle isn't trained."

"I think Miss Walton must have shown her the ropes — so that Myrtle could watch the square while she went to speak to his lordship. Funny goings on, if you don't mind my saying."

"Yes, very funny. I hope they don't disturb you. How is the cooker turning out?"

"Very nice, thank you. In fact, this is a nice little kitchen, and the cold shelf is wonderful."

"I'm pleased to hear it."

"Would you like breakfast?"

"I can do it."

"No, you won't. I'll have it ready faster and I know where everything is. You sit down. The kettle's hot, and you'll have tea in no time."

"Thank you very much. But I'll be back in a minute. I must find out why Lord Laneford is here first."

She did as she said, and returned fully apprised of the situation.

"Unbelievably, he's acting as a messenger today. The Home Office neglected to send anyone to collect reports or to follow the Communists."

"Whatever can they be thinking of?" Mrs Barker looked annoyed with them. "Tea's on the table, and your eggs are almost ready."

"Excellent. I'm so glad you came." Sophie sipped her tea. "How is Myrtle's work?"

"Not at all bad. The main thing is, she listens to what she's told. If I ask her to do something a certain way, she does it without answering back. She's just like an extra pair of hands. I think, with a bit of training, she might get on in the cooking line."

"I'll talk to her about that after this is all over."

"Here are your eggs."

Upon her return from the shops, Ada decided she would turn the tables on the young woman following her. As she approached a corner, she increased her speed. Then, when out of her pursuer's sight, she stopped to wait, and put down her heavy bags. Ada had the satisfaction of seeing her follower hesitate, come to a hasty decision, and walk forward, trying not to return her look.

"Mornin'," said Ada, as the woman passed her.

"Good morning," said the woman, without turning.

Ada picked up her bags and followed. On the way, she analyzed the person in front. *Definitely a maid*, thought Ada. *Probably gives herself airs because she thinks she's clever*. Most satisfying for Ada was that she believed the maid's dress was of inferior quality to her own, although she had to allow that the short jacket she wore was very becoming. Ada wondered where she had got it from.

They walked through St. George's Square and along St. George's Road. When they neared Alexandra Gardens, it became apparent that the maid worked for a neighbour in the square. Eventually, the maid entered number two, and Ada crossed the road.

She entered number seven and headed straight for the kitchen, where she found Sophie just finishing her breakfast.

"Hello, miss. You're up early."

"Good morning, Nancy. I woke up and couldn't get back to sleep. You won't believe this, Lord Laneford's arrived."

"*Never.*"

"Yes! Apparently, someone at the HO got the wrong end of the stick and let all the agents go. Lord Laneford found out this morning from Archie and came hot-footing it round here. How about that? We have a baron for a courier."

Ada grinned. "That's a treat."

"Anyway, they're putting everything straight and he's only with us for the morning."

"Is his valet, Mr Philpott, 'ere an' all?"

"I haven't seen him. Did you see a valet, Mrs Barker?"

"No, but the way things are going, one should turn up at any moment."

"I agree. It is all rather potty."

"May I ask something?" asked Mrs Barker.

"Yes, of course," replied Sophie.

"Are Lord Laneford and Miss Flora, stupid me, I mean Miss Walton, are they...? Well, you know."

"Um, yes, they are."

"Well, I never. To think of her with a title... Oh, I *am* glad I came. This is so exciting! They've not made any announcements, have they?"

"Not yet. I think these are early days."

"Oh, I see." Mrs Barker stirred a pot. "He seems like a very pleasant gentleman."

"We've met 'im before," said Ada, "and he's right proper, quiet, and ain't stingy like some of them. He puts his 'and in his pocket when he should, and brings out more than what's 'oped for."

"Well, that's all right, then," said Mrs Barker. "Are you, er, are you hopeful for them?"

"I think I am," replied Sophie. "Of course, I am, only it will just take some getting used to if they marry."

They were all quiet for some moments.

"Do you know what I'm thinking of?" asked Mrs Barker. "Wedding cakes with royal icing."

They all laughed. Then someone knocked on the back door.

"I bet that's Mr Philpott," said Ada, who went to answer. "I've got something to tell you later, miss, so don't let me forget."

"I won't."

Ada was wrong. Instead, Len Feather, Mr Yardley's oversized chauffeur from Yorkshire, filled the doorway. Ada was amazed.

"Hello, Miss Carmichael. I've come, like, because I heard you were short-handed." He was well-dressed in civilian clothes rather than his usual chauffeur's uniform.

"Hello... Sorry, I'm just so surprised to see you. Is Mr Yardley with you?"

"No. He's down at his mum and dad's."

Ada started giggling. "I've never 'eard a peer's estate called that before. Come in."

"Hello, Len," said Sophie.

"Morning, Miss King."

While he was being introduced to Mrs Barker, Myrtle entered the kitchen.

"Would you like some tea?" asked Mrs Barker of Len.

"Ta very much. I could murder a cup," said Len. "But I'll tell you what. I can't abide just sitting here with everyone busy. Give me summat to do, and I'll be right happy."

"You might let yourself in for more than you bargained for," said Mrs Barker.

"I might, but I'll risk it."

"That's very adventurous of you," said Sophie. "I'll just inform Lord Laneford you're here."

"Thanks, Miss King."

As she left, she noticed Ada bring Len his tea, and then sit down at the table across from him with her own cup. It caused her eyebrows to rise.

In the parlour, Laneford was reading. He got up when he saw her.

"Sorry to disturb you, my Lord."

"On the contrary, Miss King. It is I who am disturbing you."

"Is it a good book? You look so engrossed."

"I don't know yet. It's Gladys' book and I've only just started. She's enjoying it, and says it's a very good murder mystery, if you can get past the odd behaviour of the narrator who goes by the name of Hastings. She said he was instantly smitten with his friend's wife, and the next thing you know, they're walking in the woods alone together for hours on end. Gladys says nothing off was implied, but it struck her as most odd. After that, I am informed, the story becomes quite engaging."

"Interesting. Who is it by?"

"Um..." Laneford picked up the book. "Agatha Christie. Ever heard of her?"

"No, I haven't." Sophie read the title. "The Mysterious Affair at Styles. Sounds intriguing." Sophie smiled. "I thought you should know, Len Feather has arrived. He's in the kitchen."

"Excellent. I'll see him in a moment. I'd like to finish this chapter first."

"Then, if you'll excuse me, I'll take the dog for a walk."

---

It was not yet nine-thirty, and with the square being almost empty, Sophie went to the park. It was sunny and the air still, although it felt cooler in the open space. She soon had the delight of seeing Biscuit running and performing the most astonishing leaps, sailing through the air in pursuit of the ball.

She took in the view from the top of the hill for some minutes. Here, she felt she could truly breathe, and felt less encumbered. Despite the immensity of London, she thought, it was really such a slight thing when compared to the sky. That simple observation seemed to sweep away all the complexities of her life, at least for the moment. Something she had heard was that a commemorative tree had been planted hereabouts in 1864 in honour of Shakespeare's three-hundredth birthday. Sophie set about finding it.

"Come on, Blast-it."

The sensibly yet stylishly dressed young woman with her dog on a leash descended the hill. They used one of the cinder paths that led nearest to a very singular-looking tree she had spotted from the hill-top. Some eighty feet tall, it stood at the bottom of the slope. As the distance closed, she saw it was indeed an oak, but was it Shakespeare's Oak? She believed it to be the right size for its age - fifty-odd years, plus whatever age it had been when planted. She turned on to a different path to get closer.

There was no sign, but the beaten path which traversed the grass to get to the tree told her it must be the right one. She crossed and, once under the broad spreading branches coming into full leaf, became *convinced* it was the right one. She touched the bark, and this conjured up thoughts of Shakespearian lines and scenes, vesting the moment with significance. With annoyance. she noted several sets of initials had been carved. Sophie looked up, and decided the tree was ill-suited for climbing, but its height had her thinking of galleons and then Elizabethan England. Her reverie was broken by a tug on the leash. She looked at the dog.

"*Oh,* how *could* you?"

Biscuit was marking his territory.

As she turned to leave the oak, she observed at a distance Kuritsyn and his bloodhound, in the company of another man. They slowly ascended the hill by a more westerly path. Unnecessarily, she looked about to see if anyone was watching her, then set off at a smart pace after them.

The men really were inching along, while Sophie walked as fast as she could, at a speed that almost verged upon the absurd. Biscuit relished this and dutifully trotted beside her, never pulling and never falling behind or getting distracted into stopping. Gratefully, Sophie assumed his model behaviour resulted from his police training.

When she got onto the same path, the men were still a short distance from the crest of the hill. They stopped. Sophie moved behind a tree. By their hand movements, it became apparent that something was under vigorous discussion. The stranger — Sophie was uncertain whether she had seen him the night before — was a little shorter than Kuritsyn, but still tall. He seemed youthful and had a moustache. The clothes he wore were on the shabby side, but his European suit had once been respectable. From her vantage point, she was certain by the cut of his clothes that they were not British made. The stranger offered his cigar case to Kuritsyn, which delighted the latter — as though he had not seen a cigar in years. Superficially, at least, they were on good terms.

They smoked. Kuritsyn did so with some extravagance, almost as if he were putting on a performance to demonstrate how thoroughly at ease he felt and what a carefree man of the world he was. The other smoked in a curious fashion.

The stranger held his short cigar close to his chest, as if to keep the smoke from straying too far. This was familiar to Sophie, and she tried to recall where she had seen the mannerism before. It wasn't her father with his pipe. Then she remembered a certain Dr Beasely, who attended the sick of Havering-under-Lyme; he had the exact same habit. Having identified him as the earliest example, later ones also then occurred to her. She analyzed them as a group, discovering their commonality was their education, being professionals or career men. The one outlier was the theatre manager whom Flora had introduced to Sophie one evening. She remembered him wearing a bowtie and large gold cufflinks. In her mind, she could see his hand now. When the manager wanted to emphasize a particular point he was explaining, he had used the cigarette to pin the meaning in the minds of his listeners. Sophie had seen the stranger do something similar in tracing a small, yet airy circle with the end of his cigar, before holding it near his chest again. She decided he must be an intelligent man, used to conversations in drawing rooms and upper-class social gatherings.

After a while, Sophie estimated how long it was possible for her to stand next to the tree without becoming an object of curiosity to others. A young workman walking towards her was about to provide a test. Sophie pretended she really was not interested in anything at all, and certainly not the two men further up the path. The workman must have noticed her, but did not turn his attention in her direction, so that came as a minor relief. This was not the first time that Sophie, while doing something she herself would consider peculiar if she were the onlooker, believed anyone who saw her must instantly know what she was up to, and, of course, condemn her for it. She finally grasped that anyone seeing her now would assume that she had a valid reason for being where she was, that it was none of their business anyway, and so would ignore her or, at least, not think to impute any hidden purpose to her presence.

This line of thought about surveillance made her think of cameras. Had she been holding a camera, might the young workman have taken notice? Might he have spoken to her, and thereby drawn attention to the fact she was behind a tree? This was completely unanswerable unless also tested, she decided. However, a camera would be very useful in Alexandra Gardens. It was a puzzle to her why the HO had not supplied one. Also, a telephone or radio or both would have been most useful, too. When Flora and Lord Laneford had mentioned why the HO could not obtain such instruments for the current operation, she would have laughed had not the explanation been so thoroughly aggravating. She decided that, if the Foreign Office was rather slap-dash in its ways, the HO was completely inscrutable, if not totally asinine. She exempted Lord Laneford, of course, from her strictures upon the HO.

Having finished their cigars, the men moved on. Sophie followed. At the point where they had halted, she paused and examined the ground. While monitoring them, she stooped to retrieve a cigar end. Informed in what to do as are all readers of Sherlock Holmes' adventures, she sniffed it, instantly regretting her action. Instead of determining the tobacco type by sense of smell, far easier, she found, was reading the cigar band which bore Cyrillic lettering. These were the stranger's cigars and of Russian or Slavic origin, which probably accounted for Kuritsyn's enthusiasm when offered one. Folding the stinky object in her pretty handkerchief, she determined to use envelopes in future. Although armed with evidence that only confirmed an almost certain fact, it was at least something tangible. She followed the men at a safe distance, feeling remarkably satisfied with herself.

# CHAPTER 9

# A WALK IN THE PARK

Avoiding the two dawdling Russians by many yards, Sophie left them to it and returned to Alexandra Gardens. She did not know whether Kuritsyn had recognized her, but thought that, even if he had, he would consider it quite normal for her to be in the park. As soon as she entered the square, Mrs Fitch intercepted her.

"Good morning, Miss King. Has Miss Walton informed you of my suggestion?"

"Good morning, Mrs Fitch. Do you refer to entering Blast-it in dog shows?"

Mrs Fitch was taken aback. "Yes… I thought the dog's name was Biscuit?"

"Did you?"

"Well, yes. Is that not correct?"

"Yes, it is."

Mrs Fitch looked nonplussed. "Am I to understand your dog has two names?"

"Yes."

"Then if you do enter him into shows, with the view of eventually trying him at Cruft's, you must call him Biscuit."

"I'm sure Miss Walton shall do that, if she so chooses. However, should I enter him, I shall call him Blast-it."

"I don't think that's a suitable name for anything, let alone a dog."

"Blast-it. Sit." The two women watched as the dog sat. "Blast-it. Lie down." He lay down. "He doesn't seem to mind, and neither do I."

"*Really*," declared Mrs Fitch, who turned to walk off.

"Blast-it. Walk," said Sophie.

When she got to the door of number seven, she found it bolted, and had to knock. Ada opened it to her.

"Good morning, miss. We have to keep the door bolted now. Whatever's the matter?"

"Good morning. In a word, Mrs Fitch. I cannot tolerate the woman. As soon as she speaks, she orders me about. Others, too, I'm given to understand." Sophie removed her gloves and unleashed Biscuit, who went to find water. "Sorry. I'm obviously..."

Ada forestalled her by putting a finger to her lips and glancing towards the shut parlour door. Sophie continued in a whisper,

"I'm undergoing a test of my patience and failing. Why was the door bolted?"

Ada smiled.

"Who's in there?"

"Mr Drysdale," replied Ada, also in a low whisper.

Sophie mouthed the word 'Oh'. She removed her hat and jacket, and Ada took them away. She entered the parlour.

In a comfortable chair, Laneford was reading. Nick, in ordinary clothes rather than his messenger's uniform, sat in a nearby chair with a book open. He grinned awkwardly at her. At a table by the window, Archie was writing. He stopped and said,

"Good morning, Miss King. Excuse me for not rising. How are you this fine day?"

"Good morning, and I'm very well, thank you... Has something happened?"

"Yes."

"Is it bad?"

"Not bad, exactly. More in the line of a dreadful bore."

"Admirably put," said Laneford, who rose, keeping his place bookmarked with a finger.

"Not one, but two Home Office suppliers of agents have decided that our little mission has A, been compromised, or B, been deemed not worth the trouble. They've pulled all their support, claiming budget cuts, lack of funds, lack of manpower, more important operations currently on the go, etc., etc."

"The usual rot," chimed in Laneford, before resuming his reading.

"As you say, sir. The usual civil service rot."

"They can't do that," exclaimed Sophie.

"They've done it, my dear old thing," said Archie. "And we're the last ones to bally well be told. Excuse the split infinitive, I'll just be a moment. I have to finish this, and then I can give you my undivided attention."

In the silence, Sophie observed Archie writing and Laneford reading. She turned to Nicholas.

"Sorry, miss. I'm not allowed to speak or move off this chair." He gave an anxious glance towards Archie.

"What is going on?" asked Sophie.

"There," said Archie. "Finished." He stood up, airing the paper to help the ink dry. He slowly walked over to Laneford. "Here you are, sir. The FO's official request to have the HO investigate the foreign nationals visiting the Communist section installed at number fifteen."

"Thank you," said Laneford, receiving the paper. He put the book aside to read through the proffered document. "Yes, that'll do. May I borrow your pen?"

"Of course." Archie offered it.

Laneford wrote a note on the document, which he returned to Archie along with his pen. "Allow me to explain, Miss King." He faced her. "Until I could accept the surveillance operation proposed by Mr Drysdale, not one of us had a legal right to be present in this building. I have noted his request, accepted the legal responsibility for the operation on behalf of the HO, but have also asked him to use all available resources at his disposal, because, as explained, the HO has none available at present. To be brief, we are back in business, but now with a smaller force."

"It's all quite baffling, really," said Sophie. "Have you re-authorized the operation, then?"

"Exactly," said Laneford.

"We had to," said Archie, "because I only came here ostensibly to clear the house and to finish up our part of the old operation. But then Mrs Barker terrified me so dreadfully, I just couldn't face ejecting her from her kitchen."

Sophie laughed. "Not an easy task. I have a question. What on earth is Nick doing in here?"

Both men looked at the boy.

"Between us," said Archie, "we have discovered that young Nick is altogether too knowing for his age. He has some bad habits around keyholes and open doors."

"Undoubtedly windows, too," said Laneford.

"I gave him two options," said Archie. "He could go to Borstal Prison in Rochester, where they would set him straight, or, as I happened to have some change in my pocket, he could work for the FO on an ad hoc basis and for a token sum that was not open to discussion, despite his attempt to discuss it."

"Very forward for his age," said Laneford. "But he also has a bicycle — let us not lose sight of that fact."

Sophie glared at Nick, who sank back into his chair, his cheeks aflame.

"Don't be too cross, unless you feel it is necessary," said Archie. "We've already hauled him over the coals."

"I'm ever so sorry, miss." Nick spoke in a small, pathetic tone.

"Stand up," said Sophie. She stared him in the eye. "When you work for Burgoyne's, your conduct must be exemplary. Even on your own time, your behaviour should be such that it does not cause any comment except those which are complimentary. Spying on these gentlemen is grounds for dismissal. If anything like this ever happens again, you will be instantly discharged. I believe I have made myself abundantly clear."

Sophie turned to Lord Laneford. "I apologize, my Lord. Burgoyne's Agency has broken your trust, and I ask your forgiveness. We will withdraw from the operation if you feel our work is not up to the required standard."

"Oh, please don't do that." He pursed his lips and addressed Nick. "Miss King has kindly given you a second chance. Make good use of it, young man." Nick nodded rapidly in response.

"Mr Drysdale," said Sophie, "I lamentably regret the lapse in our standards, and it will not happen again. Do you wish that anything further be done to repair the situation?"

"Um... I don't think so... Nick. Stay inside on the ground floor where I can find you. Don't you dare go near the windows at the front. You may leave now."

"Yes, sir." Chastened, he took his book with him.

When he had gone, the two men laughed.

"It isn't funny to me," said Sophie.

"I know," said Archie. "But that little blighter is going to get on in life."

"Hopefully, it will be within the law," said Laneford.

"My Lord, he's a very good boy, quite trustworthy and talented in useful ways. Clever with it. It's just that, of late, he's been getting rather above himself."

"Growing up, no doubt. I think we should now craft a plan of action. But we'll need a report from you first. Sorry, Drysdale. You're in charge, of course."

"Think nothing of it. Miss King, would you summarize the situation as it stands, please?"

"Certainly. I'll omit all references to the police investigation, as there seems to be no connection between the two operations at present.

"Last night, a group of four men entered number fifteen together. I identified one of them as an inhabitant. Because of the poor light and the speed with which they moved, of the other three, only two could I say were definitely unknown to me. I searched the log book and, by analyzing yesterday's entries, I can confirm the group was composed of two strangers and two inhabitants.

"Subsequently, at 9:25 p.m., Kuritsyn and a muffled stranger who carried a suitcase left number fifteen in a somewhat furtive and deliberate manner. Kuritysn came out first with his dog. He checked the square and gave a signal to the other man, who had remained just inside the hall. They walked away in a direction that would have them pass both our front and side doors. I decided to follow and take Blast-it with me."

"Blast-it?" enquired Archie.

"A term of affection. His actual name is Biscuit."

"Please continue."

"While we walked towards the side entrance, this most sensible of dogs alerted me by a low growl that someone was standing outside the garden door." Archie and Laneford looked at each other. "I waited, trusting the dog's instincts. After some minutes, I began to doubt, but then, quietly, Kuritsyn and the other man parted company."

"A trap?" suggested Laneford.

"It appears so, my Lord. In retrospect, I believe it possible the suitcase was a blind and part of the subterfuge, to test and to see if the agents were still present here. If so, it means the stranger who left with Kuritsyn had accompanied the other stranger, the more important agent, who remained inside the house."

"Do you believe he is the one we are expecting?" asked Archie.

"I'm uncertain, but I feel he is not. I've seen him, by the way."

"Yes, we know," said Archie.

"How do you know?"

"I arrived a few minutes after you left, as did Nick. Miss Walton, who has a powerful voice, by the way, alerted the house when Kuritsyn and the interesting gentleman departed from number fifteen. Len followed them to the park. Around the square, Miss Walton informs us, Kuritsyn was quite vigilant, and the Russians walked at a brisk pace. Away from the square, Len states both men were relaxed. Once in the park, they slowed their walk to a crawl. Len kept them under observation until he saw that you had started to follow them. Believing the men were simply strolling in the park to talk and with you on their trail, he returned."

"Aha. The two of them appeared to be old acquaintances."

"Len said something similar," said Laneford.

"What happened next?" asked Archie.

"Well, as they weren't going anywhere and were unlikely to be meeting anyone, because by then they were more or less retracing their steps, I gave them a wide berth and returned."

"Did you notice anything interesting about the new fellow?"

"Actually, I did." She took her handkerchief from her pocket and unfolded it. "Oh, my handkerchief is stained. I'm going to use envelopes in future." She held out the cigar end for their inspection.

"Russian," said Laneford.

"Is there any significance to this butt?" asked Archie.

"Yes. The stranger, a man of thirty or so, dropped this one. My observation of the way he smoked is that he is a professional, such as a doctor or an engineer. He could even be a theatre manager. A good conversationalist, he listened intently to Kuritsyn. Probably a likeable man, with a mild tendency towards showing off, but he does so in an engaging manner. He may be selfish, but I think, on the whole, he is considerate of others. Intellectual, he undoubtedly is well-versed in the latest Communist Party news and modes of political thought. However, I think he loves his country more than he does his communism."

"You deduced all that from a cigar end?" asked Laneford. "No, of course, you didn't. It was your astute observation of the man."

"Theatre manager?" asked Archie. "How did you arrive at that?"

"By simply comparing his behaviour to that of people I have known or met. I'm sure Russians are fundamentally no different from Britons. I have met Kuritsyn, and for him to get on so well with the stranger, they must have a similar outlook on life. Whatever else they have in common, I don't know, but it's certain they have similar views on communism. Kuritsyn is going through the motions. Astoundingly, his dog was originally named Czar. Then he called it Lenin, but got into trouble, so named him Vladimir. He is giving the appearance of fitting in with the Communist Party because he must do so to survive. Kuritsyn found the other gentleman's conversation highly diverting. It follows, therefore, that they have a similar outlook and can only air their opinions away from the others at the house for safety's sake."

The two men glanced at each other.

"Very good," said Archie. "Is there anything else?"

"I'm afraid not."

"If your delineation of the man's character is correct," said Laneford, "then we are waiting for another person to arrive."

"That's my feeling."

"And my feeling is that the agent won't come to the house," said Archie. "Too risky. The chap here is a courier of sorts. He has instructions from the Kremlin and will meet someone else. That someone is the one we're after."

"A British national, do you think?" asked Laneford.

"Looks increasingly likely. Whoever it is must be well-placed if he is to run a network of agents and because the Russians are going to all this trouble."

"What do you mean by well-placed?" asked Sophie.

"A man such as a high-ranking civil servant, but probably not a diplomat. He could be an officer in the army or navy, or someone in a key industry."

"Could also be a financial chap," added Laneford. "Or, heaven forbid, in the Secret Service."

"Oh, dear." Sophie frowned at the thought. "Here's something I've been meaning to ask. Why did the Russians choose this Primrose Hill group for the meeting or whatever it is? Are there not other communist groups?"

"We can only guess," said Archie. "There *are* other sections, but they are more or less devoted to working within unions and around the fringes of the Labour party. They get the word out about their cause, and seek to change the minds of the working man and woman. By contrast, the section here doesn't seem to do very much in that line, which makes it seem all the more important in a way. The workers who live at number fifteen rarely agitate for their cause in any meaningful manner. Really, one would not know they are in the pay of the Russian government unless told. It's as if the Russians have set up this particular cabal in Primrose Hill for special operations, such as aiding their more valuable agents."

"What is the Doctor's role in all of this? And why is his full name not in the reports?"

"He uses a false name, which I cannot reveal," said Laneford. "He is only ever referred to as The Doctor. We're fairly certain about his true identity, but the only definite thing is that he is a friend of Lenin. Apparently, certain high-ranking Communists hate him sufficiently to want to kill him — Stalin or Kamenev being strong candidates, but we're not entirely sure. All we can say is that he's hiding here and is in charge of the house. The Doctor rarely goes out but, when he does, he dines very well with one or two Russian friends."

"Could he be the murderer?"

"I shouldn't think so," replied Laneford. "I'm informed there is no traceable connection between the inmates of number fifteen and the death of Hamilton. However, if the Doctor is who we think he is, he's quite capable of murdering someone."

"Well," began Sophie, "at number fifteen, Mr Kuritsyn is the prime candidate for killer, because of the dog biscuit bag found at the murder scene. I suppose he could be the murderer, but why? Yet a man in hiding who fears for his life — surely that's a real motive for murder should he feel threatened."

"I wish I could help you on that score, Miss King. Even if we had more facts, I'm unable to reveal details. From the little we know of the Doctor, there's nothing I recall that suggests he's your murderer."

"Thank you for that much, my Lord."

"I say, it's rather an encumbrance for you to say, my lord, so often."

"Ah, not exactly. I must set an example for the staff. But that's kind of you to mention it."

"As you please, Miss King."

They planned the operation. The flat used previously by the other HO agents was still available to house those assigned to follow the Russian and, as Sophie learned, it also possessed a telephone. Afterwards, Sophie found Flora to see how she was getting on and to inform her of the new arrangements. Flora reported that little had happened, except for the return of Kuritsyn and the stranger.

In the kitchen, work was progressing amid a steady flow of conversation.

"So, when you were boxing, didn't you meet up with anyone who scared you?" Ada asked the question, but Mrs Barker and Myrtle were also interested. Len was good at keeping them entertained.

"Not scared, exactly. The only person who's ever scared me was me mother. She has a bit of a temper, like, and I've felt the sharp end of her tongue many a time. But," he added significantly, "it always blew over quick. Funny thing is, when I said I were going into boxing, you know what she said?" He paused as he peeled a strip off a carrot. "She was against it, so she said, 'You're a bit of an eyesore as it stands. Perhaps boxing will improve your looks.' That's me own mother, mind you. Anyway, she weren't so put out when I started bringing home the prize money." He picked up another carrot. "Now there was one fella I were up against, and even me second looked worried. Now I'm a big fella, but this bloke was a couple of inches taller and had to be a good eight stone heavier. But there were two things that worried me. The size of his stomach... No, no, don't laugh. Because in the clinch, he'd force me back with it. He'd get me in a corner, like. But that wasn't the worst of it. He had long arms, like a gorilla. Hung down to his knees, they did. That meant he could keep me at a distance, and if I tried to close, then there's his stomach to consider."

"What 'appened then?" asked Ada.

"Well, I'm nervous, because I don't know what to expect. The referee gets us in the middle, gives us the talk, we touch gloves, the bell rings, and off we go. He comes out and takes a big swing at me head. I duck, then pop back up to give him a trial tap on the side of his noggin. There weren't much power in it, but blow me if he didn't go down like a log. I thought he was going to break the boards. The ref and me, we were both that surprised. So he counts him out, but takes a close look to make sure the bloke hasn't been paid to take a dive. No, he's out proper, and I won. Crowd was annoyed, though. Robbed of their entertainment, see. That caused some ructions."

"I don't know. I think I'd be scared to get in a ring, knowing some fella wants to knock me block off."

"It's all about the training and setting your mind to the task at hand."

"I s'pose. So you've never been scared?"

"During the war, but that's summat else."

"Hmm."

"I'll tell you when I *was* really scared. Like my heart stopped beating. I was fifteen and had started working down the mine with me Da. At the beginning of the shift, twelve men at a time used to get on the lift and there were three platforms to this thing, but it were old and rickety like." Len gave Mrs Barker a slow wink without Myrtle and Ada noticing. "So it kept stopping and starting with a jolt as the next lot of fellas got on. We're all in a huddle with nowt but a bit of old wire round the edge to stop us from falling down the shaft. Nigh on half a mile of drop. That's a nice way to start your first day, with all that on your mind. Well, I'm with me Da, as I said. We've just got on. The first jolt, and summat breaks. We heard it, and the old hands all knew it was summat bad. Then we began moving again. Only now we picked up speed, and we're going down faster and faster. My poor old Da, his face was as white as a sheet, but he says, 'Son, this is the end. Bear it like a man, and say your prayers.' We're hanging on, and going so fast, knowing that the crash is coming any moment. We looked like a desperate bunch, clinging to what we could for our dear lives. Then the crash came. Boom! And we went straight through the gallery floor. You'll never guess what happened next."

"What 'appened?" asked Ada, her eyes agog.

"We come out in Australia."

Ada struggled to speak. "What a thing to do! To speak about your dad and prayers like that."

"You should have seen your face... It were only a bit of fun."

Mrs Barker, occupied at the stove, kept her face averted and shook with silent laughter.

"At my expense, thank you very much."

"I know, but no harm's meant. If it's any use to you, I got caught out the first time I heard the story."

"Did you?"

"Oh yes, only I was told it the very first time I stepped onto the lift. I was right scared, but that's how miners cure a lad's fears. Scare him half to death, then make a joke out of it. How they all laughed at me. It's funny now, looking back, but it weren't at the time."

Ada laughed, no longer annoyed. "But I'm not a miner."

"You never know. You might find you're handy with a pick-axe."

"I should say not. Thankfully, I'll never find that out."

A little later, Sophie entered the kitchen tasked with telling the others, particularly Mrs Barker, about the changes to be made.

"I have to inform you of some necessary alterations to the household arrangements. Mrs Barker, may I have a word first with you in private? It will only take a few moments."

"Yes, Miss King. I'll just put these on the glimmer." Mrs Barker turned down the gas on two saucepans and wiped her hands. Then, with a face as long as a tombstone, she followed Sophie into the dining room, knowing full well that the coming discussion meant changes to the menu.

"I'm dreadfully sorry," began Sophie. "The Home Office pulled the plug on the spying operation. Without informing us until an hour ago, they've taken all their agents away as of yesterday. However, Lord Laneford and Mr Drysdale have restarted the operation. With the change in personnel, there is also a change in the eating arrangements. The HO made shift for themselves. You see, this is rather difficult but, because I know these gentlemen, I couldn't very well say that we wouldn't feed them."

"I can understand that, Miss King." Mrs Barker stared at her bleakly. "How many and for how long?"

"Well, the idea is that some men will take up residence in a nearby flat. Until Monday, it will be three or four in total. That includes Mr Drysdale and Lord Laneford, and Len, if he's staying. The fourth person is a Mr Philpot, Lord Laneford's valet. From Monday onwards, the number of agents on hand will be in a state of flux, but there will be at least two, and possibly four, agents present. His lordship and Mr Drysdale have other duties, you see, and they're not yet sure who they can get."

"I see. How many for lunch and dinner today?"

"There are the six of us, including Nick, and three of them. Mr Philpott will arrive in the afternoon, but Nick, and possibly Len, may have gone by dinnertime."

"That's nine for lunch and seven to nine for dinner." Mrs Barker's stony mien had yet to soften. "We have Lady Shelling arriving tomorrow."

"I'm so sorry to impose on you like this."

"It's not your fault, Miss King... These things happen... Right. I'll do plain cooking only. Lord Laneford will have to put up with it. I shan't do their breakfasts, and they'll have to eat their lunches and dinners here. All I can say is, thank goodness Myrtle came."

"Yes. No doubt, Nancy will have to go to the shops for more supplies."

"Oh, yes. And she'll have to go soon or there'll be nothing left."

"It's just after ten now," said Sophie. "Lunch at one?"

"I can manage that."

"Thank you, Mrs Barker. I know how tiresome this is for you."

"It's happened before, and it'll happen again."

"By the way, how are you finding Len?"

"He's pleasant. A lively man, I'll say that. And helpful, too. He's told us some funny things."

"Does Myrtle get on with him all right?"

"I think so, but then she's quiet."

"And Ada? I mean Nancy, of course."

Mrs Barker hesitated. "Like a house on fire." She raised her eyebrows.

"Ah," said Sophie. "I thought as much."

# Chapter 10

# Many, many biscuits

At eleven on Saturday morning, and with the new plan in place at number seven, Sophie took Biscuit for another walk. With the changes in the operation, she thought that the division of surveillance duties might also need reworking and improvement. A walk would aid her in deciding what was best to do, and she wanted the fresh air before her time came to go to the attic. She had decided that once around the square and then off to the park would do the trick.

She and Biscuit had barely got off the steps when Alan Mellish not so much emerged as came hurtling out of number 19.

"Come on, Topper! Spring is in the air."

Sophie presumed Mellish spoke to his dog, although as yet she could see no canine presence. His master, however, was very noticeable. His clothes were more muted today, far less the riotous jumble they had been the day before, but he still wore his orange and white scarf. Sophie took a deep breath to prepare for walking over to meet him. However, Mr Mellish had now espied her.

"I say!" he shouted at Sophie. "Miss Number Seven! Hold up a moment!" He, with dog now in tow, began running, so Sophie waited.

"Phew. I'm glad you stopped. I have something I want to give you. Well, it's for your dog, actually."

Seeing him close up, Sophie thought he had a pleasant face beneath his tousled hair. She watched him fish in a pocket and then produce a bag of dog biscuits. He held them out, and they stared at each other.

"Hello, I'm Miss King."

"Didn't I say hello? Hello, I'm Alan Mellish, and that's Topper."

The dogs were already introducing themselves. Biscuit remained placid, while Topper, a Jack Russell, was a bundle of energy but evidently friendly.

"These are a sample of dog biscuits from my new and improved second batch. I make them myself, but I'm still in the experimental stage."

"Are you?"

"Yes. One cannot rush things to market, no matter how good they are. I've fine-tuned the ingredients and Topper has given the enhanced biscuit his seal of approval."

"I'm glad to hear he has. How, exactly, does he do that?"

"Eats them without restraint and does not regurgitate. He's had three tastings, and this batch has now passed with flying colours. Go on, try one."

"You don't mean me personally?" Sophie laughed.

"I eat them for purposes of quality control," said Mellish in all seriousness. "You would suffer no harm whatsoever if you tried them. I assure you, they are quite tasty. But I was referring again to your dog, of course."

His reply rendered Sophie speechless. She took the bag of biscuits from him.

"Thank you... Blast-it. Sit." The dog obeyed. "Good boy." Sophie gave him one of the bone-shaped biscuits. He crunched on it eagerly and made it disappear in seconds.

Mellish, who had been watching the process intently, said,

"If he is going to regurgitate, he will do so within the next four hours. But I'm sure he won't."

"I sincerely hope not."

"I also sincerely hope not. And I doubt very much that he will. Blast-it? That's quite an original choice. I'm undecided upon a name for the biscuit, and would appreciate your opinion on my ideas. I'm leaning towards Vita-Bone, although Cerebone, the one I currently use, is also a strong candidate. What I actually want to call it is Osteonio, but the public is so easily confused that it may not understand the significance of the name. What do you think?"

"Vita-Bone."

"Ah, a good choice. The only problem there is that some of my other formulations contain the word vita."

"Do they? Could you give some examples, please?"

"There is my Vita-Chemic line, which is a range of compounds in tablet form based on Dr Schuessler's most excellent work in bringing the elements in the body into a state of harmony. Naturally, I have made significant advances in many areas, with the result that my preparations deliver the most astonishing results. I have many testimonials extolling the virtues of the Vita-Chemic line. Some results are nothing short of miraculous. Then there is Vita-Mars, which enhances maleness, and Vita-Venus, which enhances femaleness."

Sophie was entering into a state of shock.

"So, you see, if I call my dog-biscuits Vita-Bone, there might be some confusion with my other formulations in the public's mind. And we can't have that, can we?"

"No, we mustn't have that... Why not call it Biscuit Bone?"

"Hyphenated or separate words?"

"Separate words, I think."

"Thank you. I shall consider your suggestion while lying in bed before sleep comes upon me."

"Oh," said Sophie.

"I'm going to the park. Are you?"

"Absolutely not."

"Then I'm sure I shall see you later on. I'm in my workshop all week, so I spend as much time as I can outside on Saturdays and Sundays for the proper absorption of ultra-violet rays. The lower the light levels, the more time I spend outdoors. You should try it. Oh, and let me know at once if Blast-it rejects the biscuit, and save me a good sample of his vomit." Without saying goodbye, he walked away.

Sophie was deciding where to go, as she watched the chemist leave. Someone spoke to her.

"Good morning, Miss King. He's a little hard to take, isn't he? One eventually gets used to his conduct."

"Good morning, Major Cummings. He was rather shocking. Actually, I'm concerned about Blast-it. He just ate one of Mr Mellish's dog biscuits, and I'm not sure they're safe."

"Don't worry, Mellish is quite careful with his products. He tests them all on himself, for one thing. And Vindaloo here has sampled the much vaunted second batch without ill-effects."

"Thank you for relieving my mind. I was wondering if I had just poisoned my dog."

The old gentleman smiled. "Not a chance of it. I'm quite suspicious of many of his items, but only in regard to how he boosts their efficacy out of all proportion to what they can actually do. Other than that, I'm certain they are quite safe."

"He mentioned his Vita-Chemic line. Are you familiar with that one?"

"I believe the tablets only contain harmless salts. Mellish is reticent about what he puts in his products. Claims they are trade secrets and all that."

"I see."

"But there was a powder he used to manufacture — called it Fluvo-Blossom. I tried it, and I'd swear he'd put opium in it. I really should have sent some away for analysis. The powder is supposed to impart a general sense of well-being, and it certainly does. A little too much, if one wasn't careful with the quantities. He's discontinued it now."

"Probably just as well, by the sounds of it... You call your dog Vindaloo. Were you in India?"

"For many years I had the honour of serving the crown in that country. Loved it there."

"Did you think of staying on?"

"Oh, yes. To be more specific, I loved the country itself — the people and the culture. I was not so impressed by the European society there. As my old friends and colleagues gradually left the services in India, I found myself increasingly at odds with the younger set. When I retired, there was no one left whom I could truly call a friend, so I returned home. My wife died many years ago, you see, and my two children live in England. I returned to be near them, otherwise I might still have stayed."

"You must miss it. I've always wanted to go to India."

"If you get the chance, you must. And, yes, I shall always miss it. But I've taken steps to ease the sense of loss... You'll discover this soon enough from our neighbours. I'm writing a book on Indian cuisine adapted for the British housewife."

"How interesting. I don't do much cooking, and I'm hardly adventurous, but your book very much intrigues me."

"Does it? Would I be a bore if I explained a little about it? Not everyone is interested, and it's quite heartening to find someone who is."

"By all means."

"Thank you, dear lady. Shall we?" He extended his hand to suggest they walk their dogs. "My main objective is to simplify the labour and processes involved in preparing a curry, for example, in such a way as not entirely to lose the authenticity of the flavour and quality of the dish. The Indian woman who cooks in the village, out of necessity does so with fewer spices and employs simpler processes than the chef who cooks in the top Bombay hotel. The villager typically eats plainer food. This does not mean the village food lacks flavour. It doesn't. And when she prepares dishes for their festivals, the Indian woman will happily bring out her most costly spices and foodstuffs to prepare those special dishes associated with the day.

"The major difference between Indian haute cuisine and that consumed in the village lies in the complexity of the flavours and, of course, the using of the choicest cuts of meat. The Indian woman must be at all times economical, while the chef prepares food for those with expensive tastes; for him cost is not an issue. It is the same for the average housewife in Britain, who must also be economical in her habits. Some imported spices are quite expensive. To reduce costs, I have designed the recipes for those with a modest budget, and who cannot devote the extraordinary amounts of time some

Indian dishes require in their preparation. Furthermore, adjustment has had to be made because many of the ingredients are not readily available, and much less so outside of the major cities."

"Then how is someone to prepare an authentic curry if she does not have access to the proper materials?"

"Ah-ha — straight to the heart of the matter. I asked myself the same question, and it desperately required an early answer. I have included in the appendix a selection of spice importers willing to supply small quantities at a reasonable cost and send them by post. I also included recommended ordering lists so that the lady who endeavours to try several recipes does not waste her money unnecessarily on items she will use infrequently. It isn't a perfect arrangement, but it will guide the reader sufficiently through the maze of unfamiliar names and the correct quantities needed."

"That's most helpful. It sounds as though you've devoted much time and thought to your book."

"In a sense, I live for it, because I'm battling against a widespread ignorance of the subject. The recipes one currently finds in Britain are too difficult to follow, or assume a prior knowledge of Indian cooking, or, and this is the greatest sin, rely heavily on commercial curry powders. Really, many recipes are little more than making a stew, adding apple and or raisins, and a tablespoon of curry powder! They call the resulting mess a Madras! That is a monstrous crime perpetrated wholesale upon the British public."

"I suppose I'm a victim of that crime," said Sophie, smiling. "When trying an English version of a curry, I found it quite edible, but not as spicy as I expected. I shall certainly talk to my friends about this."

"Thank you. There's something I ought to add. At present, I'm looking for volunteers to try out my recipes. I have several kind people helping me, but there are quite a few recipes still to be tested. If you know of anyone willing to participate, I would be most grateful, and supply them with the necessary ingredients and a sum of money to cover the cost of the food they purchase on the condition they fill out a small report card."

"Then I shall most definitely pass the word along and inform you of any interested parties."

"I would be much obliged. Are you going to the park?"

"Not now, I think. There are several things I must do in the house."

"Then, Miss King, I hope to see you again soon. Good day."

"Good day, Major Cummings."

She hung about for a minute and, when Cummings was out of sight, rushed back into the house more excited than she had been for quite a while.

---

Mrs Barker viewed the new arrangements with the acceptance of a hardened fatalist. Things had been going along nicely. Now there was much more work to do, which meant the attendant worries of her occupation had increased with the extra mouths to feed. As a professional servant, she had not allowed her emotion to get the better of her and, in creating new lists of meals and supplies for those meals, she had kept her irritation at bay. Gradually, she was becoming acclimatized to the new household order. As it was almost mid-day Saturday, there would be no further shocks. An extra person, or even two, might show up and require food, but such tests of her culinary readiness were to be expected. She always cooked extra because you just never knew.

Sophie entered the kitchen at a rush, saw Mrs Barker, and her steps faltered. The cook looked up, and long experience informed her that trouble had entered the kitchen again.

"It isn't want you think," said Sophie.

"Oh, but it's something, isn't it?"

"Yes. Can we speak privately?"

"I can leave this, Miss King."

They left the room.

"I'm so sorry to disturb you with your extra work and everything. I understand how severely trying it must be when you've only Myrtle to help you, but something's come up."

"I know it must be bad, Miss King, so it's always best to say it straight out."

"No, it's not bad. Can you cook Indian food? Not like we do here, but as they do in India?"

"Indian food." Mrs Barker answered as if mesmerized and heeding a pied piper's call. "Real Indian food with all the spices? No. I can't, but I've always, always wanted to learn how."

Sophie laughed and clapped her hands. "Then you won't believe what I'm about to relate."

She explained all about Major Cummings and the recipe tests.

"Oh, I'd love to have the chance at that," said Mrs Barker, "but what happens if he's the murderer?"

"I don't know how to answer. He seems to me to be a kind and patient man, but he's as suspect as any of them until we can find evidence to exonerate him — or find the guilty party, of course. My plan was this: if you agree to it, and you are under no obligation to do so, we will have the means of getting inside his house. You and I could visit on various pretexts. Let's say I get the recipe and the spices, etc. from him. Then you and I would go to his house to get some advice on a particular point. The way I see it is, he would invite us in, and I'll look over such rooms as I can, while you're in the kitchen having your questions answered. I won't achieve much, I know, but it's worth a try. Ooh, he employs an Indian servant. Perhaps we would all troop into his kitchen for discussion, and then I'd excuse myself for a reason, but really it's to find out what I can. Something like that. It all depends how the situation unfolds."

"That doesn't sound too bad."

"No. And then we'll have real Indian food, too. I've always wanted to try it."

"Have you? It's lovely, but it can be very, very hot. Spicy hot, if you can imagine it. Years ago, there was a big weekend party at a house. They sent me to assist with the preparation of the lunches. But the dinners were all Indian, every scrap of them. Two women and two men prepared them. They didn't speak a word of English, but we got along after a bit. They gave me some of their food to eat. Oh, Miss King, I've never tasted the like before. It was delicious. It's hot, but I found I didn't mind it, although it takes a sight of getting used to. Anyway, if it's too hot, you can add this stuff called raita, which I did. It's cucumber in a white sauce. From that moment on, I've always wanted to learn how to cook Indian food, and I thought I'd never get the chance. What a turn up… That's it. We'll go. I don't care if he *is* a murderer. I'll not miss this opportunity."

"Well done, Mrs Barker. And I'm looking forward to trying your results."

"It'll have to be in the week, though. We have her ladyship coming tomorrow."

"Then I'll tell Major Cummings we'll conduct the test on Wednesday. Would that be suitable?"

"Yes, Miss King. Was there anything else? Because I must get back."

"No, there isn't, and I apologize for taking you away from your duties."

"Oh, no, don't apologize. This is one interruption I haven't minded in the slightest."

Sophie went upstairs to Flora.

"You're ten minutes late for the start of your shift," said Flora.

"Sorry. Things keep happening, but I have lots to tell you."

"Is Mr Mellish very peculiar?"

"Much more than that. He is a crank. Rather rude, very abrupt, self-absorbed, and he eats his own dog biscuits."

"Really? Did he do it in front of you? I couldn't see you both properly from here."

"No, I'm glad to say he didn't. He says he eats them for testing purposes but, frankly, if he lived on them exclusively, I wouldn't be at all surprised. When you meet him, be prepared for a shock."

"Your caution is duly noted."

"Now, let me tell you about Major Cummings."

Sophie informed Flora of the plan of action to get into Cumming's house and eat Indian food.

"Have you ever tried it?" asked Sophie.

"Only a few things which included curry powder. Devilled eggs, I recall, but I've never tasted the real thing. I'm interested, though. It's supposed to be very hot... Oh, I know why you're so excited. You've always wanted to go to India. So eating the cuisine is like a substitute?"

"I'll never get the chance to travel there, so I suppose it is."

"And Mrs Barker's all gung-ho, is she? Excellent. I hope she doesn't have a failure. I couldn't stand it with you both moping about."

"I'm sure she'll be fine."

"We'll see," said Flora. "Now, between Major Cummings and Cranky Mellish, which one's the murderer?"

"Mellish. The Major seems so unlikely, and Mellish seems capable of anything."

"Anyone who wears such a scarf must be deranged."

"He was a lot worse yesterday. Which reminds me. Because the biscuits are still being tested, Cranky Mellish asked me to do something. Should Blast-it vomit, you're to save a sample for him."

"I'll do no such thing. If you volunteered to collect it, then that's entirely your responsibility."

"I'm up here, so it's your responsibility now."

"Oh, no. You can't get away with that. You made the agreement, I didn't. I would have refused. The utter cheek of the fellow. I can't believe you didn't put him in his place."

"Um, I think it's because I've been blundering about so much. I'm more or less at war with Mrs Fitch, and I find Mr Bristow boorish. I didn't want to add Mellish to the list, although I easily could have."

"Ah... Being alone up here for so long, I have achieved a rare clarity of mind concerning Alexandra Gardens. There is a small pack of dogs present. More importantly for us, there is also a small pack of dog owners. Who is the leader of the human pack, the top dog owner?"

"Mrs Fitch."

"Who is the second top dog owner?"

"Bristow... Although Kuritsyn might be, because we've yet to see the two together."

"See what I mean?"

"I do. Shouldn't there be an underdog owner, too?"

"If my theory holds true, yes. Within a couple of days, we'll probably know who it is."

"Very perceptive of you. I shall keep it in mind."

"Right. First, I'm off to see what Sidney's getting up to. Then I'll take Biscuit for a walk and find a few suspects to interview."

In the split second of silence before Sophie answered her friend, they heard the light noise of quick paws on the stairs. A moment later, Biscuit entered the attic with the lead in his mouth.

"He doesn't miss a thing," said Flora.

"That's because he's most intelligent."

# Chapter 11

# A Stranger in the Garden

On her way out, Flora, with Biscuit trotting beside her, stopped off in the parlour to see Lord Laneford. He was alone and stood up, book in hand, as soon as he saw her.

"How are you finding the book, Sidney?"

"Very Interesting. Hastings is an amiable ass, like Watson, while Poirot's the one with the brains."

"I'm almost at the end, so try not to finish before me. I would be aggravated if you knew the murderer's identity before I did."

"I won't do that." He put in a scrap of paper as a bookmark, the second one it held. He put the book down on a side table. "Did you hear anything back about the part you tried out for?"

"No, and I don't know why they're dragging their feet. It's not just me they haven't contacted, though. They've called no one yet for the summer season. The rumour is, there have been money troubles."

"So, it might never start... I'm sorry, my dear. I know you were rather looking forward to the new production."

"I can't deny that I was. I expect my career to have ups and downs, but not that the downs should so predominate!"

"All I can say is keep your chin up. I'm sure a good part, a better part, will come along soon. But don't you need to meet people, you know, to put yourself forward?"

"Yes, but I detest doing it. The parties can be fun, but the people I have to approach know exactly why I'm approaching them — to beg for a part. If they haven't already thought of me, it's because they've cast a friend in the part or they're doing someone a favour. I have little pull, and even that's in decline."

"It's a closed world to me, otherwise I'd help." Laneford put his hands on his hips and studied Biscuit. "He looks too friendly to be a police dog. Does he lick people into submission?"

"I know, but he's awfully clever and so agile. You should see how high he jumps. It's quite remarkable."

"I take it you're going to the park? Why don't I follow at a discreet distance to observe young Biscuit? I can slip out the side entrance easily enough."

"But it's so close to lunch."

"*You're* missing it."

"I'm eating later."

"Then I will, too. I'll talk to Mrs Barker. I'm sure she can accommodate the minor change."

"But you'll just be dragging about after me. That'll be such a bore. Remember, we mustn't be seen together and so we can't talk."

"Even if it were at a respectful distance and in silence, my dear, I would follow you to the ends of the earth."

"How lovely of you." She kissed him on the cheek. "I must go. There's a chance I'll meet a neighbour, so prepare yourself for some serious hanging about. Don't get spotted."

"I'll use a different route to the park." He picked up the book.

From the attic, Sophie observed Flora go once around the square, and to be accosted by Kuritsyn. Sophie trained her binoculars on him. He was obviously haranguing her for more than a minute, which only seemed to end when she accepted one of his leaflets. Then, for several minutes, they talked normally until Mellish joined them. He approached the pair with an outstretched hand. Kuritsyn put several leaflets in it, then Mellish, without a glance, stuffed them in his pocket. A few minutes later, they parted on their several ways.

Over the course of the next hour, during which Sophie ate her lunch alone, a few suspects came out singly, at intervals, including Mrs Fitch. Sophie considered how she might come to peaceful terms with the woman. The problem was that Sophie's back was up the moment she saw Mrs Fitch. She considered various people she had met before, those whom she always wanted to avoid or found irritating. In particular, she recalled a Mrs Winters in Havering-under-Lyme. Sophie realized it was the unbridled meddling of certain people that caused her to take a dislike to them. However, she had reconciled with Mrs Winters when the women's son had died on the Western Front in 1916, and the change that had brought this about had not all been on Sophie's part. The sad woman, sad Mrs Winters, permanently lost her combative nature. In the period of her deepest grief and desperation, she had turned to Sophie as if to her dearest friend. It came as a shock to the young woman. That act and Sophie's sympathy had washed away all their prior acrimony. They were friendly now and even wrote to each other occasionally. The memory made Sophie think harder of ways to repair the situation with Mrs Fitch.

Kuritsyn went to the shops, returning laden with heavy bags. Three Communists came home from work. She was sure one of them was more than slightly inebriated. Flora and Biscuit returned from the park. As soon as they entered the square on the other side of St. George's Road, Mr Clark and his dog emerged from number one right by them. Flora stopped because he spoke to her, and they conversed. It was by chance — Clark had obviously not been waiting to meet her. A thought occurred to Sophie, so she swung the binoculars towards number twenty. Sure enough, and within a minute, Mrs Pringle, carrying Nankin, came down her steps.

"Aha," said Sophie.

Then she witnessed a curious thing, which had her turning her binoculars from one end of the square to the other. Flora and Clark were deep in conversation, while at the other end Mrs Pringle started in their direction, but abruptly turned aside. Her change in course took her the long way around the central garden. She set down Nankin so that he could walk. Now that Mrs Pringle was on the nearer side, Sophie stood up and dispensed with the binoculars. She moved closer to the window and hid behind a curtain which was tied back to one side. She surmised that Mrs Sandra Pringle intended to spy upon Mr Clark and Flora. The definitive proof of this came when the woman halted at a place where the hedge was thinner and lower. She was almost motionless, her gaze fixed upon the conversationalists.

"Oh, dear." Sophie did not doubt for a moment that Mrs Pringle was jealous of Clark talking alone to Flora.

Mrs Pringle resumed her walk and eventually joined them. Through the binoculars, Sophie tried to gauge Mrs Pringle's demeanour. She was vivacious and talkative, as if nothing were the matter. Sophie knew something was wrong, and anxiously awaited Flora's report. After a while, Flora said goodbye and crossed the road, while Clark and Mrs Pringle slowly walked off in a different direction. An instant later, Dulcie Villard came out with her poodle. She looked towards Clark and Mrs Pringle, but then turned and pursued Flora, calling to catch up with her.

"Blast it," said Sophie, almost simultaneously thinking she really should stop using the expression.

She had a clear view of Miss Villard and Flora until they got too close to number seven to be seen properly. She noticed that Miss Villard's mouth was working rapidly and incessantly, as though filled with a bulging store of words that she must transmit all at once, but could not blurt them out fast enough.

Several minutes elapsed before Flora came charging up the stairs, with Biscuit in her train.

"What happened!?" asked Sophie.

"Did you see it!? La Pringle is jealous because she's in love with Clark! I couldn't believe how she behaved. It was so unexpected."

"Was she nasty to you?"

"Oh, yes, in that very pleasant type of voice that sounds friendly but really means 'leave my man alone or I'll scratch your face to pieces.' I did nothing! I honestly didn't say a thing to Mr Clark to warrant her attitude towards me."

"Jealousy. Unbelievably, I could see it all play out from here. Do you know she spied on the pair of you?"

"I can quite believe it of her. Mr Clark was pleasant and remained so even after she joined us. Either he didn't notice what she was doing or ignored it."

"Which do you think?"

"Um... Ignored it."

"So he knows what she's like. Therefore, she's often prone to jealously."

"Yes, that must be true."

"And what did Miss Villard say?"

"That is a whole other matter. I would say she is some type of evil genius inflicted upon humanity. It was as if she knew all about Pringle's jealousy and came to me only to comment on it at the ripest of moments. Do not make friends with her or tell her anything. Promise me."

"I promise."

"Miss Villard says that La Pringle flirts with every man under sixty. She reeled off names, but I only recognized our Mr Bristow. She went on to say that Mrs Pringle had been infatuated with Mr Hamilton, and that the affair became quite torrid."

"Really?"

"Yes. Then, after he was murdered, she hit the bottle."

"No."

"Oh, yes. I think she secretly hates Mrs Pringle."

"Do you think she thinks she murdered him?"

"Do you mean, does the Villard think La Pringle murdered Mr Hamilton?"

"Yes. That's what I said."

"Not exactly. To answer, she didn't speculate at all on the murder, and certainly didn't hint La Pringle was involved."

"Hmm... I'll take notes. Start from when you went out."

"Comrade Kuritsyn tried to recruit me. The way to escape from him, I learned from Cranky Mellish, is to take one of his leaflets, and then Kuritsyn switches off the propaganda. He did the same with me, only I didn't realize it at the time. He becomes quite normal afterwards."

"I saw that."

"Well, I asked Mellish why he took three leaflets, and he said to roll into tapers and use as firelighters. Kuritsyn didn't blink an eye when he said it. I'm sure that his only real concern is that he goes out of the house with fifty leaflets and comes back with none."

"There are some real oddities living in the square."

"Aren't there just? Cranky said little and seemed rather bored. He's friendly with Kuritsyn. I mentioned Biscuit's lack of vomit-sample, and he looked unimpressed. Anyway, Kuritsyn actually seems a decent fellow. Before Mellish arrived, he was explaining the relative merits of three local greengrocers."

"For any particular reason?"

"I imagine it's because it's what he's interested in. He volunteered that he's in charge of both household security and the shopping because he speaks the best English. He cryptically said he was the only Chekist in Primrose Hill, which he found immensely amusing. What do you think he meant?"

"The Cheka are these dreadfully vicious secret police in Russia. They also seize and then redistribute food. They kill, without trial, anybody who disobeys them."

"How dreadful! So they steal a farmer's crop, and if he protests, they shoot him?"

"More or less."

"So why does anyone want to be a communist if that's the sort of thing they do?"

"I have no idea."

"It's completely inexplicable. To continue, Kuritsyn much prefers his shopping duties to security, and knows the price of everything at the shops. He always goes as late as possible on Saturday — his reason being that the greengrocers and bakers then want to get rid of as much as they can at a discounted price because they're shut on Sunday. He says he saves a lot of money that way and passed the tip on to us. That's rather decent of him, wouldn't you say?"

"Yes, it is. I'll mention it to Mrs Barker and Ada. She's already been to the shops three times today, so she won't go again. Do you know Miss Villard's maid followed her earlier?"

"She told me. And good for her in dealing with the creature."

"By recruiting her maid, Miss Villard shows just how systematic she is in her approach to gossiping."

"She tries to make herself important by it, I suppose," said Flora. "Villard's quite vitriolic, though."

"Yes, so it seems." Sophie paused for a moment. "We must remember that we are also likely to be the victims of her tongue."

"Possibly, but if we avoid doing anything that attracts her attention, she will probably be harmless enough. It's people's secrets and weaknesses she's after... Wait a moment. What if she finds out our secret?" As she said this, Flora's eyes became as big as saucers.

"Um, we'll threaten her with dire consequences yet to be determined," Sophie replied, laughing.

"Right. The best dire consequence would be to give her a taste of her own medicine." Flora was emphatic.

"That would be very fitting and quite just," replied Sophie, "except that all we have on her at present is that she's a malicious gossip, which everyone must already know."

"She's bound to have a hidden secret... Did you like what she was wearing?"

"I couldn't see properly, but she looked well turned out. I got an overall impression of elegance, which was greatly emphasized by her well-trimmed poodle."

"That dog hasn't a hair out of place. She must groom it daily. And Villard's clothes are very expensive. Lovely gloves, and she was wearing a gorgeous chiffon blouse over a camisole. I'd have asked her to remove her jacket to see the sleeves if only she had stopped talking for a second."

"Was she wearing jewellery?" asked Sophie.

"I think all of it was gold, and looked like it cost something, anyway. I know little about watches, but her gold half-hunter was on a thick gold chain. All good quality, nothing showy."

"She would hardly wear a diamond-encrusted evening watch to walk the dog."

"No... But Miss Villard must be comfortably off."

"More comfortably than a hairdresser's income should allow, do you mean?"

"Absolutely... You're thinking she's a blackmailer."

"Of all the types of crimes there are, it's the one that would suit her best."

"How true, and beastly if so," said Flora.

"Did anything interesting happen at the park?"

"Nothing worth recording. Biscuit drew an audience with his acrobatics. I'm certain he knows more tricks than we realize, such as jumping through hoops and over fences and things. I think it best we just stick to ball-throwing, otherwise people will wonder why we have such a highly trained dog. It makes my arm stiff afterwards, though."

"I had a touch of that, too. Not bad enough to use White Horse Oil."

"The relief that vile stuff brings is barely worth enduring the terrible smell. When I had a nurse, she used to smother me in it. That, and Vick's."

"My mother did the same," said Sophie. "No use complaining. I believe their motto was 'If it smells foul, it does you good.'"

"How true... That's closely related to the one for medicines, 'It tastes horrible now, but you'll be better tomorrow. If not, you'll get more.' The thought of taking medicine compelled one to feel better."

"And Friar's Balsam, with that dreadful inhaler and the required towel over one's head. My face always flushed bright red from the steam."

"I quite liked the process. It used to send me into a trance."

Sophie laughed. "That's another thing I didn't like about it."

"I'm going downstairs now. Is there anything you'd like sent up?"

"No, thank you. I can last until teatime."

At around three-thirty, clouds moved in, delivering a brief shower. The distant sky threatened more, which meant the unusually long run of good weather had come to its end.

It was just after the shower, with the streets still wet, that the woman and dog whom Sophie had seen, and Flora had spotted in the park, entered Alexandra Gardens. This was the woman who had variously screamed and muttered to herself. Sophie now watched her with interest.

The first odd thing the woman did was to enter the gardens and sit down on an obviously wet bench, although admittedly her heavy raincoat must have been proof against the damp. The woman sat there, allowing her dog to roam about. Other than her knowledge of this person's previous behaviour, Sophie could detect nothing wrong with her. She glanced towards number 24, in case Mrs Fitch came out to say something. All the while the woman remained in the gardens, Mrs Fitch did not appear.

It was difficult for Sophie to estimate the stranger's age — the woman's hat and buttoned-up raincoat hid many clues, and she therefore could be anything between forty and sixty. All that Sophie could observe was part of an inexpressive pale face and a fringe of short, dark, perhaps grizzled, curls peeping below her round and almost brimless hat. Both her clothes and shoes looked old, dated, but well-cared for. The hem of her dress had risen a little, and Sophie espied thick brown woollen stockings. As the woman was in no hurry, Sophie indulged herself by surmising a possible character and background for the stranger. She settled upon a retired teacher who had experienced various disappointments in her life from which she had never fully recovered.

The woman reminded Sophie of an aunt on her mother's side. So unchanged was her Aunt Lucy by the passing years while Sophie was growing up, that she had assumed her aunt had been born old. One day, her mother showed Sophie some surprising photographs. There were several of the staid aunt, but she was unrecognizable. Sophie could not reconcile the bright, pretty face of the laughing eighteen-year-old by the beach at Bournemouth to the deadpan expression of her Aunt Lucy whom, if she had smiled once during a visit, was said to have been in high spirits. In one photograph, her aunt was perched on a donkey, displaying a very trim figure in her Edwardian blouse and long skirt while holding on to her straw hat. Sophie had found this quite incredible. Sophie now stared down at the woman in the gardens. Had she, too, once sat on a donkey clutching her hat in the summer sunshine? It seemed equally impossible that her aunt, as a lively young woman, could ever become the lonely, emotionless, and dour person *she* had. It was all tricks of time and place, memory, and state of mind. Sophie decided she would take Aunt Lucy to the seaside and stick her on a donkey, whether she liked it or not.

The woman was careful with money, of that Sophie was certain, although less so when the lady took a packet of cigarettes from her handbag and lit one with a match. Beyond this, Sophie could tell no more than that the woman was middle class and alone, except for her dog. Indeed, the woman looked lonely, personified loneliness, and it touched Sophie's heart. She studied the dog, deciding it was a girl. The animal was affectionate, devoted to her mistress, and often returned to her even while investigating the gardens. The streak of collie in the dog's heritage gave the impression she was a typical friendly family dog. Sophie heard trudging footsteps on the stairs to the attic and wondered who it was.

"Hello, miss," said Nick. "Mr Drysdale says I can go home now, but that I should see you first, in case you wanted something doing."

"He's over at the flat still, is he?"

"Yes. Him and Mr Len are there. He said he didn't want to compromise the mission here with too many people in the house. Might get noticed, he reckoned."

"What did he have you do?"

"Nothin', miss. All afternoon I've done nothin'."

"While doing nothing, what did you do?"

"I read for a bit. But I've really done nothin'."

"I imagine that's what he planned for you."

"But why? He gave me a florin."

"Then he's rather nice. What did you think about this afternoon?"

"Well... you know. I was about to mention it. I'm ever so sorry for what I've done. If I'd known it was going to get you in trouble like that, I honestly wouldn't have done a thing. I'm sorry, I am that, miss. It won't happen again. I'll treat everyone proper."

"It appears you may have done exactly as Mr Drysdale intended — considered your behaviour and come to a proper understanding of how your conduct can affect or reflect upon others."

"Yes... He did that deliberate?"

"I'm sure he did."

"That's clever of him."

Sophie smiled. "He is an intelligent gentleman, and a brave one. He received a medal for bravery during the war, but he won't say how he got it. That's the type of man he is. If he asks you to do something, make sure you do it to the best of your ability. Then, in some small way, you will work for the good of the country, because that's what he does."

"Blimey, that puts it on a chap, don't it, miss?"

"Yes, it does. It's called responsibility. The older you get, the more you will have to bear. One day, you will become responsible for others, either through having a family, or in the type of work you do. Put the support of your family first in your considerations, because they will always vitally depend upon you. Do you follow me?"

"I do, miss, but I think that's all a long ways off."

"Hopefully, it is. First, you need to establish your character, who it is you are going to be, and how you will discern the right conduct from the wrong. If you wish to train yourself to be an agent, spying on gentlemen is not how you set about it... How did they catch you, by the way?"

"They were right tricky. They was talking about the weather. Then that Lord Laneford must have been lowering his voice, and speaking as though he wasn't moving any closer. But he was. Next thing I know, he throws open the door and catches me looking like a right chump, doubled over with me ear to where the keyhole used to be. He grabs me by the collar and pulls me into the parlour. Then both of them kept on talking about prisons and which one would suit me best. I felt right sick."

Sophie laughed. "Do you know who they are?"

"I know they're both spies. Mr Drysdale blew his top when I said he was a spy. Then he handed me the money and said I now work for the FO, and if I tried to leave the house without his permission, he'd have me arrested and put in the nick before going to the Old Bailey. 'Course, miss, he didn't say nick. He said jail."

"Let us put the entire matter behind us. We shall not refer to it again."

"Thank you… I hate to bring this up, but I s'pose the driving lesson's gone down the plug 'ole."

"It very nearly did… But I gave my word and you shall have your lesson."

"Oh, miss. I don't know what to say. I'd do anything for you."

"Is that so? Then look out of the window… Do you see that woman on the bench? I'm sure she will leave at any moment. Follow her and don't let her catch you or allow it to appear as though you're following her to anyone else. That's most important. See if you can find out where she lives and memorize what she does. Take note of anyone who talks to her."

"That's the woman who had the screaming fit. Shall I report back here afterwards?"

"Yes. What time are your parents expecting you?"

"Seven. It takes almost an hour to get home from here."

"Right, that should still allow ample time. Make a quick sandwich in the kitchen to take with you, then wait by the side gate with your bicycle. When she leaves, I'll signal from the rear attic window."

"Got it, miss. I'm on my way."

Nick charged down the stairs, jumping some of them several at a time.

Sophie resumed her observation. The woman sat a little longer than expected, but eventually stood up to leave. The dog came over and she attached the leash. Sophie hurtled towards the rear window. Nick was waiting, and although he was not directly watching the window, noticed her immediately. Sophie gave the thumbs up signal. He responded similarly, then left by the side entrance. Sophie rushed back to the front to find the woman was closing the garden gate behind her.

Now the woman did a second odd thing. She stopped in front of number twenty-four, Mrs Fitch's house directly opposite number seven, and stared at the façade. Sophie could not tell whether the woman's stare was directed towards a specific window because of her angle of view, but knew it was not on the top floor. She scanned all the windows but could neither detect movement nor any motionless figure behind the net curtains.

After half a minute, the woman moved away, and Sophie was unsure if she actually looked more dejected now or if she just imagined she did. Some seconds passed and then Nick came into view, lazily riding his bicycle as if he had no particular place to go. He looked like any of the thousands of youths on bicycles around London, and Sophie instantly perceived the excellence of such a disguise.

The third odd event occurred the instant Nick disappeared from view. Mrs Fitch came out, descended her steps, and went to the side of the house to look along St George's Road after the woman. She stayed a short while before going back in.

It was getting close to teatime, and Ada had done all she could in the kitchen for the moment. The men were over at the flat, including the newly arrived Mr Philpott, Laneford's valet. One of them would be returning soon, so, in their absence, she tidied the parlour. On the table she found a novel with two bookmarks protruding from it. Curious, she examined the front and back covers before opening it. She began reading. Within minutes she had drifted from Primrose Hill to a place called Styles. She turned a page, read it, and then another page. Suddenly, she remembered she had things to do. Ada took a piece of paper from a nearby desk, tore off a strip, and wrote Nancy Carmichael on it. She put the book on a shelf where anyone could find it and left the room.

"Everything all right, miss?" asked Ada, carrying a tray to Sophie.

"Yes, thanks. I could do with a cup. Have you had yours?"

"I 'ad some downstairs. So what's Nick up to?"

"He's following the woman who screamed and walks about muttering. It's very interesting. She sat in the gardens earlier — her dog was with her. When she left, she stopped in front of Mrs Fitch's house and stared at it. She just stood there. Then a minute later, just as Nick went past in pursuit, Mrs Fitch came out to look down the street after the woman. What do you make of it?"

"Ooh... I don't know. She wasn't watching Nick?"

"No. That seems highly unlikely. The speed with which she came out suggests she was standing on the main floor, in her parlour, perhaps. It must be that Mrs Fitch and the woman were staring at each other, with only the net curtain blocking the woman's view. It's very odd, but I'm sure they must know each other, and something has happened between them."

"The poor soul might not be all there," said Ada. "She might do it all the time, and Mrs Fitch don't want to get involved, but did come out to make sure she got 'ome all right. She lives nearby, don't she?"

"She does, and you're probably right. I keep reading too much into the smallest things."

"Speculating, that is."

"Exactly. I should be patient and wait for Nick's report."

They spoke of the changes in the household arrangements and a few other things, while Sophie sipped her tea. Eventually, they heard Nick ascending the stairs and awaited his arrival in silence.

"Hello, I did it." He was breathless. "Nobody saw me or nothing."

"Excellent!" said Sophie, notebook and pencil in hand.

"Her name's Miss Boddington, and she lives at 37 St. George's Square, and she owns the whole bloomin' house and lives by herself."

"How on earth did you find that out?"

"I got talking to a couple of local boys younger 'an me. I said I was going down the sweet shop, and they'd get a gobstopper each if they told me about the old lady who talks to her dog. I'd already followed her, and she'd just gone in. They weren't doing nothin', so they said yes."

"Didn't they ask you why you wanted to know?"

"Oh, yeah. I told 'em, confidential like, that I worked for the police. They fell about laughing and never asked again."

"I wish life were always that simple," said Sophie. "Go on."

"They told me all they knew. They reckon she's got lots of money. One boy said she's got millions, but he was being stupid — showing off, like. The best bit is, she always keeps to herself, but was friendly 'til recent. Always had a dog and was fine until she went a bit loopy after the murder. The stupid boy reckons she did it. The other one said he don't know who it was. All he knows is, since the murder, he has to be indoors before it gets dark, which, he says, is a crime. I bought 'em a liquorice stick each as well, because they were so helpful."

"Very good," said Sophie. Ada nodded her approval.

"That's all there is about them. Anyway, I followed her when she left here. When she came to the murder scene near the pub, she crosses over the road to avoid it and then crosses back when past it. Now, I can't swear to this, miss, but I don't think she was muttering to herself. She walks along a bit hunched over, like this." Nick hunched and rounded his shoulders and brought his hands up to chest height. "She holds on to the dog and carries her handbag like that. Looks right awkward. Although it seems like she's moving quick, she takes little steps. I know that, 'cause I was having trouble riding so slowly; it made me wobble on my bicycle. I followed her to her house, and she went in through the basement. It's big. Like this house... I think that's everything, miss." He grinned, pleased with himself.

"Did her house look rundown or well-cared for?"

"Er... In the middle."

"Did she talk to anyone?" asked Ada.

"No. That reminds me. She looked behind her once, early on, and then again a bit later, looking back at the murder scene."

"Hmm... When she looked back the first time, did you happen to look back, too?"

"No. That would have made it like I was watching what she was doing. It would give me away."

"Of course, it would. How many seconds elapsed after her leaving Alexandra Gardens, would you say?"

He puffed out a noisy breath. "I don't know, miss. Maybe ten seconds. Not much longer, though. Why do you ask?"

"Mrs Fitch, who lives in the house directly across from us, went to the road to watch Miss Boddington. If your and my time estimates coincide, then they saw one another when Miss Boddington turned around and looked back."

"Is that important?" asked Nick.

"It's peculiar, and I don't yet know if it's important to us. It may mean nothing."

"I reckon," said Ada, "that Miss Boddington and Mrs Fitch used to be friends and 'ad a row. She wants to make it up, but Mrs Fitch won't 'ave none of it. She still thinks about her old friend, but won't climb down off her 'igh 'orse." Ada suddenly tutted and looked annoyed. "Nick, say 'igh 'orse."

"High horse."

"I don't believe it! You live near me. Why don't you drop your 'aitches?"

"My mum used to clip me round the ear if I did. Her family was a bit on the posh side, but they lost all their money. She had the habit, and gave it to me."

"Oh, I see. That explains it." She stared at Nick. "You should be really thankful to your mother for taking such care over you. I wish my mum had known to clip me round the ear. Too bloomin' late now."

"It's never too late," said Sophie, "if that's what you want to do. But we'll talk about it another time. Nick, thank you very much for an excellent bit of work. You may go home now but be very careful around traffic. Drivers of vehicles can't always see someone on a bicycle."

"I'll be careful, miss. Good night."

"Good night," said Sophie and Ada.

"What do you think now?" asked Sophie.

"About the same. But if Miss Boddington went funny after the murder, that looks right suspicious."

"It certainly needs investigating. I'll explain all of this to Miss Walton."

"Yes. Has Lord Laneford come round because Gladys is 'ere or because of the mission?"

"I suspect he came for the mission, but will stay for Miss Walton."

"I should call her Miss Walton, an' all, now I'm an' 'ouse-keeper. It's 'ard, I mean *h*ard, to stay in character sometimes, ain't it, miss?"

"Very hard. I've no idea how double agents manage it."

"They must go off their *h*eads."

"Are you trying again?"

"I'll give it another go. It might *h*elp if I stayed with Nick's mother."

They laughed.

# Chapter 12

# Embarrassment

At five-thirty, towards the end of a long, tiring workday, Mrs Barker surveyed her larder. Yesterday morning it had been empty, apart from a few scraps of things the previous agents had left behind. Now it was crammed with food, some of it in preparation for Sunday's lunch, but most of it for the ongoing demands of the household. In baking four large meat pies and five small fruit pies, she had utilized every pie dish in the kitchen. This was her standby, her strategic reserve, to be deployed should an unexpected guest or two arrive. The way things had been going, Mrs Barker felt sure there must be a horde of unexpected guests milling about outside just waiting to be invited in. If there were, she was ready for them. Satisfied by what she saw, she decided she would have a lie-in tomorrow morning and get up at eight.

She had never kept a dog, and was indifferent to them. They had not figured in her life, and never had she permitted one in her kitchen. This particular Saturday had wrought a change. Mrs Barker had been carefully saving scraps all day. The quality of the scraps in the bowl had started out as being that which a dog *might* eat. After several sightings of and interactions with Biscuit, the quality of the scraps changed to include that which a dinner guest would choose above all else. She was ready to bestow the bountiful bowl upon the favoured canine. With the bowl in one hand and a sheet of newspaper under her arm, she opened the kitchen door to the hall.

"Biscuit, Blast-it, whatever your name is! Come here!"

She heard him quickly descend three flights of stairs. Biscuit turned at the bottom and presented himself to Mrs Barker.

"You knew it was food. Come in, and don't make a mess."

In a corner of the kitchen, she bent down with some difficulty and placed the bowl on top of the newspaper.

"There, that's for you."

Biscuit sat staring up at her.

"I didn't save it all for nothing. Go on, eat it."

He did as commanded.

Having broken one of her own cardinal rules, Mrs Barker now smiled as she watched him.

"That was quick," she said when he had finished. "Good boy." Unfamiliar with dogs, she gave him the lightest and most tentative of pats on the head.

"Blast-it!" Sophie called from somewhere upstairs.

The dog gave Mrs Barker a look, which she swore later meant, 'I'm terribly sorry, but I have to go. Thank you for the food.' Biscuit then answered the summons.

"Get your leash," said Sophie to Biscuit, while on the stairs. Flora was behind her. Ada was in the attic.

They quickly got themselves ready to go out in a whirl of coats, hats, and gloves. Mr Saunders was walking past their house, and the agents, come what may, intended to interview the only witness to the murder.

At thirty-one, David Saunders had his entire life mapped out before him. He was completely and utterly a banker. He came from a family of comfortable means. When he married, he bought the house, number twelve, in which he and his wife, Colleen, now lived. She came from an Irish family, also of comfortable means. Colleen was practical and artistic. She painted and had articles printed in magazines for women. Together, they awaited the arrival of their firstborn, which was now only a matter of a few weeks away. Therefore,

Colleen now rarely appeared in the square. They had already purchased everything necessary for the baby's advent, except those things exclusive to a boy or a girl. In Colleen's family, two avid and rather competitive knitters were eagerly awaiting the pronouncement of either boy or girl to start their needles clicking on the baby's behalf and get in first with their output.

Ginnie, an English setter, was old now, pre-dating the Saunders' marriage by several years. She moved slowly and methodically. David Saunders was quite content to walk at her pace. He was content with almost everything in his life. The park was not far away, but their slow speed meant the walk always lasted the best part of an hour. As Sophie and Flora left the house, Saunders was still at the railings close by number seven.

Flora took the initiative because Sophie was rather shy about accosting strangers.

"Good evening," said Flora, as they approached. "You must be a near neighbour of ours."

"Good evening," he replied, raising his hat. He was already thinning on top. His father had gone bald at an early age, so Saunders did not think it unusual or complain about his condition.

"We're from number seven. What number are you?"

"Oh, ah, number twelve," he replied cautiously.

"We arrived only yesterday and we're liking the house very much. This is my cousin, Miss King, and I'm Miss Walton."

"Please to meet you. I'm Saunders."

His caution became apparent to the two women. His dog was looking warily at Biscuit, who sat patiently.

"We're thinking of buying a house in the area," said Sophie.

"Yes, only we're unsure of the property values," added Flora.

"Ah."

"We decided to pool our inheritance money and invest it in a house."

"Ah, I see. A commendable approach, and your timing is most advantageous, if I might say so."

It occurred to both Sophie and Flora that he was on the defensive in case they asked him for a mortgage. They glanced at each other.

"Do you think house prices have stabilized now?" asked Sophie. "We're eager to buy and don't need a mortgage."

"It just so happens that I work in a large bank, so I'm quite familiar with the state of the house market."

"Then you're *just* the person to talk to," said Flora. "Unless it's inconvenient, or you'd rather not. I can appreciate that, being a bank official, you must be very careful to whom you speak."

"Thank you for understanding. I find I must be a bank officer outside of business hours as well as within them. It so happens that I approve loans and mortgages, but I have made it a rule not to involve myself professionally with my neighbours, to avoid even the hint of a conflict of interest. As you require no mortgage, that puts a different complexion upon any discussions we have."

"I can't help having an eye for a bargain," said Sophie. "If we bought now, and the prices went lower, I'd be very, very upset."

"There are no guarantees, Miss King. To understand the whole picture, the war produced an overall slump in demand. The dreadful loss of life has further depressed the demand for housing. Distasteful as it is to include, it is a factor that cannot be ignored in financial considerations. In the current state, I see the market remaining depressed for several years, but I doubt, or I should say, it would surprise me if the market fell further. Another five to ten years, and houses will be double the price, particularly in an area like Primrose Hill."

"Why Primrose Hill and not across the board? You see, although we're leaning towards something around here, we are yet to commit ourselves."

"All the bargains are being snapped up. Properties in Central London and in the most prestigious or fashionable areas have already rebounded. With economic stability, this effect will widen into other parts. I like to think of Primrose Hill as being in the third tier of select residences. The houses were solidly constructed and well designed. As prosperity increases, this area will quickly become an attractive alternative to those moving up in the world, but also to those moving down, so to speak. Events have decimated the finances of the upper classes. The war, taxation, and the inheritance laws have all taken their toll. A property once valued at fifty thousand now goes for twenty-five. If the owner who must sell buys one of the better houses in Primrose Hill for only two or three thousands, he keeps something substantial to live on."

"Thank you so much," said Flora, who touched Mr Saunders' arm, "for explaining the matter so clearly. We'll go to the estate agent's on Monday."

"I agree. But remember, we said we would try out Hampstead and Kensington, too," said Sophie.

"But if we like it here, why need we go to those places?"

"For comparison," answered Sophie.

"Mr Saunders, please guide us in this matter."

He laughed nervously. "Oh no, no. I mustn't do that. Both those areas are, in many ways, equivalent to Primrose Hill. The distinct advantage this area possesses is its isolation from so much of the traffic and noise found elsewhere. I often think of it as a fertile island which contains a complete community and protects it from the bustle of London as a whole. It is a genteel and peaceful area. It has its issues, yes. All places do. You might find similar pockets elsewhere, but if a tranquil life in one of London's well-to-do areas is what you desire, it is most readily found here."

"You should become the mayor," said Flora.

Saunders laughed heartily. "That is such an amusing thought, Miss Walton."

"We must go to the park now," said Sophie. "We don't want to be late back."

"Are you going to the park, Mr Saunders?"

"Yes, I am."

"Would it be a bother if we accompanied you?" asked Flora. "We don't know anyone in the area and you have been so kind."

Trapped and unable to refuse, Saunders replied, "Why, yes, of course. It will be no bother at all."

They set off together, the agents fully cognizant that Mr Saunders was bothered and would rather go alone.

"Tell us about your lovely dog," said Sophie. "An English setter, isn't it?"

"Yes, she is. Ginnie's a marvellous old girl…"

They walked and talked all the way to the park, and the conversation became illuminating.

"So you avoid walking Ginnie in Alexandra Gardens?" asked Flora.

"I cannot name names, you understand."

"Of course, you can't," said Sophie.

"I find the gossip quite distressing. I'm forced to distance myself from it."

"Is it only among the dog owners?"

"I'm sure there are others who do, but I'm not aware of them if there are."

"Phoebe. We must be careful in future."

"Yes. Has it always been that way?"

"To a certain extent, but it worsened last year, and again more recently. To tell the truth, I only go out with Ginnie at the least likely time to meet anyone."

"Oh, I see," said Flora. "But you must be friendly with some of them."

"Only Major Cummings and Mr Kuritsyn. I talk to them still."

"We've met Mr Kuritsyn. But he's a Communist?"

"Strange, isn't it? Here am I, a capitalist, yet I like the fellow. The truth is, he would like to stay in England and have nothing to do with Communism. He's still a socialist, of course."

"I know nothing about it," said Sophie. "But I find it odd that so many communists can just set up house the way they have."

"Yes, I've also wondered about that… I don't think they do very much. Makes one wonder why they're here. Still, none of my business, and it's all within the law."

They walked further into the park. Biscuit fetched the stick Flora threw, while Ginnie kept near Saunders. Sophie waited for Flora to return before saying,

"Someone mentioned there was a murder last year in Primrose Hill."

Saunders hesitated before commenting. "It was this year, actually."

"This year?" Flora looked shocked. "I hope they've caught him."

"Unfortunately, they haven't."

"How absolutely dreadful," said Sophie. "The police really should do something. I'll search the newspaper back numbers to find out all about it."

"Well, yes. In doing so, you'll discover soon enough that I was the only witness to the crime."

"My goodness!" said Flora. "That must have been devastating for you."

"It, er, it is an unpleasant memory, but one learns to live with it."

"I should imagine you would never want to think of it again," announced Sophie. "I know I wouldn't."

"Oh, I don't think so. They say talking things over makes a rotten thing easier to bear." Flora turned to Saunders. "That's what I would do. I'd go to a psychologist."

"Nonsense," said Sophie. "If you must talk about something like a murder, all you need is a sympathetic ear. What's the point of telling the same person the same old thing all the time? And paying a hefty sum for the pleasure of it."

"A psychologist could be expensive, although I really know nothing about it. Do you?" Flora asked Saunders.

"They charge quite a lot, I understand. But, fortunately, I feel no need to resort to one."

"But don't you feel burdened?" asked Sophie. "You must feel burdened."

"I wouldn't object to hearing about your experience, if that would help," said Flora.

"Not much to tell, really. I had taken Ginnie for a walk. You might recall an evening in February when there was heavy fog…"

He more or less recited verbatim his witness report, which Flora and Sophie knew by heart. They heard him without interrupting. He added a few extra details he had learned afterwards, but he was ignorant of the police suspicion that the murderer was a dog owner in Alexandra Gardens.

"So you knew Mr Hamilton. How ghastly that must be for you," said Flora. "Makes it so much worse!"

"I knew him, but I never had much to do with him. It still struck home, though."

"You told your interesting narrative so well," said Sophie. "The part that intrigues me is that the murderer took the weapon away with him and, you said, it clanged against the railings. Did it sound like a big, heavy object?"

"It was a slight but definite sound of metal against the railings. I've thought it over, but can't identify what it was."

"Something like a hammer?" she suggested.

"The coroner ruled that out at the inquest. He said it was a very straight wound. Excuse my mentioning that."

"Makes one wonder what it could have been," said Sophie.

"I've thought about it often. I keep a toolbox at home and, after considering what the coroner had to say and matching it with what I heard that evening, I tested a few items. A heavy file with a handle seemed most likely to fit the bill, but when tested on the railings, it didn't sound the same. Neither did a large chisel. There was not much else suitable, so I tried a hammer. It sounded more like it, but it's the wrong shape entirely to fit or match the wound."

"Sounds like a hammer, but shaped something like a heavy file… I have no idea," admitted Sophie.

"Neither do I," said Saunders. "So I no longer dwell on it."

"Naturally, you don't," said Flora. Sophie signalled with her eyes that they should leave. Flora continued, "We've inadvertently stirred up some disturbing memories you'd certainly rather forget, which is poor of us."

"That's true," said Sophie, "but I confess to being quite fascinated by it all. If you ever care to talk it over again, I'd be most interested in hearing what you have to say. For now, I think we should leave. We've taken up your valuable time for far too long."

"Interrupted your constitutional, don't you know?" said Flora.

"The interruption, as you call it, has been most welcome. In a way, talking it over has helped."

"When the police catch the criminal, I think you will feel much better," said Sophie.

They parted, with Flora and Sophie trying to appear as natural as possible.

"We won't talk for two minutes," said Sophie, "in case he's watching."

"Throw the ball, then. Poor Biscuit is dying to run about."

They both walked and threw the ball for the dog. Eventually, they came to a stop but continued with the game.

"I feel rotten deceiving him like that," said Sophie.

"I know. We wouldn't get anywhere if we didn't."

"We have no choice... Shaped like a file, sounding like a hammer. What am I?"

"Very strange. I'm useless at riddles."

"Put your thinking cap on."

They were quiet.

"Do you suppose the murderer was carrying a file *and* a hammer?" asked Flora.

"That's possible. Do you think he used both when he struck Mr Hamilton?"

"How could he do that?"

"Well, he'd have to hold the file straight like this." Sophie used her flattened left hand held high and horizontally to demonstrate the file's position. "Then he'd strike against the file so."

"I'm not impressed. He might have done it that way, but it seems idiotic to me. The murder took place in a fog, remember? What's more likely is that he would flail about with the hammer until he struck Hamilton."

"More than likely. Also, the murderer would have to plan it that way to bring those particular tools out with him... so we can forget the idea."

They were quiet for a long time.

"I can't think of anything," said Flora.

"Neither can I. The answer does not lie in a toolbox, unless it's some obscure item."

"Wasn't there a mention of spanners and adjustable wrenches?"

"That was Sergeant Gowers. He wasn't convinced it was either of those."

"I barely know what they are."

"As a budding detective, you must familiarize yourself with such things."

"But they're all so dirty. I know you fiddle with your car, but why do you do it to yourself?"

"I don't fiddle. I perform maintenance to keep the car in good running order."

"Let me look at your hands."

"Certainly not."

"They're probably ruined beyond hope by scars, broken nails, and ingrained dirt."

"They are not. I'll show you." Sophie took off a glove. "See."

"Make sure you keep them that way. Mr Yardley won't marry you if you have the hands of a mechanic."

"Flora, don't."

"Has he asked you yet?"

"No. Has Lord Laneford asked you yet?"

"No, but I'll say yes if he does. What will be your answer?"

"Part of me wants to say yes. I fear he'll expect me to settle into the role of Mrs Yardley and leave everything I've built up at Burgoyne's. I can see why, because of his position as the heir to a viscountcy, but I can't do that so easily. It's the people who rely upon me more than anything. I can't let them down and it makes it frightfully hard."

"What about his spying work?"

"He'll continue with it, I'm sure. Although, that brings up another item. He frequently puts himself in great danger. One day, he might not return home. I'd always have the worry of it... Not exactly a bed of roses."

"I've never understood that expression. Roses have thorns. Why would anyone lie on them?"

"If you were correct, it would be a far more apt expression to describe my situation. I believe a *flower*bed of roses is meant."

"It is? Then they should say what they mean and not confuse me."

"What will you do if you marry Lord Laneford?"

"Give up acting, although I might try amateur productions. If I have a say in it, I'd cast myself as the leading lady. For once, I'd be certain of getting the best part. As for spying and investigating, it's an absolute fixed condition that I continue on. Sidney has to put up with it."

"Oh... I suppose I could do something similar should things progress that far with Sinjin."

A man approached them, enquiring about Biscuit. He left them after a minute.

"It's getting dark. We ought to go home," said Flora.

They turned about. Flora spoke again.

"You're very quiet. Are you still thinking about Mr Yardley?"

"No. The reason we can't find the murder weapon in the toolbox is because it was never there. It has to be another household item."

"Like a poker?"

"A poker has too large a diameter. If the diameter is too thin, it has no weight behind it to do the damage. Now the edge of something might answer. Such as, and I know this sounds absurd, the metal stands the cobblers use with that foot shaped thing on it. That part goes crosswise, you see. So does the base. The murderer stood directly behind Hamilton and hit him with something like a cobbler's stand."

"Try as you might to talk me out of it, I now picture a deranged cobbler running about foggy streets, his stand raised up high, ready to strike. However, we clear away the unimportant, like so, pfft! You comprehend? My dear Phoebe, always arrange the facts in their proper order. That is the only method, so *never* neglect the use of your natural faculties."

"I *beg* your pardon?"

"Take no notice. It's just something I've read recently."

---

In Alexandra Gardens, the only person out and about was Captain Bristow. Upon sighting Sophie and Flora entering the square, he waved and smiled before starting towards them. His Newfoundland pulled in eagerness to meet others, particularly Biscuit.

"Hullo, hullo," he said at a distance. "Making use of the last light? Days are getting so much longer now, aren't they?"

"Indeed, they are, Captain," said Sophie.

"I'm looking forward to the summer. It means I can go sailing again. Staying away from the sea for too long gets on my nerves. A nautical life is in my blood."

"I can understand that. Where do you sail?"

"Oh, um, Cowes, mostly."

"I know Cowes."

"You sail, do you?"

"I don't have a boat, but I sail with friends off the Hampshire coast. I missed it terribly last year. A few things cropped up that had to be dealt with."

"Really?" He glanced at his wristwatch. "Good heavens. Look at the time. And here's me babbling on about the light. I'll probably see you both tomorrow. Good evening, ladies."

They both said good evening.

"How extraordinary," said Sophie.

"He obviously didn't want to discuss sailing."

"That's very suspicious. Do you think he's lying?"

"Has to be."

They stood across the road from number two.

"Hello!" It was Miss Villard.

"This is like a farce," whispered Flora. "Hello! Come and join us."

"She'll talk about Bristow," whispered Sophie.

Miss Villard joined them, saying,

"So. Have you fallen in love with Primrose Hill yet?"

"It is certainly wooing us," answered Sophie, smiling back at her.

"That's very good... I wanted to talk to Captain Bristow, but I see he's gone. Did he seem all right to you?"

"I think so," said Flora.

"Is he ill?" asked Sophie.

"No, no, nothing like that."

"He was rather abrupt," said Flora.

"Was he? I wonder why?"

"We were only talking about sailing," said Sophie, "then suddenly he took off."

"Ahh." The level of awareness in her tone begged a question.

"Do you know something about him?" asked Flora.

"I know a few things about the Captain."

"Oh, Miss Villard, you can't keep us in suspense," said Sophie.

"I shouldn't really say anything without him present, but..." A slow smile spread across her face. "I'll tell you this much. Throughout the war, he was a lieutenant in charge of launches carrying supplies to ships at anchor in Portsmouth. Two months before the end of the war, they promoted him to captain just to increase his half-pay after the war ended. A friend got him the promotion. What can I say?"

"You mean he was only a captain for two months?" asked Sophie.

"And it was because a friend wanted to get him more money?" asked Flora.

"Yes!"

"I don't think he should call himself Captain," said Sophie. "What do you think, Miss Villard?"

"I think you should call me Dulcie. Concerning Mr Bristow — it makes him happy. Why not?"

"This is Phoebe, and I'm Gladys, seeing as we're all friends together. Naval officers work hard to earn their rank. To hear of someone getting a promotion through a friend simply to get more money is far removed from the spirit of the Royal Navy."

"I don't say it isn't. But lots of bad things happened during the war, and this seems of little consequence to me. Perhaps I'm used to the idea, whereas you have just heard of it."

"You could be right," said Flora.

"His captaincy is one thing, but your reaction suggested something about sailing?" said Sophie.

"Phoebe, he doesn't have a boat. Not so much as a canoe. Yet he claims he sails. Do you sail?"

"A little. I have for years."

"You probably know more about it than he does. He had a desk job, you see. Once in a while, he was out in a small boat, that's all. I saw him run indoors, and it was to avoid *you* because you sail."

"That explains it," said Sophie.

"Then what does he do for a living?" asked Flora. "I mean, isn't he in that big house by himself? How can he afford it, Dulcie?"

Miss Villard smiled again. "He's not short of money. He is a designer and a very good draughtsman. To you, he'll say he designs boats and things, but that's not where he gets his money from. Oh, no. He has designs of boats that he will show you. Hm! However, Mr Bristow has another office. In there is where he does his actual work, but he won't show it to anyone."

Flora leaned in a little closer. Sophie waited expectantly.

"He designs lavatories."

"The rooms, you mean?" asked Sophie.

"No. The bowls."

"The porcelain?" asked Flora.

Miss Villard nodded. "He does very well, considering. His top model is 'The Pedestal', but he has another he sells to local governments. That one he calls, 'Straight Back - County Council Fashion.'" She ended by nodding significantly again.

"What does that even mean?" asked Flora.

"Who knows, but he sells thousands of them to the councils. Me, if I designed such receptacles, I would call myself the Queen of the Lavatory, or some such thing. He should make himself famous by what he does, not hide it and be ashamed. It's better for business."

"Yes," said Flora, still in control of herself.

"That reminds me of Sir Henry Doulton," said Sophie. "He made his father's pottery business famous by manufacturing clay sewage pipes. It was only later that he concentrated on the art pottery for which he's remembered."

"Oh, that's interesting. I don't think Mr Bristow will ever be so successful, but he should never hide his light under a bushel."

"We won't mention a word," said Flora.

"I don't see how we could!" said Sophie.

"Of course, you won't say anything. I'm going now. It's getting too cool for me."

They all said good night. Sophie and Flora hurriedly returned to their house in complete silence. Once inside, they broke down and laughed like anything. Even Biscuit barked. Their laughter was short-lived, however. Inspector Morton opened the kitchen door.

"Good evening. Sorry, I'm late. A few things held me up, and Sergeant Gowers is off today."

"Good evening. You've come for the daily report? It's only partly finished. There's more to add, you see."

"I'm going upstairs," said Flora. "Good evening, Inspector."

"Oh, ah, good evening, Miss Walton."

Annoyed, Sophie shot her a glance. She smiled at Morton. "Why not sit in the parlour, Inspector, while I get organized?"

"Yes, I'll do that."

Sophie rushed up the stairs after Flora.

"You can't leave me alone with him."

"Ooh, the mind boggles."

"Don't let it. I fear he's going to propose to me."

"No!"

"Ssh. Yes."

"What will you say? Are you going to accept?"

"Flora, what do you take me for, after what I confided in you about Sinjin?"

"Then explain yourself."

Sophie let out a long sigh. "I like Inspector Morton as a friend. Never have I encouraged him, but I know that he likes me."

"We all know that."

"I suppose you do. However, the situation is becoming awkward. It's obvious what's going to happen, but I can't bring myself to hurt his feelings. Never mind about the awkwardness of having to continue to work with him afterwards. I... I don't know *what* to do."

"Don't worry, I'll not desert you in your hour of need. This is an absolute corker of a situation, and I couldn't possibly miss it."

"What do I do, though?"

"It is a simple calculation. Tell him you love Mr Yardley..."

"I couldn't possibly..."

"Shh, shh. Let me finish. You, or I, or both of us, could do so by hints that he cannot mistake. Do you see? Then it would be for him to decide that he cannot or should not marry you. He has to see it. But Sophie, it would be simpler and kinder if you introduced the subject. In fact, the kindest thing would be to tell him plainly he hasn't a hope in the world, and he's wasting his time."

"Auntie says similar things, only she's absolutely brutal about it. She told me that in rejecting a suitor, I should be as harsh as possible. She told me that in rejecting one, her response was, 'I couldn't possibly consider marrying a worm like you.'"

Flora laughed, "She's dreadful sometimes. But that was years ago..."

"No! This was in 1918, at the end of the war. Her reasoning is that it's better to be insulting for the sake of the man's soul. He'll get angry, then realize he's had a near miss. He'll go to his club, down a few drinks, and be laughing with his friends by the end of the night. The next day, while nursing a hangover, he'll go out. That's when he'll either decide to swear off marrying a woman forever by becoming a monk, or fall in love with the next suitable candidate who crosses his path."

"She's got it all worked out, and it even sounds true. You can't do anything like that, though."

"No. Your plan of dropping hints is much better."

In the parlour, Sophie and Flora dropped hints while discussing the case with Morton and, although occasionally irritated by the mention of Mr Yardley, he ignored everything and stayed an hour longer than necessary.

## Chapter 13

## Sunday spies

Shifts in the attic were beginning to deprive the agents of sleep. After some discussion, they found they could rearrange the schedule. Flora could stay awake into the wee hours without ill effect, as long as she got a solid eight hours afterwards. Therefore, she stayed up until three a.m. during the night shift that nobody wanted to do. Sophie would go to bed early, then wake to cover the hours from 3 to 6, and afterwards get a few more hours of sleep. Ada took over from six until nine, when Sophie returned to stay until twelve, at which time Flora took over once more. The rest of the day they divided into two-hour stints, which they shared equally. In their off hours, Ada attended to the household duties, while Sophie and Flora took the dog for a walk in the hope of interviewing a suspect.

During the night, it had rained heavily off and on. By daybreak, this had tapered to intermittent showers, swept in on a strong breeze. By seven, it was still rather dark in the attics and the rain pattered on the roof, while Ada sat below it, a blanket around her shoulders, listening to the mournful noise above her head. There were twenty things that needed doing in the house, while she stared at dull number fifteen, in the dull light of a dull, dreary wet morning. She tightly clutched her hot water bottle before the very last of its warmth faded away. She felt like going back to bed, especially as nothing whatsoever was happening in the square below. Number fifteen looked as enigmatic in the grey light as it had in the dark. Ada yawned. She picked up the binoculars. Although their novelty had worn off, they were still useful. She looked for any sign of life in the Communist stronghold, window by window. There was none. They were all asleep while she was staring uselessly at their house. She put down the binoculars, checked the time by Sophie's wristwatch, which she had borrowed, discarded her water bottle, and pulled the blanket more tightly about her.

As she stared, the door of number fifteen opened, and a man rushed out.

Ada jumped up. "Godfathers! It's 'im!" She stood rooted to the spot. There was a plan in place for just such a contingency, but she struggled to recall it.

The man was probably hurrying for no other reason than to lessen his time in the rain. She noted which direction he took and then ran to Sophie's room.

"Wake up! Wake up! The Communist bloke's scarpered! You know, the stranger!"

"What? He's what? Where?"

Ada pulled the bedclothes back. "Either you go or I do. Which is it?"

"You go, you're dressed."

"Right. He's heading towards the shops." Ada fled downstairs, stopping long enough at the umbrella and coat stand to equip herself, then left the house, still pulling on her raincoat.

Sophie felt slightly deranged from lack of sleep and from being so rudely awakened out of her dreams. The house had cooled overnight, so she shivered in her old, thick dressing gown as she wearily lumbered to the attic. Reaching the rear window, she picked up the pale yellow duster next to the torch, then cleaned the top left-hand pane. By cleaning that particular corner, she signalled that the Russian had gone north west on St. George's Road. She stared towards the flat, then repeated the signal. A white handkerchief fluttered the answer. Sophie sagged in relief, and hoped the responding agent had not seen her night attire and long, brown hair in a braid over a shoulder. No more sleep for her. She went down to make some tea and light a fire if Myrtle had not already done so.

Mrs Barker was in the kitchen with the kettle on. She, too, was in her dressing gown with her long silver and black hair hanging in a braid down her back.

"Good morning, Miss King."

"Good morning... Look at that, we're twins." Sophie waved the end of her braid at Mrs Barker.

"I have to," said the cook, "otherwise I get terrible knots."

"So do I."

"What's happened? I heard the noise."

"The Russian agent left the house. Nancy has gone after him, and I've alerted the men. They should also be in pursuit by now."

"I knew it had to be something like that. Do you think she'll be all right?"

"I'm sure she will. Nancy's very careful."

"Let's hope so, for her sake."

"I'll make some toast," said Sophie.

"No, you won't. You can have a proper breakfast, or toast, if you like. But I'll make it. You just sit there, Miss King."

"Thank you. Just the toast, please." Sophie sat down. "Is Myrtle up?"

"Yes. She's lighting a fire in the parlour, or should have by now."

"Has she said anything about sleeping in the basement by herself? It's rather gloomy, with all the old furniture stored in the unused rooms."

"Myrtle hasn't said anything, and she was bright enough when I saw her first thing. She's got her room looking nice. Never had one to herself before."

"If I had this house, I'd do something with the basement. It's very spacious."

"It is. But I'm right thankful they moved the kitchen from down there to up here."

"The old kitchen looks a bit of a wreckage."

Someone knocked smartly on the back door. The two women froze, staring at each other in horror.

"Who can that be?" whispered Mrs Barker.

Sophie got up and peeked through the window.

"It's a man," whispered Sophie.

Mrs Barker's mouth fell open.

"I must answer," said Sophie. "You go and get dressed."

Needing no encouragement, Mrs Barker switched off the stove and hurried from the kitchen.

Sophie, clutching the lapels of her dressing gown to her throat, opened the door barely a foot. Standing nonchalantly on the step was Ralph St. John Walter Gossuin Yardley.

"Sinjin!" He was the last person she wanted to see her in her present state. "What are *you* doing here?"

"Hello. I'm delighted and honoured that the lady of the house opens the door to my unworthy self."

"But you can't see me like this. I'm not dressed."

"True. Nevertheless, I do see, and you are beautiful."

"It's only eight o'clock."

"Loveliness clearly has no regard for the time of day. We can stay as we are, or I can wait here on the step while you dress. Will you be long?"

"You're enjoying my disadvantage a little too much. Come in."

Yardley entered and quickly glanced around the kitchen before turning to Sophie. "I see I've chased your cook from the kitchen. My apologies for being so disturbin'." He smiled. Whenever he did so, he looked handsome and boyish. At rest, his features took on a sullen, almost grim aspect. He took off his hat to reveal short, thick, yellow hair. He unbuttoned his heavy raincoat, revealing a grey lounge suit beneath, and a crisp white shirt which accentuated his healthy colour.

"Who's pursuing the Russian?" asked Sophie.

"Laneford and his man, Philpott. Archie's tagging along in case an extra hand's needed. As I was on the spot, I thought I'd come over to save all that signalling business."

"Len's gone, I take it."

"He was to have had the weekend off, so I took pity on him as he'd already lost a day of it. He didn't seem to mind being here, but left last night after we spoke on the telephone. Anyway, I arrived around seven."

"I thought you were at Elflund Hall for the weekend."

"I was supposed to be. Deirdre's nineteenth birthday was yesterday, but there was nothing planned for today. She was intrigued by the card you sent her. Asked a few pointed questions."

"I was just thinking of her on her birthday. I have met her briefly, you know. Did she enjoy her celebration?"

"Yes… The truth is, I think she would have rather been at a jazz club last night, instead of with the family."

"Oh, dear. Is she headstrong?"

"Not that one would notice, because she first listens politely, and then ignores completely, and is secretive in doing so. My concern about night clubs is that she'll get involved with drugs through the characters who frequent such places only to make money. I know she's been once, and that was to one of the more innocent places. However, I'm pretty certain she's drifting towards that wrong type of nightclub life."

"Likely she will, unless something's done. What attracts her to it, do you think?"

"The excitement and the supposed glamour. I imagine she finds elements of daring and danger in bucking convention, which undoubtedly adds to the allure."

"The burden of being an older brother. I recall, in very different situations, behaving similarly to my brother, Peter. Whatever you say won't work."

"I have an ace up my sleeve. At least I believe I do. I have a doctor friend who runs a small clinic for the rehabilitation of addicts. I've visited the place, and found the experience quite harrowing. By hook or by crook, I'll get Deirdre to visit the clinic to talk to a few of the patients. If anything can set her straight, that would."

"Yes… She might surprise you, though, and be quite sensible about everything without your intervening."

"You could be right, and I hope you are... Shall I make the tea? No one has ever died after drinking one of my brews."

"Thank you, but only if you wish to face the wrath of Mrs Barker. You have driven her from her kitchen. She's bound to return at any moment to wrest it back from you. If she finds you with a kettle in hand, you're likely to be wearing it the next moment. Sit there, and be good, so I can get dressed."

"I'll be as meek as a lamb heeding the command of the shepherdess."

"Why did you say that?" Sophie looked down at her old dressing gown. "I look like a shepherdess in this? Oh, really!?"

"Just a little."

Ada had to walk quickly to keep up with the tall man ahead. She slowly gained on him, but was mindful not to get too close in case he turned around. The rain eased off, but it was windy, so she kept her umbrella furled as they walked the length of St. George's Road. At the end, the Russian turned onto curving Berkley Street, but kept to the northward branch. *Going towards the shops*, thought Ada. *They ain't open.*

Along Regent's Park Road, they passed all the shuttered and darkened shops that had been so lively yesterday. There was no litter on the street, which surprised Ada. She was about fifty yards behind the man, and they were near to the end of the parade of shops. The bridge lay ahead, with the station entrance on the other side of the tracks. He was going somewhere further afield. Ada hurried. As he stepped off the bridge, she stepped onto it.

To her surprise, the station right by the bridge was shuttered, she being unaware it had been so since closing to the public during the war. The Russian followed a short road before entering a cross-street. Ada reached the corner of Adelaide Street. Now she could see where he was headed. On the other side was the wide low front of Chalk Farm Underground Station, and the man was walking directly towards it.

With no traffic about, Ada charged across after him. Before she had reached the pavement, he had entered a newsagent and tobacconist shop next to the station. She did not know what to do. Go in? Wait outside? Wishing not to be discovered, she walked past to wait unobtrusively in the tube station entrance. Passing the closed door, she could see nothing inside the shop.

Ada did not want trouble with the ticket, so she must find out first where the man was going in order that she should pay the right fare. She waited in the entrance to keep an eye on the newsagent's door. Then she remembered she was still wearing Sophie's watch. It was eighteen minutes past the hour. To her, the station seemed busy for a Sunday. She wondered if a market was open nearby. Several people entered, blocking her view. When they had passed, the Russian was in the street again, preparing to cross the road and go back the way he had come.

*What a bloomin' waste of time*, thought Ada. She felt, at first, that there was really no need to follow if he was only returning to number fifteen. However, she then supposed she had better follow him, anyway. *All that, to watch him buy a newspaper.* Then an idea occurred to her, and she went inside the newsagent's.

"Mornin'. Where's the nice weather gone, eh?"

"Morning. It'll be back soon," answered the middle-aged newsagent.

"I 'ope so. That fella what was in 'ere. What newspaper did he buy?"

"He bought two. Why do you want to know?"

Why did she want to know?

"Well, I work in an 'ouse, and the lady got a nasty letter. One of them very nasty ones. All cut out from newspapers, it was, and quite disgusting."

"I've heard of those. Do you know him, then?"

"He's a neighbour, and we don't 'ave nothing to do with him usually. He's a funny bloke... Have you seen him before?"

"Never, that I recall. But then I get a lot of customers."

"Well, you would, being right by the station, an' all."

"That's right. He bought a Daily Herald and a Times. Yes, and a box of a hundred Navy Cut."

"I'll take them two papers, but not the Navy Cut."

"Quite right. They're too strong."

Ada had already noticed a display of Cadbury's chocolate.

"And a small Dairy Milk... No, better make that five."

"Five? You'd be better off with the largest bar. More for less, see."

"All right. Thanks!"

The newsagent put the items down, and Ada paid. He leaned forward on the counter.

"Now you listen to me. I can see you're a smart girl who wants to get to the bottom of things. Don't you go near that bloke, lovey. If you think it's him what sent the letter, you go to the police. Let them handle it."

"Thank you, I will, an' all. I wanted to get the evidence first. You can't go to the police without 'aving something to back up your word. Anyway, it won't be me. I'll leave it to the lady of the house."

"That's right." He stood up straight. "You do that. Enjoy your chocolate."

"I will. Bye-bye."

He waved to her as she turned to leave.

Ada hurried back. In crossing the bridge, she met Archie Drysdale.

"Hello, Miss Carmichael." He raised his hat. "Are you all right?"

"Yes, I am, thank you."

"What happened? Whoops, we'd better move first, or the smoke will choke us."

They left the bridge before a heavily smoking engine passed beneath them.

"Is he still being followed, or do I have to catch up with him?"

"Lord Laneford and Mr Philpott are taking care of that."

Once safe, they stopped to talk. Ada briefly related what had happened without Archie interrupting her. He smiled when she explained the story she had told the newsagent.

"Excellent work, Miss Carmichael. May I relieve you of those newspapers?"

"Yes, sir... Do you think there's something in them?"
"I hope so. Let's return, shall we? Showers still threaten."

---

In the parlour at ten, a coal fire hissed and jetted in the grate. With the doors shut, the room had overheated. The newspapers had been apportioned and each of the four men present were scanning every square inch of their assigned pages.

"Are you sure this isn't a wild goose chase?" asked Yardley, sitting on the floor, propped up against an armchair.

"No," replied Archie, sitting at the table. "Even if we discover nothing of interest, we can't be certain we didn't miss something. The newsagent might be in on it. Highly improbable, but still possible, is that someone concealed a handwritten note inside a newspaper."

"If they did that, we'll never know."

"Nothing promising, and no extraneous writing in my section," said Laneford. "Do you think he purchased the cigarettes for himself?"

"Can't say, Lord Laneford. If they are his, he likes them rough, strong, and cheap. They were a favourite in my battalion."

"Mine, too," said Yardley.

"Hopefully, we'll receive a list of possible names for the fellow by mid-week." Lord Laneford folded up a page and set it aside. "Found anything, Philpott?"

"I regret to say, I haven't, my Lord. I've circled several things that may be of interest, but I'm doubtful of them."

"Do they really put messages in an advertisement for a product?" queried Yardley.

"It happened once, so now we always look to be sure. It was quite good, actually. Some of it was coded — the shape of the hair tonic bottle meant one thing, and the direction it pointed in another. Fortunately, we caught the rascals. Because so few people were interested in their revolution, it failed in its aims, but it was a well-crafted message, nevertheless." Archie was coming to the bottom of his page of the Times. "Here, I should shout Eureka, but I won't embarrass us all."

"You found it?" asked Laneford.

"What does it say?" Yardley got up.

"3 plus 2 at 2 by Long Neck."

"Which means?"

"I don't have it complete, but I would say that three people are meeting two people at two o'clock today, because it's in the Sunday paper."

Yardley picked up the sheet and read the advertisement. "That part looks obvious now you've explained it."

Lord Laneford looked over Yardley's shoulder to read, then remarked, "By Long Neck appears to be a name, because it's capitalized. Also, it suggests authorship."

"It's unusual to put a name or identifier in such a message," said Archie. "The capitalization may be an attempt at camouflage. There's no punctuation, so it probably should be read as one phrase, with the 'by' referencing a location. Three of us and two of you meet Sunday at two by... Any suggestions for long neck?"

"May I make an observation, Mr Drysdale?" asked Philpott.

"Observe away," said Archie.

"The Giraffe is known for its long neck, as are ostriches."

"Splendid. Regent's Park Zoo, it is," said Archie. "Less than a mile away, a public place with plenty of secluded spots. Can you get anyone to assist, my Lord?"

"A couple, perhaps, seeing as it's such short notice. I'll telephone, but there's one chap I'll have to hunt down. Where shall we all meet?"

"The main gate at one?"

"That's cutting it fine, but I'll do my best. Philpott, you remain here." Laneford left the room.

"Yes, my Lord."

"I'll bring Len back if I can find him," said Yardley.

"The FO doesn't have anyone else available at the moment, but two of the ladies in the house can pitch in."

"Right," said Yardley. "If I can't raise Len on the line, I'll go home to pick up a few things and change cars. There's plenty of time. Can I bring you anything?"

"I don't have my revolver with me."

"Anything else?"

"The usual kit."

Within minutes, Laneford was driving to meet someone, and Yardley was doing likewise in his Rolls Royce after having failed to reach Len.

---

There was a small room, an office and study combined, on the second floor, and it was here that Sophie went to avoid the men downstairs, and keep out of Mrs Barker's way. Myrtle had been sent to the attic to maintain the watch. Sophie lit the fire and found a comfortable chair. Biscuit was now lying on the rug at her feet. Sophie had noticed the mystery book with three bookmarks on the shelf downstairs and taken it up with her. She was interested, but the warmth, a good breakfast, her tiredness, and the still quiet all combined to make her nod. She nodded, and then she slept.

A noise outside made her start, and she pulled herself together.

Following a soft tap on the door, she heard, "It's Archie. May I come in?"

"Of course."

"Hello," he said. "Hope I'm not intrudin'."

"No. I think I dozed off."

"I very much like this little room. It's so welcoming. The perfect place to doze."

"It is. Did you find anything?"

"There's a chance we're wrong, but I'm fairly confident that we cracked the message in the Times. A meeting of five Russian agents will take place at Regent's Park Zoo. This is important because, as of this moment, we don't know any of their identities. All I can think is that this will be the initial meeting of those agents who will undertake the establishment of Russia's spy network. It's a tremendous chance for us, which is all thanks to Miss Carmichael's vigilance and quick thinking. Yours, too, I might add, for supplying the environment in which Miss Carmichael could work so well on her own initiative."

Sophie smiled. "That's nice to hear. And thank you for giving us the chance."

"Aren't we all good fellows? I really should say, comrades."

"When does the meeting take place?"

"Two o'clock this afternoon in Regent's Park. Either near the giraffes, or the ostriches and emus. The pre-arranged codeword was 'long neck.' Philpott cracked that part of it."

"How quaint. Well, I wish you the best of luck. I'm sure you'll be successful."

"Change that to *we'll* be successful. I need two of you to join in the chase. We're understaffed, and it's Sunday."

"Far from objecting, I'd be happy to participate. But there's a snag. Auntie Bessie's coming."

"Bessie's coming here? Ring her and put her off."

"I can't possibly do that. You tell her."

"No, thank you. She wouldn't listen to me. It's your invitation, which I object to on security grounds, so it is also your responsibility to cancel. If you can't bring yourself to do that, Bessie will have to stay here and twiddle her thumbs."

"I don't think Auntie has ever twiddled in her life. I'll think of something to tell her. She won't like it, whatever it is."

"Who will you send? And where's Flora?"

"Gladys, as you should call her, is currently dead to the world, but rises again on the stroke of eleven. It's no use trying to wake her beforehand. It can't be done."

"I've never heard anything like it. Anyway, decide who it is you can send and let me know. I'll leave now, but will return by half-past eleven. Try not to doze off again."

"I'll go to the parlour and tidy up the mess."

"We left no mess, because we are all clean gentlemen."

"I bet I find something."

"If you do, one of the others will have left it. It certainly was not I. See you later."

Smiling, he closed the door quietly.

# Chapter 14

## Among the animals

Sophie had to see Mrs Barker about delaying luncheon for so long that it had to be called dinner. A gloom settled in the kitchen.

"I seem to be continually apologizing, but there's no getting around it. Identifying the Russian agent is one of the vital reasons we are here."

"Yes, Miss King."

"Now, if we could aim for six o'clock, I think that would give sufficient time."

"Will there be extras for dinner?"

"I honestly don't know how many there'll be. I'll try to stick to the original list, but it's very difficult if we have to accommodate someone."

"Yes. What do we do about lunch, Miss King?"

"Don't do anything special. I know you made some pies; those would do perfectly."

Mrs Barker envisioned her crucial reserves decimated before their time.

"I could make some pasties."

"Good idea. I must go to speak with Miss Walton. Let me know if you need anything."

Needing was one thing, getting was another. All the shops were shut and Brick Lane market, half-way across London, would be closed in an hour or so.

"Where is it you're all going?" asked Mrs Barker.

"To the zoo."

Left alone in her kitchen, Mrs Barker stood motionless. They were going to the zoo, and this scrap of news churned up a lifetime of memories for her. She had been there once when she was nine, in 1874. It was so long ago and, though she had adored her visit, she had never considered going again. Having gone into service outside of London, a second visit was impossible, so she never even thought of it. Mrs Barker learned her craft and advanced her skills, rising up the ranks slowly, but surely. Finally, she became a cook and never seemed to have a moment to herself. Marriage came, eventually followed by the great disappointment that sorely wounded her. Depression next, then alcoholism, and she reaching her lowest point where there seemed no point to anything. She had tried, unsuccessfully, to find work, and it was only Miss Burgoyne's offer of a second chance within the last year that had put her back on her feet. Through all of this, she never thought of going to the zoo. Now, she realized, she had wanted to go all along.

"It's very difficult, isn't it, Mrs Barker?" said Myrtle.

"I'm sorry? Difficult?"

"Them changing their minds like that."

"Happens often... Myrtle, have you ever been to Regent's Park Zoo?"

"No, I never have, and I've always wanted to. Never had the money, you see."

Mrs Barker stared at Myrtle, who continued working.

"Would you like to go with me? My treat, so don't worry about that... We could take a lunch and buy tea there. They might have ice cream."

"You mean you'd pay for me?"

"That's what I said."

"Oh, I'd love it, Mrs Barker, I really would."

"We'll be finished here in a week. A fortnight this Sunday, if the weather's fine, that's what we'll do. We'll go to the zoo."

Myrtle smiled. "That rhymes, Mrs Barker."

She thought for a moment. "So, it does."

Mrs Barker hummed to herself a little later, a thing she rarely did while cooking.

---

The moment had come. Lady Elizabeth Shelling was punctual. Sophie watched the minute hand on the parlour clock make its jerky move to half-past twelve. Mrs Barker, sitting in the kitchen at the ready, heard the knock and answered it.

"Good afternoon, Lady Shelling. Please, come in."

"Good Afternoon... You're Mrs Barker, aren't you?"

"That's correct, my Lady."

"Excuse me for invadin' your kitchen in this manner, but the powers that be have left us no alternative."

"That's quite so."

"I rarely visit my own kitchen, but even I can detect lunch has been delayed. Why's that?"

"I don't understand it myself, my Lady. All I know is, it's been put back because of... I'm sorry, I'm not supposed to say."

"Where's my niece?"

"Miss King is in the parlour."

"What, counting out her money?"

Mrs Barker smiled at the reference to the old rhyme. Lady Shelling did not. Instead, she waited.

"It's this way, my Lady."

They left the kitchen.

"Auntie. How lovely to see you." Sophie got up and went to her aunt as soon as she entered the room.

"It is not lovely," said Aunt Bessie, accepting a kiss on her cheek. "You're not going to feed me."

"Of course, we're going to feed you. Something important has turned up, though, and it's disarranged everything."

"Only the death of a monarch or one's husband is sufficient reason for displacing Sunday luncheon. The latter may even be a cause of celebration for some."

"How about following Russian spies around the zoo?"

"The zoo! What is the matter with those people? Can't they choose a decent time and place for their intrigues?"

"Apparently not. We must forego our lunch because this is of the utmost importance. The Russians are at the very beginning of establishing a spy network in Britain and, if we can identify them, we can prevent them from doing harm to the nation."

"I'm all for that sort of thing, Sophie, when it's convenient."

"You must call me Phoebe... I thought you were coming in disguise?"

"I *am* in disguise. These are my old clothes."

"But your coat's immaculate, and you still look like Lady Shelling."

"These are the oldest clothes I have. I haven't worn these shoes for three years. And the coat is six years old."

"They look brand new."

"My servants are properly trained to take care of them."

"The idea was that you should *not* look like Lady Shelling. I suppose it doesn't matter as long as no one saw you entering the house through the back."

"Marsden was careful to park well away. Hawkins is with him. He's wearing that dreadful suit he dons when visiting racecourses. It should be burnt, and I've told him never to wear it when he accompanies *me* to the races. I allowed him to wear it today as an exception."

"Why is Hawkins here?"

"I envisioned we would eat first, and then, at three-thirty, Hawkins would arrive so that we may properly discuss the suspects in the murder case."

"You're up to something — Hawkins — You intend betting on the suspects."

"Yes. There is a lot of interest in the idea among my sporting friends."

"No, absolutely not!"

"Hawkins is an exceptional analyst when it comes to horses and greyhounds. He is not emotional and is unswayed by popular opinion in these matters. I have benefitted greatly from his guidance. If we allow his mind to concentrate on the suspects, I firmly believe it will be of service to yourselves and the police."

"And you and your friends."

"Very much so. For Hawkins to flourish, he must do so in an appropriate manner. He must approach the data you have collected as if it came from the racing form found in newspapers, weather forecasts, and tips gained from grooms or other knowledgeable individuals. Now you have blown the whole blasted afternoon to pieces."

"I didn't detonate a thing."

"Then it was those for whom you work. I suppose Archibald's at the bottom of denying me lunch."

"In a very slight way, but he did not know you were coming."

"Doesn't that make all the difference? Young squirt."

"I know you're put out, but please, don't be annoyed with him. We'll have a light lunch and a proper Sunday dinner later. Mrs Barker is an excellent cook. Unfortunately, I and either Gladys or Nancy are going out. One of them will stay. Hopefully, we'll return well before six, but I know nothing for certain. Who would you like to stay with you?"

Aunt Bessie thought for a moment. "If Nancy would sing some of her songs, then her. If not, Gladys. Why do you all use these wretched names when you don't need to?"

"To stay in character, thereby minimizing the making of mistakes at crucial moments. I'll ask Gladys to stay. Asking Nancy to sing all afternoon is preposterous."

"Am I to understand that you, also, will chase about after Russians? Of course, you are."

"It's a long story, but there's a shortage of agents available this afternoon. Then, we must also continue to observe number fifteen and the murder suspects in the square. So you and Gladys will be in the attic doing just that."

"I shall do no such thing. I cannot believe you even suggested it."

"I knew you would be difficult."

"Then why bother asking? Anyway, I have a much better idea. I'll go with you. If you put the kitchen maid in the attic, then Gladys can go, too."

Sophie frowned. "That's not such a bad idea... We brought disguises in case we had to follow someone."

"What are you going as, dare I ask? "

"I'll be in mourning, so that the veil conceals my face."

"Ah. Do you have the appropriate widow's weeds?"

"I'm out of deep mourning, so it is dark colours and the veil."

"Immediately after Shelling died, I was glad of the veil because my poor eyes were so red. I felt safe, you know. Everyone knew I was mourning, but I was thankful they couldn't see my face. After two months, I detested the thing. Shelling wouldn't have wanted me sorrowing, or seeming to be so, for months and years. I got rid of it. I burnt it myself, and told him, though I doubt he heard me, that I loved him still, and would always treasure his precious memory. He would have understood that... Dear man."

"It's a shame I didn't know him better."

"Yes... He once said it was easy for him to see in you, me, as a young girl. I recall it was one of the last times he saw you."

To this sudden openness on her aunt's part, Sophie returned a compassionate look. Aunt Bessie asked,

"What time are we to be at the wretched zoo?"

---

Just after one, inside the zoo by the side of the Monkey House and out of public view, the men were arranging how to monitor those areas where the Russians were most likely to meet. They found they had underestimated the number of long-necked animals there were.

"What about snakes?" asked Laneford. "They must have long necks."

"Yes, they must... They're in the Reptile House." Archie consulted his map of the zoo. "That's in between the deer terraces and the storks and ostriches."

Philpott cleared his throat. "May I say something, Mr Drysdale?"

"What?"

"It is my understanding that snakes do not possess necks."

"Are you sure?" asked Yardley. "They're so long there must be a neck in there somewhere?"

Philpott stood his ground. "I apologize for adopting a contrary stance, Mr Yardley, but there isn't."

"Ah, but the Russians might *think* they have long necks," said Laneford.

"Yes... A good try, Philpott," said Archie, "but the Reptile House goes on the list." He studied his map. "There are four of us present. Another agent, Mr Smith, is arriving soon. We can't count on Len receiving the message in time to join us. Your other agent..."

"Mr Brown," said Laneford.

"Mr Brown will follow whoever leaves 15 Alexandra Gardens and proceeds to the zoo. Shortly afterwards, two of the agents from number seven will follow in his wake, in case the inhabitants of number 15 leave separately. There's a chance all the inmates of number fifteen will be in on the jaunt to the zoo, but only the two or three of them that were specified in the coded message will actually attend the meeting. Now, any loose Russians could cause problems, so we must be very careful to look natural. We can't all walk about pretending to consult the guidebook. A loafing attitude or an interest in a particular type of animal while maintaining a good sight-line on a path is the sort of thing we want. We must blend in. And absolutely no standing behind a tree or using binoculars, if you have them."

"Rotation's important," said Laneford.

"When everyone's here, we will implement something to address that. Lord Laneford, please take the South Gate until two, then join Mr Philpott on his roving commission from the deer terraces to the geese behind the Lion House. Yardley, for you, it's giraffes, zebras, and gazelles by the canal. I'll remain by the main entrance until two, and then take up a position by the camels, which is also the rallying point. From there, I can observe the east tunnel which leads directly to the kangaroos. Any questions?"

"Yes," said Yardley. "Where are the llamas?"

"I haven't the foggiest, old boy."

---

At around the same time in Primrose Hill Park, Mr Brown trailed a hundred yards behind two men from number fifteen. One of them was the man referred to as the Doctor, whom the agents from Burgoyne's had not previously seen. He proved to be a pasty-faced, bearded, and rather portly man of about forty years in age. His middle-class clothes were noticeably old. He was over the average height and walked quickly with a slight roll in his gait, as though at sea. Flora and Ada, who followed a further hundred yards behind the Home Office agent, could plainly see this side-to-side movement.

His taller companion, the man Ada had followed, they pronounced to be handsome. He, too, wore old clothes. He was about thirty and, in having fine features and an attractive moustache, gave the impression of a young Russian Boyar and military man come down in the world, but still filled with a noble and daring spirit.

The sky had brightened and there was barely a wind. Amongst the high cloud were a few scattered blue patches, although these had yet to allow for actual sunshine to rest upon Primrose Hill. When Flora and Ada were halfway down the hill, the Russians were already leaving the park through the south-east exit. From there, it would be a short walk along Prince Albert Road to cross the Broad Walk, a small bridge over the canal, and into the Outer Circle of Regent's Park.

After a light lunch, another group of hastily assembled agents was conveyed in Lady Shelling's blue Daimler Limousine, piloted by Marsden. Her footman was forbidden to exceed thirteen miles per hour because her ladyship found the swaying in the back to be unsettling at any higher speed. Next to him sat her butler, Hawkins.

Whatever Marsden knew about today's events, Hawkins did not care to enquire, and this latter hoped the footman knew or thought nothing. For himself, he understood that Miss Burgoyne was a daring spirit and often up to something that would one day Land Her In Trouble. He knew about the police cases and reflected that he may well have now landed in a degree of Trouble himself. Her ladyship had asked, and he dared not refuse, for him to go to the zoo and look for Russians. This activity was on top of the other, and perfectly reasonable one to his mind, where he would rate suspects in a murder case according to their likelihood of having committed the crime — an unusual request but, as it was for the purposes of betting, he did not see it as unreasonable. Upon first hearing of the zoo proposition, he had assumed her ladyship's mind had finally gone. He changed this view after overhearing a word here and there, which made it apparent that a fairly significant number of others in polite society were also indulging themselves in the same activity. He held his own counsel at such goings on, but could not fathom why the zoo was deemed the best place to find a Russian. *Surely, he thought, you found them at the embassy or in certain restaurants.*

In the back of the limousine, Sophie adjusted her veil as they approached the main entrance.

"You look like the mysterious woman frequently encountered in Victorian novels," said Aunt Bessie. She peered closer. "Yes, quite effective. No one will recognize you. If we meet someone I know, pretend you are your cousin Fiona."

"But she's ten years older than I am and her husband is very much alive."

"All that's immaterial. Who can I possibly say you are otherwise? A stray widow I found wandering about? I hope you can mimic a Scottish accent."

"I can, but I doubt it's authentic. I used to practise sounding like Fiona, because her voice is so musical."

"Not when she's shouting. I don't know why but, when riding, Fiona sounds as though she's raising the clan because the English are upon them. Quite grating and completely out of character. She's normal to the point of being dull in all other respects."

"She's not dull. Fiona's a very charming woman."

"Yes. But then you have an inordinate love of Scotland, believing it is beautiful and romantic, when really it's just cold and wet."

"You go up every year to see Uncle Raymond."

"Family duty. I go in the only two weeks of the year when the sun comes out. No wonder they drink whisky — it allows them to endure all that lashing rain and dreadful wind."

"Absolute rubbish. You're exaggerating only because Tormodden Castle sits in an isolated glen and gets cut off once in a while during winter. That sounds like fun to me."

"Fun, and I profoundly detest the word, is found on the Riviera, in Italy and occasionally in London drawing rooms, but never in a Scottish snowdrift."

"There is a photograph in Tormodden Castle, and it's of you in traditional Scottish dress doing the Highland Fling during Hogmanay, which is the last day of *December*. There, care to change your opinion now?"

"It was wonderful. A thoroughly delightful time, but very long ago, so it doesn't count. If you're pretending to be a widow, kindly act like one, and don't always be arguing with me."

"You're lucky we're nearly at the entrance."

After Lady Shelling gave instructions to Marsden to be at the main gate waiting with the car when she came out at an unspecified time, without suggesting how he might accomplish this when there was no nearby parking, they left the car, bought tickets, and entered the zoo. Hawkins did so separately, partly to make it appear as though he were a stranger to Lady Shelling, and partly because she found his suit revolting. It was not exactly a garish check. At a distance, it looked pale grey but, on any closer inspection, the material resolved itself into one of a jarring black and white hound's tooth pattern. Wearing a black bowler, and a pale blue silk handkerchief in his jacket's breast pocket, Hawkins, the usually austere butler, gave the impression that he had set off for the races yesterday, got profoundly lost, and had ended up in Regent's Park Zoo today purely by mistake or by misadventure. His consulting the guidebook, staring about to get his bearings, and watching for Russian gentlemen, tended to amplify the impression of his having no clue as to how he got where he was.

# Chapter 15

# Who is watching whom?

Two men purchased their tickets at the zoo's main entrance at 1:50 p.m. The younger man spoke English while buying them. Otherwise, he and his companion exclusively spoke Russian. They stopped just inside the entrance.

"Does he still follow?"

"No, Doctor. He has walked past. I do not think he is secret police."

"Unless he is one of many, and has now done his part, letting another take over."

"How can they know?"

"Vasily, you can never be too careful. I will be in the Tortoise House. Go. Check the rendezvous to see who's there."

"Yes, Doctor."

"We will not traipse needlessly around the zoo looking for the other agents," said Aunt Bessie, examining the map in her guidebook. "It won't rain now, so we shall sit outside the tea pavilion, here. They can come to us."

"By the camels. It seems ridiculous just to sit in one spot when there are so many spots in which the meeting could take place."

"If I were a spy, I would choose the refreshment rooms as the most convenient for a meeting."

"Oh, very well."

They were near both Fellow's Tea Pavilion and the adjacent Refreshment Rooms, so they crossed the large open space in front of these buildings where children were lining up for rides on camels. They found a table against the wooden wall of the pavilion. Aunt Bessie sat down while Sophie went to get their teas, which took her several minutes.

"I'm glad the queue wasn't any longer than it was." Sophie had returned with a tray. "They're rather slow in there."

"Did anyone remark upon your veil?"

"No. I got a few stares, and the cashier didn't want to look me in the face."

"Ah. You've bought buns, I see. Are you still hungry?"

"I just fancied one."

"Obviously, you are intent upon ruining your figure."

"A bun won't hurt. Aren't you going to eat yours?"

"I'll give mine to an elephant."

"Are you hinting at something?"

"Don't be sensitive, dear. I implied nothing. You are trim and I sincerely hope you remain so, as I have done by always being careful with my portions. But permit me to give you some advice. The most dangerous time for a woman is around childbirth. Before, eat as much as you can, because you eat for two. Afterwards, eat next to nothing and exercise by getting plenty of riding. Daily, if you can manage it."

"Auntie, I'm not married."

"Yes, but you will be. Surely somebody will marry you. I hope it's Mr Yardley. He's very well off in his own right."

"Please don't, Auntie."

"The trouble with you is you're not grasping enough. Yes, I know, I said it. But the truth of the matter is, everyone wants to live in comfortable or exceptionally comfortable circumstances. For a woman in society to achieve a comfortable life, she must connive at some level, even if it is only by flattering an intensely boring but wealthy man to capture his attention. You refuse to do even that much."

"That is not my inclination, and never shall be."

"I know. And now you're eating buns. How is it?"

"Surprisingly good, but it seems I'm not allowed to enjoy it."

"Once you're married to Mr Yardley, eat all the buns you want. But not beforehand."

"There's Archie, talking to a keeper."

"He's a good rider, but I wonder how the boy sits a camel. Although, Bactrians are comparatively tame creatures."

"I was trying to remember what the two-humped camels were called. I suppose there's little chance of falling off while sitting between the humps."

"Not like a dromedary. When Shelling and I were in Egypt, we trekked on camels. If one can stomach a small boat in a choppy sea, one can endure a running dromedary, but tie your hat on first. Lady Balham was with us, and she made such a display of herself. Every possible affliction one can have in a desert, she had it and more. To top it all, she lost her hat and supposedly got sunstroke while we were in the Valley of the Kings. What a fuss she made. I'm sure it was acting — she put it all on because she hated everything about the trek and wanted to go home.

"Now let me tell you something very interesting. We heard her shouting at Lord Balham in their tent one night. Positively shrieking. Shelling and I were sitting by a fire together under the brilliant stars. It was remarkably lovely and so still. The night was suddenly shattered when she began pitching into Balham. We couldn't help but overhear several outrageous things. Apparently, Lord Balham's sister, Rosemary, had gone completely off the rails. She was living with not one, but two..."

"We should pay attention to why we're here, Auntie."

In the Tortoise House, Vasily found the Doctor.

"The tables outside the restaurant are not all occupied. A few families with children, some women, no men by themselves. No one in the area looks suspicious."

"Good. We go."

The Russians walked towards the refreshment rooms, but then the Doctor pointed towards a table outside the pavilion.

Where they sat down was also against the wall, and a single empty table separated them from Sophie and Aunt Bessie.

"Auntie," whispered Sophie. "Don't say a word."

Aunt Bessie shot a glance at her veiled niece, understood her warning, then looked away into the distance.

"The older man is from Alexandra Gardens. He's known as the Doctor," said Sophie.

As she was nearest the Russians, particularly the Doctor, Aunt Bessie turned slightly away so as not to be seen whispering. "What do we do?"

"Wait it out and not give ourselves away. Don't look at your watch, it's almost two."

"Should we sit quietly or speak?"

"Act normally, speak occasionally. Don't look at Archie or signal to him."

"I wouldn't do that... Why is he walking away? Did he not see them?"

"I don't know. If he's missed them, we must do our best." Sophie leaned closer to her aunt. "Can you hear what they're saying?"

"They're not speaking. If they are, I can't hear them."

Sophie lifted her veil to sip her tea. "This is awful, but we should make it last." She had only just put her cup down when she heard the low rumble of male speech from the Russian table.

"What did they say?"

"Something unintelligible in Russian. The way the Doctor growled, he may also be unintelligible in English."

Chairs moved. Sophie risked a glance. They were not leaving. She looked across the open space and could see three men walking abreast. A very tall man, a short man, and an average-sized man.

"They're coming," hissed Sophie.

From a window in the Parrot House, Lord Laneford used binoculars to examine the five men at the table. Three others stood near him.

"The two on the left — I've met them several times. They are both not only Soviet politicians and diplomats but also money men. The tall, distinguished, and very dapper gentleman is Leonid Krasin. Has a flat on Curzon Street and is intelligent and very suave. The shorter, professorial one, is Victor Nogin, a Deputy Labour Commissar. That's not his actual job, because he's far too capable. He also has a flat in Mayfair — New Bond Street, as I recall." He handed the binoculars to Yardley. "Those two negotiated the Anglo-Soviet Trade Treaty. They are also two of the three founders of the All-Russian Co-operative Society — usually, and mercifully so, shortened to ARCOS. The company is the financial conduit for every Russian purchase of British goods, and all sales of Russian food and goods to Britain. In other words, through ARCOS, those men control a colossal amount of money, which will only grow with time."

"As they're known, we needn't worry about *them*," said Yardley. "The other chap's British, and certainly upper class."

"I believe so, too," said Drysdale. "Let us say that we have two financial wizards bringing a British subject to a meeting with two slightly down-at-heel Russian men from Alexandra Gardens. The Doctor is a friend of Lenin and out of the country at present for his safety, so we are told. However, I'm beginning to doubt that part. The younger man, from number fifteen, who I'd swear is a Russian gentleman down on his luck, and who, we hypothesize for the moment, has recently arrived from the Kremlin. I'm sure he isn't present to enquire into everyone's health because Uncle Lenin is worried about them. What do we extrapolate from these things?"

"Krasin and Nogin are proposing a candidate," said Laneford.

"Entirely credible," said Drysdale. "This meeting must be more than just an introduction."

"Then the Doctor is the one who approves him," said Yardley. "The other is a messenger of some type."

"A trusted and highly respected one, I imagine," said Drysdale. "A personal touch was needed, and he brings orders from the Russian leadership on where the network must concentrate its efforts to produce the desired results. To sum everything up:- the Doctor will in fact control the new spy network, and was sent here well in advance to blend into the scenery. Krasin and Nogin will finance everything through ARCOS. The person selected to recruit British spies is the fifth man, whom we must not fail to identify."

"Messrs Brown, Smith, and Philpott, as well as myself, shall undertake to follow him."

"The party of three must have walked across Regent's Park to enter by the South Gate, so our new man is probably local."

"I sincerely hope so, Drysdale," said Lord Laneford. "I haven't eaten lunch and neither has Philpott."

Two tables away, a loud Russian greeting, including embraces, firm handshakes, and a backslapping took place.

"Good heavens," whispered Aunt Bessie. "They must be drunk."

One of them pulled up an extra chair to the table. The younger Russian entered the pavilion to buy tea. The men who remained spoke Russian and seemed in high spirits. Gradually, they lowered their voices. When the young man returned and served out the tea, the table quietened. Someone made a joke while holding up his cup. Everyone laughed.

"This tea may be poor," whispered Sophie, "but it is not a thing to be ridiculed by visitors. Our tea is as good as theirs, even when it's foul. I have a good mind to say something to them."

"I don't think you should," said Aunt Bessie, "considering everything."

"Of course, I won't. But the idea of it!"

The Russian table went quiet, with only the young man speaking, and he did so at great length.

"Oh, I don't believe it!" whispered Aunt Bessie. "What can he be doing here?"

In the middle of the open space, between the camels and the tea pavilion, Hawkins the butler stood, guidebook in hand, looking at every person within view in a slow, painstaking manner. His loud hound's tooth racecourse suit set him apart from every other living creature, as if he were the only zebra among brown horses in a paddock. Eventually, as he turned, his gaze lighted upon his mistress, Lady Shelling. He stared. The Russian table made quiet comments. One of them, his back to Hawkins, turned to look at the man who had been pointed out.

The crisis came. Hawkins stared. The Russians stared. Sophie stared, while Lady Shelling buried her face in her hand. The longest five seconds of Sophie's life slowly and grudgingly ticked away. Hawkins turned towards the east tunnel, consulted his guidebook, then walked off to study the kangaroos. There was a gust of shared hilarity at the Russian table, and a deep, heartfelt wave of relief two tables away.

"See what I mean?" whispered Aunt Bessie. "Even the Russians find his suit hideous. I shall destroy it tonight and send the stubborn man to a proper tailor tomorrow."

"Poor Hawkins," said Sophie. She glanced towards the Russians and noticed the young man had resumed speaking. Turning away, she saw Flora and Ada entering the open space and was again horrified. Her mouth fell open in shock.

"They can't come here... Auntie, you must do something dramatic... and very loud. I'm in mourning, so I can't. The signal is thumbs down."

"What can you be talking about?" whispered Aunt Bessie.

"Do it now, whatever it is. Just shout, thumbs down."

It took several seconds for her to comprehend what she was being asked to do. Then she blared so loudly, a camel looked around.

"No! Thumbs down! Don't be silly — in the Roman Colosseum it was always thumbs down!" Accompanying her outburst, Lady Shelling raised both arms high, clenched her fists, and gave a dramatic demonstration with her thumbs decidedly pointing earthward.

The Russian table turned its startled attention to the shouting woman. People in the open space slowed to gawk.

"What in blazes does Bessie think she's doing!?" asked Archie, watching from the Parrot House. "What is she even doing here?"

"'Streuth, we'd better 'op it," said Ada.

"The Russians are outside the tea pavilion," said Flora. "We'll go to…" She read from the guidebook. "… there, the Parrot House." They hurried away.

"My uncle has a parrot," said Ada. "I 'ope the parrots in 'ere don't talk like his one does. Children aren't allowed near it."

"I'm sure we'll soon find out if they're respectable parrots." Flora smiled.

At the table, Sophie flushed under her veil.

"We must leave at once," said Aunt Bessie. "Everyone's gaping at me as though I'm a lunatic."

"I know, and I'm so sorry, but we had no choice."

"I'm going, even if you're not."

"Of course, I'm coming. But don't go off in a huff in case the Russians are watching."

"Don't be ridiculous, Sophie. *Everyone's* watching. Which way do we go?"

"The East Tunnel, so we can keep our backs to the Russians as we leave."

They vacated their seats and, like early Christians crossing the sand in the Colosseum so recently invoked, endured the ridicule and censure of their audience gathered en masse outside the Refreshment Rooms. It was a small yet adequate mob, possessing a distinctly thumbs-down attitude.

Aunt Bessie ignored them. She measured the distance to the tunnel's mouth, hoping she reached its safety well before anyone she knew recognized her.

Sophie, technically better off beneath her veil, thought similarly, although more in the abstract — strangers had seen her at a table where there had been Bad Behaviour. She glanced at her aunt, certain a row was looming. Probably not in the tunnel, neither in the car, but sometime, while it was still today, there would be a row.

They got into the tunnel. Aunt Bessie stopped and put a hand on Sophie's arm.

"Look to see what's going on."

Sophie did so by peeking around the corner.

"It's all back to normal. The Russians are talking again."

"I don't care about the blasted Russians. Let me see." Aunt Bessie methodically surveyed the people in the open space. She turned and clapped her hands while smiling. "I don't see anyone I know, so I believe we got away with it. What do we do now that our cover's blown?"

The girlish glee on her aunt's face surprised Sophie. "We may as well leave. Archie can find us at the house."

"What a pity… It was such a near thing, wasn't it? I believe I pulled off the diversion remarkably well."

"Yes, you did. And you made me jump."

"Did I?" She laughed. "Serves you right for putting me on the spot like that."

They began walking. Other pedestrians were in the tunnel, but not close enough to overhear.

"I noticed there were three gentlemen of means among the Russians," said Aunt Bessie.

"One of them was impeccably dressed," added Sophie. "There was another, though, whom I've seen before. The youngest man — he wore respectable but rather shabby clothing, yet he had a good table manner."

"Who is he?"

"The Home Office is working to identify him. He arrived in the country within the last few days, so he can't be that hard to find."

"Will they deport them all?"

"Apparently not. The idea is to leave them in place to monitor what they do and limit their effectiveness."

"How tame of Archie. He has no flair for the dramatic."

"I think he has flair. I'm sure an agent will infiltrate the Russian network, and Archie shall turn others into double agents."

"I'm not convinced. I'd have them all soundly thrashed, clapped in irons, and put on the ferry. Then, in the middle of the Channel, I'd keel-haul one of them as an example to all Communists of what they may expect for rude behaviour. One must stand up to tyranny early on."

"Yes, Auntie." Sophie had heard similar pronouncements before, and it was pointless disagreeing with her.

## Chapter 16

## Shouting the Odds

Before the lunch that had become dinner, Archie had visited number seven. Marring his jubilance were two large flies in the ointment of his day's success. The names of the flies were Bessie and Sophie, and the three of them had been conversing for some minutes.

"I cannot believe you did that," said Archie to Aunt Bessie, "and that you sanctioned it," he said to Sophie, during the private family meeting.

"She didn't sanction, she commanded," said Aunt Bessie, "and I had to obey. But don't go blaming her, Archibald. All's well that ends well."

"All is not well. It put everything in extreme jeopardy."

"Nonsense. We were in control of the situation, and the Russians were on the point of asking us to join them."

"That is a lie."

"Yes, but it demonstrates their docility while we were two tables away spying on them. How close did *you* get to them?"

"That isn't the point," said Archie.

"It may not be *your* point, but it's mine. Where were you? Hiding in the Parrot House squinting through binoculars. Where were we? Within earshot!"

"Our reason for being there was to study them without creating a disturbance that threatened the operation."

"I saved the operation," said Bessie. "But you won't write that in your blasted reports."

"Archie," said Sophie. "I know you feel we caused problems, but we had no other course of action. Nancy and Gladys were sure to see and approach us. Who knows what they might have said, not realizing the Russians were at the next table? If we tried to stop them by ordinary signals, they might have behaved uncertainly in their view, and someone would have been bound to notice we knew each other and were avoiding attention. The Russians would become suspicious, and suspicion would have had them break up their meeting and be extraordinarily vigilant about being followed."

"I see that... My chagrin is over what seems to be the inevitability of something similar occurring in each and every case. That's not your doing, Bessie, but yours, Sophie."

"Leave the gel alone. You wouldn't get half the stuff you do get done if it weren't for her."

"I am not diminishing her contributions. I am explaining why I have become prone to unwonted and unnecessary headaches in recent months."

"You're calling me a headache?" asked Sophie.

"Despite success, name one operation where you haven't caused trouble?"

"You know I can't."

"We often have similar conversations. Today's example is tempered by the hasty way in which everything was organized. It is probably the least egregious because it couldn't be helped. However, the effect of your antics could have been disastrous. Where you were at fault, although I'm sure you had the best intentions, was to bring an untrained person into the affair. I surmise that Bessie did not want to walk around the zoo, so you sat with her only to keep her company as a dutiful niece should. As an agent, you were supposed to report to me and not run your own operation with your aunt and her butler... Was he supposed to be in disguise? Never mind, I digress. In an operation, you report to me, and do not defer to your aunt's desire for tea."

"Don't go blaming her for all the bungling," said Bessie. "Blame the Home Office for taking all its agents away."

"I'm sorry, Archie. I thought I was doing everything for the best."

"I'm sure you were. Dash it all, consult with me first, so that I know what's going on and we're not at cross-purposes."

"I understand."

"Good. Let this be the end of it. Now, what did you learn?"

He was very interested to hear that they only spoke Russian at the table. It meant that the man they assumed was British was fluent in the language. Archie received confirmation that the young man was of noble birth, with the addition that he was subservient to the Doctor and the others because he purchased and served the tea. Only the lowest ranking man would do that. That the young man also spoke at length, with the rest listening intently, meant that he brought important information necessary to establish the spy network. He had brought orders for each of them, which meant the directives came from someone who outranked them all. Few outranked Krasin and Nogin and, if the instructions were issued after a Politburo meeting, it ultimately meant that Lenin was behind it. Archie explained this to Aunt Bessie and Sophie before he left. What he did not explain, and that which was uppermost in his mind, was his impression that, beyond the ordinary need for spying, Lenin was up to something particular concerning Britain. He did not know what it was, yet he had persuaded himself there was definitely something.

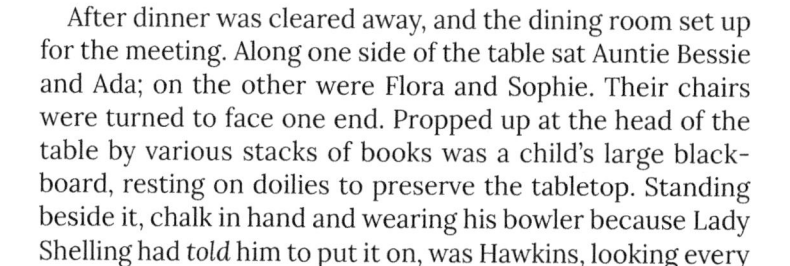

---

After dinner was cleared away, and the dining room set up for the meeting. Along one side of the table sat Auntie Bessie and Ada; on the other were Flora and Sophie. Their chairs were turned to face one end. Propped up at the head of the table by various stacks of books was a child's large blackboard, resting on doilies to preserve the tabletop. Standing beside it, chalk in hand and wearing his bowler because Lady Shelling had *told* him to put it on, was Hawkins, looking every inch a prosperous bookie, ready to shout the odds and take bets. There was no trace of the butler about him.

"Let's have the runners' names," said Aunt Bessie.

Sophie had notes in front of her. "By house number. One, Mr Clark. He's a musician for the LSO, but works mostly as a pianist at a cinema. We haven't met him yet."

"A dark horse," said Aunt Bessie. "There's often one in a race."

At the top of the blackboard, Hawkins wrote, Alexandra Gardens Stakes. Beneath this he put the first entrant, No. 1, Mystery Man — 100/1.

"We don't think much of dark horses," said Aunt Bessie. "Information is what's needed."

Hawkins spoke. "To employ a racing term, my Lady, that is bang on the nose."

Sophie, Flora, and Ada were stunned to hear the butler speak so but, as Lady Shelling gave no reaction, neither did they.

"Number two, Miss Villard. She is the most wicked of gossips."

"And her maid's in on it, an' all," said Ada.

"We can't fathom how she can afford her expensive clothes," added Flora.

"A possible blackmailer," said Sophie. "Definitely, there's more to be found out there."

Flora added, "There's something else — something she said. Excuse me, Lady Shelling, for what I'm about to repeat. She said that if she had designed a porcelain receptacle, she would call herself the Queen of the Lavatory."

"She said what?"

The conversation and its context had to be explained to Aunt Bessie.

Hawkins then wrote, No. 2, Queen of the Lavatory — 10/1.

"Eight to one, surely," said Aunt Bessie.

"The blackmail is not proven, my Lady. If it were, I would agree with you."

"Have it your own way."

"Number nine is Major Cummings. He is a well-mannered gentleman." Sophie went on to describe his character and explain the cooking test.

"His servant walks the dog first thing in the morning," said Ada. "Wears a long white coat done right up to here," she put her thumb and fingers around her throat, "and a white turban what's got a bit of yellow in it. Does he count as a suspect?"

"Do you mean Major Cummings sent his servant to do the deed?" asked Flora.

"Or the servant did it on his own account," replied Ada.

"Although that might be true," said Sophie, "we should consider them as one entrant. What do you think, Auntie?"

"Remind me to tell you about my experiences in India when we are at home. I don't wish to derail the proceedings. Yes, one entrant."

Hawkins hesitated before writing, No. 9, Hurry Curry — 20/1.

"Why so high?" asked Sophie, who liked the Major.

"It is not very high, Miss King. These prices are merely a start until the strength of the field become apparent. As the servant cooks, he also has access to knives. Furthermore, it is typical of gentlemen stationed in India to bring home mementoes. Among such things is often found the kukri knife. It is a heavy blade, long for a knife, with a highly curved edge. The spine is flat and angular. You explained the nature of the wound to me, and it is possible that the spine of the kukri could be the cause of such a wound."

"Well done, Mr Hawkins. That is a definite possibility and one I'll try to confirm."

"Thank you, Miss King."

"Next is number 12, Mr Saunders. As you know, he's the only witness to come forward. He is as unlike a murderer as can be. He strikes one as safe, sound, and secure. Why would he put himself through police interviews when he could so easily hide the fact he was nearby at the time?"

"As an alibi," said Flora. "He's a witness only to disguise the fact he's the murderer. It's done all the time!"

"Where's it done all the time?" asked Sophie.

"Mainly in stories but, if murderers read of it, then they know they can do it themselves."

"I suppose you could be right." Sophie looked at Mr Hawkins.

The entry he made was, No. 12, The Witness — 20/1.

"Captain Bristow at number fourteen." Sophie explained what they knew of him.

"He pretends to sail, but doesn't? How absurd can the man be?" queried Aunt Bessie. "Is this Miss Villard creature to be trusted in what she says of him? Perhaps she's only making up things or guessing. There are people like that, you know."

"She speaks with certainty," said Flora. "Undoubtedly, she embellishes, but an outright lie...? The Villard would if she had to, although I'd say she hasn't had to yet."

"I haven't spoken to her, my Lady, but I think that, an' all," said Ada.

"She's been very quick to establish herself," said Sophie. "It's as if she's trying to beat everyone else in moulding our opinions."

"Aha, that's very telling," said Aunt Bessie. "It's important, because it means others hold a contrary opinion, and she's rather cleverly getting in ahead of them. They probably don't like her much."

"I hadn't even considered that aspect," said Sophie. "Then those who are against her most likely are the people she defames."

"Exactly! She makes her acid remarks about Bristow, because Bristow knows something about her. You can be sure of that. He might not repeat it under ordinary circumstances, but Miss Villard can't be sure he'll remain quiet. Hence, she strikes first... Hawkins, what do you make of Bristow?"

"Mr Bristow has his accomplishments, but is embarrassed to mention them. Therefore, he makes himself of more importance in other areas of his life through an unseemly yet harmless subterfuge."

Sophie said, "What we can't understand is how Miss Villard knows so much about him, even in private matters."

"I certainly can," said Aunt Bessie. "It's plain to me they were intimate in the past, and it ended badly."

"Why didn't I think of that?" said Sophie.

"Because your mind is too pure. I have heard so many stories that very little shocks me now. Hawkins, write something down or we'll be here all night."

He did — No. 14, Flush with Success — 20/1.

"The Communists complicate matters," began Sophie, "and we need not bring in everything we know about them. The basic premise is this: the Doctor is a man of some standing within the Communist leadership. He is present in Britain for a specific purpose, as we discovered today. Would he resort to murder if threatened? The answer is, of course, he absolutely would. From top to bottom, the Bolsheviks are bloodthirsty and vengeful, employing violence to achieve their aims. Although risky on British soil, to murder someone who found out a little too much about their enterprise is a tactic to which they would resort. Of the Communists in Alexandra Gardens, Mr Kuritsyn is the best placed candidate because he spends so much of his time outside. Setting aside his constant propaganda, he is quite affable and entertaining. Several in the square, such as Mr Saunders, for example, readily converse with him. Also, it has become apparent he is not thoroughly ardent in his communistic beliefs."

She searched through her notes to reassure herself on a point before continuing.

"It would be easy for us to blame the Communists for the murder merely because they happen to be present. Now, I have no idea if this theory is true and I have no factual foundation to support it but, it seems to me, the Doctor might order a murder to protect their operation. He is the authority in the house. Of the other four men, we know very little. They do not socialize locally and seem only to exist for their work, which is, I am told, to proselytize on some small scale. The Doctor may have committed the murder himself. He may have sent one of the four workers. He may have ordered Mr Kuritsyn to kill Mr Hamilton. Kuritsyn did say he was a member of the Cheka, the Russian secret police — we thought he was joking. Anyway, this is the most likely, in a technical sense, because of the evidence of the dog biscuit bag. We don't really have anything more concrete than that."

"How dependable as evidence is the dog biscuit bag?" asked Aunt Bessie.

"Quite conclusive in its way. Very few bags have been distributed and only within Alexandra Gardens — the biscuits aren't for sale to the public yet. Two were found at the murder scene. One was in Mr Hamilton's pocket and the other was lying on the ground. It had been dropped very recently. The police believe it was dropped at the time of the murder."

"Hmm... How do you rate the evidence of the bag, Hawkins?"

"At two to three on, my Lady."

"You've convinced him, and it seems quite definite to me, too."

"It could hardly have been planted, Auntie, so it must have been dropped by accident. Only the dog owners in Alexandra Gardens received them, so that is more or less that."

Hawkins turned to the blackboard. No. 15, Red House — 5/1.

"Things are hotting up. What's next?"

"Mr Alan Mellish at number nineteen. If there were a competition for the rudest and most peculiar man in Britain, he would be a finalist. He has to be seen and heard to be believed, and when one has seen and heard him, one wishes one hadn't."

"You don't like him, then, I take it," said Auntie Bessie wryly.

"I'm told one gets used to him, but that comes from neighbours who cannot easily move away. They're saddled with him — they must endure his presence, while everyone else can escape."

"It's true, Lady Shelling," said Flora. "In terms of the case, he's more interesting because he's the source of the bags. It's more likely that one fell out of *his* pocket than anyone else's."

"Interestin'."

Hawkins put on the blackboard, No. 19, Dog Biscuit — 15/1.

"Mrs Sandra Pringle at number 20. Almost certain to be romantically entangled with Mr Clark, and completely jealous if his attentions wander elsewhere. She's an attractive woman, well-dressed, and may be flirtatious. We've noticed a few small things in that direction. I witnessed her spying on Mr Clark when he was talking to Gladys."

"Yes," said Flora, "but the Villard has the daggers out for her, and ran across the street to tell me all she could to shred La Pringle's reputation to pieces."

"Oh, yes. This is more like it," said Aunt Bessie. "What did she say?"

"She linked La Pringle's name with those of a dozen different men, including Mr Bristow. Reeled them off like a shopping list, putting a passionate affair with Mr Hamilton at the top."

Aunt Bessie considered the matter before replying. "You say Mrs Pringle is flirtatious. Miss Villard says far worse about her out of spite. The truth lies somewhere in between."

"According to the Villard," said Sophie, "La Pringle was in love with Mr Hamilton. He was supposed to be handsome, and attracted the attention of several ladies roundabout."

"She briefly took to drink, after he died," said Flora.

Aunt Bessie looked from one young woman to another. "It's my opinion, Villard and Pringle were *both* in love with Mr Hamilton. They both pursued him, but Villard lost the contest to Pringle — the result being:- she is bitter and vengeful towards her successful rival. Mrs Pringle is also a jealous woman. Her current concern is that she does not lose the affections of Mr Clark." She looked at Flora. "You must always be careful not to make enemies, my dear." She turned to Sophie and then Ada. "That goes for both of you, too. I once had a tremendous enemy, and it took much effort on my part before I finally crushed her. Don't fall into the trap I did. There is no satisfaction to be had in such contests, and I still regret the entire episode. Avoid that sort of confrontation at all costs, if you can. If for some reason you can't, then to blazes with them. Now, Hawkins, what do you make of all that?"

What he made of it was, No. 20, La Pringle — 4/1. Then he adjusted the odds for the Queen of the Lavatory, making them also 4/1.

"Ah, do you see? Hawkins is a veritable Solomon. And we have two joint-favourites. Absolutely splendid. Is there any sherry?"

"I got in a nice amontillado yesterday, my Lady," said Ada, rising from the table.

"We'll wait until you return," said Sophie. "Please, Mr Hawkins, take a seat."

With the sherry poured and Ada settled, they resumed. Hawkins sipped his sherry and took up his position.

"One left," said Sophie. "Mrs Fitch, aged 46, lives at number 24, which is directly across the square from us. She is tyrannical, and I've already had a couple of run-ins with her. Without exception, she orders everyone about, dogs included. Mr Bristow, an overbearing person himself, calls her the Supreme Authority. We're sure he meant across the board and not just regarding dogs. She's also the chairwoman of the garden committee."

"An inveterate organizer," said Aunt Bessie. "Give them a cause and those around them live in misery. I'm familiar with the type... Hawkins. Who was that dreadful woman who came to dinner, and I said I'd never invite her again?"

"The Duchess of Branterbury?"

"Not her."

"If you could be more specific, my Lady, as there have been several ladies barred."

"The charity woman. Announced she wanted a hundred pounds from everyone at the table to send to her missionary brother to feed the poor in Matabele Land."

"Mrs Worthington."

"That's the one. Where was I...? Yes! Mrs Worthington was six feet tall, a misfortune she could do nothing about, but if she had only married a man her own height, I'm sure she might have been happy. Instead, she married Mr Worthington, who was only five feet six and looked like a rabbit. Poor man, I felt so sorry for him. She controlled him like a slave. I also sensed that Mrs Worthington was a stranger to soap and water. Some people believe that by not washing they strengthen the body, which is idiotic, of course. The point I'm coming to is this. After she rudely made her demand for money, much in the same graceless way as would a threatening extortioner, the other guests politely, I thought, refused to get involved. This reaction to her demands precipitated an incoherent tirade. Not getting her own way, she left, dragging her hapless husband with her. When the organizing type is foiled in its efforts, it goes insane. I don't say it's permanent, but people like Mrs Worthington seem to live on the verge of a maniacal outbreak more or less all the time. I hope that assists everyone in their deliberations."

"Good grief," said Sophie. "I'm glad I wasn't present. But applying what you've just said to Mrs Fitch, I can see she possesses a faint strain of that attitude. She's obsessed with dog shows — Cruft's in particular. She was trying to be helpful in guiding us in the entering of Blast-it in a show, but she was dictatorial. And when I jibbed at her suggestion, she got quite shirty with me."

"Very bossy and intrusive," added Flora. "She examined Biscuit's hindquarters without my permission."

"There's your proof," said Aunt Bessie, "which I find nauseating. *She's* obviously the one to watch."

"But she's a very doggy person, Auntie."

"Yes, but takes control of dog and owner in one go. Who's her family?"

"We don't know."

"That bears looking into. I doubt her complaint is hereditary, although one can never be sure. A domineering personality is not always transmitted from one generation to the next, but if there's a prevalence of lunacy — ah, that's an entirely different matter. Are we finished?"

Sophie answered her by saying, "No. Without revealing names to us, Miss Villard hinted during a general conversation with others present that several ladies living nearby were enamoured of Mr Hamilton. I assumed the gentlemen present while she said this knew whom she meant, and that it included Mrs Fitch. I might be mistaken in that assumption. Mrs Fitch is nearly twenty years older than Mr Hamilton."

"Hmm, the age difference doesn't mean anything. Take my word for it. If Mrs Fitch finds herself attracted to Mr Hamilton, what difference does age make? She can't help it striking her if she's seventeen or seventy. But acting upon that attraction and with impropriety, that is a different matter entirely. Now if the handsome Mr Hamilton, who has women flocking after him, was attracted to Mrs Fitch, then there can only be one reason. She has money and property while he does not."

Sophie wrote shorthand notes before she spoke. "We have several points to follow up. Also, I'll ask the police if they have discovered anything further. Does anyone have a question?"

"No. We all want to know what Mr Hawkins thinks," said Flora.

Although he acknowledged Flora's request, Hawkins looked to Lady Shelling for permission. She gave it with a nod.

Hawkins took his chalk and wrote, Number 24, Royal Command — 10/1.

"Oh, I am disappointed," said Aunt Bessie. "Why, Hawkins?"

"During my career, I have met many ladies possessing a forceful personality. My experience is that they are no more likely to murder someone than is anyone else. If they have a temper, I could see a sudden blow in the heat of the moment, as it were, my Lady. To plot an assassination, as I am inclined to believe the murder of Mr Hamilton in the fog must have been, speaks of a heart filled with hatred and desire for revenge. A jealous nature might sink into such a state. I have heard nothing to convince me that Mrs Fitch is a jealous woman. Miss Villard did not say so. She may have hinted, but she did not say. On the contrary, Mrs Fitch endeavours to be of use after her fashion. To wit, she offered advice on how to enter dog shows. Her examination of the dog was the same as any breeder might do upon meeting a new animal. Being ill-mannered in her approach and not waiting to be invited are her defects. Her intentions, however, were of a helpful nature. My Lady, I asked myself, is Mrs Fitch a petty tyrant?

And I answered, yes. I asked myself if Mrs Fitch had been rebuffed by Mr Hamilton? My answer is that there is no proof that she ever made such an advance or even had hopes in that direction. The only evidence provided was from Miss Villard — a very doubtful source of information and, in any case, the inference was so slight that it could have been mistaken. I apologize, but I could not include it in my calculations."

"So we've been building castles in the air?"

"Lady Shelling, I could never think such a thing. Tonight has been a most invigorating airing of facts and opinions. You asked me to render the information into a practical form. If I were opening a book, although I believe it far too early, these are the odds I would stand behind."

"No front-runner, eh?"

"That is the issue at present, my Lady. We need a clear favourite. The odds can then be adjusted to reflect that, in the event of the favourite winning, the book is either balanced or modestly profitable. At present, without a strong contender, I can only suggest a sweepstake."

"What on earth is that?" asked Sophie.

"If I may explain, Miss King. We have on the board nine runners entered, which permits up to nine punters to enter the sweepstake. As it is a blind draw, the stake at risk will be small. The names of the contenders in Alexandra Gardens, including Mr Saunders, would be written on slips and drawn at random well before the contest is concluded. One slip is given to each punter. The one who holds the paper bearing the winner's name receives all nine stakes placed. In effect, the punter will sweep up all the stakes, hence the term sweepstakes."

"That sounds fair."

"It is, Miss King, yet it excludes the art and science of studying the horse's form, the experience and track record of the jockey, expected weather conditions, and a host of other considerations both objective and subjective. The sweepstake merely employs the luck of the draw."

"Going to be a punter, are you?" asked Lady Shelling of Sophie.

"No, but I'm curious about how the scheme works."

They heard a knock on the back door.

"Good grief! I forgot every last word about him coming today," said Sophie, jumping up. "Quick! Hide the blackboard and don't mention the case. And for goodness' sake, Auntie, don't admit you know anything about it, or Inspector Morton will be greatly annoyed with me." She rushed out of the room.

Aunt Bessie looked at Ada and Flora to say quietly,

"How dreadfully tempting it is."

## Chapter 17

## Brittany in Britain

"*Oignons!*" A deep, gravel voice rang out in the square. The call was followed by three pulls on a croaking, ratcheting bicycle bell.

"*Oignons!*" Wedged in the corner of his lips was an unlit, half-smoked French cigarette. The man in the beret, ancient suit, and dark jersey fraying at the cuffs varied his call. "*Gar-lique!*"

He slowly rode along the middle of the road, his ancient bicycle so laden with long, heavy double strings of onions, it was a miracle it could move. With knees almost at right-angles and barely protruding past the thick mass of onion festoons hanging from handle bars, frame, and the carrier at the back, he propelled the whole in an easy, unrushed way. It was a moving heap, a veritable mound of onions in motion, and the man responsible for its propulsion was swarthy, stocky and, when dismounted, not tall.

Flora beheld him from the attic eyrie and dashed to the top of the stairs.

"Onion man! Quick! It's the onion man!"

Sophie was in the parlour writing, and she leapt up. In the hall, she collided with Ada.

"What's gone wrong, miss?"

"Nothing. It's the onion man."

"Onion man!" Ada turned and hurried to the kitchen.

"Mrs Barker, the onion man's 'ere."

"Stop him. Don't let him go!"

"'Ow many?"

"One. No, better make it two. The bhajia recipe calls for a lot of onions."

"Right."

"Get some garlic, as well."

"Right." Ada hurtled from the kitchen.

"You have money?" asked Sophie, ready to open the door.

"Yes."

"Get one for me. I'll take it home to White Lyon Yard. And have the man bring them down to the basement. I'll wait for you there."

"Right."

Sophie opened the door, and Ada launched herself into the square. She ran towards him waving furiously, because the onion man is a person of great importance. One can never be certain when he will appear, and to just miss him is one of the greater tragedies in life. He travels widely, appearing at odd times and according to his season but, when sighted, every housewife and servant runs to him, because, as they all declare, he has the best, biggest, and tastiest onions the world has ever known.

"'Allo," said the Frenchman, coming to a stop.

"'Ello," said Ada.

"Combien?"

"Can I 'ave three strings, please?" She held up three fingers.

"Trois?" The Frenchman also held up three fingers. When Ada nodded, he replied, "Bon!"

"And some garlic." She held up a finger.

"Gar-lique, oui, oui." He was smiling. In fact, he was more or less ready to smile all the time. With an effort, he pushed his bike over the kerb and onto the pavement. He expertly propped it up against some railings.

"Où habitez-vous?"

"What?"

"Ehh, où est votre maison?"

"Oh, 'ouse, you mean. Number seven." She pointed.

"Numéro sept." He wheeled the bike further along the pavement and propped it against the railings of number seven.

"Can you take them downstairs, please?"

"Comment?"

"Down there." She pointed to the basement area.

"Oui, d'accord." He handed Ada the bunch of garlic, then picked three strings off his bike. He held one up. "Magnifique, hein?"

"Yes, they look lovely."

The fat, firm, light orange-skinned onions, tightly plaited together by their dry stalks, were indeed magnificent. Ada held the gate open for him, glad it was him carrying them and not her. The moment he stepped off the steps into the basement area, Sophie opened the door. Myrtle stood behind her, ready to take the onions away. Ada paid him and added sixpence to the total.

"Bonjour, monsieur," said Sophie.

"Bonjour, madame."

"Je m'appelle Mademoiselle King."

"Ahh." He came more to attention and buttoned his jacket. "Je m'appelle Henri Gautier, citoyen de Roscoff, Bretagne.

Sophie knew he was from Brittany, as were the majority of onion men. She told him that long ago her family had once lived in Colombel, on the eastern side of Brittany. Although delighted, he had never heard of the village. She had trouble understanding some things he said, because he used so many Breton phrases — a language of Celtic origin. However, they continued their dialogue in French, as Sophie was unsure of how much English Monsieur Gautier would understand.

"Did you hear about the murder?"

"Yes. A terrible affair, is it not?"

"Terrible. Were you in the country when it happened?"

"No, my brothers, uncles, and nephews, we arrived in March."

"Then how did you hear of it?"

"Mademoiselle, everyone speaks of the murder. They speak, but no one saw a thing. It was in the fog, you understand."

"So I have heard. I no longer go out at night. The police have not caught the man, so how can it be safe if the murderer is still about?"

"It is a bad affair, *but* you should not worry. He is gone, and I think the police shall never catch him."

"What do the neighbours say?"

He took out some matches and lit his cigarette. Then he leaned comfortably against a doorpost and unbuttoned his jacket. Sophie leaned against the other doorpost opposite him.

"It is like this," he said, enjoying his cigarette. "They do not know, so they guess." He pointed at her meaningfully. "One person says, I saw a man with a funny leg the day before; another says, a man glared at me the day after. So," he shrugged, "they don't know anything, but that does not stop them talking, no. Especially the ladies."

"What do *you* think happened?"

"I say, to find a man in a fog to kill him, you must live close by. The victim lived in St. Georges. Then his killer is from St. Georges." He drew on his cigarette. "Although he could live in Alexandra Gardens. He might have lived here, in this very house, before you moved in."

"How can you say such a thing, Monsieur Gautier? You frighten me."

"Don't be scared, Mademoiselle. He will never come back. Why would he? It makes no sense. He has gone far away, and this is what the police must do. They must investigate everyone who has left the area since the murder. That way, they shall find him."

"Such an interesting thought. I often imagine the killer is someone in this square, and he stares at me through the windows."

"No, oh, no, no. The people here are fine people."

"But fine people murder sometimes, like anyone else."

"That is true."

"Then just suppose... If you had to pick a name from Alexandra Gardens, who would you say did it?"

"I cannot do that."

"Oh, really, Monsieur. You meet so many people, and know so much. You see things no one else sees. I believe you have a name in mind, hein? There is someone nearby, someone very close, whom *you* know, and you have said to yourself, 'Yes, it might be him.'"

"No. Never have I thought of such a thing... But since you have asked me, I say... Monsieur Bristow."

"Why him?"

"He knows everything, but really, he knows nothing. It is all a front, a show. He hides something, that one. Also, last year, he complained about my onions. There is never anything wrong with my onions. He wanted his money back, but he had eaten half of them and stored the rest in a damp place until they *rotted*. Pah! He shouted — Let him shout, but he does not cheat me, no. I am not easily fooled. I sell him no more onions. *Never!*"

"Oh, how could he behave so badly towards you?"

"Because he is the *miser* and wants me to pay for his mistake. What can you do...? Mademoiselle, it is with the deepest regret that I must leave. The neighbours are waiting, you understand."

"When will you be back?"

"Two weeks, a month. Who can say? Au revoir."

"Au revoir. Knock on the door if we don't come out."

"Mais oui, bien sûr."

In closing the door, she suddenly remembered that she would not *be* at number seven the next time he came.

It was only Monday morning, yet Mrs Barker was already in the grip of an intense excitement. Last night, Sophie had sent a note by Myrtle to Major Cummings. The note said that her cook, Mrs Barker, would submit to the test and prepare a dinner of Indian cuisine this Wednesday. Within the hour, Major Cumming's Indian servant, Farhan, came to number seven bearing an envelope. He had smiled warmly at Ada, and had so gracefully put his hands together in salutation as if praying, that after he had gone and Ada had shut the door, she practised the gesture.

Inside the envelope was a note of thanks from Major Cummings, and an explanation of how they all would proceed. Also, he had included a set of recipes with a list of ingredients Mrs Barker would need. On Tuesday, she would go to number nine, to have explained anything she did not understand and receive the spices she could not otherwise obtain. Major Cummings did not know this, but Sophie was going to accompany her.

Mrs Barker had read and re-read the recipes. She understood them in part, but a few unfamiliar terms threw her off. She could not yet 'see' how the dishes would turn out.

"Nancy," said Mrs Barker, pointing at something in the recipe, "take a look at this. How do you pronounce that word and what is it?"

"G H E E… Jee, I reckon." She sounded out variations. "No, it must be Jee. I don't know what it is."

"It says to fry things in it, but I've never heard of it. Where can I get some? It's on the list, so it must be important. This is all very worrying. I wish I'd never agreed to it."

"Can't you ask on Tuesday?"

"I suppose I'll have to. I'm to learn how to make yoghurt the Indian way, na'an bread, and a few other bits and bobs, so I'll need my wits about me, otherwise I'll have no idea what I'm doing. Then they'll teach me about the spices. And I have to look for kukri knives, when I've never seen one. Miss King was very insistent about that. I hope I don't spoil the dinner, because Major Cummings is dining here Wednesday."

"Can't help you with the knives, neither. What's yoghurt?"

"Fermented milk. The consistency is close to a clotted cream, but it has a slightly sour taste. Nobody cares for it much, so I never make it, but I quite like it with fruit."

Although the need for surveillance on number fifteen had diminished, the agents from Burgoyne's had to keep it up, as they had received no order to cease operations. The agents were also unaware of what had happened to everyone after the meeting at the zoo. Archie had told them that two of the men outside the tea pavilion were well known, and Lord Laneford and his men were actively pursuing the man who had arrived with them. Since then, they had been told nothing and, yet again, the Home Office was conspicuous by its absence. No couriers or agents of theirs had returned. Sophie found it all very annoying.

Flora called down the stairs.

"Comrade Kuritsyn's out and about! Guess who's with him!"

"Who!?"

"The dashing Russian!"

"No! Should I try to talk to him!?"

"Can't hurt, can it!?"

"I don't think so!" She was about to call Biscuit, but he was already trotting towards her with his leash in his mouth.

It was impossible for Kuritsyn and the visiting Russian to have walked any slower than they did. Neither could they have walked any faster because they were so deep in discussion. A two-year-old, stumbles or falls included, could have finished a lap of the gardens while the Russians would still have been only half-way around. Sophie walked out of number seven and crossed the road to allow Biscuit to investigate the hedge and railings. She blocked their path. The Russians saw Sophie and sped up.

"Good morning, Comrade Miss King," said Kuritsyn in a hearty manner.

"Good morning, Mr Kuritsyn," replied Sophie.

"Permit me to present my good friend, Comrade Vasily Ivanovich Razov."

"I am delighted your acquaintance to make, Comrade Miss King," said Razov. He was not so much handsome as superabundantly alive. Courteous and attentive with flashing eyes, his hair and neatly trimmed moustache were thick and vigorous. Sophie was struck with the idea that he must be a man of extremes — laughing, he would laugh loudest; crying, he would cry soonest, angry, he would bay for blood and revenge before everyone — a dancing, daring cossack of a man, who would be wounded to the heart upon seeing a child's treasured flower broken.

"I'm pleased to meet you," said Sophie.

"Comrade Razov is a great man," said Kuritsyn. "He comes from Moscow, and has the confidence of Comrade Lenin!" Kuritsyn nodded, and seemed to imply, 'What more could you want?' "Thursday evening, he shall give a stirring speech at the meeting. Do not forget to attend, comrade."

"Oh," said Sophie. "What will your talk be about?"

"I shall bring to oppressed people of Camden and Primrose Hill, the only thought our great Comrade Lenin had last ten days ago. All in Russia who hear are transported in blazes of delight. His idea is a greatness profound, and very startling to us all. We to ourselves say, how can a man ever think like this? But he does. All the time, he does, because there is no end to his thinkings. Then, ten days ago, as I said you before, after the conclusion of his thinking, he speaks to Politburo. There, everyone falls down at his knees, and says, 'What is this that comes from his mouth now?' Then they applaud like ones deep in the vodka."

Sophie believed she understood, so, she therefore asked, "What thought can this possibly be?"

"Profuse apologies, comrade, but I have put the wax on my lips until Thursday evening."

"Sealed," said Kuritsyn to Razov. "Putting wax on lips gives wrong idea." Then he said to Sophie, "Comrade Razov is learning English very quickly."

"Very quickly!" said Razov. "A month ago, I knew nothing. Next month, I will know everything. Helping gratefully, Comrade Kuritsyn has lended to me some books."

"Which ones?" asked Sophie, now curious.

"Which ones, you demand of me? I shall say, Shakespeare, who is imperialist lackey. Clever man, but talents wasted in being toad of the court. Bourgeois Jane Austen... Not bad. Silly woman runs about after silly man, and they clasp each other at the end. Nobody dies. Not dramatic. The greatest book I have read in England while visiting is Robin Hood. What a hero!? If he were alive, he would come to Russia and be loved by Comrade Lenin and all Russian peoples. Robin Hood was Marxist ideologist long before anyone think of Marx. Take from the rich; give to the poor. Marx stole his idea. Then, brave Comrade Hood, he fights tyrant capitalist Sheriff of Nottingham, and steals from the wicked church. Ah-ha! Everyone in Russia does that now with rifles and artillery, and many dying, but Comrade Hood did it first with bow and arrow. He is national hero, yes? And why? Because his socialism is pure. I think the English secretly want revolution, but dare not stick up their heads because they have no Comrade Hood to lead them. I would like to shake his hands. All of Russia will want to shake his hands when I tell them."

"His English improves every day," said Kuritsyn. "It was very bad just two days ago. By Thursday, we hope, he will be ready for his first speech in English. Promise me you will come, comrade?"

"I certainly hope I can," answered Sophie.

"You are not blue-blooded communist?" asked Razov. Kuritsyn whispered to him in both Russian and English, causing Razov to amend his question. "Red-blooded?"

"No. You haven't convinced me yet to join your cause."

"Ha! In Russia, it is no longer a cause, but way of life. Be convinced by the miracle of co-operation at the Mylovar Soap Factory. There, all peasants sing revolutionary songs when bringing their sunflower seeds, because they are so happy. If I told you the tonnage of soap produced, you would want to bring your own sunflower seeds."

Sophie, momentarily baffled by his logic, said,

"I don't think knowing the tonnage would do it," said Sophie.

"Better still is the monumental canning and sausage factory in Kourgan. Astonishing! 50,000 tins of meat a...

"Comrade, a moment, please. I explain matters, Comrade Miss King. Comrade Razov is one of the top men at Centrosojus, the organization responsible for controlling output from the consumer societies all across Russia. He is devoted to his work."

"So it seems. Thank you, Mr Kuritsyn. Mr Razov, are you in Britain to promote the export of Russian goods?"

"Yes. Very clever of you to guess."

"I wonder if you would be so kind. I have a question and I'd like to ask you both as you are such devoted communists. It's a technical question to help me understand how communism works on a personal level. If someone gave either of you a gift of a hundred thousand pounds, would you redistribute your own wealth? And if you did share it with your fellow workers or gave it to some committee, what percentage would you donate?"

They stared at her.

"Let me understand this," said Kuritsyn. "Someone gives *me* a hundred thousand pounds, and you want to know how much I would give away?"

"Yes."

"Oh."

The men looked at each other.

"Excuse us a moment," said Kuritsyn. "We confer in Russian. Our native tongue is easier for us."

"By all means," said Sophie.

Razov began. "If we say we give it all away, she won't believe us."

"And if we keep it all, she will say we are capitalists. This is very dangerous. How much would you keep?"

"No, you say first," urged Razov.

"Er, huh... If it was known I had received the money, it would be seized, but if, somehow, I could keep the gift... Um, probably quite a lot."

"Yes, anyone would, but we cannot say this."

"Don't worry, Vasily Ivanovich, I know how to answer her."

In English, Kuritsyn said to Sophie,

"This is a very deep matter, and must be referred to a higher party member."

"Would that be the other gentleman staying at your house?"

"You mean the Doctor?" asked Kuritsyn. "Yes, we will ask him."

"He is a clever man," added Razov, "an enormous intellectual who understands political matters. He will tell us what to think according to socialist principles and party guidelines."

"I believe he might," said Sophie, who then had a brainwave. "If he's so intelligent, what does he think about the murder?"

"Murder?" asked Razov. "What murder is this?"

"Some fellow was attacked during a fog in February," said Kuritsyn. "They attacked him from behind and broke his neck."

"Does this happen often in London fogs?"

"No. It was around the corner by the pub. I knew Hamilton, the man killed."

"Probably just drunken brawl in street. One dead — that can't be helped sometimes."

"Maybe it was drunken brawl. The Doctor says the police should round up everyone, interrogate them until they find the murderer, and then hang him from a lamppost as example to others."

"Good grief," said Sophie. "Surely he wasn't serious?"

"He is always serious," said Kuritsyn.

"But what about a trial?"

"In Russia, trials are a thing of the past. The Cheka now decide everything during the interrogation."

"Do you agree with that?" asked Sophie, horrified.

"Yes," said both men together.

"That's only because you *must* agree," she said. "Mr Hamilton was an innocent man. His death demands justice. Unfortunately, there's no evidence that leads to a suspect."

"Then it will remain unsolved." Kuritsyn shrugged.

"Mr Kuritysn, did you not hear or see anything that night? Surely, you were out with Vova?"

"Earlier, we went out to Camden, before the fog came down, so I know nothing. But you say Hamilton was innocent. Perhaps. Yet he was the type of man who makes enemies. Sure of himself, always arguing with men, and insincere towards women. I detested him. I explain the glorious revolution to Hamilton, and he insults me, Russia, and Comrade Lenin."

"Filthy reactionary," said Razov. "How dare he ever live!"

"Yes, but they're allowed to live in Britain. I was sorry to hear he was murdered, but I cannot weep for someone I did not like."

"Oh, I see," said Sophie. "You believe he brought it on himself? That he made an enemy who was volatile enough to attack him in the fog?"

"I don't see why not. Comrade Razov, if this man insulted you, how would you react?"

"Kill him — face to face, so he knows why he dies."

"Let's hope it never comes to that, but I think so, too. Comrade Miss King, there would be no satisfaction in killing an enemy from behind if one wants revenge."

"What if Hamilton and his killer had an argument first?" asked Sophie. "Then Mr Hamilton turned away, and the killer struck from behind in anger."

"Yes, that could be," said Kuritsyn. Razov looked bored.

Sophie noticed they were tiring of the subject. "Do you have any leaflets?"

"Yes," said Kuritsyn. "Would you like one?"

"May I take five? I believe everyone should be exposed to new ideas."

"Five! I wish all comrades were as helpful as you."

## Chapter 18

## A WHIFF OF SOMETHING

At one o'clock, Monday afternoon, an unnamed Home Office department attacked number seven. It approached stealthily and, without warning, knocked on the back door.

"Who can that be now?" said Mrs Barker, throughly fed up with the amount of traffic passing through her kitchen.

"I'll see who it is, Mrs Barker," said Myrtle.

She opened the door to find four men lined up along the path with boxes and suitcases. One had a camera tripod balanced on a shoulder. The nearest man, tall and stern with a light-coloured moustache, could only ever have been an army officer.

"Good afternoon," he said in a crisp voice. "Breed-Dankworth's my name, and I'm here to take charge of the house."

Myrtle heard the words, but what she was supposed to say and do next eluded her completely. She looked helplessly at Mrs Barker, who came over.

Mrs Barker had one shot in her locker. "There must be some mistake," she said. "Have you got the right house?"

"We don't make mistakes. This is number seven, and it's now under my control."

She was momentarily speechless until the thought came that there was yet another thing to be done. She smiled and said, "Excuse me a moment," before slamming the door shut, bolting it, and telling Myrtle to run and fetch Miss King.

Upon first hearing the report, Sophie was equally confounded. She rose from her chair. By the time she got to the back door, she was furious. Biscuit accompanied her, even daring to enter the kitchen without invitation because he knew something was up and was not prepared to miss it.

Sophie opened the door.

"I am Miss King and I am in charge of this house."

"Breed-Dankworth." He briefly raised his hat. "I take it you haven't been informed? That's bad of them. Anyway, I'm in charge now, and I'd like a report from you explaining how matters stand."

"Here is my report." Sophie genteelly cleared her throat. "If you do not leave my garden in the next two minutes, I shall summon a constable and have you all arrested for trespass."

"Come, come..."

"Blast-it! Guard him!"

Biscuit normally had a friendliest-dog-in-the-world air about him. Since entering the kitchen, he had eyed the visitors warily, while still giving out the impression he was essentially a dog of peace. Upon the command, he transformed into a dog of war. Biscuit crouched, as if preparing to spring. His hair bristled and his ears flattened, all the while growling with increasing intensity and tempo. The visitors saw his fangs, and Biscuit's mouth quivered as if he could barely restrain himself. The dramatic change even took Sophie by surprise.

Breed-Dankworth shot down the steps in ignominious retreat. From the path, he said,

"Well, look, obviously the changeover has not been co-ordinated properly. We'll go, and um, come back when everything has been sorted out. Good day."

The other men hurried out of the garden, but Breed-Dankworth backed away cautiously, fearing to turn his back while Biscuit still fixed his unwavering, baleful stare upon him. When the side entrance door shut and the Home Office men had gone, everything returned to normal. The dog wagged his tail and Sophie made a fuss of him.

"Do you want a... Vita-Bone? Do you want a... CereBone? Do you want a... Biscuit Bone?" He woofed enthusiastically and received his reward.

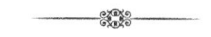

---

"Are we in trouble with the Home Office?" asked Flora, seated in the attic.

"Bound to be," replied Sophie.

"It's despicable that a gang of men in detachable collars should dare try to throw us out of our lovely home."

"I didn't notice if their collars were detachable or not."

"Good old Biscuit put a stop to their games... I wish I'd seen him."

"I want to keep him," said Sophie.

"You're setting yourself up for a great disappointment."

"I know... and leaving this house."

"Yes. I'm beginning to loath spying from an attic, but there's no house in the world I'd rather be doing it from than here... You see that woman?" Flora passed the binoculars to Sophie. "She talks to herself."

"It's rather tawdry, finding out petty things about people that they don't want known."

"Yes, it seemed so, at first," agreed Flora. "My scruples have been thoroughly suffocated, though. It's addictive, in its way. Now I want to find out everyone's juicy secrets. From up here, I feel as though they all belong to me, and they owe me their lives, their thoughts, and their hidden passions. Clearly, I'm going off my head."

"I don't think you are. I, too, sometimes feel as though I have a right to know everything about everyone."

"Yes... Wouldn't it be ghastly if this were habit-forming? I mean, suppose we become inveterate snoopers and did it all the time without being disgusted with ourselves?"

"I'd hate it. We despise Miss Villard because of what *she* does, but we're no better."

"I disagree. Firstly, we're being paid to spy, and for good reasons. Secondly, we don't gossip. We are not and never shall be gossips. Thirdly, we don't do this for our enjoyment... At least, I didn't start out doing it for enjoyment, but now have an interest bordering on the morbid."

"It isn't the done thing, and yet, here we are doing it! What a very peculiar way of life we've landed ourselves in. Sometimes, I feel it is so absurd, I just want to laugh."

"Don't do that, otherwise you'll be committed. I'll do all I can to prevent them from institutionalizing you, but laughing by yourself will get you into trouble very quickly."

"Oh, really, Gladys."

Flora laughed. "Ooh, who's this? Yes, it's your dashing Russian returning from the shops."

"He's not *my* Russian." Sophie observed him through the binoculars. "Comrade Razov is definitely of the Russian nobility, so what's he doing being a communist?" She passed the binoculars to Flora.

"Surviving, I imagine. It must have been awful for many Russians. Say the wrong thing, and they shoot you. One must quickly adapt or else."

"The funny thing is, I'm sure Kuritsyn knows him. It's as if they've met before — in Russia."

"They could be from the same county. Do they have counties in Russia?"

"Something similar, no doubt. Probably Russia's smallest county is larger than Britain."

"Yes, and they're not all Russian there, are they? There are others, like the Armenians and Turkomans... Do you see how he swaggers as he walks? You're right, Phoebe, only a nobleman could walk like that... He seems not to have a care in the world."

"Yes. I told you he's learning English. I hope he hurries up, because it's excruciating to hear him. He called Shakespeare a toad, and he waffled on about a soap factory and sunflower seeds. It isn't so much his grasp of the language as what he's talking about. Most surprising, and in very unexpected ways."

"I must speak with him to observe the phenomenon, although you say he's delivering a speech Thursday evening."

"I'd like us all to go... Myrtle could sit in for us."

"I hope we can. Are the Russians important still?"

"Not as much as they were. They're the same as any other suspect in Mr Hamilton's murder, except we know a spymaster lives there, so we have to be extra careful. It makes me wonder why the Home Office sent those men. Do you know they had a camera with them? We should have a camera."

"Which brings us back to the question of what trouble we might be in. What lies just below the horizon?"

"There's no point worrying. We'll find out soon enough. I was not going to allow that dreadfully rude Breed-Dankworth to take over and order us about. We're FO and he isn't. No warning, no plan... Archie should have informed us, but I bet he doesn't even know. The HO can jolly well get on with it, and we don't need them. If they come back, I will forbid Mrs Barker to boil so much as a kettle on their behalf."

"Where will they sleep?"

"In the garden shed, if they like. This house is for ladies only, and they shan't enter except to perform their duties... Good grief, if they lived here they'd drop ash on the floor, swill beer, and not wipe their feet upon entry, never mind the impropriety of the arrangement. I won't put up with it. We're not leaving until our job's done or we're recalled. After that, the house is theirs to turn into a pig sty if they wish."

"Ahh, an Englishwoman's home is her castle."

"Exactly, even when it's temporary."

"Wait... Movement at number 20 and... here she comes, La Pringle, wearing her mooching about dress again because Mr Clark's gone out."

"I'll ambush her," said Sophie. "Blast-it!"

"Good afternoon, Mrs Pringle," said Sophie, hailing the woman from a distance to make sure she could not escape.

"Good afternoon, Miss King," she answered coolly. It was as if for her the afternoon had suddenly become not as good as it had been the moment before.

Sophie realized Mrs Pringle was tarring her with the same brush of jealousy with which she had daubed Flora.

"I so enjoy meeting you and our other neighbours. I never thought for a minute that everyone would be so friendly."

"Yes," said Mrs Pringle. She put down her Pekinese.

"The weather helps, of course." Sophie glanced at the clouds. "It doesn't look like rain. What do you think?"

"I don't think so, either. I hope not, anyway."

"Is anything the matter?"

"Whatever makes you say that?"

"I don't know… You look pensive."

"Do I?" She smiled. "Just things on my mind."

"Yes, there's always something, isn't there? For me, it's often money worries."

"Money worries?" said Mrs Pringle, her interest sparked.

"Yes. I'm a dyed-in-the-wool worrier, really. Although we received an inheritance, as I think we explained, the upkeep of the house will be very expensive, what with the rates and repairs, and the price of coal always going up."

"It certainly never goes down."

"How true. We'll get jobs, of course, and I'm sure we'll manage somehow, but it's the worry of it, you see."

"I completely understand that. I have to be careful, too. What type of work do you do?"

"Well, Miss Walton is quite creative, and hopes to find something in the advertising field. I'll find secretarial work."

"I was thinking about secretarial work,' confided Mrs Pringle, warming to Sophie's openness. "My typing's not bad and I have a machine, but I don't know shorthand."

"You absolutely need it to apply for the better-paying jobs… I know shorthand."

"Do you?"

"Yes. Would you like me to show you? I also have a book you could borrow. I won't say it's easy, especially at first while training oneself to think phonetically and learn the symbols, but practise and repetition are all you need. Some employers require a college certificate, but not all of them, and you could always attend Pitman's College or take a correspondence course if you feel you should."

Mrs Pringle stood in thought, imagining for herself a future where she went to an office and earned her own money.

"I'm very interested indeed... What a kind, gracious offer. May I take you up on it? I promise not to presume on your time, and you must absolutely tell me off if I do." Mrs Pringle laughed.

"I think it will be fun. When shall I come over?"

"Oh. I'm not fit to be seen in the mornings." Sandra Pringle spoke confidentially, then laughed again. "In the afternoon?"

"Two o'clock tomorrow?"

"That would be perfect."

"I won't have my book with me; it's still in Winchester. But I can definitely get you started with some exercises. Do you have a fountain pen or soft leaded pencils? I use pencils, but some prefer a pen."

"I have both."

"Then you're all set." Sophie smiled. "I'll leave Blast-it at home, of course. We don't want the dogs to interrupt us."

"No. Nankin is always well behaved, but if Blast-it — I can't believe you call him that — but if he were present, Nankin would turn snippy. He's quite territorial in his way and would fuss terribly."

"Yes, dogs are like that. Good as gold, until one wants them to be quiet, which is when they choose to make a noise."

"Yes... Although Blast-it seems very well behaved. Um, doesn't Miss Walton call him Biscuit?"

"She does, and that's his other name... It was something of a joke, my calling him Blast-it, that's really not worth explaining."

"And is it true you're entering him into Cruft's next year?"

"We're thinking about it. Mrs Fitch is very keen on our doing so."

"Oh, Cynthia would be. Completely mad about dogs, but she knows what she's talking about."

"Has Nankin been to Cruft's?"

"Yes, twice now. The first year, he won first place in a qualifying championship. Didn't you, Nanky?"

"He did very well. That must have been very satisfying."

"It should have been, but I thought he should have won at Cruft's. I'm not just saying that because he's my dog... Well, I suppose I am. But the dog who beat Nanky the first year only came third in the competition that Nanky won. I put it down to poor judging."

"I would have thought that impossible?"

"One would. However, I must explain this: we of Alexandra Gardens have an enemy in St. George's Square."

"You mean just down the road?"

"Yes. We have all entered our dogs in Cruft's, and have nothing to show for it between all eight of us, despite placing in numerous qualifying competitions. However, there are only three people living in St George's who enter their dogs, and they have won four first class ribbons, and a best of group." She raised her eyebrows. "That's five wins."

"Why is that?"

"Because Mrs Murray is great friends with the Cruft's family, and she's won three of those ribbons."

"Oh, I see."

"Yes. It's not that we mind her dogs winning so frequently; it's that she also prejudices the judge against *us* in whatever class we enter. Mrs Murray makes the most of her position in prosecuting her vendetta."

"How astonishing. But surely the judges are impartial — impervious to suggestion?"

"One naturally believes so. But she's been seen talking to the judges before the adjudication. We don't believe she's recommending which one should *win*, but rather that she's hinting at which one should *not* win. Then, of course, with her being known as a friend of the Cruft's family, the judge will think more severely of the dog Mrs Murray has singled out. I'll never put Nankin through such an ordeal again."

"Poor thing," said Sophie. "What's caused this bad feeling that Mrs Murray would stoop to such a thing?"

"Mrs Murray and Cynthia Fitch used to be friendly, but they had a dreadful falling out. It was a terrible row, all because Cynthia made a pointed comment about how Mrs Murray was training a dog. But that's how she is with everyone. Mrs Murray knew that and could have ignored it. No one knows exactly what they both said, but it was bad enough for them to never speak again."

"Oh, that all seems so unnecessary," said Sophie, recalling her own reactions to Mrs Fitch's meddling. "I haven't met Mrs Murray, but surely she wouldn't be so actively vindictive?"

"Mr Bristow's Newfoundland, Bo'sun, is a magnificent example of the breed. Cynthia helped train Bo'sun, and the Captain, too." Mrs Pringle laughed. "I attended the show. He didn't even get a ribbon, and Bo'sun behaved himself so splendidly. He was by far the best-looking dog, and he got no recognition. I saw it all for myself. Mrs Murray talked to the judge, another friend of hers, by the way, before he made his decision. Unless someone signs a confession, what more proof is needed?"

"None, I'd say. How unfair it all is."

"Isn't it? The Captain got very depressed around that time. He slacked right off with Bo'sun's training and now the dog pulls him about as though never trained at all. That annoys Cynthia, of course, but she rightly blames Mrs Murray for being the cause of it."

Sophie was not sure she agreed on this point, but responded sympathetically anyway.

"There were other incidents." Mrs Pringle stopped suddenly and changed her mind. "But they're not worth mentioning."

"I understand. It must be frustrating for all of you."

"A little more than that, but we don't let it get us down. I'm sorry I mentioned the subject. You must find it tedious."

"I really didn't."

"That's kind of you to say. I have to go in and get my dinner ready. Two o'clock tomorrow? I'm looking forward to learning shorthand, but you'll probably find I'm a complete dunce at it."

"You shan't be anything of the kind, and we'll have a lovely time."

After Mrs Pringle had gone, Sophie began walking but did not get very far, because Alan Mellish lounged into the square. Topper, the Jack Russell, scampered freely about his feet. Mellish caught sight of Sophie, changed direction, and lounged more rapidly in her direction. It looked to Sophie as if Mellish had fallen into a theatre costume department's clown and pirate trunk at night in the dark, and then struggled to dress himself by touch alone. The orange and white scarf was gone, but the hat, with only the feather missing, must certainly have belonged to a cavalier. "Coo-ee!" he shouted.

Until she came to Alexandra Gardens, Sophie had never been shouted at in public before. Mellish had now done it twice to her.

"Before you say another word," she said, as he came within speaking range, "please, do not shout at me in the street again."

"Get's the job done, though."

"It is unnecessary and disturbing."

"Am I in your bad books?" He smiled sheepishly.

"Yes."

"Then I promise not to do it again. Do you forgive me?"

"No, you're on probation."

"What a severe young woman you are. Can I buy myself forgiveness with another bag of dog biscuits? I've got one here somewhere." He started looking through his pockets.

"Perhaps you've eaten them."

"That was a low, sarcastic blow. Ah, found 'em." He held up the bag. "Is that a sufficient bribe? Old Blast-it thinks so."

"Bribe accepted." Sophie laughed.

"I should bribe you more often since it makes you laugh so prettily. I have to tell you, I'm in a stupendously good mood."

"Why's that?"

"Testing on my new product is going extraordinarily well."

"You mean the dog biscuits?"

"No, I mean, Fructo-Fragrante."

"A perfume?"

"Much more advanced than any perfume. Are you aware of the number of bad smells one detects in a day? It's a horrific number. Most of them we avoid by washing or throwing away kitchen refuse — that sort of thing. While *we* might devote ourselves to cleanliness, others don't. For example, you might wear perfume, I might not. To me and to yourself, you smell nice. To you, I might be so repellent that you need to stand some yards upwind. This is a problem demanding a solution, and I have solved it. Two drops of Fructo-Fragrante in a handkerchief are all it takes. By placing a nostril to the handkerchief and inhaling deeply, then repeating the procedure with the other nostril, you will find relief from the stenches of the world for up to four hours."

"But that's just a scented handkerchief."

"My dear, Miss King. It is not the same at all, because I haven't finished my explanation. The intended effect of Fructo-Fragrante is to coat the interior of the olfactory organ with a thin film. Upon encountering an odiferous tramp after such an application, he will smell like a delightful blend of oranges, apples and coconut."

"But wouldn't everything smell the same?"

"That was the main difficulty I encountered and conquered. An active ingredient within the preparation reacts with specific enzymes contained within the offending odour. The catalytic reaction is such that it quickly unlocks, so to speak, the blend of scents stored within the film. In the very instant one stands next to a tramp, one can only detect a slight scent of citrus or coconut emanating from him. I've just finished an exhaustive battery of tests with the help of three such gentlemen of the road."

"You did what?" Sophie took a second to recover. "I don't really understand your explanation, but are you saying you found tramps and sniffed at them?"

"Oh, I *paid* to smell their necks, of course, and thank goodness Fructo-Fragrante worked." Mellish gave a short, loud laugh. "I had them lined up in my workshop. They were also happy that my test was a success. Now, tell me. How is Blast-it getting on with the biscuits?"

"He loves them, and has suffered no ill-effects. Have any other dogs experienced an adverse reaction?"

"No, except for Topper, who helped himself to the first batch when it was cooling on racks."

Sophie stared at Topper, amazed at how he had survived so long with such a master.

"Where is your workshop?" she asked.

"Ethelred Street, next road over. It's a dead-end, and I have no neighbours, so I don't get complaints any more. Not like I used to when experimenting in my house."

"Ah... That's further away from the murder scene, so you wouldn't have seen anything from there."

"No. But I was working when it happened. Why are you interested?"

"I think the murderer should be apprehended."

"So do I. What has my workshop got to do with it?"

"Nothing. It was too far away."

"Do you have a suspicion I'm the murderer?"

"Ah, um, yes, I do."

"How frightfully interesting. Do I look like a murderer?"

"It's hard to say what you look like, but you don't strike me as *looking like* a murderer. Are you?"

"No. I didn't like Hamilton. He was sarcastic and dismissive of my work, but that is no cause for me to kill him."

"Who do you think murdered him?"

"It could be any one of dozens, I should think."

"Dozens? Please, explain what you mean."

"Hamilton had a very condescending attitude, and nothing is more irritating than that. He didn't actually insult people, but he made fun and laughed at their expense as a matter of course. He thought he was being entertainingly epigrammatic when it was really just him showing off."

"Mr Hamilton did this to everyone?"

"He did it to me, Bristow, poor old Cummings, and Clark, so it's a reasonable assumption he did it to others."

"I suppose it is. Am I to understand he paid special attention to Major Cummings?"

"Yes. He ragged Cummings about India all the time, and he was quite nasty to Clark."

"I haven't met Mr Clark."

"He's all right. On the moody side, because he's a musician. A talented one, though."

"What I can't understand is why Mr Hamilton was so offensive?"

"He wasn't all the time. With women, he was charming, but not with men. And he hadn't always been that way, either, not until Georgie, his Sheltie, won at Cruft's... That went to Hamilton's head."

"I see. Is Cruft's really so competitive?"

"Some people will resort to *anything* to win. I entered once, but never again. The judges kicked me out for not following a rule they literally made up on the spot. All because I had trained Topper to lick the judge's face. It was only a gesture of friendliness, nothing more."

"Don't you think you overstepped the mark?"

"Probably. But a mark's only real purpose is to be overstepped."

"I disagree."

"Good for you."

"Something you said interests me. Did Mr Hamilton 'resort to anything' to win?"

"I don't know. He might have, but he didn't *need* to. Not when he was Mrs Murray's protégé."

"Ah, I've heard mention of her before."

"Very likely. We burn her effigy in Alexandra Gardens once a week."

"Why is that?"

"The consensus now is that she sets the judges at Cruft's against anyone from Alexandra Gardens, especially anyone friendly with Mrs Fitch. It might be true, but I have had my doubts. That consensus was just a vague feeling up until this year. Then Mrs Murray did the dreadful deed that can *never* be forgiven."

Sophie supposed the way he arranged his features was meant to suggest a great mystery. "Aren't you going to tell me?"

"I'm not allowed to."

"I thought you enjoyed overstepping marks."

"I do. But you mustn't tell anyone. You, as an observer of marks, will lose your soul if you repeat what I'm about to say. Cynthia Fitch gave her Cruft's application and fee to Hamilton. He said he delivered it to Mrs Murray. She said she never received it. By the time Cynthia found out her application was lost, all the places were filled at the show. One of those two, or both, did the dirty on Cynthia. She was dreadfully upset, of course, and out the money."

"When was this?"

"Early last December, but Cynthia didn't find out until January. A shame, really. Her dog, Titus, has all the makings of a champion. Won two firsts to qualify. Still, he's a young dog, and there's always next year."

"Didn't she think to complain to Cruft's, or to go to the police?"

"Cruft's wouldn't do anything. She spoke to the police about laying charges. They said they could, but the chances of a conviction were low and, as the sum involved was small, was it worth her bother? She decided it wasn't."

"Hmm... There's something that puzzles me. I was informed that Mrs Fitch and Mrs Murray had a dreadful row over how a dog was being trained."

"Which row was that?"

"There was more than one?"

"Good heavens, yes. Putting aside Cynthia's continual and habitual sniping, and long preceding Murray's nobbling the chances of the Alexandra Gardens dogs, there was a first volcanic eruption between them years ago. It is from that point, it's believed, that all the trouble stems. Then there was a period of armed peace. The second cataclysm occurred recently, after the application disappeared. First, Cynthia took against Sandra Pringle for some unknown reason. Soon after, it became ridiculous, really. Mrs Murray, Hamilton, and

Cynthia glossed over the missing application as if nothing had ever happened. Then, dear Cynthia went and meddled with Murray's training. It's her habit to meddle, you know, and that's when the second almighty explosion ripped through Primrose Hill. Everything came crashing down, and they drew up the battle lines."

"Oh, dear. Is it thought that Mr Hamilton might have been the culprit?"

"Well, he wasn't flush with money, but to steal a few shillings from a neighbour in so obvious a way? He wasn't that idiotic. Speaking of which, I'm looking for investors. I need about twenty thousand to fund the launches of both Vita-Bone and Fructo-Fragrante. Do you have any cash? If not, do you know of anyone who has?"

# Chapter 19

# Awkwardness

Sophie had taken so long in the square talking to suspects that, when she returned to the house, visitors had arrived.

"Sorry I'm so late for tea," she said to Ada, as she removed her hat to hang it up.

"Don't be sorry, Miss King," said Ada, removing Biscuit's leash. Then she stood up straight and whispered. "You might wish you'd stayed outside. They're all in there." She nodded towards the parlour and ominously added, "All of them."

Sophie took a breath and opened the door. The parlour occupants had been served tea. Sergeant Gowers and Lord Laneford were discussing football. Archie Drysdale and Nick were playing cards. Inspector Morton, sitting by himself, looked morose and uncomfortable. Mr Breed-Dankworth sat on the settee with another man in his forties and bespectacled, who similarly had that distinguished and commanding appearance of a former military officer. They talked quietly together. Upon Sophie's entrance, they all, as one, stood up.

"Hello," said Sophie, who had not the faintest idea how to proceed.

They greeted her. With that out of the way, and in the two seconds of calm before the inevitable storm of conflicting or puzzling speeches that would bewilder her, Sophie analyzed the situation according to the people present — an office matter, a police report, a marriage proposal, and a row with the Home Office.

"Before we go any further, gentlemen," she said, "I should speak to Nicholas first. Excuse me for a moment, please." She motioned to Nick to come and speak with her.

"Er," he began, awkwardly standing at attention and as sotto voce as a teenaged boy can manage, "Miss Jones says everything's fine, but wants to know when you're coming in next, because she got a few things to tell you, and one of them is, um, private."

"Wednesday, as early as I can." Sophie suddenly feared that Miss Jones might be leaving. "Did she say what the private matter was about?"

"No, miss, but I know what it is." Nick suddenly saw the peril in admitting to spying, but continued anyway. "It's getting noticeable that one of the typists is expectin'."

Sophie, as aware that she and Nick could be overheard by the roomful of men as she was that all her typists were unmarried, said "Oh, how wonderful," in what seemed to Nick a vague kind of way. "Is there anything else?"

"Mr Burroughs paid his account in full."

"I don't believe it!"

"Miss Jones couldn't believe it, neither. But he did. Must have had a winner at the dog track, I reckon."

"Please don't speculate, Nicholas."

"No, miss. Is there anything I can do?"

"Yes. On your way back, go to Parker Street. It's near the Kingsway. Find the Pitman's Company and purchase their book entitled Pitman's Shorthand Rapid Course. Ask Miss Carmichael for the money before you leave here. It used to be three and six, but get five shillings from her."

"Yes, miss. I know the Kingsway, and it's a Shorthand Rapid Course what's wanted. Is that the lot, miss?"

"Be careful on your way back."

"Yes, miss."

He left the parlour.

"Do forgive me, gentlemen, but I wanted him to get somewhere quickly in case the place closed early."

They murmured, in their various ways, how sensible a precaution that was.

"I take it you've all met," said Sophie. "I believe I know why Inspector Morton and Sergeant Gowers are here, but I'm not sure why all you other gentlemen are present."

"Miss King, we shall come to that," began Lord Laneford. "We discussed before your having joined us what the order of precedence should be. Inspector Morton?"

Morton cleared his throat. "Miss King, do you have anything to report on the murder case?"

"Yes, but I need to write it down first. Nothing is immediately actionable, but some interesting lines of potential enquiry are emerging."

"Very good, Miss King. Sergeant Gowers, you may as well go back to the Yard. I'll wait for the report."

"Yes, sir. Goodbye, Miss King. Thank you for the tea. Goodbye, your lordship; gentlemen."

When Gowers left the room, Morton faded into the background, and picked up a book that had four bookmarks protruding from it.

Inspector Morton had been spiralling downwards since his brief meeting with Lady Shelling the evening before. He had gone to number seven for the report — his duty; intent upon asking Sophie to marry him — his desire; and had unexpectedly met Aunt Bessie — his slap in the face. Sophie had been pleasant, as she always was, and Morton did not doubt that Lady Shelling had been thoroughly courteous towards him. But oh, the gulf that had opened at his feet and had widened in his imagination ever since. He had always known that Sophie was a lady, both by breeding and by nature. That she had called Lady Shelling, 'Auntie', and even argued with her slightly — demonstrating that they were equals in so many respects — had given him to understand that, if she should marry him, he would never fit into her world, and she could not fit into his.

'Above his station' — he lashed himself with the phrase. If they were shipwrecked on a desert island, they could have been man and wife and equals. But in Britain, never. It dawned upon him, further lacerating his sense of worth, that, although he told himself he loved her, she had never once given a sign that she reciprocated his feelings. She had been friendly towards him, but no more so than she was to Gowers. Now, with the discovery that Sophie's aunt had a title, was wealthy, and was so remote from his own circumstances in every sense, he came to see that he had been infatuated with Sophie, and his love was one-sided.

They did not need him in the parlour. Indeed, he sensed he was holding up the proceedings. Gripping the book hard, he went to find a quiet place to read the mystery in which everyone was so interested, fully prepared to curse the inept policeman and wretched amateur detective he found within its pages.

"You have met Mr Breed-Dankworth," said Archie to Sophie. "Mr Kell is from the same department."

"Miss King," said Kell. "I'm delighted to make your acquaintance, and apologize for the former misunderstanding. I'm sure we can set everything straight between us."

"I'm sure we can, Mr Kell. Mr Breed-Dankworth, in the same spirit of reconciliation, I hope we can put all previous irritants behind us."

"Of that I'm certain, Miss King."

"Excellent," she said.

"If I might explain what it is we want to do," said Kell, "perhaps you can find a way to facilitate the matter."

"I will try my utmost, Mr Kell."

He smiled. "I'm informed you have a thorough knowledge of the situation on the ground. So, without rehashing everything, what we want is to get full information on the gentleman known as the Doctor. I understand he's rarely seen."

"We saw him for the first time yesterday, and not at all today. He has a very pasty complexion, so I doubt he even uses the back garden at number fifteen."

"A proper recluse. Yesterday, two men had to be identified. We managed one, thanks to Laneford, but the visiting Russian's identity eludes us. We must find out who he is so we can pigeon-hole him."

"I know who he is," said Sophie.

"You do?" asked Kell.

She looked at Archie. He nodded for her to proceed with her explanation.

"I only met him today in the company of Mr Kuritsyn. His name is Vasily Ivanovich Razov, about thirty." While she spoke, all four men took out pens to record the name. "He is a very intense, active man, who comes from the landed classes or nobility. I'm not sure of the terminology used in Russia. He works, at least I was told he works, in the head office of an organization called Centrosojus. During the conversation, he uttered some statistics about factories for no particular reason other than to convince me to become a communist. It struck me as absurd at the time. This was another thing. Apparently, he's learning English, but it sounds very peculiar, and it made me think both men were not being entirely truthful. Overall, his English is good with some rather lamentable and inexplicable lapses. So I don't know if it was just a show or real. The funny thing is, he's giving a speech in Camden this coming Thursday evening, and he's trying to improve his English between now and then by reading Robin Hood, whom he greatly admires."

"You learned all this in a single conversation?" asked Kell.

"Yes, and there's more. I carefully questioned them about the murder and tried not to arouse their suspicions. They gave me no new information and could only offer their opinions. However, because they were blaring away about the glorious revolution, I asked them an awkward question and they couldn't answer it." Sophie laughed. "They said they must refer the question to the Doctor, which means he's the one in charge at the house."

There followed a silence, which was broken by Lord Laneford.

"What question did you put to them?"

"I asked that if someone gave them a hundred thousand pounds, would they redistribute their own wealth? If they did, how much would they give away? That completely flummoxed them. I wish you could have seen their faces."

"I can readily imagine it, Miss King," said Kell, smiling. "Will you attend their meeting?"

"We're all going," said Sophie. She remembered Archie and turned to him. "That's if you think we should."

Archie Drysdale stared at his cousin, knowing full well that if he had not been sitting in the room, she would have gone to the meeting without telling him. They were *all* going, which meant they thought the speech would be hilariously entertaining. He would not upbraid her now, but later... He decided there really was not much point in saying anything. Sophie was, as she had always been, his little cousin who liked adventures, larks, games, and fun. Now she was a spy, and she had hardly changed her habits at all. He could still see the girl in her.

"I think you should go," he said.

"Exactly my thought," said Kell. "I'll send a man separately but, if you can share your findings, Drysdale, I'd be much obliged."

"Of course, sir."

Sophie now wondered who Mr Kell could be. He spoke again.

"We come now to the use of this house as a place of operation. I have no wish to interfere with the police case. Mr Breed-Dankworth needs a man in the attic at all times to observe number fifteen. Miss King, we must be absolutely certain we identify all the important players in this network. There is a high degree of probability that we shall see more agents — Russian or British nationals — visiting number fifteen. Whenever the Doctor goes out, we will follow him. I do not ask that you involve yourself or your agents in any of this. There are three things required of you. The first is that we be given leave to station an officer in the attic. That would relieve you and your agents of the necessity of keeping the square under surveillance. The second is that, during the day, you would be so kind as to assist the officer in the attic by passing any messages he needs sent to the others in his section. The officers present will not make any demands upon your household economy." Kell smiled. "But I'm sure the occasional cup of tea would not go amiss. What do you say?"

"I can agree to all of that, Mr Kell, tea included. However, we rely upon watching suspects in the murder case entering or leaving their houses so that we can time our departures to intercept them. We usually just shout down the stairs. The real difficulty is that Mr Kuritsyn, and possibly the Doctor, are also suspects in the case."

Kell nodded. "Yes, yes." He turned to Breed-Dankworth. "Can your men call out the neighbours as they appear?"

"I don't see why not, sir."

"Is that satisfactory, Miss King?"

"Most satisfactory. I can provide a list of the houses and people we're watching."

"Good. Now the third item is that you would kindly document your meetings with anyone from number fifteen. I'm sure you do so anyway, but we'll need a copy as soon as you can provide one after such a meeting."

"Yes, I can do that."

"Thank you. Those are all our requirements. Do you have any, Miss King?"

"Only that your officers or agents remember that this is a ladies-only house. For example, they must not startle our cook by sudden hammerings on the back door. If a schedule can be organized and adhered to, I believe things can run smoothly."

"We will settle the matter to your satisfaction, Miss King," said Breed-Dankworth.

"Thank you. One concern I have is this. The volume of traffic through our side entrance far exceeds that which is normal. Two houses across the road overlook it and, during the day, they can see everyone. At night, the nearest lamp-post is far enough away that it casts no direct light on the side entrance but, if someone were suspicious, they could still detect a steady stream of people — all men." Sophie began to blush. "Gossip runs through this square faster than anything one cares to name. We cannot allow the frequent use of the side entrance to become known. The Russians will hear of it and be put on their guard."

"Have a word with the occupants across the road," said Kell to Breed-Dankworth. "If necessary, warn them off."

"Right, sir."

"Comments, anyone?" There were none, so he got up. "Thank you very much, Miss King, for being so accommodating. I hope we meet again soon."

"I hope so, too, Mr Kell."

The meeting broke up with only Archie lingering behind.

"Do you know who he is?" he asked.

"A pleasant gentleman from the Home Office."

"That's one way of describing Vernon Kell. I've never seen him so affable before. That you chased off four of his agents with a police dog... well, let me just say this, wonders will never cease."

"Who is he, then?"

"A very important and serious-minded person who bestowed an honour simply by being here. Don't think you've made a friend. It doesn't work like that in the more exalted circles."

"You're all so mysterious."

"Yes. Keep it that way for your sanity's sake. Anyway, I hope you enjoy your meeting with your fellow comrades on Thursday. In the past, I've found such get-togethers on the dull side. They like to use fifty words when five will do."

"Thank you for the warning."

They were on the point of leaving the parlour.

"Archie? Are you still thinking of buying this house?"

"Yes, but the Russians being here complicates matters, so I'm no nearer a decision."

"If you do decide to buy, don't keep a dog."

"Why do you say that?"

"To protect *your* sanity."

In the sitting room upstairs, Sophie and Inspector Morton went through the day's findings. He had watched as she efficiently wrote her notes in shorthand, explaining them to him as she went. She was methodical and concise, and he appreciated the clarity of her reports. Morton could just watch her working and derive pleasure from it, but he was also attentive to what she said.

"This business with the lost application is a puzzler," he said. "Someone's lying. Cynthia Fitch gave it to Hamilton, which he admitted. For her to lie, he'd have to be in on it. Their reason might be to embarrass this Mrs Murray. If Fitch is telling the truth, then Hamilton lied about giving it to Murray. He chucked the application away and put the money in his pocket. Now if Hamilton gave the lot to Murray, then she lied about never receiving it, knowing that Hamilton had given it to her. It would have to be a bald-faced lie on her part... That seems the least likely to me."

"It does to me, too," said Sophie. "Far easier for Mrs Murray would be to accept the application and then have it get lost within the Cruft's system. I don't know how she would do that, but I'm sure there's a way. It would save all the embarrassment of a public row."

"Exactly, Phoebe."

This was the first time Morton had ever called Sophie by her first name, even though it was her alternate one. She gulped.

"So I take it that Mrs Murray is telling the truth," said Morton. "We'll have to interview her, but that'd be after, um, everything you're doing here."

"Yes."

"From what you've learned from Mellish, Mrs Fitch took the loss of the application very hard. Couldn't get her doggy in the show, lost money, and was put out by this underhanded behaviour, as anyone would be, of course. Therefore, Hamilton lied, and mostly did it on his own."

"That's how it seems to me," agreed Sophie.

"Well, the big question is why? They're all chums — supposedly. Why did he nobble her chance at the show?"

"It's very mean-spirited of him if he did. I can't think what he could have had in mind."

"He was getting back at her over something, that's what that was. We need to find out what."

"At the moment, I don't see how anyone can know what it was, except possibly Mr Mellish. He may know, but has chosen not to divulge the details."

"Maybe. I'd like to know, because it might be useful."

"We'll try our best to find out. One thing is for certain — everyone in Alexandra Gardens appears to have sided with Mrs Fitch, and have assumed it was all Mrs Murray's doing. According to our reasoning, it was Mr Hamilton who destroyed the application. They leap-frogged him to blame her. I get the sense that Mr Hamilton was a great friend of Mrs Murray's."

"Yes, he was," agreed Morton. "That came out in a few of the interviews, but this is the first we've heard of the application business. They all kept quiet about that... too quiet."

"Do you mean that some of them, or all of them, believe one of their own number is the murderer?"

"No one volunteered that information, but they had to have been thinking of it as a possibility right enough." He smiled. "The first glimmer of hope in a long while. Something like a motive has popped up."

"Thinking along those lines, it could apply to *any* of them. They're all mad about their dogs, and I believe most, if not all, have entered their dogs in local shows with the view to qualify for Cruft's. So far, I know for certain that Mrs Pringle, Mr Bristow, Mr Mellish, and Mrs Fitch have all had them in Cruft's. The sense I get is that the others have, too. We'll research that point."

"If you could, Phoebe, that would be very kind."

They stared at each other.

"Do you know I've been wanting to speak to you for some time?" Morton struggled.

"Have you?"

"Yes. I, um, I was going to ask you to marry me, but I don't think it would work."

"Oh."

"I'm probably doing this all wrong, but, um, I wanted to tell you how I felt, just so you'd know. That's all... I couldn't help it, and it would be all wrong for us. I know you don't love me. That's obvious, but I just had to say that I have loved you. I can't feel something so strong and then let it go without a murmur. Can you understand what I'm saying?"

Sophie looked at him and compassion welled up. Tears almost did, too. She wanted to touch his arm in the tender affection of friendship, but knew she could not.

"I can sympathize. We can't choose whom we love, and there's nothing wrong with you speaking out. I'm glad that you did, and I truly wish you weren't hurting. I count you as a very dear friend, but I cannot return your love."

In the silence, Morton nodded. "I think I'd better be going." He stood up. "Thank you very much for the report, Miss King. Goodbye."

"Goodbye, Inspector."

# Chapter 20

# The Old Country

"Talk to her," said Flora, holding Biscuit's lead.

She and Sophie were descending the steps of number seven in the early evening.

"No, you talk to her."

Cynthia Fitch was on the other side of the gardens with her dog, Titus.

"You won't patch things up with that attitude."

"I've had a day of it, as you well know, and what with Inspector Morton on top of everything! You start the conversation, and perhaps I'll chime in later."

"Coward."

"Yes, I am, so you go first, and we'll see what happens."

"That's right, leave it all up to me. But if you stand around like a pudding, you're going to look very odd."

"If I'm holding Blast-it, I won't look odd."

"Absolutely not. You've monopolized Biscuit all day, and now it's my turn."

Sophie laughed. "Then I'll be a pudding."

They rounded the hedge to discover Mrs Fitch was in the middle of training Titus. By a series of commands, she was having him walk, stop, sit, lie down, and turn by himself. At the end of the sequence they watched, Mrs Fitch rewarded Titus with a treat.

"Oh, well done, Mrs Fitch," cried Flora.

Sophie grimaced at how false Flora seemed to her, but it was not so for Mrs Fitch. She turned and smiled.

"Yes, he's coming along rather well. Heel." They all drew nearer. "I know I'm rather abrupt sometimes, Miss King, but it's just my manner and I ask you to overlook our past…" she hesitated, trying to find the right word.

"Passage of arms?" suggested Sophie.

"That's it exactly!" She laughed. "You see, I'm interested in doing what's best for the dog, and so I tend to ride roughshod over the owner's feelings."

"We understand," said Flora.

"No need to mention it again, Mrs Fitch," said Sophie.

"I hoped you would understand. And how is… I'll call him Biscuit, if I may. How is he today? He looks in superb condition."

"He's doing very well, thank you," said Sophie, who realized she need not be a pudding after all.

"I notice he's very well behaved. What commands does he know?"

"Oh, the usual," said Flora, trying to recall what they were.

"Please try a few so that I may see."

Flora had him sit, stand, and lie down.

"Very good. Does he ever become overexcited or uncontrollable?"

"No," they both said.

"Would you mind if I tried him?"

"Oh, ah, yes, by all means," said Flora. She handed her the leash.

"Titus, stay." Mrs Fitch then turned her attention to Biscuit. "Walk." They set off together by the side of the hedge. She had a fast, ungainly, almost stomping walk. Her tweed jacket and skirt, and brown hat and shoes were all of a style more often seen in villages or on estates. She gave commands and Biscuit obeyed. Upon their return, Mrs Fitch said,

"He's exceptionally well-behaved. Did you train him?" She couched her simple question in a way that conveyed she did not believe it possible.

Ready for such a probing question, Sophie answered,

"No. We got him through a friend. The gentleman who trained him was in the army, but couldn't look after him anymore."

"Oh, I see. Yes, that makes sense. He obviously knows other commands… There, Titus, you have some competition now."

"Will you enter Titus in Cruft's?" asked Flora.

Mrs Fitch hesitated for a moment. "Next year, I most certainly will."

"Cruft's was last month, wasn't it?" queried Sophie. "I think he might have won if he had entered."

"The competition is fierce, so I don't know about *winning*," she said archly. "Also, there's a lot more to it than just entering a dog in a show. I want him to be at his peak, which he hasn't yet attained. It was too early for him this year."

"We're still learning," said Flora. "It all sounds complicated."

"Yes, there are many factors to be considered, but there's nothing so difficult it can't be dealt with."

There seemed to be no easy way to divert Mrs Fitch into talking about Mr Hamilton and the application, so the conversation drifted to other subjects.

"What do you think of Mr Mellish's dog biscuits?" asked Flora.

"Excellent. Superior to all the other biscuits I've tried."

"That's reassuring," said Sophie. "I was hesitant when he offered some of his latest batch."

"Alan does himself no favours by dressing as he does. I said to him, 'It's hard to take you seriously,' but he doesn't listen. I think he enjoys the role of mad genius, and makes the most of it."

"He comes across like that," said Flora. "Did you find his second batch an improvement on the first?"

"I couldn't really tell the difference, and I had none of the first batch left to compare it to. But when Alan speaks of a batch, he really means he's made a larger quantity than usual for a test. He's always making biscuits for Topper and, if he has a few left over, he shares them with others, whoever he happens to meet."

"In the bags?" asked Sophie.

"Sometimes, but he usually stuffs them loose in his pocket. Is that of interest to you?"

"Not particularly, other than I wish he would sell them. It makes it awkward not being able to buy from him when one wants another bag."

"I understand what you mean, but he won't take money for them. I've tried. He sells his other items, but not the dog biscuits. Alan explained he wants to launch the brand on a large scale and, if he sold them beforehand in dribs and drabs, someone would steal his idea and he'd never get the chance he's hoping for. I can't say I understood exactly what he meant, but he was most emphatic."

"I suspect it's the bone shape," said Sophie. "It's a clever idea. I don't think dogs care what shape they are, but then, they don't have any money. The novelty is designed to appeal to the owners."

"That must be right!" Mrs Fitch laughed. "It certainly worked on me, and I never considered how important the shape must be." Mrs Fitch noticed the position of the sun. "I must give Titus one more turn and then go in. It's my ironing night."

"Your ironing night?" asked Flora.

"Yes. I have a woman come in to do the washing every Monday. She does all the heavy work, but I insist upon doing some of the ironing. Not only because I'm more careful than she, but I also find it very calming. It's been my habit for years, and we're all creatures of habit after all."

"Very much so. Then, good evening, Mrs Fitch," said Sophie. "We won't hold you up."

Sophie and Flora left Alexandra Gardens and walked to the park.

"What do you think?" asked Sophie.

"She can do my ironing any time she likes. I loathe it."

"I know. The thought of ironing a huge pile makes me cringe. Although, once started, it's not so bad."

"Did you see how she dodged the Cruft's question?"

"Avoided it completely with a fib. None of us like bringing up sensitive topics in front of strangers. I don't see how we can mention it again without raising her suspicions or putting her back up."

"We must be sneakier than usual," said Flora.

"I'm all out of sneakiness for the moment. Tell me what you think we should do next."

"I must study the psychology of the Fitch before I can give my answer. However, during my long, cold, lonely vigils in the attic, it crossed my mind that we're all too taken up with dog biscuit bags. I looked in the file at the list of things Mr Hamilton had in his pocket. Outside of the expected handkerchief, loose change, etc., there were several items of interest to which we should turn our attention."

"Please continue. I'm fed up with dog biscuits."

"Not literally, I hope. Cranky Mellish didn't persuade you to eat one?"

"Not yet. Go on."

"There was a communist tract. So, I ask myself, when did Mr Hamilton put the tract in his pocket? This could be of great significance."

"Yes, I suppose it could. We'll look into it. What's next?"

"A booklet describing the virtues of Mr Mellish's chemical products. I ask myself the same question. Was it in his pocket for a week, a day, an hour, or a minute? Had Mr Mellish given the booklet to Hamilton and then killed him?"

"When he received the booklet should be verified. Cranky says he was in his workshop at the time of the murder."

"So he says, but can we trust him? Who saw him?"

"We can ask Inspector Morton that. The police must have confirmed everyone's stories as far as they could."

"Now we come to the business card belonging to Miss Villard. I say to myself, 'Why does Mr Hamilton keep the business card of Miss Villard in his pocket?' They are near neighbours, are they not? *She* has a telephone. The question first to be answered is, 'Did Mr Hamilton also have a telephone?' If not, then no matter. It is of no consequence. But if he did? Then, it is highly suggestive, yes?'"

"I know where you're getting this from. You're acting like Poirot in the book."

"Non! How could you even think such a thing, mon amie? Please, let us continue, my dear Phoebe. Last is the cinema ticket stub. Not just any cinema, but the very one where Mr Clark works. Why does Mr Hamilton keep the ticket stub? As a memento because they are friends? Non. All the men detest Mr Hamilton, yet all the ladies sigh when he is near. He and Mr Clark are not friends. But consider this, my dear Phoebe. Does not La Pringle make the eyes at Monsieur Hamilton? Certainement. And does not Monsieur Clark make the eyes at Madame La Pringle? Oui. Therefore, Monsieur Hamilton decides to kill Monsieur Clark, because he wants to eliminate his rival. He attends the cinema where he works to study his victim. He is making the preparations, deciding how he shall approach the matter. However, Monsieur Clark sees Monsieur Hamilton in the audience. His thoughts fly to Madame La Pringle and how his enemy steals her from him. He goes mad with jealousy and thoughts of vengeance. The audience, they hear it in his music — the passion, the towering rage, the death blow. Clark, immersed in a tempest of music, decides Hamilton must die!

"Two nights later, he gets his chance because there is a fog. Clark lives close to the murder scene, non? He hears Hamilton talk to his dog outside. He creeps from the house, et voilà, he strikes his enemy dead while the cinema ticket that explains everything is still in the victim's pocket."

"Oh, Gladys, *really*."

"I'm not making light of it. I'm trying to analyze the evidence like a real detective. I thought it was rather good."

"It was very good and just like the book... and it's quite thought provoking. But that's absolute rubbish about the cinema ticket. It explains nothing."

"I know. I wanted to add a bit of drama, so I took what I thought was the least important item and make it crucial to the exposition. Mr Hamilton probably just stuffed things in his overcoat pockets as a matter of course, and turned them out only every so often."

"It's funny how a little thing can suddenly seem so important because Mr Hamilton died. Am I to understand that he went to the cinema two days before his murder?"

"That's what it said in the file."

"I must have missed that."

They walked a few paces before Sophie spoke again.

"Suppose Hamilton spoke to Clark after he had finished playing. They *might* have talked about La Pringle."

"There's no way we can find that out without going to the cinema."

"Yes. One of the cinema staff may have noticed them. I mean, they would if there had been a heated discussion."

"Why not ask Inspector Morton to interview the staff?"

"Could you do it? I'm not sure I can face him again just yet."

"Of course, I will."

---

It was after dinner, and Sophie, Ada, and Flora were relaxing in the parlour. The overhead light was off and the room lit by warm pools of light emanating from a standard lamp and two table lamps. A faint tick from the clock on the mantlepiece, a settling of burning coals in the grate, and a gentle snore coming from the dog on the rug were the only sounds.

"I have to go to the office Wednesday morning," said Sophie, throwing away a five of diamonds.

Ada picked it up. "Will you be there all day, miss?" She re-ordered her hand, then put down a card.

"No." Sophie drew a card and discarded it. "Just a few things to sort out."

Ada picked up the card.

"You're picking up everything I throw away," said Sophie.

"That's because you dealt me a hand what looks like a foot."

Sophie laughed. "I must remember that one."

"Shh!" Flora was lying on the settee reading.

"Sorry," said Sophie. She and Ada grinned at each other.

The card game continued in whispers, Biscuit dozed, and Flora read.

"Finished!" she called, then came over to the table. She looked at Sophie's hand.

"Away with you," said Sophie, hiding her cards.

Flora looked at Ada's hand before joining them at the table.

"Did you solve the mystery?" asked Sophie.

"No. It was awfully clever, though... I'm annoyed with Sidney. He finished before I did and then had the cheek to write 'The Winner' on the paper he used for his bookmark."

"Did Lord Laneford work out who done it?" asked Ada.

"He says he did, but I don't believe him."

"Do you mean to tell us he read the entire book while he was 'ere?" exclaimed Ada.

"Apparently."

"I'm not being rude or nothing, miss, but what does Lord Laneford do?"

"Yes, I'd like to know that," said Sophie.

"As far as I can tell, he drifts from meeting to meeting just being himself. Sometimes, there are no meetings, so then he's just Sidney, twiddling through life. Honestly, his reading that book is the most work I've ever known him to do."

"Come off it, he must do something."

"Nothing discernable. I think he makes decisions once in a while, and that's about it. He knows a lot about finance and spying, so I suppose those are what he discusses with his counterparts, but he won't tell me anything. He also likes cricket and fly-fishing, and I suspect those are the actual things they discuss, and the fate of the nation is secondary."

"That's right an' all," said Ada. "Remember that dinner party we did in Grosvenor Square? I 'eard an American navy captain and a British captain talking. What were they discussing? The war? Who's navy has the best ships? No, none of that. They was talking about which country made the best teddy bear."

"How did they decide?" asked Sophie.

"They're probably still arguing. They was polite, though. The American was goin' to send one from Macy's when he got back, and the British captain was sending one from 'amleys, sorry, Hamley's. There you are, teddy bears, that's what they all talk about. Well, things like that, anyway."

Before anyone answered, someone rapped gently on the door. They looked at each other, puzzled.

"Come in," called Sophie.

The Home Office agent from the attic put his head in while keeping the door barely open. He stared briefly at Biscuit, who stared back from his comfortable place on the rug.

"Excuse me for interrupting you, but Kuritsyn is walking his dog in the square. I didn't shout because I didn't want to disturb the house."

"Thank you for informing us," said Sophie.

"Oh, not at all, not at all. Good night." He shut the door.

"He's scared of Biscuit," said Flora quietly.

"Yes. Um, what to do?" mused Sophie. "I don't think we can go out unaccompanied."

"We'll have Biscuit with us, and *he's* a boy," said Flora. "Does that count?"

"I don't think so."

"Mrs Pringle goes out at night with her dog," said Ada.

"Of course, she does! Then that makes it all right for us. Let's go."

Biscuit was ready first. Sophie and Flora hurriedly put on their coats and hats, and Ada closed the door behind them after they left.

"Ah! Comrades Misses Walton and King! How are you this fine evening?"

"Very well, thank you," said Flora.

"We had to come out because of the, you know, the dog." Sophie rushed out her excuse.

"Of course, of course."

"How is Comrade Razov getting on with his English?"

"Hmm, I tell you this privately. He improves, but he's still an embarrassment. I have doubts about his coming speech. Hopefully, he will keep it short, but probably not."

"What book is he reading now?" asked Flora, who had heard all about Mr Razov.

"I got a pile of secondhand books very cheap from the man at the Bomb Shop in Charing Cross Road. But Razov is reading through them too quickly. He can't be taking everything in. Tonight, he started Alice in Wonderland. It will cause trouble. The story might even destroy his mind. I hate to think what will come out of his mouth after he's read it."

The conversation was proving difficult for both women. Sophie governed herself enough to say,

"Did you know Comrade Razov in Russia? I have the impression you did."

"Yes. I am from Yaroslavl, a town north-east of Moscow. Now, what I am about to tell you goes no further. All comrades are very sensitive about their past before the revolution."

"We promise not to breathe a word of anything you say," said Flora.

"Say none of this to Razov. Understood?"

"Absolutely, we understand," said Sophie.

"Very good. I trust you, comrades. Before the war, my family sold agricultural machinery. Some of it came from Britain. That was the reason I learned English, to permit me to talk to the representatives if their Russian was bad.... Vova, come away from that. You don't know what it is." He pulled on Vova's leash. "Dogs are disgusting sometimes."

"Yes, they can make things awkward," said Sophie.

"Very true. Now, Comrade Razov comes from an old family which had an estate of eight hundred souls near to Yaroslavl. Yes, a big one. Often, the chief of the estate would come to my father's warehouse. Sometimes, the Count would visit, and he would bring his son, Vasily. That is how we met. I am older, but we talked together, and he was all right for one of the nobility. But neither of us can mention our past, now that we are comrades in the revolution."

"How dreadful it all must have been for you," said Sophie.

"Dreadful?" He paused for a moment. "No. Communism is the best thing for mankind since the invention of the wheel. It liberates all the workers."

"How did you become a communist?" asked Flora.

"It's a long story that won't interest you."

"Yes, it will," said Sophie.

"You really want to know?"

They both nodded.

"Do either of you have a cigar or a cigarette? I'm all out."

"Sorry," said Sophie.

"No, I didn't think you would. The Kuritysn family used to be prosperous and had an excellent reputation. We lived well, and had a beautiful house, servants, carriages, and motor cars when they came. The family business was important to the area, and we had no competition. We brought in the first tractors, sold trucks, and had an interest in the Automobile Works. While we are busy with the family business, everywhere people talk of socialism. For a long time we all think it is just talk. Even though there are troubles, we think them temporary, that it will all go away."

He sighed deeply and played with the end of Vova's lead.

"The war came, and it was a disaster for Russia because of poor leadership and lack of ammunition. That led to the February Revolution in 1917. Between the war and the revolution, we Kuritsyns woke up. My father died. In a way, it was a blessing he did. His death left me as the head of the family. I could see plainly how it was going, so I sent my mother and younger brothers and sisters to America. Others in the family went around the same time. One uncle said he would go to New Zealand. We all think, 'Why would you choose New Zealand? It's so far away,' but, because nobody liked him, we encouraged him to go."

"Seeing your family split up must have been very difficult for you."

"Heartbreaking, Comrade Miss Walton, but there was no choice. We were of a class that was hated, and the government had fallen to pieces. Who shall protect us? No one. We must do what we must do. So, I stay behind in the hopes I can salvage something. My mother takes some valuables, but others I hid in the forest. I kept the business going, but it became more difficult each week. The worse part is no one knows what they are doing or what will happen next. I think to myself, if I stay, they will kill me. So, me and Vova, we go into the forest. I build cabin, take supplies of food and tobacco, and wait."

"That was rather brave," said Sophie. "I can't imagine living in a forest by myself."

"There were many people hiding in the forest. It wasn't so bad. I met a sweetheart at a meeting we had. It was a fine gathering. There was roast boar, music, dancing, you could get a haircut, and someone who ran a still kept everyone supplied. It was like English village fete under the trees with vodka."

"How extraordinary," said Sophie.

"Yes, but it all ended. After October Revolution, a Bolshevik government was installed in Yaroslavl, but they had the brains of a flea. They shoot some people and seize everything. However, they couldn't be bothered to come and find us because *we* shot at *them*. They left us alone, because there were troubles enough in Yaroslavl. However, the winter was hard, and many returned to Yaroslavl or wherever they came from. Then, in the summer of 1918, there was an anti-Bolshevik rebellion. A big one, because the White Russians believed France would help them. Savinkov, a socialist, hated Lenin, and was in control. He captured Yaroslavl and shot all the Bolsheviks. Then, everyone is shooting everyone. I think to myself, Who should I shoot? I couldn't decide, so I got more supplies and went back to the forest with Vova.

"It didn't take long before the Red Army arrived in force. There was a huge battle. I heard the Red Latvian Riflemen were among them, and I say to myself, why are the Latvians in Yaroslavl? I think more and ask myself, why are Germany, Austro-Hungary, Mongolia, Persia, Britain, France, America, Japan and the Ottomans in Russia? Then there are the separatists of Poland, Ukraine, Belarus, Finland, and the rest of them. It's too many. Much too much. So, I decide, whoever wins in Yaroslavl will win everything in the end. The Bolsheviks won, so that settled it. Of course, they shot everyone, and I couldn't stay where I was, so I left the forest and became a good Bolshevik. I put a cut on my head. Here." He showed how and where. "I acted like a crazy man. I told them me and Vova got into a fight while chasing anti-revolutionaries, and I blacked out and didn't know where I was. They believed me."

"Couldn't you have escaped to another country?" asked Flora

"I might have got through, I don't know. I left it much too late to try, because I was happy in the forest."

"What a fascinating story," said Sophie. "I imagine Comrade Razov had a similar experience."

"Do not ask him about it, for his own safety."

"We won't do that," said Flora. "Something we've been meaning to ask you. Has Vova been at Cruft's? Mrs Fitch suggests we enter Biscuit."

"No! Cruft's is a decadent, bourgeois, imperialist show. No self-respecting comrade would think of such a thing!" He lowered his voice. "Now, if I entered Vova and he happened to win the championship, they would erect statue to him in Russia. If he won first in class, he would get medal. If he won nothing, we would both get bullets. Besides, he has no papers."

"You mean the breeding paper things," said Sophie.

"Yes."

"Those are important. And what is this controversy between Mrs Fitch and Mrs Murray?"

"I can't stand listening to it," said Kuritysn, raising his free hand expressively. "Everyone talks about an application form. It's so petty. It's obvious Hamilton took the money. Arrest him, don't arrest him, but stop talking about it. Anyway, he's dead, so it's all over."

"Why would he *do* that?" asked Flora.

"Maybe he wanted a drink. He drank, he fell down, he lost the paper, then he lied. Simple."

"You don't think there was anything going on between Mr Hamilton and Mrs Fitch?" asked Sophie.

"What do you mean, comrade?"

"Like a business venture or something of a more personal nature."

Kuritsyn breathed in through his nose and the corners of his mouth drooped.

"She's a widow with a good house and an income. Very desirable. Of course, he wanted to marry her. He would marry any woman who came with property and an income."

"But what were her feelings towards him?" asked Flora.

"I don't know. Why don't you ask her, comrade?"

"She wouldn't tell us if we did, so we shan't ask."

"Then why would she tell me?"

"Sorry, I shouldn't have asked. I'm just very curious about it."

"Well, all I can say is that if she had a passion for him, she hid it well. But remember, she's a very strange woman. Cynthia's passion, assuming she had any, might come out in an unrecognizable way."

"Such as?" asked Sophie.

"Hmm. Cynthia is devoted to dogs. Lives, thinks, and breathes dogs. So! Her desire for Hamilton might have appeared if she made a big fuss over his dog. I say *if* because I don't know that she did. It's a nice dog, a Sheltie. The people in the pub have stolen him... That gives me an idea! Perhaps they killed Hamilton to get his dog."

"I don't think they did that," said Sophie.

"You never know, comrade."

"I suppose not."

"Time for me to go. I have performed the security check of the area and must report my findings. I will say, I met two very good communist sympathizers who are likely to join the revolution on Thursday, only if the speech is kept short." Kuritsyn laughed with a deep, sudden immensity that surprised his audience. "Good night, comrades."

"Good night, Comrade Kuritsyn," they replied.

He walked away humming — basso profondo — a Russian song that pre-dated the revolution.

# Chapter 21

## Shockwaves

Mrs Barker was awake before her alarm went off. She stared into the gloom of her bedroom, worrying about ghee. It was Tuesday. She had fretted about many meals over the years, especially dinners for important guests, but today she was beyond fretting. None of her usual coping tactics served her purpose. Being that hardworking type of cook who prepares ahead, she usually pictured the proper sequence not only of every dish, but every part of every dish, because of her long experience and natural flair. To her, it was just a question of putting in the work at the right time and, if anything went wrong, she could always substitute. She had never really suffered a culinary disaster thanks to her organizing abilities. When a large tom cat had run off with a roasted leg of lamb and hid with it under a bed, where, on hands and knees, she had to fight him for possession, even that near disaster had turned into a triumph by her quick repairs to the savaged joint of meat and a sauce which disguised the fact that she had had to wash the lamb to remove fluff. After the diners had partaken of the leg of lamb, they summoned her to the table. On her way to the dining room, she had felt as though she were about to faint, so nervous was she as to what was going to be said. However, the summons had been only to commend her for such excellent cooking. Mrs Barker could deal with any circumstance, and any menu — *if* it were European. But India was in Asia and there they used spices of which she had never heard to make things with which she was completely unfamiliar. Everything she knew did not apply. This left her feeling like a kitchen maid on her first day at work, certain someone would shout at her least mistake. Irritated at being beset by repetitive and inconclusive thoughts, she got up to switch off her alarm before it rang. Then she washed and dressed.

In the morning, the rooms at the front of the house were gloomy. Conversely, the rooms at the back, including the kitchen, were quite bright. It was still dark outside at present but, later, the sun would stream through the kitchen windows. She liked that because, when she sat down with her tea at the kitchen table, the light's reflection from the liquid made a bright dancing shape on the wall, which amused her. As she put the kettle on, she looked through a window for a trace of the dawn, but there was none.

Mrs Barker was long habituated to the dawn and found nothing poetic in it. Instead of the sunrise, she much preferred electric lightbulbs, which she still considered a miracle, and was happy to have two of them in her kitchen. It was *her* kitchen, of course. She had reorganized it to make it so. Granted, it could do with a new chopping board, and some of the knives needed proper sharpening but, overall, it was a decent kitchen, in a decent house, in a decent neighbourhood. Apart from the cold shelf which she would have liked to take with her when she left, what Mrs Barker truly appreciated was that everything came to hand so readily. Some kitchens in which she had worked were the size of a warehouse and about as cheerful as one. Others had a more medieval theme, possessing the gloom of the dungeon, and with kitchen equipment that seemed to be dual-purposed for use in a torture chamber.

She got a few things ready while she had her tea and then she wandered into the parlour. The room felt quite warm from the previous night's fire, so Mrs Barker, curious about all the goings-on in Alexandra Gardens, pulled the curtains back to peer into the square. It was still dark outside. For two seconds she stood there, looking along St George's Road where the street lamps were brighter. She noticed the dark shape of a stationary man at the edge of a lighted area opposite number three — about forty yards away. He was hard to distinguish, and impossible to identify. While she watched him, he partially turned in a sudden movement. Mrs Barker heard the cry of a man in pain, saw the man stumble back, and then fall to the ground. She gaped. Someone came running down the stairs shouting.

"*Oh, mercy!* Whatever next!?" she, almost breathlessly, said to herself. Then she remembered the officer awake in the attics. As she entered the hall, the agent was on the last flight with Biscuit close on his heels.

"A man's been attacked in the street," said the officer in commanding urgency. "You must help him. I can't — the operation. I'll send someone, but go, and shout loudly to scare off the attacker."

She stared at him.

"Go, woman!"

"Yes," she said.

She hurried out hatless, coatless, but carrying an umbrella as if she meant to stab someone with it. Biscuit went with her.

"Leave him alone!" Shouting belligerently, Mrs Barker bustled down the steps, while the dog raced towards the prostrate figure.

---

By 8:30, many inhabitants in the area had become acquainted with the name of Mrs Barker. The fame of a cook depends normally upon her kitchen skills. Mrs Barker was now famous for saving a man's life, and going after his attackers with either a rolling pin or an umbrella, accompanied by her trusty dog. Because the Home Office agent in the attics could not appear in the matter, her modified statement to the police unavoidably gave the impression that she alone had heard a man's cry, and had rushed out at once with no thought for her own safety.

The excitement of the affair was now dying down because Alexandra Gardens had to earn a living. The police took Mrs Barker's statement after the man had been taken by ambulance to a nearby hospital. Now, Mrs Barker, ensconced in the parlour, was regaling her attentive audience with an account of the incident. Myrtle, who had already heard it all three times, also listened spellbound.

"As soon as I heard that *dreadful* cry, like that of a lost soul it was, I knew I had to help the poor man. So I went into the hall and, just then, that man from the attic came down. He said he couldn't go into the street on account of the operation. I thought at first he meant he'd had a surgery, but, of course, he didn't. He meant the Russian case. So I said I'd go out and see that everything was all right. I didn't like the idea, but I made up my mind there and then to do it.

"Usually, I don't take kindly to dogs, but Biscuit is one of the best. What a lovely dog. All quiet and good manners, but brave as *anything* when he has to be. I hope you get to keep him, Miss King."

"Unfortunately, we can't."

"And we can't steal him," said Flora, "because the Yard would be on to us straightaway."

"I know what you mean, Miss Walton. Such a pity. You should have seen him, though. He stood over that poor fellow like he was saving his own master. I've *never* witnessed such a thing."

"How long did it take you to reach Mr Clark from the time you heard the cry?" Sophie was taking notes.

"Less than a minute."

"And the street was empty?"

"As far as I could tell, it was. It was dark, and there were plenty of places for someone to hide or creep away in the shadows, but not along St. George's Road. I'd swear to that." Mrs Barker suddenly laughed. "I already *have* sworn it — to the policeman!" She laughed again.

"Was Biscuit looking in any direction in particular?" asked Ada.

"I don't think he did, and I made a point of taking notice of him."

"Were there any odd noises or sounds of doors shutting?" asked Flora.

"No, it was as quiet as the grave. That is, until everyone started coming out."

"This part interests me very much," said Sophie. "Take your time, Mrs Barker, and try to remember in what order they arrived, and how they were dressed."

"The first was the old gentleman, Mr Owen, as I found out, from number four. He was in his dressing gown. Between us, we made poor Mr Clark comfortable. He went for a blanket, a cushion, a bowl of water and a towel, because he said, with a head wound like that, we shouldn't move Mr Clark. I completely agreed with him."

"Did Mr Clark say anything?"

"He wasn't unconscious, but he was woozy. He tried to get up and said, 'I must go.' When we stopped him, he said, 'I have to tell Sandra.' Otherwise, he only groaned and fidgeted."

"What happened next?"

"A woman came out of number three and said she would telephone the police. Mr Owen told her to call for an ambulance as well. Then, one of the Russians came over. He was dressed for work and, although he couldn't speak any English, he knew exactly what to do. Very gently, he made Mr Clark keep his head still. I wondered what he was doing at first, but then, in Russian, mind you, he spoke to him like a baby, all soft and cooing. That settled Mr Clark right down. Then Farhan, Major Cummings' servant, came over, and he had brought a blanket for me. Wasn't that thoughtful of him? And do you know what? He speaks perfect English, and I was *that* surprised. I suppose he was fully dressed. He had on that long tunic coat. He was very nice to me, and asked what had happened, and then we got talking. Do you know, ghee is only clarified butter? I had been worried about it, and I needn't have been, after all."

"I think he was keeping you company, in case you were upset," said Flora.

"Well, he was, really, come to think of it. How kind of him."

"I thought it was jee," said Ada.

"So did I, but, no, it's ghee, and he says it so beautifully. Have a listen to how he speaks whenever you get a chance." Mrs Barker turned to Sophie. "There was a bit of a lull, and then a good few came out all at once. Captain Bristow was first in his dressing gown. He brought that great big dog of his. It's a silly creature, and kept jumping about and the Captain could barely control it. Not like Biscuit, who's a wonderful dog. Wonderful. So well behaved he's almost human. Then about three turned up together, including Miss Villard's maid, who was dressed. Then came, er, Mr Saunders in his pyjamas, wearing an overcoat over the top. He was very concerned and helpful. There were a lot of others, some were just looking. After the police constable arrived, Mrs Fitch came out, and she was dressed. Then you and Nancy. You saw for yourselves the arrival of Mr Mellish, and Mr Kuritsyn... I don't think I remember any more."

"Lots of people on their way to work were staring," said Ada.

"I wanted to throw something at the nosey parkers," said Mrs Barker.

"It *was* annoying," said Sophie. "We were just in time to see Mrs Pringle."

"*Quite* the exhibition," said Mrs Barker primly. "She obviously has feelings for him, but to let herself go like that."

"She thought he was dead," said Ada.

"I know, but he was better by the time she saw him. If she'd stopped for one second, she would have seen he was not so badly off."

"I tried speaking to the constable," said Sophie. "He wouldn't tell me anything. All he kept saying was, 'Move back, please,' and that type of thing."

"Coppers never will tell you what you want to know," said Ada.

"I did hear him say the assailant might have used a hatchet," said Mrs Barker. "There was some blood coming from his head, and more from his left shoulder. He couldn't move his arm. I reckon it was his hat that saved him from being done in."

"Was it as if the attacker aimed for his head, but the blow somehow glanced off and struck Mr Clark's shoulder?"

"Oh, to think of such wickedness! It has to be something like that, Miss King, although I wouldn't know."

"Perhaps we'll learn more later. I think that's all for now. If you remember anything, Mrs Barker, be sure to tell me. And may I say this on behalf of us all, you behaved splendidly in a very difficult and dangerous situation."

"Yes, you did, Mrs Barker," said Ada.

"Absolutely marvellous," said Flora.

"Well done, Mrs Barker," said Myrtle.

"I don't know what to say. Thank you, but please — not another word or you'll have me in tears, that you will."

"We can't have that," said Sophie, smiling, "when we have to prepare for the training session at Major Cummings' house, or would you rather put it off?"

"No, Miss King. I'm as fit as a fiddle, and I couldn't bear to miss it."

Before they went, Sophie reviewed her notes on the case. She consulted the blackboard with the odds listed by each name and changed Mr Clark, Mystery Man, to 200/1. He seemed now to be the least likely to have murdered Mr Hamilton, unless there were a convoluted set of circumstances wherein someone knew Clark had murdered Hamilton and had then zealously set out to avenge him. She deemed the scenario so implausible it was not worth serious consideration. Glancing down the list, she pondered a question. If Mr Clark was less likely to have killed Hamilton, did it make everyone else more likely to be the murderer? If so, how should the odds be adjusted to reflect the change? She decided such calculations were Hawkins' department, so she had better send a message to her Aunt Bessie.

Although number nine was only two doors along and the house was in almost every respect identical to number seven, when Farhan opened the front door with a silent bow, Mrs Barker and Sophie knew they were entering an abode that was altogether as different as could be. Despite the building having the same proportions, it was unrecognizable to them as being of the same London terrace that they themselves inhabited. It took only a few cues, but the women, without remarking the fact, felt they had been transported to India. Simla, the town with a temperate climate in the forested foothills of the Himalayas — Sophie had read and idly dreamt about it, but really knew nothing of the place. Today, she somehow felt she was there.

The interior had a spareness of decoration bordering on austerity. The sideboard in the hall was of a lighter hue than was typical of most British furniture, and certainly possessed more drawers, which had round rings for pulls, recessed in metal scallops. It seemed a practical and sturdy design, the type an army officer might choose because it was serviceable and durable. Although the sideboard was the focal point in the hall, its light chestnut wood with a golden overtone looked well against a pale orange wall. Her eye travelled further and, although all the woodwork was white, the walls were different hues — light tan, yellow, or orange, which gave an overall impression of warmth and cheerfulness. There was also a scent to the place, but it was faint and elusive, as if incense had been burnt several days ago, leaving the merest suggestion of jasmine and sandalwood. Sophie looked at Mrs Barker. Farhan was helping the cook with her coat. She realized they should both be wearing saris to fit in properly. Just then, Major Cummings descended the stairs, which were carpeted with a Turkoman runner. He wore a light cotton jacket of a green that suggested both an army uniform and the verdancy of a lush forest. It was not a British colour, neither did the jacket have a European cut.

"Good morning, Miss King and Mrs Barker. I trust you are both recovered from the ugly episode?"

They both greeted him.

"Thank you for inquiring. We're all right so far," said Sophie. "Although it's Mrs Barker we should be concerned about."

"Thank you, sir," said Mrs Barker, clutching a shopping bag. "I'm fully recovered, and am glad that Mr Clark is no worse off than he is. It could have been very nasty."

"So true. By the time Farhan informed me of what had happened, I could see there was little point in my coming out and only adding to the number of useless bystanders." He paused to smile at Mrs Barker. "Shall we proceed? The kitchen is downstairs."

Farhan noiselessly disappeared down the open staircase to the basement. The Major preceded the ladies saying, "I cannot express how thrilled I am at your participation in this little test."

"I'm looking forward to the results," said Sophie.

"I'll do my best," said Mrs Barker, still nerve-wracked at the thought of the coming ordeal.

The kitchen was spacious and the creamy-white walls brightened it considerably. Mrs Barker could see everything was clean and orderly — that is, until she surveyed the gas stoves. One was an ordinary British stove and well-cared for. A foot from it was what Mrs Barker assumed had to be a stove, but it was a jumble of iron pipes and hotplates, with a rough-looking box for an oven below. Use had heavily blackened every part.

The Major was talking. It was often his way to explain many things before he explained the one about which his listener wanted to know. He was pedantic without being boring. His pedantry revealed he was methodical and organized and, if he lacked the ardour of a zealot, he possessed the obsession of one who thoroughly knows his subject and wishes to communicate what he knows. He could pick a spice at random, as he did now, and explain its history, its cultural significance and symbolism, where the best was produced in India, and where it could be obtained at a reasonable cost in Britain. He finished up by saying,

"I've spoken for far too long. Now it's time for Farhan to give a small demonstration."

Farhan stepped forward, having exchanged his coat for an apron.

"Permit me, memsahib," he said to Mrs Barker, "to demonstrate the cooking of a poppadom."

He floured a large, flat board on the kitchen table. "I use gram flour, which is ground chickpeas, but you can use urad, lentil flour." His voice sounded like warm honey.

He removed a muslin cloth from a bowl and took out a round lump of dough. He pointed to it. "Gram flour, chili — not too much — coarse ground black pepper and cumin seeds. The recipe is in the Sahib's most excellent book soon to be published and enjoyed by all the British public." He broke off three walnut-sized pieces of dough. Then he took the thinnest rolling pin Mrs Barker had ever seen and rapidly rolled out a piece. His hands were quick, and his long fingers stiff, curving upwards, as he controlled the movement of the pin with the palms of his hands. The dough was now circular and thin, speckled with black pepper and cumin seeds. He approached the unusual cooker, turned a tap and lit a gas ring. A tall, roaring flame sprang up. With deft movements, he held a shallow frying pan and warmed oil in it over the flame before lowering the heat. He transferred the poppadom from the board to the pan. Within seconds, it was transfigured from raw to crisp. He put the wafer on a plate.

"Please to try it, memsahibs."

He quickly rolled out and cooked two more before his entranced audience had tasted anything. When they did, they responded enthusiastically.

"I've never tasted anything so unusual and wonderful," said Sophie, breaking off another crisp piece.

"Did you see how quick it cooked?" said Mrs Barker, visibly impressed. Then she added, "It's very nice."

"Memsahib Barker," said Farhan. "I have an apron for you to use. Now it is your turn on the British stove."

"Right, Mr Farhan," said Mrs Barker, seizing the apron from him. "I've been looking forward to this." She was raring to go.

Sophie's main purpose for being at number nine was to find something — anything that might tie Major Cummings to Hamilton's death. She hoped she might snoop unobserved, even if in a limited way. The Major accompanied her upstairs, which disallowed any searching on her own.

"I must say, Major Cummings, I very much admire how you've decorated your house."

"That's kind of you, Miss King. Actually, although I may take credit for overseeing the renovations, the inspiration was my wife's. We often discussed how we would set up a house in England, and she wanted the warm colours that reminded her of India."

"How lovely."

"Would you like to see a few of the rooms?"

"I would indeed... Have you removed some walls?"

"Yes, they were only partition walls. So do not fear; the roof shan't cave in. I particularly wanted to open up the basement."

He opened the door on a lounge that was furnished with good Georgian furniture and a pair of modern, dark blue leather sofas. The walls were warm yellow, and the Major had chosen several good European paintings for their vibrant contrasting colours. Covering the dark wooden floor was a large intricately patterned rug, primarily in rose red and orange. There were a few Indian decorative pieces, mostly brass, but the room itself said 'India' in some subtle, quiet way. Sophie assumed it was the association of ideas more than anything she could see. She would never have imagined such an interior, yet its serenity pleased her. Glancing sideways at the Major, she noted that, although he was talkative on his pet subjects, he was otherwise quiet, as he was now. A man at peace with himself. How could he then be a murderer?

"This is a lovely room," said Sophie.

"Thank you. I've always enjoyed it. Friends visit less frequently than they used to, but we often spent hours and hours in here just talking." He smiled. "Retired army officers talking about the old days in India, Burma, and Afghanistan. How dreadfully boring we would seem to an outsider."

"I'm sure you all had many interesting stories."

"Many, Miss King, although we've all heard them so often."

"I haven't. But there's one story I'm really interested in. How is it that Farhan has followed you from India?"

Major Cummings smiled. "His name is Farhan Cummings. My wife and I adopted him."

"Oh," said Sophie, very surprised and having several thoughts start at once. She did not know quite what to say next.

"You see him as my servant," said Cummings, "but that is by *his* choice, not mine or my wife's. If you care to hear it, I could tell you his story."

"I am very much fascinated, Major."

"Please," he said, offering her a seat.

Sophie sat on one of the comfortable sofas while the Major spoke.

"In many Indian villages, there has been a longstanding custom for dealing with people when they are sick. They are taken to the priest who employs traditional medicines to treat the patient. Some medicines are efficacious, some are harmless and do nothing. Some diseases, as you know, are not treatable. Then the only recourse the priest and the village have for a serious, wasting disease is to isolate the patient — much the same as we do in hospitals. For some types of disease, they install the patient in a particular hut, hoping he or she will recover. The priest may recognize that the disease is virulent and the patient will die. This is when they send the patient into the forest to wait out their time."

"How dreadful," said Sophie.

"It seems so to us, but similar practises are still quite widespread around the world. In part, they do it to appease the local deity, so that no further misfortune befalls the tribe or village, and, in part, as a practical procedure to stop the contagion from spreading to others. Often, children are patients, and it must be heartbreaking for a mother to take her child to the priest or shaman, and then be told the only thing to do is to abandon the child in the wilderness."

"I can't imagine how horrific that must be."

"Occasionally, the child survives and is restored to his parents. Even rarer is that the child wanders away and survives on its own."

"Like Mowgli in Jungle Book?"

Major Cummings nodded and smiled. "Farhan was one such child, only he wasn't raised by wolves, Miss King. He became feral and eked out a wild existence by finding food in the forest and stealing from villages and small holdings. Villagers often drove him away with stones.

"As luck would have it, my wife and I were visiting a friend's house, a captain, a mile away from where Farhan was captured. Some villagers and two soldiers had caught him and sent word to their captain. Imagine it, a wild naked boy, some eight or nine years old, who cannot speak or understand any language, and who has lived by his wits for several years. He was suspicious, frightened, and ready to bite and scratch. When first meeting Farhan, he actually snarled at us like a dog. The only thing he understood at the time was food, and he ate it like an animal.

"There's a great deal more to tell, as you can imagine. Almost immediately, my wife took charge of him and started the slow process of winning his trust. My goodness, she was so patient, and wouldn't give up." Cummings sighed. "He was tremendously difficult, and there were many setbacks, but she stuck to him."

"Your wife must be an angel."

He answered slowly, "Yes, she was." He got up. "After a year, you wouldn't have recognized him, would not ever have imagined he had such a past. He learned Hindi, some Bengali from the soldiers, and English from my wife. He soaked up his education like a dry sponge. Farhan exchanged his wildness for patience, suspicion for devotion, and his savage ways for gentleness. He counted himself as a redeemed lost soul, attaching himself to my wife with as strong a bond as any son has for his natural mother. He also devoted himself to me.

"Six months before my wife died, we adopted him. He was, by then, a part of the family, and our own children accepted him... up to a point. But Farhan did not presume; it was he who cast himself in the role of servant. He and I had several discussions in which I encouraged him to become independent and to learn a profession. What does he do? Learns to cook, so he can prepare meals just how we like them. He has always been interested in food, which, I believe, arose from his doing without for so long."

"And so he followed you to England out of loyalty?" asked Sophie.

"I asked him if he wanted to stay in India, and emphasized he should establish his own life. I offered to set him up properly, but he wouldn't hear of it. He said his life belongs to me to do with as I please. I thought of sending him away for his own good, but how could I? We would both be miserable."

"Is he happy here?"

"Based on your brief meeting, how does Farhan seem?"

"Um, he's polite and attentive, with a sort of inward contentment."

"That's him, and he never varies. Farhan, as far as it is humanly possible, possesses a faultless and unselfish nature. If those things approximate to happiness, then, yes, he is happy."

"What a remarkable story. I've never heard the like."

"Unusual, yes. I've heard of several similar instances of children saved from the jungle, so to speak. One, I know, became a Christian evangelist. Another, a girl, was reunited with her family after a year. She became a local celebrity as a holy woman."

"Going through such an experience clearly has a profound and life-altering effect. Thank you for telling me."

Major Cummings smiled again. "There's more to see if you like."

"Very much so."

Sophie rose. The story of Farhan had touched her, and she felt very well disposed towards Cummings.

"What was your wife's name?"

"Glenda."

"She must have been a very kind person."

"Indeed, she was."

They entered the dining room, and it was a companion to the lounge. It was not for formal English dinners; it was set up with comfort and ease in mind. Sophie was about to ask from what type of wood the table was made when she noticed a small collection of Indian swords and knives arranged around a shield on the wall. Her reason for being present suddenly came flooding back.

"I rather shied away from the typical trophies that officers bring back from India. I didn't want to be pigeon-holed as one of *those* types. The two swords and the shield were a gift from a prince. The others I picked up here and there. But the one I truly treasure is this plain knife. A Gurkha officer, a good friend, gave it to me when we exchanged mementoes. It was his personal knife that he carried as part of his equipment." He took down the knife in its hard scabbard and held it out for Sophie's inspection. The dessicated black leather and worn rosewood handle testified to long service. "Its heavy and very sharp." Major Cummings drew the blade. "They call it a kukri, and it's commonly worn by farmers and soldiers from Nepal. It's an effective working knife, and an efficient sidearm when carried by a soldier."

To imagine its utility was difficult for Sophie. She saw the broad, well-used knife only as a lethal weapon, imparting an ugliness beyond which she could not see. The curving blade seemed wicked, or so she thought. She studied the squared spine and noticed a ridge within it. She struggled with her thoughts, fearing the Major, who stood so close by, must surely know what she was thinking. From what she knew, the knife he held could have been the weapon used to kill Mr Hamilton. In fact, it was perfectly adapted to inflict the wound except for one obvious fact. The curve of knife and handle were so pronounced, it made it almost impossible to use except in the one direction for which it was designed. The spine was all wrong as a striking surface, unless the murderer deliberately meant to hurt Hamilton instead of killing him.

"May I hold it?" asked Sophie, appearing calm but not feeling so. She studied the Major's face.

"Of course, but it's sharp, so please be careful."

She took the handle, and it fitted her hand well. It was an unusual weight and, in trying a small chopping movement, immediately saw how useful the knife would be for a farmer. Sophie concentrated on the back movement even while Major Cummings watched her closely. She discovered the blow that struck Hamilton could be managed. But what of the attack on Mr Clark? Cummings was still watching her.

"They use it for everything, from felling trees and harvesting crops to fine work like making pins and pegs."

"Very interesting," said Sophie. "I'd better give it back to you. I feel as though I might damage something."

Cummings took the knife carefully and then hung it back on the wall. Sophie believed it could be the weapon — could *easily* be the weapon. But was Major Cummings the man? Perhaps it was Farhan, the devoted servant who would do anything for his master.

"What do you make of the attack on Mr Clark? What can be the reason behind it?"

"I don't know. It's a monstrous business, and thoroughly inexplicable. Perhaps he was in an argument with a drunk or a tramp, although it was a very odd time of day. At about six, I understand."

"Yes. Do you think the attack is connected to Mr Hamilton's death?"

"That crossed my mind, but I would say not. Mr Hamilton died weeks ago in February. Would the assailant return in the night to kill *anyone* he might find in the area? There's no sense to that. If the murderer is intent upon harming and killing others, surely he would have returned at an earlier time? If he's deranged, he would have returned several times by now. I imagine when Clark regains his faculties, we'll find out what actually happened and learn it's a straightforward matter after all."

"That may be the case, but I can't help feeling the attacks are by the same person. They were very close together geographically — some thirty or forty yards apart."

Major Cummings was quiet while staring through a window.

"Yes." He spoke more softly than usual. "It makes you think, doesn't it?" He turned to Sophie. "I pray it isn't someone from Alexandra Gardens."

Sophie understood why he would wish that, why he would not want a neighbour, someone he knew, to be responsible.

"It's very worrying," said Sophie.

"Oh, I agree. Has it upset you, Miss King? Can I get you anything?"

"No, thank you. That's very kind." She smiled. "I should go… Things to do."

"Yes, of course."

"I very much admire your house. It is highly individual and agreeably surprising."

Major Cummings became awkward. "It incorporates just some little ideas that Glenda and I had when we used to daydream about our return to England. I wish she could have seen it."

"I'm sure she would have been pleased."

"I like to think so."

They said goodbye and, in response to Sophie's question, Major Cummings said he believed that Mrs Barker would be returning to number seven within the hour.

# Chapter 22

# Visiting hour

On Tuesday afternoon, Ada returned from the shops yet again. She had already been for ordinary British shopping. This time she came in with extraordinary Indian shopping. Not that the items themselves were extraordinary, but Mrs Barker apologetically had to request that Ada go out again for several items she realized were lacking for the looming Indian Extravaganza — the name for the test dinner at number seven.

"What's that smell?" asked Ada upon entering the kitchen.

Mrs Barker had received a package of clearly labelled essential ingredients from Farhan.

"It's a combination of several things, but don't worry about that. Here, Ada, come and smell this."

"I'm Nancy," said Ada.

"Oh, sorry, Nancy."

Mrs Barker held out a small white porcelain pot.

"What is it?"

"It's labelled asa...foe...tida, but Mr Farhan called it hing. Just you have a sniff of that."

Ada got ready, Mrs Barker took off the lid, and Ada sniffed.

"Cor blimey, that stinks!"

"Doesn't it?"

"You're never putting that in the food?"

"I have to. The recipe says I must."

"But it's gone off. It's like a dead animal."

"I know. What shall I do?"

"Take it back, Mrs Barker. If you put that in, I won't eat it."

"Will you come with me?"

"All right. Let me put these things away first."

There are two methods of returning an item to a British shopkeeper in the hope of a refund. The first, the reasonable and yet least successful approach, is to take the shopkeeper to one side in private conversation and explain why the item was mistakenly purchased or what was wrong with the product. Any response is highly dependent upon the shopkeeper's character and mood. The hoped for answer is, 'Of course, madam, I will exchange it (or give you a refund) at once.' This may have happened somewhere in Britain, but there is no evidence that such a transaction has ever taken place. Usually, the shopkeeper turns nasty, but begrudgingly accedes to the request and, if a refund is involved, slams the till drawer shut afterwards. Just as often, perhaps more often, the shopkeeper declines to redress the customer's grievance, and does so with comments ranging from: 'You bought it, you keep it,' to 'Never come in my shop again.'

The return of goods is a high-risk business and the outcome very uncertain. Because everyone understands this state of affairs, families and neighbourhoods quickly identify who it is amongst themselves who makes for an excellent Returner of Goods. This class of person adopts the second and far more effective method of dealing with shopkeepers. Ideally, the Returner waits until the shop is full, marches to the head of the queue, slams the offending item down on the counter and loudly proclaims something like, 'This was off when you sold it! I want my (my friend wants her) money back! And I'm not moving until I get it!' Frequently, the customers in the queue do not mind such an interruption. After all, it is free entertainment and they naturally side with the Returner. The beleaguered shopkeeper, taken at such a dreadful disadvantage, usually settles quickly. His alternative is to fight a verbal battle until the police arrive, both of which 'unpleasantnesses' are bad for business.

It takes an extraordinary spirit to rise unilaterally to a high level of truculence, enter the quiet intimacy of a shop where customers are meekly awaiting their turn to be served, and loudly demand immediate satisfaction. Mrs Barker could establish her authority in a household and manage the trades who came to the house, but she was not a Returner. Ada was, which was why she was asked to assist.

It was a short walk to number nine. In the time it took, Ada had it roughly straight in her mind what she was going to say: 'Your 'ing's — Hing's — gone off. Mrs Barker can't cook with something like that. Do you have a fresh pot of Hing she can 'ave?' Ada had allowed for Farhan being foreign and a domestic, rather than a shopkeeper, as well as for there being an important test hanging in the balance. As a consequence, she would hold her fire, and not shout to inform Alexandra Gardens of the outrage unless it became absolutely necessary. However, she would not stand for any nonsense or have Mrs Barker put out. So, in her mind, that was that, and the matter was as good as settled.

They descended the stairs to number nine's basement area. Ada knocked loudly on the door. By a look of understanding alone, they agreed that Mrs Barker would open the negotiations, hold out the offending pot, and, if there were even a hint of prevarication, Ada would begin. The door opened.

"Good afternoon, memsahibs. How may I help you?" Farhan had come from the kitchen wearing an apron and carrying something wrapped in a drying cloth.

They both answered, 'Good afternoon.'

"Sorry to trouble you, Mr Farhan," began Mrs Barker, "but we think there's something wrong with this hing." She had to use the Indian name, because both she and Ada had found the word asafoetida far too challenging.

"Many pardons for the inconvenience... I do not understand how it can have happened. Excuse me." He put down the cloth on a small table near the entrance. Part of the cloth fell away. It shocked Ada to see he had been drying a square-bladed cleaver with a straight spine.

"Permit me to examine?" He smiled as he asked the question.

"Yes, please do," said Mrs Barker, holding out the questionable pot a little further.

He took it and removed the lid. Then he sniffed.

"It is perfect. Just how it should be." He looked from one astounded face to the other. "It is very pungent. The saying is, a little goes a long way. Yes?"

"Oh, yes," said Mrs Barker uncertainly.

Ada came loose from her moorings, deciding it was probably unwise to shout at a potential murderer who had a lethal-looking weapon near at hand. There also seemed to be nothing to shout about. Farhan could see their hesitation.

"Hing is used like an Oxo cube, or Marmite, or a few drops of Worcestershire sauce."

As if drowning in a river and then, unexpectedly, finding she could stand with her head above water, Mrs Barker seized upon the familiar names.

"*Ohhh,*" she said. "I know just what you mean."

"Excellent," said Farhan. "Hing is made from the root of the fennel plant. I am accustomed to the aroma, and I apologize for not warning you."

"Please don't apologize, Mr Farhan. You've been ever so thoughtful and patient. I feel a bit silly for troubling you."

"No trouble at all, memsahib. If I can assist you in any way, please do not hesitate to knock on this door." He turned to Ada. "Is there anything I can do for you?"

"No, thank you, Mr Farhan... I only came because I was interested."

He smiled and put his hands together as if in prayer. They said goodbye.

"What a lovely voice he has," said Mrs Barker on the return journey. "And as for his manners?"

"He's very polite," said Ada, who hoped he really was as he seemed, and not as she feared.

A shower blew through mid-afternoon and, after the morning's excitement, Alexandra Gardens became just another place in London. The agent was in the attic, Mrs Barker was preparing for tomorrow's dinner, while Myrtle was preparing for today's evening meal. Ada was cleaning the cutlery from the silver drawer, puzzling over how the fully equipped house did not appear to have an owner. Biscuit was sprawled on the rug in the parlour, listening to the rain, hoping it would soon stop so he could go out. Also in the parlour were Sophie and Flora.

"The way I see it," said Flora, "is that we should strike Mr Clark and La Pringle off the list."

"No, we can't," said Sophie. "This morning's attack might be a separate event."

"It doesn't look like it to me. Clark didn't bash himself, therefore, he's out."

"Of course, he didn't, but what was he doing outside in the street so early and without his dog? That's suspicious behaviour on his part."

"Are you thinking he met someone, and it turned violent?" asked Flora.

"It's possible," replied Sophie. "Supposing it was La Pringle. They had an argument and she... No. It couldn't be all of a sudden, because she would have been carrying the hatchet. I know — this must be it:- They were discussing a serious matter, and La Pringle had decided to kill Clark if he made the wrong decision, or whatever. So, she had brought a hatchet along with her, whacked him when he said the wrong thing, and then regretted doing it, because she really loves him."

"That's preposterous."

"I know it is, but it accounts for everything."

"She wasn't acting when she fell to pieces."

"Remorse," said Sophie.

"Rubbish. You're grasping at straws."

"Yes, I am, and it's because we don't have enough information."

"Then we'll have to be patient and wait for the police to tell us more."

"That's it!" Sophie stood up. "You said it!"

"What?"

"Patient. We'll visit Mr Clark in the hospital."

"But we hardly know him?"

"Well, a visit by two ministering angels will cure that."

"Steady on... You don't mean we'll pretend to be nurses?"

"No. Concerned visitors bringing gifts and books and things. Chocolates and... flowers."

"There'll be a scene if La Pringle is present."

"Um... We'll make a fuss of her, too."

"Should be interesting," said Flora. "Biscuit has to go for a walk first."

The sprawling dog was immediately up and ready.

"You can't come to the hospital," Sophie told him.

Flora looked out of the window and studied a puddle. "Barely a drizzle now."

"Right. I'll take him out, and then we'll go over to Camden to find a taxi."

---

Clark was resting in the farthest bed from the door in a general ward. At that moment, the long room at the end of a wing was bright because the sun had come out. The white walls needed painting and there was a pronounced antiseptic smell. The monotonous ward had twenty beds. Two had curtains around them and three were empty. Lying in one bed was an old man sitting up and vacantly staring across the room while his wife, sitting by him, held his hand and stared at him. A youth had his bandaged leg raised in the air by pulleys, a man was reading a newspaper, and another coughed incessantly. Sophie and Flora passed a bed where the patient gave them a pathetic smile, as if hoping they would visit him to relieve the boredom of just lying there with nothing to do.

Mr Clark was sitting upright, well supported by pillows. They had bandaged his head and his left arm was in a sling tightly strapped to his body. He turned a white, puffy face towards Flora and Sophie when it became plain they were coming to see him. Clark had met Flora, but not Sophie.

"Good afternoon," said Flora. "We simply had to come to see how you're doing."

"Good afternoon," he said, confused as to why they were visiting him.

"This is my cousin, Miss King."

Sophie and Clark greeted one another.

"You're probably thinking it's a fearful cheek, us just turning up unannounced like this," said Flora.

"Not at all," said Clark, who nevertheless thought it odd.

"Of course, we're absolutely dying to know what happened, but more importantly, how are you?"

"Oh, tired, naturally."

"Tell us all about it in a moment," said Sophie, "while we beautify your little corner." She held up the flowers she carried.

"You really shouldn't have, Miss King."

"But we have, Mr Clark."

Flora brought over an extra chair, while Sophie went to find a vase for the large bouquet of spring flowers. On the table by his bed, they put several newspapers and magazines, a box of chocolates, a tin of assorted biscuits, and some mints.

"You're too kind," he said several times.

By the time they had set everything in place, he knew he could not avoid giving a full account.

"We were absolutely shocked when we heard," said Sophie. "That's why we came out immediately."

"Yes... Please thank Mrs Barker for all she did. What an excellent woman. I didn't realize at the time who she was or even what she was doing."

"You wouldn't," said Flora, "not after such a horrific attack."

He smiled wanly.

"What are the extent of your injuries?" asked Sophie.

"I was concussed, but I didn't black out... I think I came close to it, though. I don't remember some things, but the Doctor said that might be from the shock. My head aches, and my arm hurts abominably. If I complain, they'll give me more morphine and I don't like that. I don't like to lose control of my faculties, you see. Anyway, the blow to the head was not as bad as it might have been. I turned just before the moment of impact, which proved to be the saving of me."

"Did you hear a noise behind you?" asked Sophie.

"I suppose I must have. Something alerted me that a person was close by."

"What happened to your arm, or is it your shoulder?" asked Flora.

"It seems that whatever he used bounced off my head," he smiled and immediately winced, "and buried itself on the top of my shoulder. It fractured my left acromion. I didn't even know I had such a thing and now it's broken. They say it should mend, but my shoulder has a deep gouge, which hurts dreadfully."

"I am sorry," said Sophie. "What about your playing the piano?"

"Not for many weeks... It's very worrying."

"I'm sure it is," said Flora.

"Is there anything we can do to help?" asked Sophie.

"That's very kind, but there really isn't anything to be done. It's a question of giving everything time to heal and learning to be patient to wait it out."

An awkward silence followed. The injury to Clark's shoulder had impacted his career, and may have done so permanently. He would not know to what extent until he resumed playing.

"Why were you attacked?" asked Flora.

"Despite asking myself that question repeatedly, I have no idea, Miss Walton. Since the fogginess passed, I've turned it over but can't find a reason."

"So there's nothing you can tell the police that would help them?" asked Sophie.

"I wish I could. I had no warning, and it was all over so quickly. The police think it was a hatchet that was used. I suppose they're right."

"You don't think it was?" asked Sophie.

"I don't know what to think. The doctor believes it might have been, and added I was fortunate that no part of the cutting edge made direct contact or I'd be in a lot worse condition... That's scant comfort, really. What puzzles me is why?"

"We think it's connected to Mr Hamilton's murder."

Clark looked at Sophie. "Do you really? That hadn't occurred to me."

"Yes," said Sophie. "It could be because your house is so close to where he was killed... And now this?"

"Good heavens... But I was playing at the cinema the night he died, so I didn't see anything. I wouldn't have anyway, because of the fog."

"The murderer may not know either of those facts. I'm sorry if this distresses you, but I believe you must be very cautious, henceforth."

"Did the police make the connection?" asked Flora.

"No. They haven't mentioned it, anyway. The constable who was summoned to the scene didn't, and then the sergeant, who visited this morning after they fixed me up, said nothing about Hamilton. Do you really believe it's a cause for concern?"

"It's only a possibility," said Sophie, "but not something to be ignored. It's a pity you didn't have your dog with you. His name's Bertie, isn't it?"

"Yes... There was a dog, though... I recall it standing right over me as if on guard... That was your dog, wasn't it?" Clark was pleased he remembered that part of the incident. "What a good boy."

"Who's looking after Bertie?" asked Flora.

"Sandra is. I mean, Mrs Pringle."

"Please excuse my asking," began Sophie, "but why were you out so early without him?"

"Oh, you know... Things."

"Miss Walton often has to think about Things, don't you?" asked Sophie.

"Absolutely. Any time day or night, I have to ponder some very difficult Things. It's my artistic temperament, you see."

"I can relate to that all right," said Clark. "When a thought seizes me, I feel quite beastly until I've worked it out."

"Had you worked it out before you were bonked on the head?" asked Sophie.

"It so happens, I had. I couldn't sleep, so I thought I would get some air. Bertie looked too comfortable to disturb, so I spent an hour walking about in the dark and came to terms with something. I really did. Then, the next thing I know, I get attacked. It's as though fate saw I had finally come up with a good idea for my music, then decided to knock me down."

"I'm sure it seems like it, but it isn't really the case. What did you decide?" Sophie looked so eager and pleased that Clark could not resist.

"Well, I haven't told Sandra yet, so please don't mention it. I've been working on a score for a musical. I was getting rather depressed over it because, although solid in its way, it was not particularly original. Well, I went for a walk, and it was as if the heavens opened to me. I can't claim genius, but the sudden clarity of what I can do, and what I will do, was of such a profound nature it was almost visionary. I know I'm not making sense, but what I realized made perfect sense to *me*. The wonderful thing is this: not only were the ideas I had something I want to do artistically, but I firmly believe it will also result in commercial success. I can't say more at the moment." He managed to seem impish despite his bandages.

"Because you want to speak to Sandra first?"

"Yes, Miss King. You're very understanding. This is important both for me and for her. I believe it solves a problem. "

"Oh," said Sophie.

"Have a chocolate, Mr Clark," said Flora as she opened the box. "I find eating chocolates solves most problems."

"I don't like to move — the shoulder, you know."
"I'll pop one in your mouth, shall I?... This one?"
"That's very kind of you."

This was the moment that Mrs Sandra Pringle chose to enter the ward. She came in, full of the desire to comfort her wounded man, but instead saw that *her* Mr Clark had two visitors. They were two attractive young women. The dark-haired one, while smiling, took a chocolate — it had to be a chocolate — from a box. Then, while laughing and with a graceful movement, she popped the chocolate into the altogether too eager Mr Clark's mouth. All desire to comfort him vanished. Mrs Pringle believed she had never before in her life witnessed such a repulsive sight. Walking almost mindlessly, but determined to do something that would wipe all smiles off all faces, she stomped her way to the end of the ward.

Sophie was able to see and understand the import of the entire scenario in an instant. It took on the character of a fairy tale that must end badly because there were simply not enough words left in the book for anything good to happen. Sophie thought suddenly of how grinning gargoyles stare down from the heights upon innocent admirers of medieval architecture. Here was a gargoyle that had assumed flesh and blood form and now seemed determined to intrude itself upon a light-hearted and blameless moment. There was no denying that the timing was awful, but how could she prevent the cataclysm that was bearing down relentlessly upon them? She thought fast, as the inexorable fury drew closer.

Sophie judged the moment nicely and then stood up. "Mrs Pringle! Let me be the first to congratulate you!"

Flora had been studying the chocolate box but now spun around. Mr Clark himself also clapped eyes upon Sandra Pringle and was completely taken aback, either by Sandra's sudden appearance or by Sophie's inexplicable utterance, but probably by both.

Mrs Pringle came to rest near the bed. Her jealous anger was not one jot diminished, but Sophie's declaration had temporarily checked it. A tense silence ensued, which needed to be broken. Mr Clark met the challenge.

"Hello, Sandra. I believe you've met Miss King and Miss Walton."

Before any more inadequate politeness was attempted, Sophie delivered the coup de grâce.

"We understand congratulations are in order, because you and Mr Clark are getting married."

Sophie's sudden and extraordinary statement shocked Flora. Mr Clark was stunned, as if his head had received another blow. Mrs Pringle could not believe her ears.

"Eh?" said Clark.

"I beg your pardon?" said Mrs Pringle.

"You're getting married," insisted Sophie, although her colour was now rising.

The second silence that occurred differed from the first. In a single second, the utterance had robbed Mrs Pringle of her adversaries, leaving her no one upon whom to vent her spleen. Instead, she and Mr Clark were thrust into the invidious position of having to come to a decision on a very private matter before witnesses. This realization came home simultaneously to the two afflicted parties.

"Sandra?" asked Mr Clark, looking pathetically hopeful and more poignantly so because of his bandages.

She hesitated before replying, "We discussed this... You know where matters stand between us."

"I know, I know, but that's the exciting thing I haven't told you. A musical I'm working on — a series of them, actually — was the reason I was out so early. I had a flash of inspiration. More than a flash. It was like the, ah, heavens opened and I could suddenly see what to do. Um." He looked at Sophie, then said breathlessly, "Excuse me, I can't say what it is, you know. Sorry." He addressed Sandra once more, and with excited enthusiasm. "There's no impediment. I have someone to do the libretto, and, ah, a rather important person I know showed interest in a project like this and we've already discussed finances. When I tell him what I have planned, I'm sure he'll be thrilled with my ideas."

"Oh," said Sandra. She glanced at Flora, then back again. "You really think it has a chance?"

"I don't think; I *know*. I've never been so sure of anything in all my life."

"But what about your shoulder? You won't be able to play."

"That doesn't matter. Well, it matters, but it's only an inconvenience. You can play well enough. I'll just write the score, and you'll play the piano part. You'll see for yourself how good it is."

"But you haven't told me what the musical is about."

They both looked towards Sophie and Flora.

"Would you like us to leave?" asked Sophie.

"No, we can't possibly go now," said Flora.

Clark had a surge of bravado. "Sandra. Marry me."

Sandra hesitated again, and she sought reassurance from Flora and Sophie. They both nodded.

"Yes, Charles. Oh, yes."

The little group visibly expanded with delight, much like a blossoming bud. Smiling congratulations were given to the beaming couple. Even Flora and the bride-to-be hugged. Mrs Pringle then asked a question of Sophie, and the latter agreed to defer the shorthand lesson to another day.

"We'll go now," said Sophie.

The secret agents left the happy pair.

"What's better?" asked Flora as they left the ward. "Solving a murder or uniting a couple?"

"They're too different to compare. Anyway, we just struck lucky."

"Yes. I almost choked when you said we'd heard they were getting married. But I'd had time to glimpse her face. My goodness, we were really going to get it."

"That will teach you to stop stuffing chocolates into men's faces."

"I hadn't intended to make a habit of it. The poor thing needed help."

"Not anymore. And we can strike them off the suspect list."

"That's something, at least. We're not getting any closer to the real culprit, though. Are we *sure* it's someone in Alexandra Gardens? I mean, the way I see it at the moment, we could strike them *all* from the list."

"I know it feels like that. Still, if it can be called progress, Major Cummings and Farhan have access to just the type of weapon that killed Mr Hamilton. But it bothers me. Why would either use the spine of a knife or chopper if they meant to kill him? It couldn't have been a mistake."

"They didn't want to get blood on their clothes?"

"Although possible, it's a very weak reason, but I can't see what else it could have been."

They descended the main staircase and met Kuritsyn coming up.

"Comrades," he asked, "have you been attending the sick?" He carried a newspaper and a tin of butterscotch sweets.

"Yes, we have," said Sophie. "He's fairly comfortable, considering what he's been through. You'll find him on the second floor at the end of the east wing. Mrs Pringle is with him."

"O-ho, the lovebirds. I will interrupt them for a few seconds only."

"I think that wise," said Sophie. "How long have they been… well, you know."

"Infatuated? Let me think. Five or six months before Hamilton, and about six weeks since."

"Really?" said Flora. "When did the Hamilton interlude begin?"

"Last year. October, before the Red Army captured the Crimean Peninsula. I was out with Vova, and I caught her and Hamilton being affectionate. I thought to myself, poor Clark, does he know of this? Should I tell him? I say, not my business. But it's difficult, you know."

"I can imagine it was," said Sophie.

"All that doesn't matter now. Hamilton's dead, and Clark nearly died. Sandra has been unlucky, but I think Clark is the better man for her. I go now. My security duties do not permit me to stay away from the house for too long. Good afternoon."

After he had gone, Sophie said,

"We had better keep Mrs Pringle on the list."

"You think she's unhinged and attacked Mr Clark?" asked Flora.

"I hope not. Otherwise, I've just made a horrendous mistake."

## Chapter 23

# What are the odds now?

Biscuit was accompanied on a walk by Sophie and Flora just after tea-time. Now accustomed to numerous daily walks, he had discerned today a definite slacking off, despite the early morning's excitement. He forgave them, though, because they were now taking him out. He forgot their past dereliction of duty entirely as they headed to where three dogs stood in a group. Could life possibly be more wonderful? When he arrived, Biscuit's tail signified it was as good as it gets. The humans involved in the gathering were not so cheerful, however.

After they had exchanged greetings, the group discussed What Must Be Done.

"There's no going out alone anymore," said Mr Bristow, who carried a walking stick. "Who *knows* when the fiend will strike again!?" He shook an impassioned finger of dire consequences at the others.

"I quite agree," said Mrs Fitch. She also had a walking stick — a thick ash. Hers was firmly planted on the ground and prominently held forward. "We shall arrange the appropriate meeting times. I suggest 7:00 a.m., mid-day, four-thirty, and seven-thirty."

"Seven a.m?" Miss Villard was horrified. "I cannot possibly come out at seven. Also, my maid often walks Lulu. They will not be safe alone."

"Dulcie, don't be alarmed," said Bristow. "There's really no need. Your maid can join us. You're all under my protection. Gad, I'd like to get my hands on this fellow. Just let him try something with me." Bristow now shook his stick.

"All dogs should be up early to begin their daily routine," said Mrs Fitch. "A walk at seven in the morning gives a proper start to the day. Send your maid out with Lulu, as Captain Bristow suggests."

"It's not you who has to listen to her grumbling about the danger. She's frightened, but I will ask."

"There's safety in numbers," said Bristow. "Just you tell her that."

"Miss Walton and Miss King, I think it best you join us." Mrs Fitch commanded as if she were a queen.

"Absolutely," said Sophie.

"Will you?"

"Oh, yes. Who else is in the group?"

"Everyone except Kuritsyn," answered Bristow. "We've yet to ask Sandra, because she's taken up with Charles Clark's well-being for the moment."

"Yes," said Mrs Fitch dryly.

"I always said she loved him," said Miss Villard. "She should never have thrown herself at Mr Hamilton."

"We shouldn't discuss such a thing," said Mrs Fitch.

"It was a fact, but I can stop. I think she will now happily marry Charles."

"Do you really think so?" asked Flora.

"I'm never wrong in matters of the heart," said Miss Villard.

"Is Mr Saunders a part of this group?" asked Sophie.

"He's not really one of us," said Bristow. "I'll speak to him, though, and see what he says."

"And Mr Kuritsyn?"

"Typical Bolshie response. Said it's all bourgeois fear and nonsense. The fellow laughed. He gets on my nerves sometimes."

"You live next door to them," said Flora. "What is that like? Are they noisy, friendly, or do they keep themselves to themselves?"

"When they first moved in, I didn't hear a peep. Not a whisper. Then they tried their socialist rigmarole on me, but I was having none of it. I suppose you could say they're polite, but I never see them smile. They've all got long faces, and so they should. Serves them right for causing so many problems. For some months now I've heard them singing, but that's not often. Mournful stuff it is, although majestic in its way. You wouldn't catch me singing such songs. All in all, they're a funny lot of bounders, but they give me no trouble."

"Are there six of them living there?" asked Sophie.

"Eight, isn't it?" said Miss Villard.

"Seven, I thought," said Mrs Fitch.

"No!" Bristow more or less brayed the word. "There are six regulars, but they sometimes have visitors and one's staying there now. He's a rum fellow. Yesterday, I was out in the garden doing something and, through an open window, I heard him reciting The Rime of the Ancient Mariner. I read it as a boy and that was enough for me, thank you."

"How interesting," said Sophie. "I spoke to the visitor yesterday, and he has a very odd turn of phrase. Come to think of it, I've seen only five of the regular inhabitants. Are you sure there are six?"

"Of course, I'm sure, Miss King. There are the four chaps who go out to work, Kuritsyn, whom we all know, then there's Doctor Teplov."

"I haven't seen him about," said Sophie.

"He keeps to himself. Mad about chess, though. I've played him a few times, but he's too good for me."

"Is he an invalid?" asked Flora.

"No, not at all. Don't ask me why he stays in all the time, although I know he writes a lot. All that Bolshevik claptrap. But I'll tell you this. I believe they have a radio in there, and it must be for him. Oh, yes. The other day, I came across two of the fellows putting up a long length of wire on the back of the house as an antenna. I asked them what they were doing, and they just grinned back like twerps and pointed to the wire. If they're going to live here, they should learn English."

"A radio?" asked Sophie. "Why on earth would they want one?"

"To talk to their comrades about the revolution, no doubt. What utter tosh it all is. I can't take them seriously. Whenever I hear them spout their propaganda, I think they're acting. I can't see how they can bring themselves to believe what they say. But enough of the Ruskies. They don't speak English properly, so they're useless for our purposes."

"I wouldn't say that," said Sophie. "One of them took excellent care of Mr Clark this morning, and he didn't need to speak English to do so."

"All right, I'll give them that. Yet I'll never understand why the government allows communists in the country. They're only here to cause trouble, so why let them in? It's this coalition government we have. It's all too stupid for words."

"We don't discuss politics," said Mrs Fitch.

"I didn't, Cynthia. I merely made an observation and raised a question, which no one can answer. However, I'll leave it alone."

"The Russians are quiet, and well-behaved," said Miss Villard. "They had nothing to do with the attacks."

"Well, I hope you're right," said Sophie, "but how can you be so sure?"

"Mr Hamilton was killed out of jealousy. The Russians don't pursue women. At least, not around here, they don't. So, they had no interest in Mr Hamilton as a rival."

"Not like some, eh?" said Bristow archly.

"And not like some *others*," Miss Villard retorted sharply, "who are only *insincere*." She almost snarled her last word. "Good night." She marched away.

"I never quite know what she's talking about," said Mrs Fitch. "Do you, Captain?"

"She's a manipulative little minx, that's all I'll say." He became hearty. "So, seven tomorrow? I doubt Mellish will turn out then. I'll find out what Sandra's doing. She'll be looking after Clark's dog, no doubt, but she doesn't rise early, either... I'm shoving off now. So I bid you all a good night. There's no need to worry. We'll stick together and the police will eventually get off their backsides and catch this lunatic."

Mrs Fitch waited until he had gone.

"I'm sorry you were forced to witness such bad behaviour. They are not always like it."

"You mean Miss Villard and Mr Bristow?" asked Flora.

"I do, indeed. They were once close. I need not say more."

Sophie asked, "Mrs Fitch, do you think the same person killed Mr Hamilton and attacked Mr Clark?"

"I'm positive it wasn't. It's an uncanny coincidence and nothing more. I imagine that, in both incidents, an attacker intent upon robbery followed his victim, but was disturbed before he could go through their pockets. After Mr Hamilton died, that same robber would surely stay right away from here for fear of being caught, because the penalty for murder is much more severe. The affluence of the area randomly drew another robber, possibly without his even knowing what had happened here before."

"That sounds reasonable," said Sophie.

"If it's not that, I don't know what it can be. All I know is that I'll be on my guard. This is a weighted walking stick with lead in it. If anyone attacks me, they'll pay a heavy price. Besides, Titus is a good deterrent. Biscuit would be, too. You both must take precautions to protect yourselves."

"I think we shall," said Flora.

"I'm going in. Shall I see you at seven tomorrow morning?"

"Yes, one of us shall join the group," replied Sophie.

Flora and Sophie continued walking.

"This is getting far too confusing," said Sophie. "There are too many undercurrents and distracting side issues. Tonight, we'll put all our observations in order. Do you think we should have Auntie and Hawkins come round?"

"The more the merrier. Only can we have Hawkins seated at the table? Otherwise, the poor fellow has to stand, and it's like watching a performing seal."

"You're right. I thought he rather enjoyed himself, but it would be more pleasant for all of us if he sat at the table. Nick should arrive soon, so he can take a message to White Lyon Yard."

---

Nick arrived, and Sophie gave him messages to deliver. One was to Archie Drysdale, concerning the new radio installation at number fifteen. The other was for Aunt Bessie, inviting her to come over later.

At about six, Sergeant Gowers visited, apologizing for being later than usual. Sophie brought him up to date on the day's events. He had already been informed of the attack on Clark, and was interested in Sophie's report of the hospital visit. It was his opinion that both Clark and Pringle should remain on the suspect list, just in case. He also promised to investigate personally Clark's alibi, such as it was. After Gowers had gone, Sophie felt sad because, since his recent revelations, Inspector Morton had not accompanied his sergeant as he had been wont to do. He was obviously now avoiding her. She hoped she had not lost a friend.

With the help of Flora and Ada, she wrote up a summary of key information for each suspect in Alexandra Gardens as it related to the murder and the attack. They all felt it was necessary because they would otherwise be overwhelmed.

"It's become apparent," said Sophie, "there are three major potential motives for murder. One, Hamilton was killed out of jealousy — the crime of passion. Two, a person killed him because of a feeling of having been insulted over something they have devoted their life to. Three, he was killed because he lost Mrs Fitch's application to Cruft's and then lied about it. On its own, the last seems hardly credible, but it is possible."

"Then for number three," said Ada, "it'd be Mrs Fitch or Mrs Murray, wouldn't it, miss?"

"Mrs Murray? What makes you think to include her?"

"See, I'm not so sure Mr Hamilton lied. People lie when they think they can get away with it. He says he gave it to Mrs Murray. Mrs Murray says she never got it. Well, one of 'em's lying. 'Amilton *knew* he'd be found out if he didn't deliver the application. Why'd he do it then? It don't make no sense for the few shillings involved. If he did it deliberate, it's because he wanted to show up Mrs Murray. To cause trouble between her and Mrs Fitch. But it's a stupid way of doin' it — putting himself right in the middle of all the argy-bargy."

"You've made an excellent observation," said Sophie. "I've been *thinking* about meeting Mrs Murray, but I believe it's imperative now. At least to clear up the matter."

"Don't forget, you're going to the office tomorrow morning," said Flora.

"I'll see her one way or another in the afternoon, then. Which reminds me. For safety, the dog owners have arranged four times over the course of the day when they will all go out together. The first meeting is at seven in the morning. I thought to go, but I think it would be better if you did, Nancy. This is for two reasons. The first is the Villard's maid will probably be there; so you can talk to her and find out what you can from that angle. The second is because if we're not present, you might hear something they would not otherwise say if we were."

"Act friendly with the maid, and eavesdrop on the others... Yes, miss. Anything else?"

"I don't think so. Thank you for doing that. Now I'll read the salient points in our records and we'll see what we make of it all. Make notes as we go along, and we'll discuss everything at the end."

Sophie began reading.

Captain William Bristow, 43.

Had an affair with Dulcie Villard that ended acrimoniously. Stated she was manipulative and ill-intentioned. He possibly hinted she was involved with Hamilton, but was, at the very least, extremely interested in him.

Reason to kill Hamilton — Jealous over Villard turning her attention to Hamilton. Along with all the other men in Alexandra Gardens, disliked Hamilton's manner and conduct.

Additional information: Henri Gautier, onion man, chose Bristow as the most likely to commit murder, but his choice was based on personal antipathy alone.

Reason to attack Clark — None.

His theory about Hamilton — A tramp did it.

Charles Clark, 40.

In love with Sandra Pringle. Had to have known of her involvement with Hamilton, but waited for her. There was some impediment to their marrying before, which seems to be removed by their working on a promising musical together. He was attacked outside his house while full of artistic well-being and matrimonial hopefulness. The only logical reason for him to be attacked was that he was a witness to the murder, or the attacker believed it was the case.

Reason to kill Hamilton — Jealous over Pringle turning her attention to Hamilton.

Reason to be attacked by another — A witness to Hamilton's murder.

His theory about Hamilton — Unknown.

Major Neville Cummings, 62.

Disliked Hamilton for general reasons, but specifically because of his slighting comments about India. Possesses knives that could produce the wound Hamilton received. However, others may have similar knives. His devoted servant, Farhan, must also be considered.

Reason to kill Hamilton — Anger over his book and love of all things Indian being ridiculed.

Reason to attack Clark — None.

His theory about Hamilton — No definite opinion.

Mrs Cynthia Fitch, 46.

Although possible, there is no evidence she had feelings for Hamilton. Her application to Cruft's was lost after Hamilton received it in order to give it to Mrs Murray, a friend of Fitch. Murray says she never received the application. Hamilton says he gave it to her. Most likely is that Hamilton lost or destroyed it. To maintain the Murray-Fitch friendship, the parties set the incident aside. The truce did not last long, and the friendship was irrevocably damaged.

Reason to kill Hamilton — Revenge, if she believed Hamilton had destroyed the application.

Reason to attack Clark — None.

Her theory about Hamilton — A robber killed him

Grigory Petrov Kuritsyn, 34.

The least affected by Hamilton's general behaviour. One of six occupants in a house used for clandestine activities on Russia's behalf. No evidence, but Hamilton may have jeopardized these activities. Although Kuritsyn is a communist, he is not a willing zealot. Said Hamilton would be attracted to Mrs Fitch (or, by extension, any woman similarly placed) because she has property.

Of interest - he was at the hospital to visit Clark. Had brought butterscotch, which is too difficult to lace with poison.

Reason to kill Hamilton — Revenge for insulting Lenin, etc., although this is unlikely due to his lack of fervour. N.B. May have been under the Doctor's instruction to kill Hamilton, but there is no evidence of this.

Reason to attack Clark — None.

His theory about Hamilton — Drunken brawl with an unknown assailant.

Alan Mellish, 31

Did not care for Hamilton. Was at his workshop just outside of Alexandra Gardens at the time of the murder.

Reason to kill Hamilton — Anger and revenge because Hamilton ridiculed his products.

Reason to attack Clark — None.

His theory about Hamilton — Unknown

Mrs Sandra Pringle, 33

Was involved with Clark but had a relationship with Hamilton. After Hamilton's death, resumed her relationship with Clark and they are now getting married. Very jealous of Clark, so was presumably the same with Hamilton.

Reason to kill Hamilton — Jealousy. Possible revenge if he spurned her, but there is no evidence to prove this.

Reason to attack Clark — Might be demented, but no other discernable reason so far.

Her theory about Hamilton — Unknown

Dulcie Villard, 28

Had an affair with Bristow, whom she now detests. She also detests Sandra Pringle, because of her relationship with Hamilton (Bristow hinted at this.)

Reason to kill Hamilton — Jealousy because he turned his attention to Pringle.

Reason to attack Clark — None.

Her theory about Hamilton — Crime of passion. Definitely hinted at Pringle being the murderer. Possibly hinted at Mrs Fitch.

David Saunders, 31. No longer under consideration.

"Any comments?" asked Sophie.

"The theories about Hamilton's death...," said Flora, "...of those expressed, they all assumed the murderer is an outsider, except for the Villard. I think she's maliciously enjoying herself. What she also does is point to a suspect residing in Alexandra Gardens, which I don't think she would do if she were the guilty party."

"That's very good," said Sophie.

"I just considered the matter psychologically."

"The Styles book again."

"Don't knock it," said Flora. "Wait until you've finished, and then you'll see."

"I hope to. Nancy?"

"Are all murderers barmy?"

"They must be to an extent. Some must be worse than others."

"Well, miss. None of them on the list *look* barmy. But from what I've seen and heard, Alan Mellish has a screw loose. All the others — you meet their types all the time. If I had to pick a suspect based on how they behave, it'd be him."

"He *is* odd," said Sophie.

"Mellish wants attention," said Flora. "That's all that is, and I should know. Work in a theatre production and you'll find there are more attention-seeking grandiose characters than there are actors. There's the drinker, the spurned lover, the god-like creature, the deathless beauty, the 'I'm everyone's friend', the gossip, the dramatic arts purist, and the list goes on. Then they all switch places. Deathless Beauty starts drinking and gossiping, and the Spurned Lover becomes Don Juan and hurls himself at his next victim."

"Good grief," said Sophie.

"Often, the drama backstage is more entertaining than the show."

"I'd like to see some of that," said Ada.

"Would you?" asked Flora. "Should a miracle occur and I get another part, I'll bring you backstage. Be warned, no matter which theatre it is, my shared dressing room is the size of a broom cupboard and colder than the North Pole."

"Would I be able to walk about?"

"Yes, within reason. As long as you keep out of everyone's way, they'll ignore you."

"Thank you. I think it'd be right interesting, I do an' all."

"Do *you* want to come?" Flora asked Sophie. "Can't be on the same night, though."

"I would, thanks."

"Now that we've settled that; Mellish might be crazed, but I don't think he's a violent maniac. He's the type who'd go off in a huff or mutter darkly to others. No violence, though. Now Bristow might turn violent if he were angry enough, but he's the type who would do so right then and there, and not save it for later."

"I agree," said Sophie. "I don't think Major Cummings or Farhan are capable of murder."

"Mind you, it'd be easy to slip poison into a curry," said Ada. "No one would ever know."

"I wish you hadn't said that," said Sophie. "The Major is coming to dinner tomorrow evening."

"Then, we should be thankful Mrs Barker's cooking it," said Flora.

"You should've seen the kitchen earlier," said Ada. "It was as mucky as a trench in there. Indian bits of whatsits all over the place, although it's clean now. Some orangey stuff stained a tea towel and I don't think it'll *ever* come out."

"What stuff?" asked Sophie.

"The sauce for tandoori chicken, miss. Here's the funny thing. Mrs Barker had to make a sort of sauce, then let the chicken sit overnight in it. Tomorrow, she has to cook it, then some of it she's cooking again another way. That sounds like a lot of work to me. A lot of work."

"Is she all right doing all that?" asked Sophie.

"Oh, I think so. She's muttering to herself when she's holding a recipe, but I'd say she's 'appy. Happy."

"Thank goodness," said Sophie. "I take it we've nothing to add to the notes as they stand? If not, I'll make a copy for Auntie's use."

---

Lady Shelling, her glasses perched on her nose, studied the report carefully. When she had finished, she slid the page across the dining room table to Hawkins. This evening, he had dressed in ordinary clothes. Now neither booky nor butler, he might have been taken for a diplomat of few words and vast knowledge. They all waited in silence while he digested the contents. They waited, and they hoped for magnificent pearls of wisdom soon to drop from his lips. If he seemed to be taking a long time, they believed that his utterance, when it came forth, would be all the greater for the intense deliberation he had given the list of suspects. He would announce a clear favourite.

He set the paper to one side, cleared his throat most decorously, then clasped his hands together and placed them perfectly on the table before him.

"I'm confused," he said.

An inward groan ran around the table. When it stopped at Aunt Bessie, it found an outlet.

"What do you mean, you're confused? Who's the favourite?"

"I am some way from announcing that, my Lady."

"Perhaps we can help," said Sophie, getting in before her aunt riposted.

"Indeed, I hope so, Miss King. In studying the document, it is apparent that Mr Clark has the most well-founded reasons to kill Mr Hamilton. I use the term well-founded within the context of the enquiry and not as an absolute statement or an approval of his moral values. Because, as you explained earlier, persons in this house witnessed the attack upon him, it is probable another suspect on the list assaulted him. Presumably, it was the murderer, and not an outsider. It is a remote possibility that there's a second violent criminal among the suspects, but the odds for that are extremely low.

"My confusion arises due to there being no obvious reason in the report for anyone to murder Mr Clark. The danger to the murderer is that the second attack draws police attention squarely back to Alexandra Gardens. The murderer was relatively safe, so many weeks having elapsed. Now that he has struck again, he is no longer safe, and I fail to see why he would take such a risk."

"It's because something is still missing," said Sophie. "We don't know what it is, either, Hawkins."

"Are you saying," said Aunt Bessie, "that there is another motif, as yet uncovered, that would explain why there were two attacks?"

"I am, aren't I? Either the answer is staring us in the face and we just can't see it, or there's more to be discovered, and then we will know."

"Or there might be two or three more things," said Aunt Bessie.

"Quite possibly," agreed Sophie.

Aunt Bessie removed her glasses. "We should continue with what we know. Besides Clark, there are eight runners to choose from, and the most likely to be the murderer is Sandra Pringle, followed by Mr Bristow. Those are my choices. What's everyone else's?"

"Mr Bristow and Mr Mellish," said Ada. "I think a man did it."

"La Pringle and Kuritsyn," said Flora. "I'm choosing Kuritsyn only because I think one of the other Russians might be involved."

"Two firsts for Pringle," said Aunt Bessie gleefully.

"I really can't decide," said Sophie.

"Pick two at random, and make one of 'em Pringle." Aunt Bessie smiled when Sophie glanced at her.

"It feels like we're picking on her. All right. La Pringle and Mrs Fitch."

"There you are, Hawkins. We have a favourite. What's your contribution?"

"My lady, I'm not entirely sure there is a favourite. Without explanation, my choices are Mr Kuritsyn, as representative of the Russians, and Miss Villard."

"If I had a third choice, I'd choose her, too," said Flora.

"Right. I'll leave now," announced Aunt Bessie. Unabashedly, she added, "As I promised, we'll open the book and we'll change the names for when my friends ask for details."

"This doesn't seem right," said Sophie.

"Not to you. Keep me informed of developments, and I'll let *you* know what a betting crowd thinks of the field. Perhaps, with more people considering the matter — and those people being willing to back their judgment with money — we might get somewhere. They may hit upon something we have not yet considered."

## Chapter 24

# Gossip

"April's showers bring May's flowers," said Ada to Biscuit as they stood under the porch watching the steady rain. "I think they've 'ad enough now, though."

It was seven, and the rain had been heavy for much of the night. She raised her umbrella.

"Come on, Biscuit."

She joined three others, also carrying umbrellas and walking their dogs.

"A lot of shirking over a little rain."

Ada overheard Mr Bristow talking to Mrs Fitch. He had his back to Ada, but turned upon her approach.

"Hello, who are you?" he asked cheerily.

"I'm Miss Carmichael, sir. Housekeeper to Miss Walton and Miss King."

"Ah, well. Good of you to turn out. This is Mrs Fitch, and I'm Captain Bristow."

Ada greeted the lady and there the conversation ended. Bristow resumed talking to Mrs Fitch. Miss Villard's maid stood apart with Lulu the poodle. Ada walked the few steps to join her.

"Good morning," said Ada.

"Good morning," said the maid with several degrees of frost in her East London voice.

"That's a clever idea — having a special blanket over the dog to keep the rain off."

"It was custom made and fitted for Lulu."

"That's your dog's name, is it? I'm Nancy Carmichael, Housekeeper."

"Mildred Plumley. I'm lady's maid to Miss Villard."

"Ooh, lady's maid, that's very nice. Where are you from?"

"Upton, near West 'am Park."

"West Ham Park? I'm from Poplar. Near neighbours, eh?"

"You might say that."

"They are sort of next door to each other."

It was Ada's opinion that Miss Plumley wanted her to clear off — probably because the housekeeper had recently caught the lady's maid following her.

"I s'pose your dog being so well groomed an' all, she goes to a lot of shows."

"Yes, she goes to a lot of 'em."

"Poodle, isn't it? You must work hard to keep your dog looking so nice."

"Very 'ard. Every day, really."

"Do you do the clipping or whatever, or does Miss Villard do that?"

"We both do it. She trained me 'ow. Miss Villard's an artist, she is."

"I bet she is. But I reckon it's you what does most of the work."

"Too right, an' all."

"Same with me. I get the place looking nice, and keep it that way, but it's the misses who get the compliments."

"Ain't that the truth? Still, it's what we're paid for."

"That's right... So, has your dog won any of them dog shows?"

"All the time. Lulu is a very superior dog. She always wins a ribbon, and she's won five shows. There was this all-poodle show, and she won it easy."

"Five shows! Blimey... What, Cruft's an' all?"

"Don't talk to me about Cruft's. Some of the dog owners, *some*, I say, not all, are a bloomin' lot of bleeders. All they do is stick knives in people's backs. Honestly, I don't know what the world's comin' to when your betters are no better than guttersnipes. They want to run that show proper, and stop all the bleedin' cheatin'. It makes me right sick."

"I can see that," said Ada. "What cheating?"

"Backhanders to judges, and favours for mates. There's one woman who's the worst of the lot. Call 'erself a lady? She should be ashamed of 'erself. But she ain't. Got a face like a brazen 'ussy."

"Ooh, brazen *hussy*, is it? Somebody do Lulu wrong?"

"I'd say they bleedin' well did. No judge in the world can ignore a dog as beautiful as 'er. But this woman done 'er down, and Lulu don't deserve such treatment from the likes of 'er."

"They sound rotten."

"Yes... What shows 'as your dog been in?"

"Biscuit *hasn't* been to a show."

"*Oh.*" Condescension dripped.

"But the misses are thinking about it."

"Oh, really." Condescension flowed.

This was too much for Ada, who would rather take a personal insult than have Biscuit belittled.

"In the past, he hasn't really *had* the time, you know. He used to be the mascot for the fire brigade in Islington, and he's ever so brave. Do you know, he rushed into a burning house and rescued a little girl from being burnt alive?"

"Did 'e really?"

"Yes, he did." Ada could see Miss Plumley was impressed, so she embellished further. "When he come out of the *house*, his fur was on fire. They chucked a blanket over him to put it out." Ada bent down and stroked Biscuit's side. "All down here, it was. But it's grown back so nice, you can't tell it ever happened."

"Let me see," said Mildred. She studied Biscuit's coat. "No, you can't see it at all. What a wonderful dog. 'Ow brave of 'im was that?"

"Very brave. I don't think he'd take to a blanket like Lulu's. It would bring back bad memories."

"Course it would," said Mildred.

They walked in silence for a few steps, then Mildred spoke again.

"I'm not really s'posed to tell anyone this. But that story of Biscuit's is like what Miss Villard did. She was a lady's maid on an estate. It had a lake out the back. So a little boy, grandson of a duke no less and in line for the title, fell over the side of a rowing boat. Miss Villard was inside the 'ouse and was the only one to see 'im, so she rushed out and saved 'im all by 'erself. She 'ad to swim part of it, but she got 'im back just in time."

"She never did."

"Oh, yes. And you'll never guess what?"

"What happened?"

"The duke settled 'er 'ouse on 'er freehold." Mildred nodded.

"He gave her the house! Well, isn't that something? Good for her, and good for the old duke, an' all."

"I should say so."

"So she knows how to swim?"

"Yes. 'Er father taught 'er at the seaside."

"I'm amazed, I am that. Her swimming and saving a little chap."

"But don't go sayin' nothin'."

"What do you think I am? Course, I won't."

"Call me Millie, please... 'Ere, that business the other day. I didn't like following you. Miss Villard put me up to it and I couldn't say no."

"Oh, I can see how you couldn't. They put upon you something dreadful whenever they like. And you can call me Nancy."

"I will, Nancy, and, yes, they do. Sorry about all that. Miss Villard likes to know what goes on, and she finds out a bloomin' lot she does."

"She would... You know there was a murder around here?"

"Yes."

"What does she reckon happened?"

"She don't tell me much but, being 'er maid, I 'ear a fair bit."

"I'm sure you do."

"She's got it in mind that only a woman could 'ave killed Mr 'Amilton. The way she sees it, it's either Mrs Murray or

Mrs Fitch because of the falling out they 'ad over something. But if it's not them, then it 'as to be Mrs Pringle. Blimey, you should 'ear what she 'as to say about 'er. Coo, it's not fit to be repeated by a decent body."

"Why does she hate Mrs Pringle?"

"'Cause she up and stole Mr 'Amilton from 'er, that's why! Cor, the tears and shouting I've 'ad to put up with. Enough to try the patience of a saint. Are your misses like that?"

Ada, put on the spot, quickly opted to sacrifice Sophie and Flora's characters just a little. "Not as bad as that. No men involved, see. They have rows now and again, and go sulky. Once or twice Miss King has thrown things if she don't get her way. Got a bit of a temper, she has. Miss Walton's different. She likes men's attention, but she isn't what I'd call flirty."

"She's the dark one, I take it. Quite the beauty, really."

"Oh, she is that, but she don't put on airs or nothing. However, she gets irritable if she's not the centre of attention. Not all the time, just now and again. Moody, you see."

"If Mr 'Amilton was still alive, 'e'd 'ave gone for 'er and no mistake."

"Like that was he?"

"Oh, yes. 'E had the looks, the charm, a wandering eye, but no money. Not a bad sort, mind you, but 'e done 'imself no favours by the way 'e behaved."

"Did he say anything to you?"

"A little... Nothing serious." Whatever Hamilton had said to Millie was a pleasant memory for her. "I think 'is charm was the problem. 'E'd say nice things to all women. The sort of thing that some might make too much of, if you see what I mean.

"I know exactly the type."

"'E's gone now, poor bloke." Millie sounded sad.

"Who do *you* think did him in?"

"I don't know. Could be anyone as far as I can see. But it was so close to the 'ouse. If it 'adn't been foggy that night, I'd 'ave seen the killer. I might 'ave seen it as it 'appened. Can you imagine that?"

"Not really. I'm glad for your sake you didn't."

"That's nice of you to say." Millie smiled. "The murder's upsetting enough, but to see it? I'd *never* forget a thing like that. I doubt I'd ever sleep again."

"Me, an' all... But what about this Mr Clark now? What do you think happened there?" asked Ada.

"It brings everything back, don't it? Now we can't walk the dogs proper when we want."

"I think it's the same bloke who done in Mr Hamilton."

"Oh, don't say that. It's 'orrible. Why can't the police catch 'im? That's what I want to know."

"They're lazy, that's why."

"Don't get me started on the police. You can never find a rozzer when you want one. All they do is drink tea and eat buns. There was a cafe in Upton, and they was always in there. Three of them, regular. They should 'ave put one of their blue lamps outside."

"It's stopped raining," said Ada, who folded her umbrella. Millie did likewise and said,

"Now, you was asking about Mr Clark. Perhaps it *was* the same person."

"Maybe Mr Hamilton and Mr Clark were criminal, and they're getting done in because they owe money or to keep them quiet."

"Could be that. I don't know about Mr 'Amilton. Mr Clark's a nice gentleman. Lives next door and 'e's no trouble. Always polite and can be 'elpful on occasion. Although 'e plays piano and other instruments and you can just about 'ear 'em through the wall, 'e's dead quiet the rest of the time."

"What would you say," asked Ada, "if Mr Clark killed Mr Hamilton, and now someone's trying to knock him off in revenge?"

"Oh, no. It couldn't be that. First off, Mr Clark's not the type — too nervy. Could you imagine 'im in a punch-up? I can't. 'E'd get slaughtered straight off. So if 'e's no good for that, 'e won't do a murder. But someone knocking 'im off? I dunno. They'd do 'im in if they thought they'd been seen doin' the other job. That couldn't be, though. It was one of 'is nights at the cinema. But if someone *thought* 'e was there in the fog... Well, you know what I mean?"

"Get rid of the witness, eh? You might be right. You just might be."

"Do you think so?"

"That's the best idea I've heard." Ada paused. "I'll go now. The housework won't do itself."

"It'd be nice if it did. Ta-ta."

Ada returned to the house, very pleased with herself. Not only had she learned vital and interesting information, but she had also not dropped an aitch all the while she spoke. Mildred's lack of aitches had provided the impetus for Ada to enunciate all her own.

---

Sophie walked to Chalk Farm Station to take the tube. For the first time in her life, she was embroiled in the underground rush hour and found it hellish. A train came and she could not board. A second arrived and, with a squeeze, she found a place to stand and held on to an upright bar just inside the door. Four others also gripped the same bar, including a very tall man whose white-knuckled fist was positioned near to the roof. His long outstretched arm threatened her hat, and she feared for its safety. In the press, with all the usual discomforts of other people's close proximity, she could only think one thought: *This is intolerable.*

Upon entering the office, she gave and received the customary round of greetings. As was her habit, she brought in some fruit from Leadenhall Market. The office was busy, and she thought about what a change a year had wrought. The typing work came in regularly, and every month saw a slight increase. Placing domestic staff had its own seasons. Requests for permanent placement were steady and unlikely to grow because the trend had not abated for large country houses to be sold off or even abandoned due to the cost of their upkeep and the ruinous inheritance tax. What continued on as it ever had were the number of out-of-work servants looking for a position. For Sophie, turning away the less qualified candidates or taking their information, knowing there was unlikely to be a job for them, was the hardest part of her business. She saw the resignation of defeat in many faces. With the surge in demand for temporary staff during the London Season, she could help some of the better trained applicants but, beyond them, there was little she could do for the others.

After discussing several matters with Miss Jones, she learned that the typist who was expecting a child had handed in her notice and would be moving to the country to stay with family. Sophie then asked Elizabeth to come into her office. Elizabeth, unlike Miss Jones, was fully in Sophie's confidence and did research for her.

"How are things?" she asked.

Elizabeth had brought with her the register containing the coming events at which Burgoyne's Agency was to provide staff.

"Extraordinarily well. If you would care to take a look, Miss Burgoyne."

Elizabeth opened the register and placed it on the desk for Sophie to read.

"May's filling up nicely," she turned pages. "June... My goodness."

"I *know*. We've been bombarded with requests. The Duchess of Hampshire has asked for eight for three days."

"Eight! That's a record... I wonder if Bunny is being kind and doing us a favour." Bunny Warren was the Duchess of Hampshire, and Sophie's father was an old friend of the Duke.

"I don't believe so, Miss Burgoyne. The measure of relief in her voice sounded quite authentic when I said we could fit her in."

Sophie smiled. "Seeing as Flora Dane and I have known her for years and were her and the Duke's guests, it might not be the thing for us to go as servants. However, I'm sure she'll see the funny side of it."

"Do you think you should?"

"I probably shouldn't, but I'll go if Miss Dane is willing. Is there anything else?"

"Not at present."

"Ah, good. I'd like your opinion on the case," said Sophie.

She informed Elizabeth on how matters stood in Alexandra Gardens, asking if, in the telling, anything had occurred to her that might help.

"I don't know if I can be of assistance. Did the police thoroughly examine the murder scene?"

Sophie explained the proximity of the murder to Alexandra Gardens as well as the dog biscuit bag that strongly suggested a dog owner was the killer. She continued by describing the suspects they had met.

"It's very disturbing, Miss Burgoyne, and I can't see any clear suspect despite all the work that's been done... Alexandra Gardens possesses some rather colourful characters. All I can really think of is a question. Why did the murderer drop the bag?"

"Why? I've just assumed they were getting something from their pocket and it fell or they had it in their hand and dropped it."

"Then why would they have it in their hand?" asked Elizabeth.

"They wouldn't, really. It's only a possibility. You see, the murderer would not have had a dog with him, so he would not have discarded the bag after giving out the last biscuit unless he gave it to Hamilton's dog. There were only two dogs present in the fog, but yet the police accounted for three bags, including the one dropped."

"Then the murderer must have taken out the weapon and inadvertently dropped the bag. I was thinking the person must be untidy in their habits, to keep a used bag in his pocket."

"Which conjecture rules out a kukri knife, as it can't fit in a pocket. Good job, too, as we're having dinner with Major Cummings tonight."

"You must be careful, Miss Burgoyne. Whoever is the murderer is concealing their hatred or jealousy very well."

"Under a well-maintained veneer of respectability and supposed decency... They are, aren't they? I'll bear your warning in mind." Sophie glanced at her watch. "I must leave soon, so I'll tell you all about the dinner when I see you next."

"Very good, Miss Burgoyne."

---

It was nearly twelve when Sophie alighted from the uncrowded train at the Chalk Farm stop. Having caught the train in a hurry, she had boarded through the nearest door. At Chalk Farm, she found she was at the wrong end of the platform for the exit. The north and southbound tracks lay in separate tunnels. As she walked, the train left. The now empty platform really looked like a 'tube', one decorated with squares of white tiles in red-brown borders. As she approached the stairs, she crossed an opening in the wall to the southbound platform. After glancing through, Sophie came to a stop. Was that Captain Bristow she had seen? She turned back. Yes, it was he, waiting for a southbound train. Bristow's back was towards her and he was holding something. Then he did her the great service of slowly turning to walk about the platform. She moved away from the opening unseen. In that brief second, she noticed he was better dressed than usual in a tan overcoat, over a suit, shirt, and tie. Bristow was also carrying a cardboard box about a foot long on each side. He held it with both hands as if it were precious, and his umbrella hung from a forearm.

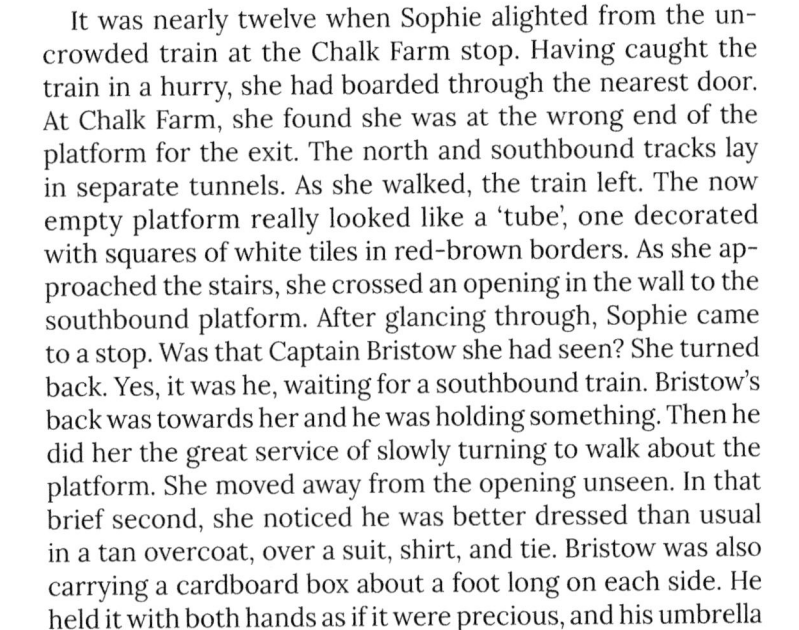

Sophie walked away in a high state of curiosity. Where was he going? What was in the box? She mounted the stairs to the lift platform with its funny little network of passages.

Neither lift was available, so she walked up the spiral staircase thinking about Bristow. She decided that whatever the box contained was valuable, and she tried fitting a theft into the murder and attempted murder cases. Twist and turn it however she might, Sophie could not see where it fitted.

From the back of her mind came a phrase which she had written down as she thought it was important, and then promptly forgot. Mrs Barker's sworn statement was that no one was in St. George's Road after the attack and there were no sounds to be heard. Biscuit had not barked or growled. This must mean the attacker had escaped by entering a house in Alexandra Gardens. The attacker was from the square. This simple revelation of confirmation left no doubt in her mind as she stepped out of the station.

Captain Bristow lived at the furthest point in the square to the attack. Even so, he could have got home before Mrs Barker came out and, if he were still in the square, could have entered his house quietly enough in the dark so that neither the cook nor the dog detected him. The only difficulty Sophie could think of was that Bristow could not easily see from his house if Clark was out in the street. And, no matter who it was, they could not have been lying in wait, because Clark's early morning walk was an aberration from his usual routine. The assailant had to have seen him through a window, or else it was his habit to be out early. Then again, the dog walkers of Alexandra Gardens would never be out early without their dogs, Mr Clark being the exception only because a unique fit of artistic giddiness had driven him outdoors. Sophie jumped as a car went past. She had crossed the road without paying attention.

She remembered Bristow had arrived at the scene of the attack in his dressing gown. At the time of interviewing Mrs Barker, Sophie was thinking the wearing of night clothes might be a significant proof of innocence. Now she realized that someone could change their clothes either way. Clark's attacker may have been in his dressing gown. If not, he may have returned home and put on pyjamas before coming out again, giving the illusion he had just got out of bed.

She was over the bridge now and passing shops lining Regent's Park Road. Negotiating the busy area put an end to her reflections.

# Chapter 25

# St. George's Square

The idea was for Sophie and Flora to amble around St. George's Square with Biscuit and 'accidentally' meet Mrs Murray. A bonus would be to just as accidentally meet Miss Boddington, too. Because such a contrivance had only a faint hope of meeting with success, they determined, in the event of failure, not to leave St. George's without knocking at number 39 — Mrs Murray's grand house, or two doors along at number 37d — Miss Boddington's basement flat, or both.

So far, the agents had only gained a bleak Alexandrian Gardens' eye view of Mrs Murray. Sophie's vague impression was that the woman was seven feet tall, shouted often, and hated humanity, but was especially vindictive towards owners who thought they might enter their dog in Cruft's. Mrs Murray was a dragon of wealth, a gorgon of respectability, and an ogre of moral rectitude. By her wealth, she could do as she pleased with whom she pleased and this included attacking anyone from Alexandra Gardens who dared to hope for a win at Cruft's. Through her respectability, she knew all the right people and, in corrupting and indoctrinating them to her cause, gained the freedom to turn to stone anyone she considered a threat to her dog's chances at the show. In her moral rectitude, a sham as far as her victims were concerned, she claimed that fair play and abiding by the rules were everything, when she secretly devoured whole the independence of judges by hints, whispers, and outright lies

— perhaps even bribes. This was the monstrous Mrs Murray the agents expected to meet.

The afternoon was as bright as it could be without a visible sun. Sophie and Flora left number seven, passed the place where Mr Clark had been attacked, then walked by the side of Mrs Fitch's house. In St. George's Road, they soon came to the place where Hamilton was killed. Nothing made it stand out or declared that here a man died by the hand of another. A few steps further and they were outside the Princess of Wales on the corner. In crossing Fitzroy, St. George's Square became apparent.

"Nothing much happened in the midday walk today," said Flora. "The way they behaved, they're all only tolerating meeting up at regulated times. I think they'll give it up soon."

"Cynthia Fitch certainly rushed to impose her will on everyone."

"And they all meekly accepted. She treated Mr Bristow earlier like a stubborn boy. More or less gave him an ultimatum to put Bo'sun back into training."

"How did he respond to her bullying?"

"He did that vague, smiling type of acquiescence which denotes that he knows he should, he doesn't want to, but certainly won't make a fuss."

"My father does the same sometimes," said Sophie. "Being a vicar, he often has to agree with everyone to keep the peace. 'Splendid idea, splendid' — that's what he says when something's proposed, when really he wishes to avoid it like the plague."

"That's Reverend Burgoyne's self-protection at work."

"Entirely so. He knows that if he approves any work in the parish on his own initiative, somebody, somewhere, will be upset. That's why he has committees look into even the smallest matters."

"I can picture Mrs Fitch thriving in such committee meetings."

"She would. I wonder if Mrs Murray is the same way."

"We'll soon find out," said Flora. "From the gossip in Alexandra Gardens, Mrs Murray is so wicked she must be Lucifer's mother."

"She can't possibly be *that* bad." Sophie laughed.

"She is, the way some of them tell it. All I'll say is this. *You* can knock on the door. When she grabs you and is busy tearing your head off, I'll run away so that at least one of us survives."

"*You* knock," said Sophie. "I'm the faster runner."

"No."

"We'll toss a coin, then."

"Heads I win, tails you lose."

"Fiddle-de-dee. Here we go." Sophie took a penny from her pocket. "Call." She tossed it.

"Heads... Oh, just my luck. I'll knock, but you speak first."

"This is getting rather silly. Very well, I'll speak, and you can be the pudding."

They reached St. George's Square. Although very similar in design to the smaller, more intimate Alexandra Gardens, the enclosed garden here was more expansive, and its northern side did not 'close the box' so to speak, but opened onto a confluence of residential roads. This gave the square an airy feel. The houses of St. George's were as large or larger than those of the surrounding area. Mrs Murray's house was one of the two most imposing residences.

"That's it, next to the end house," said Flora, pointing towards the north side.

Number 39, when viewed across the small park, was what estate agents would term a 'desirable and prestigious residence,' 'a villa among villas,' and 'a paragon in aspect, setting, and location!'

"It's very large for just one person," said Sophie. "Seven or eight bedrooms, I should think."

"Has to be. Perhaps members of her family live with her."

They took a slow tour around the railed communal garden.

"It's so quiet. Peaceful, even," said Flora.

"Yes... What did you make of the Villard story of saving a child and being rewarded with a house?"

"Ha, I'm not sure I believe it." They turned a corner and moved closer to number 39.

"Knowing what she's like, it makes one skeptical. We've been thinking she's all one way, but her saving a child from drowning in deep water demonstrates an immense amount of selflessness." Sophie sighed. "I hope it is true, yet it's brought me up short."

"The way she's behaving obliterates whatever she may have done in the past. The Villard's a troublemaker at the very least. We must deal with her as we find her."

"Sage advice," said Sophie.

The front door of number 39 opened, and through it came a smiling young woman so well dressed she might have stepped out from a magazine. In charge of a pair of King Charles spaniels, she hurried down the steps, coat open, and laughing. Then she briefly waved to someone at the door before proceeding to a car.

"Lanvin coat and Callot Soeurs dress," said Flora.

"Whose dress?"

"Callot Soeurs. Très chic. Every fashionable woman who goes to Paris buys one to prove she's been."

"Don't ask me how I know this," said Sophie, "but her new little two-seater is a Lagonda 11.9."

"How do you know?"

"Elizabeth and I have regular discussions about cars and their relative merits."

"You're both becoming very peculiar... I say, that must be Mrs Murray."

The very person they sought had come out of the house and, from the top of the steps beneath her porch, was waving goodbye to the young woman. Mrs Murray wore a long, belted, beige and black cardigan over a dark calf-length dress. According to the records, she was forty-eight. Although tastefully dressed and her hair well-groomed and surprisingly short, she seemed at once both older and younger than her years. Her movements and face were those of a woman in her thirties; the broad white streak of poliosis in her otherwise thick chestnut hair suggested a much older age was breaking out. Simultaneously and independently, Sophie and Flora wondered why she did not dye her hair to hide the white forelock.

As the car was driven away, Mrs Murray looked about the square. Her gaze was arrested by the sight of three newcomers to the area. From the agents' point of view, in that face-to-face moment, her distinguishing streak of white arching back from her forehead in a way ennobled her. The two young women could now appreciate why she had kept her streak, bold choice though it was.

Mrs Murray hesitated. She was very interested in Biscuit but, being disinclined to speak to two strangers, was about to go in.

"Hello!" Sophie called cheerily and started walking towards the woman.

"Hello," said Mrs Murray. She descended several steps when Sophie and Flora were close. "I couldn't help noticing your dog. A Laekenois, isn't it?"

"That's correct," said Sophie. "Many don't know the breed, so we're often asked."

They watched as Mrs Murray studied Biscuit. "May I?" She held out her hand partway towards the dog.

"Of course. He's friendly," said Flora.

"And well-behaved," added Sophie.

Mrs Murray smiled and put her hand close to Biscuit's muzzle. He dutifully sniffed and wagged his tail as though recognizing a friend. She stroked his head.

"You're Mrs Murray, aren't you?" asked Sophie. "We were actually on our way to see you."

"Were you?" the lady answered cautiously.

"Yes. This is my cousin Miss Walton, and I'm Miss King. We're from Winchester originally, but we're hoping to move to Primrose Hill."

"Oh?" said Mrs Murray, puzzled as to why she was being told all of this.

"Yes. We've been given to understand you're an expert on Cruft's."

"Ah... Do you intend entering your dog?"

"That's correct," said Flora eagerly.

"Well, I wouldn't hold myself forth as any type of *expert*, but I am familiar with the inner workings of the show."

"Then you're just the person."

"May I ask how you found me?" asked Mrs Murray.

"We're temporarily staying in Alexandra Gardens," said Sophie, "and several of the dog owners there said you were the person to talk to if one wanted to know exactly what to do."

"I'm surprised they directed you to *me*." Mrs Murray become guarded, making it apparent she was about to end the conversation. "I can supply the address of a person who can help you with your application."

Sophie saw that the chance to find out anything about the murder was rapidly receding.

"I believe you never received Cynthia Fitch's application."

"What did you say?"

"Mrs Fitch's application. Mr Hamilton never gave it to you, although he said he did."

"This is outrageous. I will not talk about it."

"We work for the police," said Sophie. Flora was as one thunderstruck.

"Our job is to gather information for the case," continued Sophie. "We were hoping you might shed some light on this application business. It's doubtful it has anything to do with Mr Hamilton's murder, but we can't ignore it, either. Also, we really would be interested to hear how the Cruft's application process works."

"Then why didn't you say you were from the police to begin with?"

"Because usually we can find out more if we don't. If you prefer, you can telephone Scotland Yard and ask for Detective Inspector Morton. If he's not available, you can always speak to Superintendent Penrose. Either of them can explain what we're doing here."

"Penrose," repeated Mrs Murray. "I shall do so. Wait here." She went into her house and shut the door behind her.

"Whatever made you say that?" asked Flora.

Sophie sighed. "We would have got nothing from her, otherwise. I took the chance only because we know she's not talking to anyone from Alexandra Gardens, so she won't inadvertently reveal our mission."

"As far as we know, she won't."

"That's the risk."

"Well, it's done now, I suppose."

Within a few minutes, Mrs Murray opened the door, obviously annoyed, and curtly said,

"Superintendent Penrose would like a word with you."

Sophie and Flora entered the house. The floor plan differed from their own number seven, and Mrs Murray guided them into a small and very comfortable lounge at the front. The telephone stood on a Georgian secretaire with its flap down. Sophie picked up the receiver.

"Hello, Miss Phoebe King speaking."

On the other end of the line, Penrose asked,

"Know of any good beers?"

"Anything but Government Ale."

"Thank you. Put Mrs Murray back on."

Sophie held out the receiver for Mrs Murray, who took it and conversed with Penrose for a minute before hanging up.

"He requested I assist with your enquiries and keep the matter private. I can't say I'm pleased by your rather underhanded behaviour, but I will be co-operative."

"Thank you," said Sophie. "We apologize for the duplicity, although it has been necessary to accomplish the task the Yard has set us." Sophie leaned forward. "Sorry for being so rude."

Mrs Murray stared at her and then, reluctantly, gave a short laugh despite herself. "You have a question?" In speaking, she returned to the calm demeanour she had possessed when they first met.

"Yes. What did Mr Hamilton say to you about Mrs Fitch's application?"

"I don't see how that can be important, but very well. He said that when he came in with it, I was busy, so he left it in the secretaire." She pointed to the open desk where the telephone now stood.

Sophie was not sure what she should ask next and certainly wished to avoid giving Mrs Murray cause for offense.

"He just left it? Could anyone have taken it?"

"No. I can vouch for every one of my servants. All I can think is that he was mistaken. I find it implausible, but there can be no other explanation."

"Who let him in?" asked Flora.

"He let himself in. He had a key."

Neither agent wanted to ask her the obvious question.

"I suppose I should tell you. Mr Hamilton, or Matthew, as I knew him, was the son of a friend of mine who died some years ago. It was his father; he died in 1910. He, Matthew, I mean, contacted me after being invalided out of the army. He, um, he had a bad time of it. Matthew had been wounded and suffered from shell shock, you know. That was in 1915, and I've been keeping an eye on him ever since. He came to live here for the first few months of his convalescence. When ready, he moved into a flat in the square. He recovered, but his nerve... Well, it had gone, you see. A small thing could suddenly send him into a panic, and then he would have an angry outburst... We managed to hide it, but it was sad to witness, and he had never been like it before. Never. In fact, quite the reverse.

"Because of the state of his nerves, I accepted his version of what happened to the application. I don't doubt he received it, but, after that, who knows what he did with it?"

"Could it still be among his effects?" asked Sophie.

"They've all gone. His uncle dealt with them after the police had finished. He gave me a few photographs and keepsakes, but all of Matthew's clothes and papers were removed."

"He lived at number 37c. Did he not own his house?" asked Flora.

"No. I own number 37. It's divided into four flats."

"Oh, I *see*."

"How was Mr Hamilton when talking to other people?" asked Sophie.

"He tried very hard to fit in, and act normally. Poor boy was nervous… He confided in me a little. Matthew tried to be humorous with men, but was often awkward and several times he caused offense. With women, he was different. He had a natural charm, but was too effusive. I know he caused more than one little problem."

"In Alexandra Gardens?" asked Sophie.

"Yes."

"How many little problems?"

"I really couldn't say."

"Please, Mrs Murray," insisted Sophie, "try to quantify these problems, as we're calling them. It is important."

"Three. I really shan't say more."

"All dog owners?"

She replied slowly. "Yes."

"Thank you. We don't like to intrude, but it can't be helped at the moment."

"Do you think someone in Alexandra Gardens killed Matthew?"

"We can't say, because we simply don't know. It's a question of our chasing down details that otherwise seem insignificant, but may lead somewhere. The missing application is one of those details."

"It would be such a relief if you could find the killer."

"We shall try."

In the brief silence that followed, Mrs Murray's eyes quickly brimmed over and several tears dropped before she could use her handkerchief.

"There was so much death during the war. It should never have followed him home."

"It's certainly most unfair," said Sophie. "I agree. There's no reason it should have followed him, even in an abstract sense. It did, though. Miss Walton and I are determined to see justice done in a concrete fashion, here, on British soil, through the proper operation of just laws."

"That doesn't bring him back."

"Unfortunately, no."

"What I can't fathom," said Flora, "is, if he insisted he left the application here, and came in especially to do so, he would have left it where he said he had. Could it have fallen somewhere, or been accidentally discarded?"

"As I said, the servants never saw it, and I searched the desk."

"Does it have a secret drawer?" asked Sophie.

"Two, but I went through them. Anyway, he wouldn't have hidden it. He was somewhat careless with papers and things."

"That seems to be that, then," said Flora.

Sophie stared at the desk. "How was he with money?"

"Ah, well, he was not well off, so he was rather careful with money."

"Then he might have hidden the envelope, knowing there was money in it?"

"But where? Matthew could have said at any time, but he maintained he had put it in the desk. Only an hour after Dulcie Villard left, I came in here to use the telephone. I would have seen it."

"Miss Villard?" queried Sophie.

"She cuts my hair. Matthew arrived during my appointment."

"Ah, I see." Sophie did indeed 'see', but kept her thought to herself. She glanced at Flora, who said,

"It seems we've gone as far as we can with that. I was thinking about Miss Boddington. Does she not also live at number thirty-seven?"

"She does. Why do you ask?"

"She's often out and about. I met Miss Boddington in the park and she was agitated, almost fearful. Is she all right?"

"Not really. I don't see what she has to do with Matthew, though."

"They lived in the same house," said Sophie. "Perhaps she knows something."

"I don't think it likely. Allow me to explain. Miss Boddington owned number 37 for many years until she sold it to me. She was already a trained nurse when war broke out, so she went to France in 1914. At the end of sixteen, she returned, but was noticeably quieter than before. Until she retired, she had always worked in London hospitals. Never a communicative person, after France she did become more withdrawn and less cheerful, but I would have said that was all that was wrong with her. I still found her pleasant and ready to help with small things. She's a dependable, hard-working type of person, as nurses often are. The marked behaviour you've noticed came about after Matthew's death. That's when she started talking to herself. It's obvious her nerves are affected, just like Matthew's."

"Has she been any worse since the attack on Mr Clark?" asked Sophie.

"I haven't really seen her to be able to comment... Do you believe the attack on Mr Clark is related to Matthew's murder?"

"It's quite possible. That they occurred in the same area and were similar in nature leads one to believe that they are. However, there's nothing definitely connecting the two at present."

"Would it be possible to speak to her?" asked Flora.

"I don't think she would talk to strangers."

"If you would introduce me and Miss Walton, it might reassure her," said Sophie.

Mrs Murray gave her a stony look. "I'll only do that if you promise you won't upset her. She rarely mentions Matthew, and she's worried about something, but hasn't told me what it is. The least thing might stir her up."

"We'll be as sympathetic as we can, but it's impossible to avoid discussing Mr Hamilton's murder. However, we'll be very tactful, and stop if she becomes at all distressed."

"As long as you do, then very well. We can see if she's in now, so wait here for a moment." Mrs Murray got up and left the room.

"The foul Villard stole the application," whispered Flora.

"That's the only answer. But what does the odious creature imagine she's doing?"

"It has to be spite or blackmail."

"Shh, she's coming back," whispered Sophie.

## Chapter 26

## Indian Extravaganza

For many people, there is a certain cachet to being seen leaving the best house on a notable street in a respectable neighbourhood. Never is it the *right* people, however, who behold such a praiseworthy event, but only an assortment of drifting strangers.

Sophie and Flora, on the other hand, descended the steps of magnificent number 39, totally heedless of such considerations. A ray of spring sunshine blessed their descent as they followed in the wake of Mrs Murray, the doyenne of St. George's Square. There *were* a few strangers in the square present, who naturally took no notice as Mrs Murray sallied forth with her King Charles spaniel. Both Sophie and Flora noticed, even if Mrs Murray did not, that Miss Villard was walking Lulu on the other side of the square.

"Blast it," muttered Sophie under her breath. Biscuit looked at her. "Not you," she added.

"We'll have some answering to do," whispered Flora.

"Good," said Sophie. "I want a word with the Villard."

They quickened their pace and caught up with Mrs Murray before going down the stone steps to the basement flat at number 37. The older woman knocked, and they all waited.

"Miss Boddington must be out," she said after knocking a second time, her spaniel sitting quietly next to her.

"Yes," answered Sophie. "May I ask if your dog is related to the two we saw earlier?"

"This is Cherry, their mother. The pups are both males, and it's most amusing how she used to dote over them, but now gets fed up with them within a quarter of an hour."

"She's such a pretty dog," said Flora. "Has she been entered in Cruft's?"

"Yes, and she did well." Mrs Murray looked from one young woman to the other. "You say you're staying in Alexandra Gardens. What number?"

"Seven."

"The Radcliffe house. The family has more or less died out. Old Mr Radcliffe's estate is in trust until a minor comes of age and can take charge of his own affairs. Do you know if number seven is for sale?"

Remembering Archie had an interest in the house and, considering that Mrs Murray already owned at least two properties in the area, Sophie said,

"I don't think it is."

"A pity. There's no point in our waiting here..."

She stopped because a figure with a dog was standing at the gate above them at the top of the steps. They all looked up. Miss Boddington was watching them, her hand tightly gripping the latch.

"There you are, dear," said Mrs Murray. "We don't want to come in or put you to any trouble. These ladies are acquaintances of mine, and they'd like to speak to you for a moment. Do you mind?"

"Not if they're your acquaintances."

"We'll come up. We don't want to be calling across the railings."

With that, Mrs Murray mounted the steps. Once they were all on the same level, Mrs Murray did the introductions.

"What do you want to see me about?" asked Miss Boddington. She seemed about sixty and there were circles under her eyes. A gaunt woman with a worried air, it appeared she wasn't taking care of herself. Sophie noticed several things — a button missing from her coat, fluff on her hat, and creases in her light scarf.

"We've seen you about," said Sophie, "and hoped we could meet. What's your dog's name?"

"Pepper. He's a real comfort to me."

"I'm sure he is."

"Our dog's name is Biscuit," said Flora, who thought it expedient to establish the correct version.

"He looks like a nice dog," said Miss Boddington.

"Oh, he is," said Sophie. "So does Pepper."

"I've seen you," said Miss Boddington, suddenly pointing at Flora. "In the park."

"I remember," said Flora.

"It's dangerous. You be careful and don't stand still or they'll creep up on you."

"Will they?" said Sophie. "We've heard some things, but who do you mean, exactly?"

"Don't know. There have been two attacks. The police can't stop them from happening, nor can they find the attacker. And poor Matthew Hamilton died, but they don't care."

"I think they do care, but they have no clues. They hope a witness will come forward."

"If a body saw something, they should do their duty. But there's seeing something and then there's *knowing* something. No one saw him die, but you can *know* who did it, right enough."

"Do *you* know?" asked Sophie.

"I'm not saying."

"We're living in Alexandra Gardens," said Flora.

"Oh. Then you know Mrs Fitch."

"Not very well, but we've met her several times. Is she a friend of yours?"

"Tell her... No. Don't tell her anything. Best I don't say a word." Miss Boddington reached into her disorderly handbag for cigarettes and matches. They waited while she lit one. While this was ongoing, Mrs Murray excused herself and took her dog for a walk.

"Alexandra Gardens," said Miss Boddington. "Nothing but trouble there with all the wagging tongues."

"We have noticed. They're not all equally bad, though. Major Cummings is a decent gentleman."

"I don't say anything against the Major."

"What about Miss Villard?" asked Flora.

Miss Boddington almost choked on her cigarette. "She's the worst. Wants to find out everyone's secrets and stoops low to get them. I won't talk to her ever again." She now began looking about the square in a furtive and suspicious way.

"Do you fear someone?" asked Sophie.

"Yes."

"Why don't you tell us? Perhaps we can help."

"I can't trust you. I can't trust anyone now."

"Not even Mrs Fitch?"

Miss Boddington's hand shook as she drew on her cigarette. "I don't know what game she thinks she's playing. She used to be my friend. Close we were. But there, I shan't speak of her."

Sophie and Flora exchanged puzzled glances.

"Then we won't mention her again," said Sophie. "What we *would* like to know is what you think of the attack on Mr Clark."

"Brought it on himself. He should never have used the oil."

"Oil? What oil?"

"He helped the murderer, and she helped the murderer. Now retribution is coming to both of them. There's no telling where a murderer will strike next, but Mr Clark is as good as dead, and she'll be dead next... Then I'll be dead."

"Oh, surely not." Sophie stared at Miss Boddington. "What is the name of the 'she' to whom you refer?"

"I'm not saying who she is," the woman replied defensively, "and I'm not saying who the murderer is. But didn't I already know that Mr Clark *would* be murdered? Only, he wasn't, but that was by sheer luck alone."

"Have you told the police any of this?" asked Flora.

"I gave a statement after Matthew Hamilton died, but I watched the constable sneer at what I'd told him. Dismissed me as a fool. Now it's all coming right... I don't want to talk about this any more, so don't you press me... You young ladies, you watch yourselves. Don't tell anyone anything I've said. I've not even told *her*." She pointed at Mrs Murray in the distance. "That's for her own good. The less she knows, the safer it is, but it's too late for me... Goodbye, and goodbye to you, too, Biscuit. He's a very nice dog."

Sophie and Flora said goodbye and stood for a moment. When Miss Boddington was halfway down the steps, she turned to them and said,

"Would you like to come in and have some tea?" It seemed the offer was being made out of a sense of propriety rather than anything else.

"Thank you, but we have a few things to do," said Sophie. "If you find yourself in Alexandra Gardens, just remember, you'll always be welcome at number seven."

"That's kind of you." Miss Boddington gave a ghost of a smile before turning away.

They caught up with and then took their leave of Mrs Murray, thanking her for her help. They walked away quickly and soon left St. George's Square.

"Does Miss Boddington know who the murderer is or only imagine she does?" asked Flora.

"It's very hard to tell. She's convinced she's on to something — we can be certain of that much. I counted four things of importance. First, she's disappointed by Mrs Fitch, although she refused to say why. The second is regarding Mr Clark and the oil. The third is that Mr Clark aided the murderer in some way, and will be killed because of it. And then there's a woman, she didn't specify whom, who also aided the murderer and who will also be killed."

"I wondered if she meant Mrs Fitch... What a beastly set of thoughts with which to be burdened."

"It's awful," said Sophie. "If Miss Boddington really predicted the attack on Mr Clark, why does she seem so much more settled now than she did before it happened? She was doing all that muttering, and then shouting, but apart from her odd ways, today I found her quite lucid up to a point."

"Almost rational. I noticed she called Hamilton by his first name. She must have been friendly with him."

"They lived in flats in the same house — her old house," Sophie pointed out. "They had both been through the war and suffered accordingly. I suppose they would well understand one another's past. And now she's lost him. What a dreadful shame it all is!"

"Do you think she'll ever be right again?"

"There's always hope, if she can get the proper treatment," answered Sophie.

"The hardest part of that is convincing her she needs treatment in the first place." They walked on in silence. "When are we going after the Villard?"

"As soon as we clap eyes on her. Tomorrow morning at the latest. She obviously stole the application just to cause trouble."

---

Later, Sergeant Gowers came for the daily reports and Nick to give and receive messages. Sophie informed Gowers of the latest developments. He was interested and took notes, and reciprocated by telling her that Clark had definitely been at the cinema at the time of the murder. He went on to say that when Hamilton attended the cinema two days earlier, as evidenced by the ticket stub in his pocket, no one had seen him speak to Clark, and Clark had acted as usual.

The rest of the afternoon was one of showers, uncomfortable dog walks in those showers, and unrewarding conversations with people who felt dull because of the rain. Yet number seven was cheerfully ablaze with lights. Inside the house, a thrill of excitement ran upstairs and down. Sophie and Flora tidied the lounge and laid the dining room table. Ada fussed over what crockery and serving implements were best to use, while in the kitchen, Myrtle prepared a salad and other things. Mrs Barker was in a life and death struggle with several bubbling pots. It was the Indian Extravaganza Night. Even the agent in the attic, bored silly with the view, attempted to identify the cooking odours emanating from below. He sniffed repeatedly and, although the cooking smells were unlike anything he had encountered before, he found himself extraordinarily hungry, to the point that his stomach rumbled.

The kitchen had three guinea pigs available to it, if Mrs Barker included herself in the count. According to a set of instructions as to exactly how much should be used, the spicy heat for the Indian dishes came from two jars she had received. One was innocuously labelled 'Red Powder' and the other 'Chilies'. Early in the proceedings, Mrs Barker tasted a few grains of the powder and instantly regretted it. The thought came to her that if she made an error with either of these two ingredients, everyone would be going to the hospital. Consequently, she made up several small trial batches and fed it to her guinea pigs. The kitchen rang with exclamations and oaths when the first sauce was tried and Ada thought she was on fire. Further, more moderate, experimentation yielded an unexpected outcome. Ada was for mild, Mrs Barker was for the mild side of medium, but Myrtle's tolerance to spicy heat surprisingly appeared to have no limit.

"You don't find that *hot*?" Ada was incredulous when Myrtle ate the first sauce as though it were rice pudding.

"No. It's just a bit strong, really."

"Could you stand it hotter?" asked Mrs Barker.

"Oh, yes," said Myrtle.

Ada and Mrs Barker stared at her and then at each other.

"Could you eat one of them chilies?" asked Ada.

"I don't know, Miss Carmichael. Shall I try one and see?"

"Go ahead," said Mrs Barker, using a spoon to retrieve a small green chili from the brine in which it was preserved.

Myrtle put it in her mouth and chewed it. They stared at her in amazement, expecting a violent reaction at any second.

"Now that's nice and hot. I don't think much of the taste, though, Mrs Barker."

"Don't you? It's meant to be used in cooking, not eaten raw."

"I can't believe you ate it," said Ada, who had sworn off chilies for life after eating a small fragment in the chicken makhani.

There seemed to be nothing else to say and, as much was still to be done, they returned to work.

They had made the old-fashioned dining room look beautiful. The glass sparkled, the silver gleamed, the white linen tablecloth looked pristine under the electric lamplight, and the old blue and white Spode plates exuded elegance. Two four-branched candelabra had fresh candles ready for lighting before everyone sat down. All was set.

In the kitchen, and only minutes before Major Cummings arrived, Mrs Barker was in that final stage of frantic anxiety wherein she believed she must have forgotten something important. According to the list, she was ready, and with only the poppadoms to cook, a fear beset her. She worried that the Major, the Indian cuisine expert, would condemn her efforts as those of a rank amateur. The test was somewhat of importance to him, but for her it would either be the culmination of a cherished dream or a hope turned into a nightmare. As far as she could tell, everything was edible, but would it pass muster?

The Major arrived a few minutes before seven. Ada took his hat and coat and showed him into the parlour, where Sophie and Flora greeted him. After a sherry, they adjourned to the dining room. Ada served the appetizers, assisted by Myrtle; Mrs Barker ensured everything went in piping hot.

Chutneys, na'an, poppadoms, and onion bhajias — *Funny lot of stuff*, thought Ada, as she watched the three diners begin their assault upon the dishes. As her taste tester, Mrs Barker had made Ada sample everything and, so far, Ada's favourites were the bhajias and chicken makhani. Mrs Barker had made plenty of everything, so she had no worries about there not being leftovers for their lunch tomorrow. The rogan josh was too hot for her. Then she wondered why Indian people, who live in such a hot climate, ate such hot spicy food. Ada found it quite inexplicable.

"I think I could live on onion bhajias alone," said Flora, helping herself to a third from the bowl on the table.

"They are *very* good," said Sophie. "What is your opinion of the food so far, Major Cummings?"

"I am agreeably surprised by Mrs Barker's culinary skills. Everything I have tasted is excellent... I should mention these tests fill me with trepidation. It is not the ingredients so much as my failure to communicate the proper methods of preparation and cooking."

"How did you manage in the army with cooking for so many?" asked Flora.

"When I started out, I was in charge of a Sikh regiment. There, I learned more than I taught. I did some cooking but, as a lieutenant, that was my choice. As part of my job, being in the Royal Army Service Corps, I had to ensure the men were well fed and to arrange for supplies. I decided to get good quality ingredients locally when I could. Some food supplies from Britain were poor quality or unsuitable for Sikhs. Later, I had the responsibility for many regiments with a mix of races. The troops were Hindu, Muslim, Sikh, and European. This meant I had the headache of ensuring no one was served with what was according to their religious practises an unclean food. That required a lot of juggling on occasion. A *lot*."

"I'm sure it did, Major," said Flora.

"Apart from the scale," said Sophie, "it's not unlike providing for a large household."

"*Exactly*, Miss King. The only actual difference was when the army campaigned. That was as unlike a picnic as could possibly be. The vagaries of teams of oxen, mules, and the peculiar class of person who drive them can wreck the most cautious and careful plans. I remember once..."

He related several anecdotes and, by the time he finished, the main course arrived. For several minutes, they served themselves and tried the different dishes. To the Major's amusement, Sophie and Flora delightedly exclaimed over every new little thing.

"We've noticed you're avoiding the scheduled walks," said Sophie. "Does that mean you think we're safe from attack?"

"In a general sense, I believe we are. I won't say the walking groups are unnecessary, because I could be wrong. Since discussing the matter with you, I've thought over Hamilton's death and the attack on Clark. To my mind, the same hand is at work because of the similarities. It seems it is the hand of a neighbour, but his or her motivation eludes me. I can't actually believe it's someone I know, but that doesn't mean it isn't... I suppose I'm avoiding the meetings in case I start suspecting someone. They might speak in an offhand manner, which will raise my suspicions, and then I'm afraid I'll convince myself of their guilt when, all the while, he or she may be perfectly innocent."

"That's a possibility, I suppose," said Sophie. "Would it not instead be better to plumb the depths, as it were, and exonerate whom you can?"

"That's what I'm avoiding, partially because I don't know how to set about it. In India, I often had to deal with men up on charges — usually, it was petty pilfering from the stores. However, I never took part in the investigation. They presented the miscreant to me for punishment. I heard the case and gave my decision. The situation here is entirely different."

"I think what Miss King is driving at," said Flora, "is that you might play a part in solving the case, because of something you know. It may be that you don't realize you have a vital piece of information."

"But I was at home when it happened."

"True, but we're thinking more about the motive for the crime."

"I see what you mean. Excuse me for my slow comprehension. I shall give it some thought."

The Major's attention returned to the food.

Downstairs, Farhan knocked on the door. Ada answered.

"Mr Farhan! Please, come in," said Ada.

"Thank you, memsahib."

"Is there anything I can do for you?"

"I beg that you permit me to assist in restoring the kitchen to perfection."

"Pardon? You mean you want to help clean up?"

"That is exactly my request."

Ada hesitated a moment, then smiled.

"Many hands make light work. There's plenty to do."

"Yes. And the reason I did not come before is that too many cooks spoil the broth."

"That's right, an' all." Ada laughed.

Because he was technically a guest, Ada set Farhan to work drying the dishes. Mrs Barker interrupted his labours to have him taste her chicken makhani and rogan josh. He pronounced both 'excellent', which transported Mrs Barker over the moon and brought a rare smile to her face.

In the dining room, and after an interlude of effusive comments upon the various dishes of the main course, Major Cummings returned to the subject of motive.

"I cannot think that anyone would have a reason to kill Hamilton. He was frequently tactless, bordering on the insulting but, to my knowledge, he never went further than that. I suppose a person might harbour some resentment, but not to the point of attacking him."

"I understand he was only like that with men," said Sophie.

"That's correct."

"Could he have insulted someone that night and they lashed out in anger?"

"If that were the case, then I can see Bristow playing the part, but not anyone else. As for the ladies... It's quite inconceivable."

"Unless it were une affaire de cœur," said Flora.

"That puts it in a very different light... Among some in India, there was, I'm sorry to say, a loosening of morals. A married lady shot an officer whose reputation was rather poor. She wounded him slightly, and the matter was hushed up and kept from the courts. It was certain, however, that in her impassioned and distracted state, she intended to kill him."

"Could not a similar situation have arisen involving Mr Hamilton?"

"It's possible."

The Major continued eating. Sophie and Flora exchanged glances, then allowed him a few uninterrupted seconds of silence in the hope he would elaborate, which he did not.

"Do you have anyone in mind?" asked Flora nonchalantly.

"Unfortunately, I do. I'd better not say who it is or give my reasons."

"Ah, it's probably Mrs Pringle," said Sophie.

"Sandra? Oh, heavens, no... I was thinking of Cynthia Fitch."

"Mrs Fitch! May we ask why?"

"Please, I'd rather you didn't."

"Of course, we won't, then," said Flora.

"However, I will say this. I cannot see *any* reason for her to attack Clark or, indeed, have anything against him. They've always been on exceptionally good terms."

The conversation turned again to the dinner. Major Cummings was delighted with Mrs Barker's efforts and pronounced everything a success. He said as much to the blushing cook and commended her without restraint. Privately, he thought her basmati rice to be a little on the stodgy side. He determined to review his instructions in case they were at fault. It might also be necessary for him to emphasize the goal of achieving a dry fluffiness for the rice, to offset the ingrained national habit of boiling vegetables to death.

# Chapter 27

# Disappearing act

At a little after nine, Flora, Ada, and Sophie sat in the parlour after Major Cummings had left. Biscuit was in his usual place on the rug.

"We almost had a revelation," said Flora. "The Major definitely picked upon Mrs Fitch, but didn't say why. That was very inconsiderate of him, when we want to know."

"Unless it's something completely different," said Ada, "Mrs Fitch must have taken such a shine to Mr Hamilton that the Major noticed."

Sophie glanced at Ada.

"I said the aitch proper, didn't I? Mr Hamilton... Glory be! There's hope for me yet. Do you know, when I was talking to Mildred Plumley, I aspirated every aitch while she missed all of hers?"

"You're coming along really well," said Sophie.

"Yes, and keep at it, because you can do it," said Flora.

"Returning to the Major's statement, it's supported by inferences from Miss Villard and Mrs Murray," said Sophie. "Are we agreed on this statement? Mrs Fitch was besotted with Mr Hamilton."

"Yes," said Flora and Ada. Flora added,

"Along with the Villard and la Pringle."

"And Mildred, only she was a mild case," said Ada.

"Then there is the friendly affection towards him from Miss Boddington and Mrs Murray... Would *we* have become besotted, do you think?" asked Sophie.

"If he were superficial, no," said Flora emphatically.

"That's a difficult question, miss. I reckon that when someone's nice, even if it's all on top and just show, you sort of like 'em despite your better judgment."

"The charming rogue," said Sophie.

"That's it."

"We've all met a few of those," said Flora. "I can't help thinking about Miss Boddington. Apart from Mrs Murray, she must have known Mr Hamilton the best, and his loss has upset her dreadfully. I can see that his violent end is *part* of the upset, but she must also miss him as a neighbour and friend. Hamilton must have been helpful or kind towards her. So there's another side to him we will never know about."

"Also about his suffering. Shell shock — it can't be easy living with those memories."

"Some turn to drink," said Flora.

"And suicide," said Ada. "A bloke down our road hung himself on the clothes hook on the back of a door with a tie. The note he left said he didn't fit in anymore. Sad that, ain't it? After all he'd been through, to think he didn't belong anywhere. He should have told someone."

"That is very sad," said Sophie. "But they never talk about their war experiences. They positively refuse to say anything, and I don't think that can be healthy for them."

"Miss Boddington suffers an' all," said Ada.

"She does. I think Mrs Murray tries to take care of her. When she said she had purchased Miss Boddington's house, I initially thought she might have taken advantage of her. Upon reflection, I can see how Miss Boddington might have got into a muddle or could no longer afford the upkeep of her house, so, perhaps, Mrs Murray was doing her a kindness."

"Let us hope so," said Flora. "Otherwise, it would be despicable of Mrs Murray."

"I don't think she is despicable. Remember, she was also looking after Hamilton who was having difficulties."

"When people go off their head like that, is it always permanent?" asked Ada.

"Some recover," said Sophie. "I don't know if this counts. There was a farmer near Havering-under-Lyme who went into a decline after his wife died. He was about fifty and became depressed and then let his farm go. Father used to talk to him often. After a while, the man came out of his bad patch. He sold up and moved into the village and, I would say, he was quite restored afterwards."

"I'm glad for him," said Flora. "I don't have any such anecdote to relate. I suppose if someone has a traumatic experience, time is the best healer. If they can see an alienist, that might help — if they can afford the expense."

"I don't understand what it is they do," said Sophie.

"No one does. That's why they can charge so much."

"This ain't the same, but me Nan was delirious once, 'cause she had a fever. Scared the daylights out of me, she did."

"What happened?" asked Sophie.

"Well, I was twelve at the time, and at home. Me Mum was busy with all the littl'uns and running the house, so she couldn't sit with me Nan any longer. She'd been sick for a couple o' days, heaving away, until she could heave no more. So I was sent to sit with her."

"Wasn't it catching?" asked Flora.

"No. It was a case of bad prawns. Did they ever make her sick. So I was sitting there, reading, and she's in bed fussing away in her sleep. All sweating, she was, and I stuck a cold compress on her forehead and it warmed up almost immediate. Then she pulled it off, so I sat down and waited. I thought I was waiting for her to die, I did an' all. Then she calmed down but was still asleep, so I read me book.

"It was as quiet as anything. Then, without any warning, she let out this horrible groan that made me jump. Then Nan sat bolt upright in bed. Her cap's come off, her 'air's sticking up in spikes, she's all of a muck sweat, and her eyes are open — all red-rimmed and *wild*. Then she turns to me and stares as if she's looking right at me but can't see me, and says in this awful, croaking voice, 'orrible it was, 'Cut your toenails straight across!' She stares for a moment longer before collapsing on the pillows... I thought she'd gone. I really did. So I ran over and picked up her hand to find her pulse, but I never found it. Anyway, she was still breathing, and that was the main thing. I ran downstairs and told Mum, and she come up and 'ad a look. She said Nan was just sleeping and that the doctor was coming the next day, so we should try an' keep her going until then, but it was best to let her sleep.

"The next day, the doctor arrived but Nan was better, so she 'ad a bit of a row with him. Asked him what was the point of him coming when she was on the mend? Why hadn't he come when she was poorly and 'ad to have the bucket next to the bed? He couldn't answer her, so he buzzed off. She ate like a horse afterwards and got up the following day. I told you all that, because she really was off her head, but come round right as rain again. I'm hoping it's the same for Miss Boddington, only it's taking longer.

"That's not really the same, because it was your Nan's delirium speaking," said Flora. "The fever raised her temperature and distorted all her thoughts."

"I'll say it did. You must be right, though."

"I'm thankful she recovered," said Sophie. "But what did she mean by saying, 'Cut your toenails straight across?'"

"Nan's always had trouble with an ingrowing toenail, 'cause she shaped them instead of cutting them straight. She's me dad's mum and didn't know. My mum knew, and she warned me. When she told Nan while she was having another spell with her big toe, she exploded. I've never seen her so bloomin' angry. Ever after she's been warning all the girls in the family to cut straight across."

"I didn't know any of this," said Sophie.

"It's those little curved scissors in the manicure sets that do it," said Flora. "They may be solely responsible for the country's ingrowing toenail epidemic."

"You knew?"

"Yes. Mama gave me the timely warning, too. How have you escaped the affliction?"

"I don't have a manicure set, so I've always used a straight pair of scissors."

"The angels are watching over you."

They heard a knock on the back door. Ada went to answer it.

"Who can that be?" asked Flora.

Her question was soon answered when Mr Breed-Dankworth entered the room. Biscuit watched him, then looked at Sophie.

"Good evening, Mr Breed-Dankworth," she said.

Biscuit settled back down.

"Good evening, Miss King and ladies. I'm sorry to disturb you, but something important has cropped up."

"Has it? Please, sit down."

"Thank you, but I can't stay. The Doctor from number fifteen has gone out by himself. I have one man following him but, unfortunately, my two others are already out trailing Kuritsyn and Razov. I can catch up to the Doctor by car, but I wondered if one of you ladies could join me. It's important we don't lose him."

"Should we bring Blast-it?" asked Sophie.

"Uh, no, thanks."

"Then I'll join you while Miss Walton remains to observe the square and can take the dog out, if necessary." Sophie got up and went to the hall for her coat. "Is it cold out?"

"No, it's not too bad, actually. They're promising fine weather for tomorrow."

"I trust we won't be gone that long but, anyway, let's hope they deliver on their promise," replied Sophie, as she put on her hat and coat, scarf, and gloves. She knew from the weight of the coat that her blackjack was in a pocket, as should be her police whistle. "Umbrella?"

"Better safe than sorry," said Breed-Dankworth. "Although I don't believe it shall rain."

Sophie thought it was colder than Breed-Dankworth had led her to believe, but it was not too bad if she kept moving. They had left Primrose Hill and were now proceeding over the bridge at Gloucester Gate. On the other side of the road was a Home Office agent and ahead of him was the Doctor. Sophie knew his name was Doctor Teplov, thanks to Mr Bristow, but because everyone had acted so cautiously about using his name, she kept that information to herself.

Breed-Dankworth had explained in the car, before dropping her off, that she was the reserve in case the following agent was identified by the Doctor. If that happened, Sophie would take over the chase while Breed-Dankworth kept close by in the car. She found the idea silly because, should Teplov spot the agent, he would surely look all the more diligently for others, and then spot her, too. Not that she minded the walking; it was welcome, almost necessary, after all the Indian food she had eaten.

At the corner with Albany Street, the HO agent and his quarry turned. Sophie hurried across the bridge to keep up. It was here that Teplov caught the HO agent, just as Ada had caught Mildred, Miss Villard's maid. But he did not see Sophie, because she cautiously peered around the corner first and jumped back without his having seen her. While she waited, Breed-Dankworth drew up in the car. He slid down the passenger window.

"What's the matter?"

"He's caught your man. If I go around the corner now, he'll catch me, too."

"Yes, he will. It's a dead straight road, and he'll also notice the car."

"Where's he likely to be going?" asked Sophie

"At a guess, the Doctor's heading to the Fabian Society, although they're not usually friendly towards Bolsheviks. 17 Osnaburgh Street is nearly a mile south from here. "

"Then why don't you drive ahead and wait for him. I'll take the next road over and come back onto Albany."

"Chancey, but there's no alternative. You'll have to hurry. Follow the Outer Circle until you get to Chester Gate, then cut back through."

"I will."

"Sorry, I can't give you a lift, Miss King. At least it isn't raining."

"There's that to be said."

"Good luck."

Sophie sped off towards Regent's Park, and Breed-Dankworth drove away. He soon parked his car in Laxton Place and then left it there while he went to shelter in a doorway on Longford Street. From this vantage point, he observed the entrance of the Fabian Society.

Sophie walked as quickly as she could, heading south past rows of extraordinarily fine Regency houses designed by Decimus Burton, and built by his father, James. In the vast darkness on her right lay Regent's Park. The road itself was well lit, but the park only had lights around its fringes. She hurried past a policeman and bid him good evening. He gave her an odd look when returning the salutation, but said no more. Soon, she was warm. By the time Sophie got to Chester Gate, she was hot. Calculate it how she might, she could not tell if she would be behind or in front of Doctor Teplov when she reached Albany. She marched along the narrow road, her attention fixed on the junction ahead, and ready to dive into the scant cover available.

To her relief, Teplov was no more than two hundred yards south of her on the opposite pavement. She charged after him, using the few parked cars as barriers in case he looked back. He did turn, and she slowed to a dawdle, becoming intensely annoyed at having been seen. What he had made of the woman two hundred yards behind him, she could not tell because his pace did not vary after he began walking again. She resumed closing the gap, but at a lesser rate. Almost immediately, he went around a corner. Sophie hurled herself after him. When she arrived, he had gone. She followed, but could not see him along Little Albany Street when crossing it. This narrow backstreet was surprisingly well-lit, but where millionaires may be living on the Outer Circle, Little Albany, four streets over, was dilapidated and ramshackle, almost slum-like and dirty.

Where she found Teplov was at the south end of Munster Gardens, standing near a lamp post, but in the shadows. He was waiting for someone and, she deduced, if he was at the rendezvous, Teplov must believe he was safe from pursuit. She looked at her watch and it was ten minutes to ten. It was difficult, but she found the suitable doorway of a darkened house for an observation post and waited there, watching.

Munster Gardens was in decline and had fallen much further than Alexandra Gardens. The bones of the houses here were good late Georgian and early Victorian, but the brickwork was blackened and the area was fast running to seed through lack of repairs. Her view across the hedges bordering the road bisecting the square permitted her only to observe his head and shoulders. She believed, hoped, she was invisible to him.

Within a few minutes, a rapidly moving figure from the south approached Teplov's position. He was a young man, taller than Teplov. He stopped under the electric lamp, but Teplov made a gesture to bring him into the shadows.

As far as Sophie knew, Teplov was a Russian spy of some great magnitude. The man he met had to be a neophyte — not more advanced than herself. She was learning a lesson while on the job — keep in the shadows so as not to be seen. It made her wonder why they had chosen a well-lit square in the first place. Both men looked about them, then they started towards the eastern end of the square.

Sophie, surprised by the amount of lighting, saw the tall chimney of a small power station nearby and now knew why there were so many lamps in the area. She more than *saw* the power station — she could taste it because the wind was light and variable. Little wonder the nearby houses were so smoke-stained.

Through a network of narrow streets and alleys, she followed them. They crossed Stanhope Street to enter a short cobbled road of some dozen low, flat-roofed and plain-faced terraced houses. Sophie watched from the corner as they entered the middle house on the north side. She observed the younger man opening the door with a key, switching on the hall light, and then standing aside to allow Teplov to enter first.

In the ten minutes it took for the young man to re-emerge and retrace his steps, Sophie had cooled off considerably. She raced away to hide behind a post box. Now she did not know what to do. Follow the man or watch the house? She supposed Teplov might stay there the night, so she determined to follow the young man. When it was safe, Sophie went to the house Teplov had entered to make a note of the number. Then she chased after her quarry.

Sophie believed she was being quite spy-like, far superior to the young man who never once looked around as he traversed Osnaburgh Street. Realizing the Fabian Society was just ahead, she stopped at the intersection with Longford Street and found a suitable place to shelter. Sophie almost jumped out of her skin when she found it was already occupied.

"It's all right, it's me," whispered Breed-Dankworth.

"Thank goodness for that," she whispered back. She took cover in the doorway.

"Did you lose the Doctor?" he asked.

"No. That man now entering what I suppose is the Fabian Society at number seventeen met the Doctor in Munster Gardens."

"Really?"

"Yes. I followed them to 8 Seaton Place. It's a terraced house close by, and in quite a poverty-stricken area. Anyway, that young man had the front door key. It seems the Doctor's staying there, although he brought no luggage with him."

"I see."

"Do you? I don't. What's going on?"

"The Doctor is moving into the house or he's leaving the country. Either way, the lack of luggage means he's obscuring his tracks."

"What do you mean...? He'll send for his luggage when he feels safe? Who is the younger man I followed, and safe from whom?"

"Safe from us or... I'm not at liberty to divulge any details."

"Then neither am I."

"What do you know?"

"Many things, Mr Breed-Dankworth. You mean the Politburo. I know the Doctor has enemies."

"How do you know that?"

"Ah," she said archly. "I would discuss it with you, but if you're not going to be communicative, then that's that. You can drive me home now."

"I have to stay here."

"Oh... I know, I'll borrow your car."

"I'm sorry, I need it."

"You're not sorry, and it's unsporting. Although I didn't do very much, I got you out of a jam."

"You did, and for that you have my gratitude, but I can't leave my post and I may need the car."

"Then, good night. Think twice before asking for another favour."

Sophie swept away, thoroughly disgusted with the Home Office.

# Chapter 28

# Another disappearance

Thursday promised interesting developments in Hamilton's case. Sophie and Flora had determined more pointedly to interview Mr Clark, Miss Villard, Miss Boddington again — if they could catch hold of her — and Mrs Fitch. They felt they were closing in on someone — a little more of the right information would disclose the murderer. Even if they found no evidence strong enough to convict, Sophie felt there was enough understanding scattered about Primrose Hill of who the killer was. This only needed to be compiled and interpreted properly in order to point unequivocably to the perpetrator. Then, with a suspect in sight, the possibility of closing the case increased exponentially.

It was eight o'clock and after breakfast. The agents met in the parlour.

"Mrs Fitch has gone out for the day," said Ada. "Gone to visit her brother. He's a dog breeder with a small farm, but I didn't hear where it is. He's come up to town to meet her for lunch, and she'll be back late this afternoon."

"Oh, that's a pity. I wanted to talk to her first," said Sophie.

"S'posin' she's the murderer and scarpers, miss?" asked Ada.

"Then at least the police will know she's the one they want. But if she returns, we intend talking to her without making her suspicious."

"Easier said than done," said Flora. "If she is the murderer, she's going to be highly suspicious no matter what questions we ask. It's the same for la Pringle and the Villard."

"So you think it's definitely a woman, miss?"

"It's leaning that way. All three of them have some explaining to do. Mrs Fitch with her passion for Hamilton, and the missing application; Miss Villard, the same; and Mrs Pringle and her jealousy. Conversely, no additional information has been provided about any of the men."

"And we can't go to the police without anything definite," said Sophie. "We're balancing out probabilities. As of today, Mellish seems no more likely to have attacked Hamilton and Clark than when we first met him."

"It's the same for Bristow," added Flora. "Whereas the good Major is beyond reproach."

"And Farhan wouldn't hurt a fly," said Ada. "He's ever so nice, he is an' all. Talk about good manners."

"Yes," said Sophie. "Then there's Mr Kuritsyn. He seems to want to avoid violence, and has an air of indolence about him that makes me believe he just could never be bothered to murder anyone! I mean, look what he does with those wretched fliers. He just wants to *lose* fifty of them every day because that's the number he's been told to offload. Recruiting for the revolution means nothing to him."

"Then test Kuritsyn," said Flora. "Ask for fifty fliers and see what he does."

Sophie laughed. "Of course he'll give them to me. I'll do it."

"Who will you see first, then?" asked Ada.

"We're going to the hospital to visit Mr Clark."

"Then let's go now before La Pringle gets there," said Flora.

They arrived at the hospital just after nine. In the ward, two nurses were dealing with a patient behind a screen as Sophie and Flora entered. The same woman who sat holding the hand of the vacant-looking man was already in her place. He seemed more animated today. In the last bed, Mr Clark was reading a book.

"Good morning," said Sophie and Flora.

"Good morning. How nice of you to come."

"We've brought you some fruit this time," said Flora.

"You're so kind."

"Someone's looking after you," said Sophie, pointing to the piles of books, magazines, and delightful things to eat.

"Sandra is making such a fuss over me, and more than that. Open the drawer, if you please."

Sophie did as requested and stared at a musical score with lyrics.

"Take it out."

She did so and read the title. "If I Wished Upon A Star."

"It's marvellous. We worked on the libretto for the song yesterday, and she came up with some tremendous ideas. We finished it together. There, what do you think of that?"

"It's a match made in heaven," said Sophie.

Clark laughed. "That sounds like another song title to me." He laughed again.

"Would you like us to sing it?" asked Flora, scanning the page over Sophie's shoulder.

"Could you?" He was touched. "It would have to be done quietly though... The other patients, you see."

"It would be *safer* if we did, too. Please forgive any *rust* you may detect," said Sophie.

"*Oh, Miss MacInnes,*" said Flora. "Our music teacher was a tartar." Then she mimicked a Scottish accent. "There shall be no R-r-r-ust found in any of *my* gels' voices!"

"She trilled the word and was an absolute tyrant," said Sophie, "but we all loved her."

Together, they looked through the score. "Ready?" asked Flora. Sophie nodded. "On the count of three." They began.

Mr Clark, with half a smile on his face, let his thoughts drift to unknown regions as he listened. They had good voices and readily grasped the melody. Classically trained as he was, he could hear the defects in their performance, but they had caught the spirit of the piece.

"Thank you, my dears," he said when they had finished.

"All the shop girls will be singing it," said Flora, "and that's the surest sign of success."

He beamed at them. "You're *too* kind."

"It's very good," said Sophie. "We expect tickets to the first performance," she said, laughing.

Unfortunately, his happiness was so expansive that his shoulder caused him to wince.

"You poor thing. How is it?" asked Flora.

"It's more of a dull ache now. Thank you for asking."

"Have the police been back?" asked Sophie.

"No, they haven't. It leads me to believe that my case is now lost among their blessed files somewhere. Have you seen them in the Gardens? Are they doing *anything*?"

"No," said Flora innocently, knowing full well that Sergeant Gowers was actively working on the case in conjunction with the local police.

"Just as I thought. As for my shoulder, they change the dressing and tell me it looks no worse, and it needs two weeks before I shall notice a difference. From what I hear, they might put it in a plaster cast if these straps don't do the trick." He sounded annoyed. "The doctor will tour the ward later this morning, so perhaps I'll find out more then. I sincerely hope so."

"I'm sure they're taking good care of you," said Sophie. "But doctors sometimes keep things back until they're sure of what to do."

"To make themselves seem more important, no doubt. Either that, or they don't really know *what* they're doing. But I shall find out. I intend getting definitive answers. Plaster cast - yes or no? When do I go home? And I'll get an exact date from him."

"Do so nicely," said Flora, "or he might tighten the straps until you shriek."

"You're right there. I should be careful... A timely warning, Miss Walton."

"Do you know to whom we spoke?" asked Sophie. "Miss Boddington. We had seen her about, and she was acting rather strangely, but we stopped and spoke to her yesterday. She seemed much calmer."

"Did you? I do wonder about her mental state. It's very sad. She used to be such a pleasant woman. What, may I ask, did you discuss?"

"I was about to say, actually. She mentioned you, and she was quite insistent..."

"Disturbed, really," interjected Flora.

"Yes, disturbed, about *you* and some oil. She said we should ask you. We couldn't imagine what on earth she meant. Do you know?"

"Oil?" His perplexity showed. "I've no idea what she can have in mind."

"She was most insistent," said Flora.

"Oil? How extraordinary." He considered the matter for some seconds. "The only oil I believe she can refer to is when I oiled the hinges on Cynthia Fitch's side gate. The gate made a dreadful sound, and it only wanted a few drops per hinge to silence it. Cynthia had no oil, so I offered to help. Do you think it can be that?"

"Perhaps," said Sophie. "How did Miss Boddington get involved?"

"She was passing while I was oiling the thing. I remember now. She said, 'About time. That door has wanted seeing to for a while.' Or something like that."

"When was this?" asked Flora.

"Let me see... Late January, I believe. I can't give you the date, because I'm very hazy about such things, but I do recall it was a Wednesday... Or Thursday. During the week, anyway. Why is it important?"

"Only to put her mind at rest when we see her next," replied Sophie.

"Ah, I see. Well, give her my regards. I often think of her... Her condition's quite sad, you know. Very sad."

They talked of several other things until it was convenient for Sophie and Flora to leave. On their way out, Sophie said,

"It's Mrs Fitch, isn't it? She had Mr Clark oil the hinges so she could get through the gate without making a noise and attack Mr Hamilton in the street. Her side gate is only a dozen yards away from where he was struck down."

"You're leaping to a conclusion but, I agree, it looks altogether too suspicious. Then Miss Boddington knows the gate was oiled, and has decided that it was used at the time of the attack."

"Yes, but she doesn't blame Mrs Fitch for the murder, does she? She holds something against Fitch, but not the murder."

"We must see Miss Boddington and find out," said Flora.

---

"Good morning, Miss King," said Nick, opening the front door for them. He was waiting for Sophie and Flora to return and had been playing with Biscuit.

"Good morning, Nick. You're early."

"Hello, Nick," said Flora.

"Morning, Miss Walton... I'm here, miss, 'cause Lady Shelling is going out somewhere in her car, and she dropped off a message for you at the agency, knowing I'd be bringing it later."

"I wonder where she's going? Where's the message?"

He helped them take off their coats like a little gentleman, and they thanked him.

"On the table, in the parlour, miss... He's a lovely dog, ain't he? Do you really call him Blast-it?"

"Yes, although his real name's Biscuit."

"I call him Blast-it like you, miss. I think it's *high*-larious."

"Hilarious, please," said Sophie. "I'm glad you've joined my team of one."

"How many commands does he know?" the boy asked.

"There's a list of thirty," said Flora. "We have to be careful what we say in front of him."

They entered the parlour.

"I'd love a dog like him, all trained up and what not. Couldn't be better."

Sophie opened the note from her aunt.

"He's acrobatic, too," said Flora. "When we take him to the park, he does these amazing leaps while chasing a ball."

Nick looked at Biscuit wistfully.

"The racing crowd has given their verdict on the murder case." Sophie held up the note.

"Do tell," said Flora.

"You got people bettin' on the murder? What, Lady Shelling an' all? Well, I never."

"Nicholas! Do not repeat a word of this to anyone. It's a sort of experiment, which is the best face I can put on it. But I don't like it at *all*."

"That's because Lady Shelling's a force to be reckoned with."

"I *beg* your pardon! Do not pass remarks about my aunt!" She glared at him. "And that expression," Sophie spoke slowly, "did *not* originate with you."

"No, it didn't, miss. I overheard it."

"Hmm… You should be careful you don't trip over those big ears of yours. Now be quiet, or I'll bung you out."

"Sorry, miss."

Sophie read out the note, which contained the following information:

No. 15, Red House — 3/1. (Kuritsyn et al.)
No. 20, La Pringle — 3/1. (Pringle)
No. 14, Flush with Success — 5/1. (Bristow)
No. 2, Queen of the Lavatory — 6/1. (Villard)
No. 24, Royal Command — 8/1. (Fitch)
No. 19, Dog Biscuit — 12/1. (Mellish)
No. 9, Hurry Curry — 25/1. (Major Cummings)
No. 1, Mystery Man — 50/1. (Clark)
No. 12, The Witness — 100/1. (Saunders)
(Final prices - book now closed. 217 bets placed.)

"Gosh!" exclaimed Flora. "Two hundred and seventeen!"

"Auntie knows a lot of people, but that number surprises even me."

"Who or what is a La Pringle, miss?"

"A lady who lives in the Gardens, and I'm not explaining any more than that."

"Oh. So almost everyone thinks the Russians or La Pringle killed Mr Hamilton? How can they know?"

"The answer is they don't," replied Sophie. "It's all guesswork... Good grief, can you imagine the conversations this has sparked?"

"All too well. Let's hope there isn't an MP among them who feels it incumbent upon himself to bring it up in the House of Commons."

"Surely, he wouldn't?"

"Not if his choice wins."

"Oh, don't. It doesn't bear thinking about... This is the first and last such escapade for Auntie. Never again. I won't stand for it."

"None of my aunts are anything like your Aunt Bessie. They're all delightfully vague except for the grumpy one."

"I have a grumpy one as well," said Sophie. She looked at Nicholas. "Do you have any aunts?"

"I have three, miss, and they all act the same. They used to pat me on the head and say, 'Look how you've grown.' Now that I'm taller than them, they say something like, 'Ooh, look at this young man. Will you ever stop growing?' I dunno, they're nice and all that, but they don't half embarrass me. It was worse when me voice broke. Coo, you should have heard 'em then, miss."

"You poor thing," said Flora. "However, they're only being kind and affectionate in their way."

"I know that, miss. But fellas like me, well, we don't like a fuss being made, that's all."

"Nick, is there much typing going out today?"

"A fair bit came in, but there's not much going out at the moment. Although it'll be a rush tomorrow, miss."

"Ah, then I might have a job for you here. We're going to Miss Boddington's in the next few minutes. If she's not in, I want you to track her down. She's most likely to be at the shops or in the park with her dog. You'll wait nearby when we knock. If there's no answer, off you go."

"Right-o... Important, is it?"

"Very, but we're not sure why yet. You see, we don't quite agree with the choice of favourites on this list." She held up the paper. "Although they may be correct, and we may be wrong."

"Who do *you* think done it?"

"Did it."

"Did it, miss?"

"At the moment, Mrs Pringle or, increasingly, Mrs Fitch."

"Number twenty, La Pringle, 3/1, and number 24, Royal Command, 8/1. She lives right across from here." Nick grinned.

"Can you recall the whole list?"

"Yes, miss."

"Go on, then," said Sophie.

Without error, Nick recited all the entrants as Sophie had read them.

"You have a very retentive memory," said Sophie. "That could be useful in the future."

They were all quiet with their separate thoughts until Sophie broke the silence.

"Come along, Blast-it. We're going for a walk."

---

Flora knocked on Miss Boddington's door, but no one was home. They climbed back up the steps. At the top, Flora gave a subtle shake of her head. Nick, some distance away by the side of the road, was examining a tyre at that moment. Deciding his bicycle was fit for use, he pedalled away.

"Where to now?" asked Flora.

"Fitch is out, so let's see Miss Villard. We must stay near Alexandra Gardens until Nick returns."

On their return journey, they bumped into Mr Mellish, who was accompanied by the scampering Topper.

"Hallo, 'allo. Taking advantage of the fine weather, are we?" As usual, he wore an odd assortment of clothes, but this time they were mostly hidden under overalls.

"Good morning," said Sophie and Flora. "It is a lovely day, Mr Mellish," added Sophie.

"Now let me see. You've been here nearly a week, and you look *fairly* trustworthy, so I think you can call me by my first name. I'm Alan, if you didn't already know."

"Well, Alan," said Flora, smiling, "this is Phoebe, and I'm Gladys."

"Phoebe and Gladys. Gladys and Phoebe. Excellent. Now that we're the best of friends, I can tell you of the significant change I'm making. I'm renaming CereBone. It shall henceforth be called Biscuit Bone. There, Phoebe. I've gone and pinched your idea. Will you sue me?"

"Only if you make lots of money."

"That's the right attitude. No point in suing me now, unless you just want to do it for the legal exercise, in which case, be my guest. However, and don't tell Kuritsyn this, I would dearly like to become a capitalist, but I shall not be a hard-hearted one. I will bestow upon young Biscuit here a lifetime supply of said Biscuit Bone. Look at that. He recognizes the name. What an intelligent animal." Mellish reached into his pocket and produced a bag of biscuits. He gave one to Biscuit. Topper looked up at him expectantly. "As if I'd leave you out, you old devil." Topper was also soon crunching away.

"Thank you for the future supply," said Sophie. "Blast-it will certainly appreciate it, as do we. Now, I've been meaning to ask you something. We met Miss Boddington yesterday. She was moderately rational, although we had seen her about beforehand when she certainly wasn't. What do you think is the matter with her? And my second question is, what has she against Mrs Fitch?"

"The war is the answer to your first question. Poor old Boddy has been in a decline ever since. I talk to her occasionally, but usually she avoids Alexandra these days. Prefers the park and St. George's for walking her dog. In the past, she used to be over here all the time. Your second question's a bit of a facer. Could be one of a few things. They used to be thick as thieves. Then Boddy wanted to have a go at entering a dog show, and blundering Cynthia told her not to bother because of Boddy's dog, Imp, being a crossbreed. I had a go at Cynthia about that. I told her she herself was a crossbreed. That didn't go down very well, but serves her right. Imp's a lovely dog. She should have encouraged Boddy instead of crushing her hopes. At the very least, she could have been more diplomatic about it."

"You think it's over that?" asked Flora.

"No. I just thought I'd tell you to give some colour. Cynthia's a bully, as you've probably found out. Most of the time, she's sensible and helpful. Once in a while she becomes tyrannical, and blunders about. We all keep quiet because it blows over quickly. The next row between Boddy and Cynthia was more spectacular. It was about Hamilton. Broadly speaking, Cynthia maintained Hamilton was evil, while Boddy, acting as defending counsel, said no one understood him, least of all Cynthia. Then, and this was the stinger, Boddy accused Cynthia of setting her cap at Hamilton when she shouldn't. Cynthia went into a towering rage. That was probably the most interesting row I have ever witnessed. They each vehemently denied everything the other was saying."

"When did this happen?"

"Um, this year. Early January, I believe."

"No wonder they don't speak to each other," said Flora.

"But they *did* speak again. Three weeks ago, Boddy came looking for Cynthia. As luck would have it, I was on hand when she found her. Poor Boddy, she was out to sea and almost incoherent. It didn't last long. She accused Cynthia of harbouring a criminal. That's all she said, but she repeated the charge four or five times. Cynthia responded in a kindly way, telling her to have a cup of tea and a lie down — that sort of rot. Boddy marched off shouting and hasn't been seen since in Alexandra."

"I saw her," said Sophie. "A few days ago, she was sitting on a bench watching Cynthia's house."

"Was she? The poor little lovey. She must be so lonely. I'll visit her later on, not that we were ever particularly close. Still, a visit from me is probably better than nothing."

"I'm sure she'll appreciate it," said Sophie.

"Yes, she will," said Flora. "You must have realized by now that we're dreadfully nosey."

"Aren't we all?" said Mellish conspiratorially and with a smirk.

"Phoebe saw Mr Bristow at the underground station and he was carrying a box as if it contained the Crown Jewels. We wondered what was in the box."

"Did you, indeed? Are you aware of Bristow's trade? I daren't elevate it by calling it a profession."

"Lavatories," whispered Sophie.

"Then you know. Is no secret withheld from you… Ah-ha. Dulcie Villard has been talking out of turn again. I can't swear to have certain knowledge of what was in the box, but I've a pretty good idea. He designs the pedestal that must never be mentioned. First, he draws the diagrams, then he produces a working scale model in clay. Bristow applies glaze, then pops them into a small kiln to fire them. Afterwards, if they haven't fallen to pieces, he tests his concept for flow and a few other things."

"How on earth does he do that?" asked Sophie.

"Holds them under the tap or, I'm told, he uses a working miniature cistern. Then, when he thinks he has developed the perfect throne, he takes the drawings, models, etc., and off he goes to meet a chum who will manufacture the prototype. What happens after that, I don't care to know."

"Neither do we," said Sophie. "So Mr Bristow makes little working lavatories. I don't know why, but I find that incredibly amusing."

"Because it's high-larious," said Flora.

"High-larious? I'll use that one," said Mellish. "Cynthia will soon correct me on it."

"Will she?" asked Flora, who smiled broadly at Sophie.

"And so she should, too," said Sophie.

Mellish laughed. "It's always interesting talking to you, ladies. I must push off, though. There's something that needs blowing up."

"You say things like that only to get attention," said Flora.

He grinned. "Works, don't you know? Until the next time."

# Chapter 29

## All change

It was still Thursday morning, and Mellish had just left Sophie and Flora walking Biscuit in Alexandra Gardens. Kuritsyn appeared in the square.

"Comrades!" he boomed from a distance, then headed towards them.

"Good morning, Mr Kuritsyn," they said when he was closer.

"Splendid day for the revolution," he said as he reached them. There was a large envelope full of leaflets under his arm.

"If you have fifty leaflets in that envelope, I'll take them all," said Sophie.

He stared at her. "Excuse me, Comrade Miss King. The explosions around the barricades must have affected my hearing. Did you say fifty?"

"Yes."

"Unbelievable. Let us move further along so no one can see us from number fifteen. I must keep the envelope, you understand? We're running low, and if they see *you* with the envelope, they will know what I'm doing and find some way of shooting me."

"Don't be ridiculous," said Sophie. They began walking.

"No, it's true. They often look out of the windows and everything they see goes into reports. The reports go to the Kremlin. Orders will come back to shoot me."

"That isn't true."

"Not exactly. This is what they will *really* do. When my time here has expired, I'll go back to Russia. There, they'll arrest me without warning, and then they'll shoot me. For myself, I don't mind so much. But what will happen to Vova if I'm dead?"

"Are you serious?" asked Flora.

"Absolutely, Comrade Miss Walton. We Russians are a very serious-minded people. That's why we never laugh unless drunk."

"I've seen you laughing," said Sophie.

"That's from the vodka I had for breakfast."

"You *are* joking now," said Sophie. "But is it true you will be returning to Russia?"

"Yes, unless I can get a certificate of naturalization, I must go back. Of course, I *could* go underground, but if I'm caught, I'll be deported. Now, my problem is this, I have to be here five years to qualify. I have nowhere near enough time in dear Old Blighty. So, Secretary of State must fix it for me. But he will say, Kuritsyn? Who is this fellow? No, we don't want him. Throw him out."

"I am sorry," said Sophie.

"Not as sorry as I am." He looked about him, and then over the hedge towards number fifteen. He lowered his voice. "You get Secretary of State to fix it for Kuritsyn... And Razov, but Kuritsyn first."

"Well, I wish we could, but we don't know him."

"Hmm. Unless I'm mistaken, and I'm *not*, you both work for the British government. I don't tell this to the Doctor. He's gone, by the way. Razov is in charge of house now."

"But we're cousins...," began Flora.

"Excuse me, comrade. You may be cousins, but why do you have a *man* in your attic? Only I know this. He has camera, and when he set it up, I saw the curtain move. Before you, there were spies in number seven, so I watch carefully to see who moves in next. The Doctor knew of the spies. I knew it. We all did, and then one of them dropped his notebook and we picked it up and gave it back to him. What a durak. At present, no one at number fifteen thinks you are spies. No. But I know you are, because I still watch. I was not suspicious at first, even with all your harmless questions about Hamilton, *but...* they made me think. In the beginning, I say to myself, no they are lovely English women, that's all. But when I see camera, I say, Kuritsyn, you have made mistake. I have eyes, I watch closer. Every time someone walks their dog, there you are, too. I think the English spies are clever to pick on the dogs, but why? Answer — to find Hamilton's murderer. Your questions now become plain to me. It is part of a plan. You disguise well, but once I see through the veil — *everything's* obvious."

"So you think we're police spies?" asked Flora, sounding as incredulous as she could.

"I *know* you are. But, you also talk to Razov, hmm? And you want to come to meeting tonight, yes? That means you are police spies *and* you keep watch on number fifteen. Cannot be otherwise. All is plain, but I don't tell Razov *any* of this. Not a word. I swear it on Vova's head."

"Mr Kuritsyn," said Sophie. "I shall see if there is any interest in your request. What can you offer the British government in exchange?"

"Of state secrets, I know nothing. Razov may have something, I'm not sure. But let me tell you this. Russia is running rings around Britain in spying matters. You are all looking the wrong way. Your laws are lax and justice is very slow. You give too many of the wrong people benefit of doubt. Russia uses this to its advantage. Remember, and never forget this: Soviet Russia is dedicated to exporting revolution, overthrow of monarchies, overthrow of democracy, and seizing *all* capital and means of production. It will use every method it can to accomplish these things. Britain fights spy war with blindfold on and both hands tied behind back. In the Kremlin, they laugh. It's a big joke. Ha-ha! Therefore, they drink and enjoy themselves. Now listen. You might catch one or two spies, but miss the other twenty who are *right* under your nose. I can help the British government with this. As for Razov... I don't know if he will help or not. Let someone else approach him.

But for me, I will assist your government, and if Razov can be given the chance of being naturalized, then I will be happy… By the way, his English has taken a bad turn for the worse. You should hear him tonight just for that. Oh, yes. I mustn't forget. Long live Comrade Lenin and the sublime revolution. I leave now, and these are yours."

He extracted all the fliers from the envelope and handed them to Sophie.

"I'll do what I can. I can't promise anything at present, but I will get an answer for you."

"You will try your best, I'm sure. I look forward to seeing you tonight, comrades." He clicked his heels together and gave a curt bow. Then he left with his empty envelope as though he meant to continue the distribution work out of the area.

"The blasted Home Office gave us away," said Sophie. "I am so annoyed with them."

"Did you just recruit a Russian spy?"

"Only began the process, really. I'll tell Archie as soon as possible, and that's probably the last we'll hear of it."

"You were awfully natural through the whole thing," said Flora. "I would have over-acted the part… I suppose recruiting a spy isn't the sort of thing one puts in one's diary."

---

Nearly an hour had elapsed by the time Nick returned. Mrs Barker had lunch ready for him. Sophie and Flora heard his report while he sat in the kitchen.

"Try to keep your mouth closed while eating," said Sophie. "All the top-notch spies do."

"Yes, miss."

He delayed reporting until he had finished a forkful.

"So I went all over the place, miss. I was about twenty minutes round the shops. I looked in the butcher's, two greengrocers, the fishmonger's, and two bakeries, then cycled up and down the road, but never saw her. After that, I went to the park."

"Have some food," said Sophie.

He quickly shovelled in two loads and ate them with rapidity.

"At the park I looked all over the place. *All* over. It was great going downhill, and I was going really, really fast, but I had to leg it. A park-keeper came after me. Poor old codger. He was shouting away and shaking his fist, but there was no way he could catch me. I steered clear of him after that. Honestly, miss, she wasn't there. By herself or with her dog, I would've seen her."

"Thank you, Nick. We'll leave you in peace. Before you go, I'll give you a message to be delivered to Mr Drysdale at the Foreign Office, and you're only to put it into his hands and no one else's. It's absolutely vital it reaches him today, so track him down if he's not in his office — even if you have to wait outside his flat for him to return home."

"Yes, miss."

"Good. I'll also give you a note for Miss Jones to explain your absence."

"Thank you. She might cut up rough, otherwise."

"I'm aware she might. When you leave on your bicycle, go through Primrose Hill Park again, and then continue through Regent's Park, just in case Miss Boddington has gone for an extra long walk. Should you see her, either return here or follow. You'll have to use your judgment on that. Mind that you're careful around traffic. There are some busy roads in the area."

"That's right, miss. I'll be careful. I don't want to die young, 'cause there's a lot I want to do."

"It all sounds dramatically important," said Flora. "What is it you want to do?"

"Drive round Brooklands in one of them racing cars, fly an aeroplane, and go mountaineering."

"And be a spy?" asked Sophie, smiling.

"Oh, yes. I've got my heart set on that, I have, more than anything else. Then I can travel to foreign countries and see the world."

Thoroughly charmed, Sophie refrained from commenting on his dreams, but they made her smile.

"In case we've gone out before you finish, I'll leave the messages on the table in the parlour."

"Very good, miss."

In the parlour, Sophie sat and wrote out her notes.

"I like rambles in the countryside," said Flora, also sitting at the table, "but I'd hate climbing a mountain. The cold must be dreadful."

"Yes... it would be. I don't know why anyone would want to be in a tent when it's freezing."

"Would you go mountaineering?"

"I don't think so... Besides, I can't. Auntie thinks any woman who goes mountaineering must be demented. I'd never hear the last of it."

"I can imagine how she would react."

In the silence, the clock ticked while Sophie's nib scratched the paper.

"There. All done." She blotted her writing and put the notes in envelopes. "Now we'll hunt the Villard and keep a lookout for Miss Boddington."

They found Dulcie Villard at home, but on the verge of leaving for an important appointment. Mildred opened the door and admitted them into the house.

"She's got it done up beautifully," whispered Flora while they waited in the parlour for Dulcie to appear.

"Even if she was *given* the house," whispered Sophie, "the furnishings must have cost a fortune. Did the duke gift her *everything*?" Sophie turned an unbelieving face to Flora.

"Blackmail or, you know, the *other* thing." Flora nodded.

"Are you suggesting her saving the child is an invented story?"

"Who can say for sure? We know she can't earn enough through hairdressing for the upkeep of this place, anyway.

I don't trust her. So if the story is not true, there has to be another reason... She's coming."

Dulcie Villard descended the stairs and entered the parlour.

"Hello. How nice of you to visit."

"Hello," said Sophie and Flora.

"We were passing and thought we'd just call to see if you were in," said Sophie.

"You have a very charming house," said Flora.

"That's kind of you to say. I'm quite pleased with how it turned out. Unfortunately, I have to leave at once. Did you call for some particular reason?"

"Yes," said Sophie. "We have learned your secret."

For a fleeting moment, Miss Villard's expression was one of sullen horror before she composed herself. "What can you mean?" Her voice was overly bright and brittle.

"Several secrets," said Flora darkly.

"What is this about? Money?"

Her answer, and the speed with which she arrived at her tentative assumption, tended to confirm Flora's suspicions. An uncomfortable silence lengthened until Sophie spoke again.

"We will not repeat what we know to anyone on one condition."

"It's a small matter," added Flora. "Quite minor, but we must have the truth from you."

"The consequences will be dire if you're not forthcoming. I believe we need not elaborate."

"You will tell us," said Flora, "what you did with Mrs Fitch's Cruft's application, and why you took it."

"That's all we require, and then you'll be safe, as we said."

"You have our word," said Flora.

"I have to go. I don't want to talk about this now."

"You absolutely *shall* talk now," said Sophie. "Tell us what we want to know, then we'll leave, and you can go where you please."

"Send us away and you'll suffer the consequences." Flora finished by raising her eyebrows.

Whatever thoughts tumbled in Miss Villard's mind, they did not show. She was in command of herself when she spoke. Miss Villard said,

"I don't know why you're interested. A silly mistake, that's all it was." She paused. "I was at Mrs Murray's house in an upstairs bedroom, dressing her hair. We heard the front door close. 'That must be Matthew,' she said. 'I can't see him now.' She couldn't, because I had only just started cutting. We were quiet, there was no noise. A little while later, the front door closed again. 'I wonder what he wanted?' she said. I continued cutting her hair, and we talked of other things."

Miss Villard put a hand to her forehead. The strain of the interview now showed in her movements and the way she stood.

"You should understand... I was in love with Matthew Hamilton. But... he did not return my love." She sighed heavily. "When the appointment was over, I went downstairs, and Mrs Murray said she would follow in a moment. I waited in her lounge at the front. On top of the escritoire was a blank envelope. It wasn't sealed, and it had not been there when I arrived for the appointment, so I knew Matthew had brought it... Well, I don't know what made me do it, but I looked inside. You must realize, I wanted to know what he was *thinking*... But I was disappointed in that. There were only some coins, a form filled out to enter Cruft's, and a short covering letter from Cynthia. So, I read it. Then I heard Mrs Murray right behind me, so I slipped everything into my bag. There was no time to put it back. That's all there is to it. I couldn't give the application to Mrs Murray after that, could I?"

"Did you destroy it?" asked Sophie.

"No, of course I wouldn't do such a thing. I posted it with the money."

"To Cruft's?" asked Flora.

"No. To Cynthia. She must have got it the next morning because it was a local delivery."

Sophie became mute. Flora noticed and took over.

"Then how do you know she received it?"

"She was in a foul mood for days afterwards," she spat out the words. "Saint Cynthia certainly kept quiet and even lied about the application being missing. She obviously thought Matthew had sent it back to her. Ha. Serves her right."

Flora and Sophie glanced at each other.

"We'll go but, as promised, we won't say anything."

The interview ended. Sophie and Flora quickly took their leave to return home.

"Good grief," said Flora, as they hurtled along.

"So much trouble because that *wretched, wretched* woman stole the application. How could she do such a thing?"

"We've seen the Villard's *real* nature... I don't think she struck the blow."

"I *know*. The Villard's meddling makes my blood boil." Sophie ran up the steps of number seven.

"What's the plan of action, then?" asked Flora.

"Get the police involved!"

They were inside the hall now.

"I agree, but to do what, exactly?"

"To hunt down Fitch, Pringle, and Boddington and have them questioned. With Fitch suppressing the fact that she received the application back, it makes her look very bad. I can't see the path clearly, but I'm most anxious for Miss Boddington. She believes someone is out to kill her, and now I'm inclined to believe her fears are well-founded. Mr Clark should be safe as long as he's in the hospital. Come to think of it, if Mrs Fitch is the murderer, Villard is at risk if the part she played in the application ever becomes known."

"That last part's a *bit* of a stretch," said Flora, "and I'm still not convinced Miss Boddington is in danger."

They entered the parlour.

"This is how it seems to me," said Sophie. "Miss Boddington rowed with Fitch over her 'setting her cap' at Hamilton. Therefore, we know that Hamilton had in the past been charming to Fitch, as he was to all women. She took it the wrong way, as probably did the Villard. Upon realizing he was not courting her, Villard resorted to petty, spiteful revenge.

His charm took Fitch differently. She developed a serious passion for Hamilton and found nothing in his manner to dissuade her from it. They're all merrily going along, misunderstanding each other, when she asks him to take the application to Mrs Murray. Remember, they were *all* friends at that time. He delivers it, Villard steals it, and then returns the blasted thing by post. What does Fitch think when she gets her application back without any explanation? At first, she would believe Mrs Murray sent it. She likely wouldn't even think of blaming Hamilton. Fitch suppresses what she believes is an insult from her long-time friend. Then something makes it apparent to Fitch that it wasn't Mrs Murray who sent the application back. Who then can she blame? Only Hamilton. Her obsessive love turns to... I've no idea what it turned into — something putrid, no doubt, but maybe it caused her to want to do away with him."

"Oh, surely no one would decide to kill someone over such a trivial matter?"

"Maybe it didn't seem so trivial a matter to someone who was already quite unhinged. Perhaps Fitch came to see the return of the application as Hamilton's abrupt, even cruel, way of saying he wanted nothing more to do with her."

"If so," said Flora, "Fitch would have gone through torments... I understand all that you've said, but where do you fit in Mr Clark?"

"I'm uncertain, but it might have gone like this. Fitch decided to kill Hamilton. She also decides that she will do so while he's walking his dog because his usual route takes him past her side gate. However, she can't use the gate as it makes a loud noise when opened. She asks Mr Clark if he has any oil. He offers to see to the hinges for her, and she accepts. Then, for some reason I don't understand, Fitch delays her attack. In February, during a thick fog, Mr Hamilton goes for his usual walk. Perhaps he wants to find another hardy soul out and about just for the fun of it. Mrs Fitch ambushes him. She might have spoken to him first, and what an eerie conversation that would have been — she full of murderous intent and he blithely unaware. She strikes him. After shutting the gate, she goes back inside, believing her veneer of respectability and own certitude in everything will allow her to escape detection, despite her house being right next to the crime scene... I don't think she's an unintelligent woman, but she must be so sure of herself that she was blinded to her plan's deficiencies — even though, as we know, it worked."

"How convinced are you?"

"It's difficult to say, because it's only a possibility. Equally likely is that La Pringle went mad with jealousy because maybe Hamilton's attention was wandering elsewhere. If it was Pringle who killed him, then maybe Miss Boddington is in no danger, and only her disturbed state makes her believe she is."

"The police should put everyone under lock and key until it's all sorted out."

"I'm sure they want to do that sometimes, but they can't."

They were quiet for almost a minute.

"If it were Fitch, she must have got the weapon from inside the house," said Flora.

"It was a Monday night..."

The women looked at each other and almost said in unison, "Her ironing night."

"The heaviness, the edge, the point and corners — that could definitely be the weapon," said Flora. "So the edge broke Mr Hamilton's neck as the coroner described... No, hold on. If she used an iron, that means the attack was spontaneous. The oiling of the hinges, however, shows premeditation."

"True," said Sophie. "That spoils the theory."

"Not necessarily... Just suppose she always planned to use an iron for a weapon. It might be that she had tried to attack him on previous nights, but there were people in the street preventing her. It just so happened that, with the fog, she had the perfect opportunity for a concealed attack, and it merely coincided with her ironing night."

"That's much better, and plausible, too, if she also used an iron on Mr Clark. Fortunately for him, he turned at the right moment. The flat of the iron would have glanced off his skull, and a point buried itself in his shoulder. Of course, if we're correct, she'll go after him again, as well as Miss Boddington. Fitch's guilty conscience had her remembering the gate being oiled. She understood that anyone who had knowledge of her actions was and will continue to be a threat to her. Their shared knowledge exposes part of her plan. So, with a total disregard for human life, she intends to murder them and will try once more in a brazen fashion, which is fitting with what we know of her."

"It's entirely possible," said Flora. "What also could be true is that *Sandra Pringle* left her house with an iron or some other thing concealed either under her coat or in a large coat pocket. La Pringle ambushed Hamilton on his usual walk. Maybe she was determined to kill him because he had jilted her, as we just discussed, and the fog provided the perfect cover for the deed. However, I can't see how to fit in the attack on Clark."

"That's quite convincing, too, as far as it goes. But just suppose La Pringle believes Mr Clark suspects her of murdering Hamilton. That would be cause enough for her to do away with him. Maybe it was only his proposal of marriage that made her feel safe and convinced her he suspected nothing after all... Dear, dear, there might be more to find out, and I feel we're running out of time. I don't know, perhaps the two events are unrelated." Sophie threw her hands in the air.

"We must do something."

"Unfortunately, we can't until Sergeant Gowers arrives. The local police wouldn't take our two convoluted theories seriously, and Fitch is out at the moment, anyway."

"The HO spies can't help because of the Russian mission," said Flora.

"Don't talk about those nincompoops. To think that Kuritsyn was spying on us while we were spying on him, and then an HO man made that blunder which gave us away... Kuritsyn was very good at concealing from us what he was doing and from those at number fifteen. Perhaps he should give Breed-Dankworth and his men some lessons. They certainly need them."

"Come on," said Flora. "We can't just sit here. Biscuit hasn't had a proper outing yet, and we can look for Miss Boddington. Remember, there's that mystery 'she' in Alexandra Gardens that she's still protecting, and we must find out who it is."

## Chapter 30

## Going for a walk

Miss Boddington left the dentist's surgery in Chalk Farm. The work was necessary and, although out of pocket for two fillings she could ill afford, she was relieved it was over. Before opening the door to the street, she massaged her lop-sided face where it sagged. The dentist had airily said the effect would wear off in a few hours, but he had not convinced her, especially so because of the size of the needle he had used.

Across the street from the dentist's was a tearoom, where Mrs Fitch had been sitting alone for half an hour. She had eaten an early lunch at a restaurant near Covent Garden with her younger brother, who had come into town on business. Naturally, with his being a successful breeder, they had discussed dogs, of which there were many, then family, of which there were few. When she espied Miss Boddington coming out of the dentist's, she quickly finished her tea. With her coat now buttoned, she picked up her heavy walking stick.

Mrs Fitch was no spy or detective, and so she followed Miss Boddington closely, a scant ten yards behind. They passed by the underground station and newsagents. Miss Boddington crossed the road but, because she was more taken up with the state of her mouth, failed to notice Mrs Fitch, who paused in a shop entrance so as not to be noticed.

They went along the short approach to the railway station. At this time of the early afternoon, there were few people about. Mrs Fitch closed the gap, knowing Miss Boddington would not be taking a train, but using the bridge to go home.

When they were on the bridge, Miss Boddington turned around, having heard a noise.

"Cynthia!" she said, astonished.

"Hello, Boddy... I've been trying to catch up with you." Cynthia relaxed from her exertions, and she smiled as she drew near. They stopped.

"Why?"

"I've been thinking we should mend fences, and put aside all those awful things we've said to one another." She paused while a noisy lorry passed them. "It's not right that a friendship of so many years' standing should end like this."

"But I can't... Not while... You know. Why ever did you allow her to do such a thing?"

"Who do you mean, dear?"

"Sandra Pringle, of course. She'll kill me, and Mr Clark, and now, I see, you are on her list, too. Why did you let her?"

"You think...? What is it exactly you believe of Sandra?"

"That she used your side gate to attack Matthew, and *you* let her use it. I've said to myself a thousand times that you couldn't have known what she was about. But there, she must be completely mad. So why have you never gone to the police?"

"Is that what you believe?" Mrs Fitch became very stiff and awkward in her manner. "I did my ironing that evening, so if Sandra killed him, she was in my house without my knowledge. I had no idea she used the side gate."

"You didn't know...? You didn't *know*!? Why ever didn't you tell me? Oh, dear, dear, dear." She began crying.

"That's right. I didn't know," said Cynthia.

"I *knew* you weren't involved, and it had to be her. Though I really can't understand what she could have against him. I know he was angry sometimes without meaning to be. I heard him in his flat shouting at Georgie."

"As you say. And remember, when I was speaking to that man in January, he actually kicked Georgie. He did it *right* in front of me. It convinced me he was capable of anything."

"That's so hard to believe. Matthew was so nice most of the time."

"Yes," said Cynthia.

A car passed. Cynthia then looked both ways along the bridge, which was empty. She glanced at an approaching engine on the tracks below. A thick plume of smoke belched from its funnel. They were always slow and smoky coming from the yards.

"Use your handkerchief, dear," said Cynthia.

Boddy looked down to reach into her pocket. Cynthia glanced along the bridge again.

"What a sight I must look," said Boddy. "And I've just come from the dentist, too."

"I know," said Cynthia.

She glanced again towards the engine.

"*Oi! Watch out for the smoke, ladies!*"

A porter from the station had stepped onto the bridge at the Chalk Farm end.

"Quick, Cynthia," said Boddy, now aware of the approaching train, "or we'll be smothered." Miss Boddington fled to the Primrose Hill end. Cynthia followed, and they were soon in front of the shops and among numerous other pedestrians.

---

From the top of Primrose Hill, Flora and Sophie had a sweeping view of the open park.

"Where on *earth* can she have got to?" asked Sophie, her hands on her hips as she surveyed the broad vista.

"I don't know, but I think we're wasting time here. We should try her house again." She threw the ball for Biscuit, who shot down the slope after it.

"I suppose so… How about we split up?"

"Bags I stay here with Biscuit."

"Oh, *no*. You're not getting away with it. Not after you had me calling him Blast-it when you knew otherwise."

"I thought you had forgotten about all of that."

"Absolutely *not*. I have my revenge planned, but I haven't been able to bring it off."

"What was it?"

"Ahhh, I'm not telling you... On second thoughts, I'll let you off completely, *if* you pay a penance."

"You mean, I go to Miss Boddington's to see if she's returned?"

"Yes."

"I'll only go if you tell me what it was you were going to do."

"That's *ridiculous*. You can't negotiate a penance. How impenitent can you *be*?"

"I am *contrite*," Flora had a hollow sob in her voice, "and my heart..., my heart is broken... Those were my lines in a play. Truly, and this is no lie, it was soul-stirring stuff, and the audience blubbered right up until I was executed. Then they fainted."

Sophie laughed. "Oh, you win. I was going to tell the Villard that you won an elver-eating competition, but then she became too much of a suspect for me to do that."

"You mean baby eels! How *disgusting*. I hate eels."

"I know you do." Sophie was smiling to herself.

"To think, she would have told everyone... I'm going. You've made me feel quite faint." She handed Sophie the ball and departed.

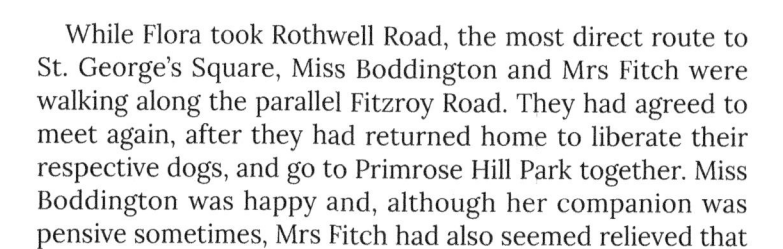

---

While Flora took Rothwell Road, the most direct route to St. George's Square, Miss Boddington and Mrs Fitch were walking along the parallel Fitzroy Road. They had agreed to meet again, after they had returned home to liberate their respective dogs, and go to Primrose Hill Park together. Miss Boddington was happy and, although her companion was pensive sometimes, Mrs Fitch had also seemed relieved that they had cleared away the misunderstanding and put the past behind them.

"What has been happening in Alexandra Gardens of late?" asked Boddy.

"Not a great deal. Two young women, cousins I believe, have moved into number seven."

"Have they? I've seen them with their dog." Miss Boddington was about to say more, but checked herself. Mrs Fitch did not notice.

"Only temporarily, because they're looking to buy a house and have selected Primrose Hill as a potential area."

"Oh... And how's Mr Bristow these days?"

"Quite himself. He had a severe cold a few weeks ago, and we feared it was the flu. Fortunately, our fears were unfounded."

"I *am* glad to hear that. Still, he's such a hale and hearty gentleman, he probably would have got through the flu all right."

"Undoubtedly... I've had to have several words with him about Bo'sun, though. That dog has lost all his training, and he just permits Bo'sun to do as he pleases. I can't understand why Bristow doesn't take steps. I... I find it quite *maddening*."

"Well, you would, when you're so devoted to the proper training of dogs." They neared the park. "Oh, look! Can you see? The bluebells are out."

"I thought they would be. We'll keep to the trees around the edge and enjoy them on our walk. The best show will be on the west side, near the reservoir."

"Bound to be, Cynthia. Imp loves that part once the grass grows tall. It's really quite countrified, don't you think? You could almost imagine being miles outside of London."

"Yes, one can. It's nice and quiet there."

At a water fountain, Biscuit slurped noisily from the little trough at the bottom, while Sophie depressed the button and drank far more decorously from the jet at the top. After they had finished, Sophie put the leash on him, saying,

"You've had your run for the time being."

He looked up at her appealingly and panted.

"You want a biscuit, don't you?"

He woofed and got what he wanted.

As it was mid-afternoon, the park was not being enjoyed for itself, but only used by solitary travellers as an easy short-cut. Sophie stopped and turned occasionally while walking south, to search every part for Miss Boddington. As the tally of fruitless surveys increased, she began to feel that Miss Boddington might never be seen again. She reached the treed path at the southern end near the zoo, and turned west, more or less parallel with Prince Albert Road. She was no longer expecting to find the woman anywhere, and it seemed even less likely to find her in the direction she was heading. At least Sophie could say she had searched the whole park — *if* anyone asked.

At the northern end of the park, under the trees, Boddy and Cynthia ambled along. Titus and Imp ran about together nearby. Imp was an affectionate dog, overjoyed to see her friend again, feeling much the same way as Boddy towards Cynthia.

Two pedestrians came towards them as the women neared a bench. Another pedestrian was following them.

"Sit here and have a cigarette."

"But you don't like me smoking?"

"An unfortunate habit you picked up as a nurse during the war. I can make allowances for that."

"If you don't mind, I will."

Boddy sat in the middle of the bench. Cynthia chose the windward side to escape the drifting smoke.

"Did you ever smoke?" asked Boddy.

"I have smoked, but gave it up. At some point you must, too."

"Easier said than done... The dogs get on so well together. See how they play?"

It was a joy for Boddy to watch them. After a while, she noticed Cynthia seemed perturbed.

"Is there anything the matter?"

"Nothing." Cynthia spoke sharply and dismissively.

"Surely there is?"

"Leave it, Boddy." She stood and looked up and down the path. "Let's walk."

As obediently as Cynthia's dog, Boddy did as instructed.

Rather than keep him on his leash, Sophie allowed Biscuit to explore on his own. He never strayed far and frequently walked beside her of his own volition. She was becoming immensely attached to the light brown and curly-haired dog. They reached the corner by the park-keeper's lodge and turned north onto a long path which ran by the side of the fence. Cars passed on the road nearby, but shrubs and bushes hid them from view. The way of the path was open for a stretch before rising and entering into a wooded section.

Sophie arrived at a point where she had followed Kuritsyn and Razov several days earlier. The path became steeper and, where it forked, she continued on the familiar open track towards the top of the hill, eschewing the darker path through a grove, which was deserted as far as the eye could see.

After about fifty yards, Biscuit, who had been nosing around, stopped and stared into the trees. He lifted a paw off the ground.

"Are you pointing?" asked Sophie, laughing. "Have you seen a rabbit?"

It was a perfect point, and he did not move a muscle while Sophie spoke. She came close and looked along his line of vision.

"Oh, look at the bluebells!"

Then she saw a dog running loose under the trees.

"Is that Imp?"

She stared for a moment, then put the leash on Biscuit. When she looked up, she saw Titus. Sophie hurried forward to where she had seen the other dogs.

"I simply love bluebells," said Boddy. She breathed out a satisfied sigh of pleasure as she gazed at a little blue lake of flowers. "They never last long enough, but they make the woods so beautiful while they do."

"Yes," said Cynthia, distracted, and often looking up and down the sheltered path.

"I think the dogs enjoy them, too."

"How can you say that?"

"Well, look at them running about without a care in the world."

"Better call them in. Come, Titus! Imp...! Imp...! Come!"

Both dogs obeyed her, Titus doing so with no hesitation.

"Oh, but they were having such a nice game."

"Too much of a good thing will spoil a dog. Give me your lead."

Boddy surrendered the leash without a murmur. Cynthia soon had both dogs under control.

"They're thirsty," said Boddy. "Did you have a nice game, Imp darling?"

"Don't speak to your dog like that. She doesn't know what you're talking about."

"Yes, she does. She always has."

"Oh, look. Look there! Has she cut her paw?"

"My goodness, where?" Boddy bent down to examine Imp's paw.

As she did so, Cynthia again quickly looked about. Then with one hand she yanked on the leads and moved the dogs away, snapping angrily, "Stay!" Cynthia turned back and kicked Boddy in the ribs as she tried to rise. She lifted her heavy ash stick to strike.

"Why?" Hurt and in pain, Boddy looked up. "It was you, after all."

There was a shout, then a police whistle blew. Biscuit rocketed through the bluebells and leapt.

# Chapter 31

# The Fog Clears

Sophie ran as fast as she could. Biscuit was now being attacked by Titus as he pulled on Mrs Fitch's sleeve. As a result of Biscuit's heroic lunge, the woman was prostrate and winded. Miss Boddington could not rise because her ribs hurt.

"Stop! Biscuit, heel! Heel!" shouted Sophie.

He disengaged, but Titus came at him again and they tussled, all growls and snapping jaws.

"No! Titus. Sit! Both of you. Sit!"

That stopped them, but they did not sit down. Neither dog seemed to have suffered any damage. Instead, Biscuit stood by Sophie, and Titus went to his fallen mistress.

"She tried to kill me," gasped Miss Boddington.

"Are you all right?"

"No. I think my rib's fractured." She was breathing heavily and clutching her side.

"Is there anything I can do? Should I get you up?"

"Not at the moment. I must stay still until help arrives."

"Yes." Sophie blew on her whistle until a man appeared in the distance. "Someone's coming."

"Where's Imp?" asked Miss Boddington. "I can't call her."

"Imp...! Come on, Imp! Heel! Here, Imp!"

Nervously, the dog came out from hiding in the trees and slunk over to Miss Boddington. Imp lay down, shivering. Sophie took hold of her leash, which was still attached to the collar.

"I don't know what to do about Titus," said Sophie.

"Don't you try. He might go for you," warned Miss Boddington.

"I ought to see how she is."

"I can hold Imp. She won't pull."

"Let go if she does. Biscuit... Stay."

Sophie hesitantly approached Mrs Fitch. Titus did not growl or threaten, so she went nearer.

Cynthia Fitch lay on her back, staring up at the sky. Although winded, she appeared otherwise unharmed. Biscuit had knocked her down and then seized her arm, almost tearing her sleeve off. Sophie looked for bloodstains, but could find none.

"Are you hurt?" asked Sophie. She waited for a reply. "Have you nothing to say?"

Mrs Fitch turned her gaze to Sophie, but did not answer. The man arrived.

"What's the trouble?" He was about twenty years old, a labourer.

"This woman," she pointed at Fitch, "violently attacked that lady. I saw her do it."

"Are you the police?" He asked.

"No, I just have one of their whistles."

"Handy that, but I think they can nick you for it. Um, who's hurt the worst here?"

"That lady. She probably has a fractured rib. She knows because she was a nurse."

"So what's the matter with this one?"

"I don't know. My dog knocked her down to stop the attack, and now she's just lying here and won't speak. I'm sure she didn't hit her head."

"Right, then. I'll fetch a copper... Do you think the lady needs an ambulance?" He nodded towards Miss Boddington.

"It's best you ask her. I can't offer much help in that department. I need to stay here to look after the dogs and make sure this creature doesn't escape."

"She just went for her, eh? Why'd she do that?"

"No, it wasn't a sudden assault. She planned it. She was going to murder her."

"*Was* she, now...? How'd you know?"

"Because she has attacked others and killed one already."

"Good job you saw it, then... She's a right nasty bit of work."

"Sad to say, she is."

The man nodded and went over to Miss Boddington.

"You've had a time of it. But don't you worry, dear. Help will be along soon. Anything I can do before I go?" They spoke briefly, then the man left to find a policeman and a doctor.

---

There were many delays before Sophie returned to number seven. A policeman had eventually arrived to sort matters out, and Sophie gave him the particulars. Privately, she told him who to contact at Scotland Yard because the woman under arrest was a murderer. Soon afterwards, a doctor came, summoned from a nearby house. He examined Mrs Fitch and could find nothing physically wrong with her. Miss Boddington he braced and bandaged and waited with her until an ambulance came. The constable took Cynthia Fitch to the park-keeper's lodge. She was held there until a black maria arrived to take her to Marylebone Police Station. The police took Titus away, too.

What also delayed Sophie's return was her going to Mrs Murray's house with Imp and Biscuit. Naturally, Mrs Murray wanted to know what had happened. The delay came because the explanation was not something to be rushed. Mrs Murray demanded the fullest details. Despite Sophie's employing the police tactics of being non-committal and tight-lipped, there was still much to tell. The story appalled Mrs Murray, and she was outraged over the attack. She quickly grasped that Cynthia Fitch had murdered Matthew Hamilton. She wanted to know why Fitch killed him and, because Sophie could not answer, the flow of questions was not staunched. By the end, Mrs Murray agreed to take care of Imp and go to the hospital to comfort Miss Boddington.

Although it was only a short walk to number seven, it was long enough for Sophie to begin to feel awful over what she had witnessed. The horrible aggression displayed by Mrs Fitch was beyond her comprehension. That the woman had secretly attacked friends and neighbours was unimaginable. The notion had worried her enough while the investigation was ongoing, but to have had such a demonstration of Fitch's unfettered malice exposed Sophie to a whole new level of savagery. The thought came back to her again and again. If Biscuit had not been present or were not so well trained, she would have been too late. Miss Boddington would have succumbed to the assault with the heavy stick. Instead, Biscuit's sudden appearance had distracted Fitch and, before the first blow had fallen, Sophie had witnessed Fitch's stare, the woman's entire face set in a ferocious mask. Sophie, from a short distance, had glimpsed the woman's features, barely recognizing her.

Her thoughts, which would undoubtedly have spiralled down, changed completely when she entered number seven at about six o'clock. The welcome distraction started with, 'Where have you been?' in the hall, moved to the parlour where the whole household gathered for an exposition of the dramatic news, proceeded to the kitchen because Mrs Barker had to attend to dinner, and was made complete by them all eating their evening meal together in the dining room. This included Biscuit, to whom they drank a toast and gave a round of applause, he being variously described as the dog of the hour, dog of the year, and best dog ever. Sophie fashioned a crown from a napkin and tried to balance it on his head, but he declined the honour. Being a dog, he much preferred the extra Biscuit Bones he received.

While this was all ongoing, Miss Walton and Miss King were 'not at home' to the residents of Alexandra Gardens. The news of Mrs Fitch's arrest and Miss Boddington's injury had somehow already become public knowledge. Two of the three callers — Bristow and Sandra Pringle — went away with their burning questions unanswered. The third caller, Farhan, only delivered a note from Major Cummings, although he chatted with Ada. In his note, the Major asked no questions, but instead he offered to help in any way he could. Sophie thanked him with a brief note in return.

"What time is it?" said Sophie, looking at her wristwatch. "Good grief! The meeting."

"Are you still going, miss?"

"Yes, as are you and Flora. It starts at nine, so we have time to get there."

"What does one wear to a communist gathering?" asked Flora.

"Um... Not one's tiara or sable fur," said Sophie.

"What would they do if someone did?"

"Throw things at them, I expect," said Ada. "You know, miss, it might be a rough crowd."

"You mustn't say 'miss' tonight, Comrade Carmichael," said Sophie. "We've all joined the revolution for the evening."

"That's goin' to be difficult, er, comrade."

There was a knock at the back door.

"That better not be the HO," said Sophie."

Ada left to find out. She returned and showed Archie Drysdale into the parlour.

"Hello, I'm glad I caught you," he said.

"Hello, Archie," said Sophie. "We're going out soon. Should we change our plans?"

"No, not at all. Excuse me, Miss Walton, but I must have a quick word with Miss King in private."

"I know when I'm not wanted. Anyway, I have to put on some overalls for tonight's adventure, Comrade Drysdale."

"No one has ever called me that before, and I hope they never do again."

"That's because you have the glorious rank of a commissar."

Archie smiled politely as Flora left the room. He spoke after she shut the door.

"I got your note about Kuritsyn. How reliable is he?"

"He often jokes and is hard to take seriously in some ways. At least, that's the case for me. Quite frankly, he's given away some details on the internal workings of number fifteen. Perhaps that was to establish himself as being forthcoming. He presents as a man who is half-heartedly involved in communism and is only keeping up a pretense. However, he was watching us. Do you the know, the HO gave us away while setting up a camera? Kuritsyn noticed the agent in our attic. What is the matter with them?"

Archie groaned. "Not again."

"Yes, and they nearly lost Dr. Teplov last night. He's moved, by the way. The HO asked us to pitch in and follow him."

"How do you know Teplov's name?"

"Mr Bristow, his next-door neighbour, plays chess with him. He told us."

"But that's the man's real name?"

"What did you expect?"

"I don't know... I've got an uneasy feeling something fishy is going on. No time to talk of that now, and I probably shouldn't, anyway. But I'll tell you this much. Teplov is the agent we were expecting, and he was here all along. So Razov's arrival would lead us to believe that *he* was the man to watch. That's a very crafty piece of work, and we don't know if they planned it that way or it was a mistake in the intelligence we received."

"Talk about tricky... I only hinted at it in the note, but Comrade Kuritsyn actually said that the Russians are running rings around us in the spy war. Those were his exact words."

"He used the word 'war', did he?" Archie looked grave.

"Yes. Does it matter?"

"To my mind, that's the most important and illuminating thing he could have said. It gives credence to his statements. We were under the impression the war had yet to start."

"Then the Russians are ahead of us?"

"So it seems."

"We can't have that."

Archie smiled. "I, and others, aim to redress the balance. Now, don't breathe a word of this to the HO."

"Ha! *Them.* Not bloomin' likely, me old fruit!" She sounded like a cockney.

Archie was taken aback, but then he smiled. "I dare you to say that to Bessie."

"I'm tempted but, prudently, I shall decline your challenge. Auntie would make mincemeat of me."

"Levity aside, Kuritsyn may prove to be important. So tonight, do not approach him or wave or anything else like that. If he catches your eye, give a simple nod as soon as he does. If he is an agent, he will be extra cautious from now on. Should he approach you, well, he might be too careless for us to use. He might also be a Cheka agent trying to infiltrate. We can't trust him now or ever. That doesn't mean to say that, whatever his motivation, he might not be useful. Sophie, give a nod, that's all."

"I understand. What about the naturalization process, though?"

"It can be done, but I think I must be very careful to whom I speak on this subject."

"Do you suspect a mole?"

"We can't be too careful. Say nothing to Bessie and don't let it go any further than Miss Carmichael and Miss Walton, because I'm sure they know already."

"Not much, actually, and I won't now say anything more to anyone."

"I'll leave shortly. How do you like the house?"

"I adore it. You should buy it, and now you can."

"I can? What do you mean?"

"Oh, of course, you won't have heard. Our dog Blast-it caught the murderer this afternoon. The vile and wicked Mrs Fitch is in jail at this very moment. You should have seen him. He was *splendid*. What a leap he made! And he *crashed* her to the ground... Sorry, Archie. I must get ready for the meeting. I'll tell you everything next time. Good night."

# Chapter 32

# Camden Lock

Kuritsyn had provided Sophie with directions to a warehouse near Camden Lock. There was no direct route, but the three women caught a bus along the High Street. They got off by the bridge over the canal.

"We're going in a warehouse?" asked Ada.

"Yes," said Sophie.

"And it's right by a canal?"

"Yes, it's just across the road from here."

"I'm not going," said Ada.

"Why, what's the matter?"

"Water rats, that's what. The thought of swimming rats makes me feel sick. Uuergh."

"The place will be full of people," said Sophie. "The rats won't come in, because they'll be too scared to."

"They won't?"

"No."

"If I see one, I'll scream, I will an' all."

"So will I," said Flora. "You and I can hold hands and run away while Sophie's beating them back."

Ada laughed. "Oh, don't, miss. It's not funny, and I can't help meself."

"I don't like them, either," said Sophie. "We'll *all* run. How's that?"

"All right," said Ada, but she sounded uncertain.

They reached the door and found it guarded by two heavy-set men in overcoats.

"Comrades," said the first man, a Russian.

"Good evening," said Sophie.

"Good evening, comrades," said the second, a large Englishman with an extremely high-pitched and nasally voice. "You're in time, and they are about to start." He opened the door.

"Excellent," said Sophie.

They entered. As she passed, Flora said to the Englishman, "Long live Lenin."

"Oh, absolutely, comrade. Indeed, I might add, may he live forever."

Inside was a single, large, oblong, and very crowded room. The smell of the tobacco smoke hanging thick in the air only just displaced the musty, pondweed and sewer gas odour that usually prevailed in the space. It was very dimly lit. Such poor lighting as there was came from a few scattered and depressingly naked lightbulbs which hung from the arched brickwork ceiling. The dinginess made the interior seem even more unwholesome. The only bright spot was the wooden platform at the far end. Here, several lamps improved matters. One lamp stood on an old wooden table around which were several occupied chairs. There sat the night's speakers.

"Watch your pockets," whispered Ada to the others, as they moved through a thick knot of shabbily dressed men and women. She had already counselled them to leave their handbags at the house.

They found a spot next to the wall about halfway along.

"There must be three hundred people here," said Flora.

"At least," said Sophie.

They were quiet as they studied those about them. Anyone further than five yards away was only a shape, and the farthest people blended together into one shifting shadow. Although it was hard to see them, Sophie did not recognize any person on the platform.

Flora whispered. "See that man? Two people in front of us, leaning against the wall? I'm sure he's a reporter, comrades.

He has a pencil behind his ear, and when he took a swig from his flask, he was holding a small notebook."

"An insightful observation, comrade," said Sophie.

"I wonder which paper he's on, comrade," said Ada.

"Not the Times, comrade," said Flora.

"Can we drop the comrading, comrades?" asked Sophie. "Use it sparingly or it will become tiresome."

"Yes, comrade," said Flora.

They took in their surroundings quietly from then on, whispering comments when they noticed something novel.

"Good evening, comrades," said a short young man, whose taller companion remained silent during the exchange but watched intently and smiled when anyone else did.

"Good evening, comrade," said Flora.

"Is this your first time 'ere at one of these meetin's?"

"Yes," said Sophie. "How do you know?"

"Oh, you 'ave that new, never-been-to-a-meetin'-before look abaht ya. Know what I mean?"

"That's observant," said Sophie.

"So it is. I'm Comrade Dave, an' this 'ere's my mate, Comrade Eric. Mind if we stand with you for a bit?" He grinned.

Sophie and Flora glanced at each other, unsure how to reply, but wanting to be rid of the young men.

He continued, undeterred. "They should 'ave dancing. I've always said that, an' it's a shame. You know, I like dancing, I do. I go down the Palais reg'lar. You ever been down the Palais?"

"Comrades!" said Ada in her Returner of Goods voice while addressing the young men. "Shove off, and chance your bleedin' arm somewhere else, you capitalist lackies. We've come 'ere to listen to blokes with brains about the revolution, not chatter like monkeys about dancing."

Sophie and Flora were aghast, expecting an ugly scene to erupt.

"Sorry, comrade," said the instantly cowed Comrade Dave. "Don't take us wrong, it's the revolution first with us, *oh* yes... C'mon, Eric."

They shoved off as instructed.

"Good grief," muttered Sophie.

"Well played," said Flora to Ada. "Capitalist lackies, though?"

"I got that from today's pamphlet. I had to speak that way, or we'd have never got rid of 'em."

There was a stir on the platform. A man got up from the table and approached the edge of the platform. The room suddenly buzzed with a flow of anticipatory comments, which immediately ebbed away.

"Comrades! Can I have your attention, please!?" He was a northerner. The room quietened.

"Thank you... First, allow me to say...."

Having caught the room's undivided attention, he then squandered it by extensively droning on and on. His subjects were: the results of the last meeting, the speeches to be given at the current one, and the guest speakers at the next meeting. He was one of those who, once they have got going, was virtually impossible to stop, except by external force. His own conscience allowed him to speak for as long as it took, because that part of the brain controlling his mouth was a marathon runner where only a sprinter was needed for the job. All members of the audience took on a glazed look as their capacity for independent reasoning withered away.

"This is *dire*," whispered Sophie.

He droned extensively and exhaustively, but even the worst speaker cannot continue forever. It came as a surprise when he actually stopped talking by introducing the next speaker on the roster.

It was a Russian, an intellectual, who wore gold-rimmed glasses. He carried a sheaf of papers, which he consulted frequently. His command of English was excellent — too excellent. He used very long words that half his audience had never heard before and he would have lost them completely save they clung on dearly to the fact that he obviously must be a genius and therefore knew what he was talking about. His subject was the reorganization of trade unions. He was thorough, insightful, but a poor communicator. The bulk of the audience was left with the idea that something must be done to reorganize, but could not have said in the least what it was.

The droner called out the next speaker, a woman from the audience. She was angry but, at least, comprehensible as she tackled her subject, which was the plight of underpaid women in British society. The agents listened to her intently, and heard much that was thought-provoking, but it was somewhat marred by the woman's vehemence. She illustrated well the poverty in northern English towns that led to women and children being underfed because of the lack of work and government money. She laid all her charges against the wicked capitalist system.

Capitalists — Sophie had met a few and been around many of them. Were they as evil as this woman painted them? Sophie recalled a particular gentleman, very wealthy, and one of the kindest and most sympathetic men she had ever met. Was he evil? She thought not. The speaker had mentioned women being trapped in poverty. The gentleman, Sophie decided, was just as strongly trapped in his wealth. Despite his charitable generosity, he would forever be wealthy, but he worked long hours with very little time off. That time off might include a few days in Paris, or taking some hours to see the sights during a business trip to New York, but otherwise he worked indefatigably all his waking hours. However, if someone in a Liverpool slum received what the man spent on restaurants in a week, it would change his or her life. It wasn't the gentleman, she decided, it was the inequities in the system, which she already knew needed vast improvement. Sophie listened to the woman again. Now it was as though she railed against the very man Sophie knew, as if she would kill him on the spot. The woman's speech ended, and it left Sophie wishing the world were a kinder place than it was.

A Scotsman next rose from his chair. He was a firebrand and he animated the crowd. A clever and effective speaker, he worked on the audience's emotions. "Come the day of the revolution", he stormed about the stage impassioned, "we will sweep all injustice away." He spoke of sacrifice, blood, sweat, and tears, and the part every person would play. They would enshrine workers' rights, putting them above all other considerations in the fairer and freer society to come. He urged them to keep alive in their souls the fire of the revolution and carry it unquenched into their daily lives. He roused the crowd, making it believe it could achieve anything if it stayed the course and all comrades worked together. When he finished, it not only cheered, the audience roared.

As the noise died down, the agents heard Kuritsyn's voice booming close by.

"Gallacher is a *wonderful* speaker, don't you think so, comrade?"

Sophie looked over at him, catching Kuritsyn as he slapped someone on the back. He returned her gaze as the man answered. This was the moment, then. Sophie nodded, as Archie had instructed her to do.

"Most excellent," he said, as if addressing the man he knew. "Razov speaks next, and I know he will tell us something interesting. No doubt, I shall see you afterwards, comrade." Kuritsyn then pushed through the crowd towards the front.

"Did he not see you?" murmured Flora.

"There's a matter I can't tell you about. We mustn't speak to him unless he speaks to us."

"Oh," said Ada. "I thought that was all over and done with."

"Only for us. It seems it will never be over, even though our part has ended."

Razov spoke. Sophie was dumbstruck as soon as she heard him. He spoke very well, in near flawless English. No more were there the semi-idiotic statements and peculiarities she had heard in Alexandra Gardens. She realized Razov and Kuritsyn had tricked her.

"What's going on?" whispered Ada, puzzled. "His English is perfect."

"I don't know," said Sophie.

After the surge of annoyance at being caught out had subsided, she listened carefully. At the end of Razov's introduction, he said,

"Allow me to tell you something first, comrades," said Razov. "I have only been in Britain for a short time. Truly, I have been made to feel most welcome. I have met such charming people and I to myself say, 'You know, Razov, it's not bad here. If not for the work of the Revolution, you should stay.'" He smiled as he spoke, and the audience smiled with him. "How can I? There is so much pressing, pressing work to be done."

While he paused, Sophie realized what he was getting at. He had signalled to her his intention to work for the British Government. Razov continued — a casual speaker, never stumbling, mildly entertaining, and believable.

"A fortnight ago, Comrade Lenin called me into his office. I don't wish to give the impression that I am an intimate of our august leader. I'm not. He gave me a commission — and it was a great honour for me, when he could have chosen any of several hundred. This is the commission he bestowed: to come to Britain and explain the great successes Soviet Russia is achieving even under the difficult circumstances of war and insurrection."

He smiled. "I warn you, comrades, I work with numbers and statistics, and I keep them all in here." He tapped his forehead with a finger. "But do not be alarmed, I shall not weary you with *those*. Although, I can if you want me to. The best way for me to illustrate how Russia improves under Soviet control is with a human story. There is a small Russian village, one of many, many thousands. It is a picturesque little place...."

---

On the bus ride home, Sophie was quiet, thoroughly understanding that two professional Russian spies had tutored her. By their conduct at the meeting, they had confirmed not only that they were spies, but had also displayed their professionalism. This meant that the Kremlin indeed had sent them to operate in Britain — now or at a later date. The meeting also confirmed that Russia was far advanced in its espionage endeavours. Kuritsyn had mentioned there were others such as they. She suddenly felt daunted while Ada and

Flora chatted together happily on the almost empty bus. How clever were the Russians? Were all their spies so adroit? How many British secrets had Moscow obtained so far? Sophie became unhappy while imagining a vast, hidden network of enemy agents, controlled by minds of immense insight and precisely calculating intelligence. As she now saw it, they were unstoppable. Ada and Flora said something that drew her back into her surroundings.

"What are we going to do with all them pamphlets?" asked Ada.

"We'll probably take Kuritsyn's supply every day until we leave," said Flora. "Can you make a paper aeroplane? I've tried numerous times, but they were all useless."

Sophie started laughing.

"Hello, Daydream. Back with us? What made you laugh like that?" asked Flora.

"I'm sorry. I was turning something over in my mind. Kuritsyn and Razov are clever spies. But they're only men, after all. I've just been imagining dreadful things, when all Kuritsyn wants to do, as you've just reminded me, is throw away the pamphlets... Except he can't." She laughed again.

"That *is* funny, but why is it so funny to you?"

"It occurred to me that the people in charge of the Russian spy network must have super intellects and consider every ramification of the slightest change in any situation. But they can't be like that. No one is. They are just ordinary people, men mostly, who have committed themselves to seizing more and more power. Yes, they will cause trouble and much suffering, but they are not gods. They're only ordinary after all."

"That's thoughtful, but hardly funny," said Flora.

"But, it is," replied Sophie. "Remember, in the recent past, we've met a man very much like Lenin. These men are only pompous and arrogant. They have no compassion for others. To put it simply, they are wicked, motivated by greed. They are difficult to deal with because they are clever, or they control many people because they go unchecked... Well, those are things we *can* do something about. Such people will always be with us. They only have to be reined in before they cause damage."

"Miss," said Ada. "I think I understand what you're saying. But what about what that woman said? She wasn't lying about the hardships."

"No, she wasn't. However, I disagreed with a few things she mentioned... I don't care for politics, but the poor must be brought out of their poverty somehow. In that, I wholeheartedly agree with her. But violent revolution and civil war are not the ways to bring about such a change. Look, Britain is far from perfect, but it is safe. Here we are on the last bus home and no one molests us. No one will drag us off, then put a gun to our heads to question our political loyalty. There *are* criminals who may act violently, as we know only too well. If poverty can be reduced by a good margin, then criminality would reduce, too. However, I don't believe either will ever be eliminated."

"Are you running for parliament?" asked Flora.

"Ha! I wouldn't stand a chance, so I won't try. But do you see my point? Ada, *you* know this. How many unsuitable candidates come into the agency looking for domestic work for which they're unfit?"

"Loads, miss. Every day."

"Precisely. So here's where *we* might help them. We need to direct them to vacant positions that suit them. I thought it over, but can't yet see how to manage it."

"You mean, to become a sort of general employment agency?" asked Flora.

"I thought of that, but the firms who use them usually demand skilled or experienced workers. It doesn't help the unskilled people who come to us."

"You know, miss, there are a lot of small factories and warehouses near the office."

"Yes."

"How about you get them to tell you what jobs they've got? They can telephone, and you can post them on the notice board at the top of the stairs."

"That's brilliant," said Sophie. "As soon as I'm back in the office, I'll start the process. Thank you, Nancy."

The bus pulled up at their stop, and they alighted.

---

Sergeant Gowers was waiting in the parlour. He had been there an hour. Biscuit dozed on the rug in front of the fire while the sergeant read the Mysterious Affair at Styles, a book he had found lying on the table. The agents arrived, and Biscuit scrambled to meet them.

"Sergeant Gowers!" said Sophie, entering the parlour. "You're working very late."

"Hello, Miss King." He was already standing. "The Fitch case kept me busy, and I'd like to tell you what happened."

"Surely you want to go home, don't you?"

Flora and Ada came in. They said their hellos.

"I don't feel tired, and I'd rather do this tonight, because I won't be back here, you see."

"Oh. Please, sit down. Would you like something to drink?"

"Thank you, no. Myrtle gave me some tea earlier."

"Getting pointers from the book?" asked Flora.

He smiled. "Not so far, but I was enjoying it."

"We're all reading it at present," said Flora, "otherwise you could take it with you. I know. I'll send it to the Yard after we've finished."

"Oh, that's *very* thoughtful of you. I'll look forward to that."

They all settled themselves. Gowers took out his notebook.

"Have any problems arisen?" asked Sophie.

"Not really. Mrs Fitch has confessed to the murder of Hamilton, and the assaults upon Mr Clark and Miss Boddington."

"My word," said Sophie. "That must make it much easier all round."

"Very much so, Miss King. We like it when arrests go as smoothly as this one has. Now there's no problem, as such, but she's being less helpful when it comes to her motives."

"She won't say what they were?" asked Flora.

"I'll tell you what she said about a motive." Gowers opened his notebook to read. "This was all Fitch would say about Hamilton. 'He was a villainous arch-deceiver. He callously toyed with people's affections. When angry, he went mad and became abusive. He kicked his own dog. Someone like that doesn't deserve to live.' That's all she said and did so very nastily, and she wouldn't say when or where any of these things took place."

"They had a row, then," said Ada, who nodded emphatically. "She upset him, and he panicked on account of his shell-shock, got angry, then he kicked the dog."

"That must be it," said Sophie. "We did wonder if they met and spoke. It seems this, though, had to have taken place prior to the night of his murder."

"Him kicking the dog, well, that obviously decided her," said Flora. "How dreadful."

Gowers nodded. "So that's how it went. I've an idea of some of her reasons from your reports, but I'd like to go over them a little more thoroughly. This way, I can finish the case off tomorrow." He found a clean page in his notebook. "When the trial comes up, the prosecuting counsel will have to make a statement about her motives, even if she doesn't. Otherwise, the judge will get irritable, and lawyers don't like to irritate judges. With a guilty plea, they'll want it all over and done with on the day, and no funny comments made from the bench. Sensitive they are."

Sophie looked towards Flora and Ada, then back to Gowers. "Um, we're given to understand that Mr Hamilton was an attractive man, and rather too charming towards women. He wasn't always like that, but became so after being shell-shocked during the war. Mrs Murray is the one to talk to for background information. Miss Boddington as well, I suspect. Have you heard how she is?"

"Apparently, she has a fractured rib and bruising, but it's not a bad fracture and she'll be back to normal in six weeks."

"Thank goodness for that," said Flora.

"This Miss Boddington... is she... is she all right, do you think?"

"Again, speak to Mrs Murray. The war affected Miss Boddington, and she's not been herself since, so we're told. She displayed some very odd behaviour when we first arrived."

"Oh, I see."

He wrote in his notebook. Sophie continued.

"So Mr Hamilton was nervous or panicky, sometimes angry, and tried too hard to fit back in. Obviously, he must have been very effusive. The result was he had an affair with Mrs Pringle, while Miss Villard was besotted with him."

"And Miss Villard's maid, Mildred, took a fancy to him," said Ada.

"Is that so?" said Gowers. "I wonder what he could have said to them."

"No one has told us," said Sophie. "However it was he acted, it sparked a great deal of jealousy and, by the end, emotional hurt. I doubt he ever knew the extent of it. Mrs Fitch got caught up in it all, and she developed feelings for Hamilton that he did not reciprocate."

Gowers wrote quickly, and Sophie waited for him to catch up, before continuing.

"I presume that because Mr Hamilton's manner didn't vary, Mrs Fitch was waiting for a proposal of marriage. The problem seems to have been that Mr Hamilton wooed, or partially wooed, each woman individually when they were alone and in conversation together. The result was, each woman thought all his affection was for herself alone. With Mrs Pringle, it so happened he *was* attracted to her."

Gowers wrote, then said,

"Clark must have been livid with Hamilton... How did Mrs Pringle suddenly switch from being all involved with Hamilton and then go back to Clark? They were an item before she got involved with Hamilton."

"She was infatuated and swept off her feet," said Flora. "When Hamilton died, she still liked or loved Clark."

"A bit flighty, eh?"

"I think so," said Sophie. "At the back of everything, she's lonely, and has money worries. To put it simply, she was looking for someone to take care of her."

"But Hamilton had no money to speak of."

"She's highly emotional," said Ada, "and a very jealous woman."

"It's true," said Flora. "Her head said she needed money, but her heart wanted love and affection."

"So her heart won out, eh?" He wrote something. "Do you know a lot of crimes are committed because people just don't stop and think for a second? They let their emotions and passions rule their heads, like you suggest. That's all a closed book to me, and thank goodness. Now, with Mrs Pringle, would you say she loved Clark still when she was with Hamilton, or did it come back afterwards? I find this type of behaviour fascinating."

"We're fascinated, too," said Flora, "but I honestly couldn't say which it was."

"Neither can I," said Sophie.

Ada shook her head when Gowers looked at her.

"Let's press on, then."

"Cynthia Fitch gave her Cruft's application to Hamilton. He delivered it, and Miss Villard stole the envelope. She was in Mrs Murray's house cutting hair at the time and took the envelope away without Mrs Murray ever seeing it."

"Why'd she do that?"

"Miss Villard took it, because she wanted to know what Hamilton was up to. She was madly in love with him, if you recall. She and Mrs Murray knew he was downstairs, and he left without seeing them. The Villard didn't intend taking it, but knew Mrs Murray would see her with the application if she put it back, so she put it in her handbag instead. Then she posted it back to Mrs Fitch without explaining she had handled it."

Gowers wrote and then looked up sharply. "That must have upset her. Fitch eventually had to think Hamilton sent it back."

"It's what started it all."

"That's it right there. Mrs Fitch felt spurned and that she'd been insulted in a heartless way because he posted the application back to her with no explanation... Yet really, it was Miss Villard's doing."

"Isn't she a cow?" asked Ada.

"That's one word for her," said Gowers. "Technically speaking, she committed a crime, but she'd get off. Not a *thing* can be brought back to her. Still, she wasn't to know what would follow."

"Yes, Mrs Fitch would have learned the truth eventually in some other way," said Sophie. "Perhaps from Hamilton himself. It's quite possible she would still have set out to kill him."

"Possible, Miss King, but not certain, because he may never have kicked the dog had they not been having an argument. Anyway, we can't put the genie back in the bottle." He leafed through some earlier notes. "I can see now that Clark oiling the gate caused Fitch to worry he could connect it to her preparation for the murder. Then, because Boddington happened along while he was doing the job, Fitch felt threatened by her as well."

"Is she insane, do you think?" asked Sophie.

"Legally or practically? There's a difference, you see. To us here, she's absolutely cracked. In court, I doubt that defence can be made. Though, believe you me, I could well be wrong about that. The preparations she undertook, legally speaking, demonstrate her mind was sound at the time... The thing that gets me, is why did she take so long to go after Clark and Boddington?"

"I spoke to Farhan earlier," said Ada. "We had a little chat about the attack today, miss, when he delivered the Major's message. He said that Mrs Fitch thought more of animals than she did about people. That made me think. I reckon she went after Mr Clark only because his dog *wasn't* with him. She's all for the welfare of animals, and didn't want the dog upset while she was doing him in."

"While true," said Sophie, "dogs were present in the first and last attacks."

"I s'pose."

"No. I think Nancy's on to something," said Flora. "It could have gone like this. She attacked Hamilton and then became distressed over the dog running loose in the fog. That decided her to wait for when Clark was alone to attack him. With Miss Boddington... That's difficult. Perhaps she felt the urgency of finishing everything as soon as possible."

"I can help you there," said Gowers. "Miss Boddington went to the dentist today in Chalk Farm..."

"*That's* why we couldn't find her!" exclaimed Sophie. "Sorry, Sergeant Gowers, please continue."

"You were looking for her...? Miss Boddington was returning across the bridge over the railway when Fitch came up to her from behind. They had some type of reconciliation over past grievances, but she said Fitch was acting strangely." He consulted his notebook. "This is what she said. 'She seemed anxious and kept looking both ways on the bridge.' Remember, Miss Boddington didn't have her dog with her at the time." Gowers nodded.

"I reckon she was going to whack Miss Boddington with her bloomin' great stick," said Ada, "then tip her over the side onto the railway tracks."

"That's a steel girder bridge," said Gowers. "Could she manage it?"

"Oh, yes," said Sophie. "She's very strong. Fitch was showing Mr Bristow how to handle his dog properly. She took the leash from him, and the dog, a big Newfoundland, began pulling, but she held him all right before bringing him under control by commands."

"Then that means her initial attempt was thwarted somehow," said Flora. "There you are, Nancy. You were right after all. The Fitch wanted to get it all done today without upsetting the dogs if she could help it."

"If correct, and I'm sure it is," mused Sophie, "then she might have visited the hospital tonight and killed Mr Clark."

"Doesn't bear thinking about, does it?" said Flora.

"No. In the end, all of it is so unutterably sad."

The room was quiet for a moment.

"So, how did Mrs Fitch do it on the night of Hamilton's murder?" asked Ada.

"Well," began Gowers. "It was simple, really. She'd been looking out to attack Hamilton for some time. He passed by her side gate most evenings, and she waited for him. She couldn't bring it off because there were often people about, despite it being dark. Anyway, that foggy Monday was perfect for her. It was her ironing night, and she was using the murder weapon to iron her blouses, if can you believe it."

"Was she always going to use an iron for the weapon?" asked Flora.

"Oh, yes. Fitch said that she had always thought an iron would make a perfect weapon. It appears murder had been on her mind for a long time. On that night, she wore a pair of suede gloves. She didn't want to spoil them, so she put her hand in the dog biscuit bag to hold the handle. Fitch was certain she would be attacking Hamilton that night, so she waited some minutes for him outside on the pavement. He came along, and they spoke briefly, but she won't tell us what either of them said. He turned away and then she hit him. Down he goes, and the Sheltie runs about loose. She meant to hit Hamilton again, but it was difficult because of the fog. She switched the iron from her right hand to her left, and that's when she lost the bag — it fell off. As she's feeling about in the fog with her right hand to hit Hamilton again, Saunders calls out. That panics her, but she had sense enough to go in her house through the front door. Because Saunders was so close, he would hear the unlatching and latching of the gate, even though he wouldn't hear the oiled hinges. I know this for a fact as I tried it before coming here."

In silence, the three women assimilated the details, and glanced at or nodded to one another.

"It is getting late, so I'll take my leave now." Detective Sergeant Gowers stood up. "Allow me to thank you for the invaluable work you've all done. An excellent job, ladies. The Yard very much appreciates it."

"Thank you, Sergeant Gowers."

"Will the Yard let us keep Biscuit?" asked Flora.

"If they left it up to me, I'd say yes." He laughed. "Biscuit's a lovely dog, and he's more than earned his keep today. Haven't you, boy?" He patted him.

They said goodbye. Sophie showed Gowers out through the back door.

"Before you go," she said. "What happened to Inspector Morton?"

He turned to her an inscrutable face — one of a policeman's tools of the trade. "He had to go up to Birmingham. I can't say why. It was another of those Government Ale jobs."

"Ah, I thought it might be other work... To think, I didn't know a word about these beer jobs a year ago."

"Neither did I." He smiled now. "Funny how life goes, eh? Good night, Miss King."

"Good night, Sergeant Gowers."

Sophie watched him leave through the side gate, sighing heavily as she closed the door. She was not sure why she sighed.

# Epilogue

The day came when the Burgoyne agents had to leave number seven, Alexandra Gardens. The Home Office decided the ladies should depart under the cover of darkness, and asked them not to say goodbye to anyone in the square nor tell anyone they were leaving.

To say they were annoyed with these directives would be an understatement. The agents found it difficult enough just to be leaving the pretty house, but not to be allowed to say goodbye? Between them, they worked up several excellent stories they could have used to cover their departure, voiced them several times, but ultimately knew they had no choice but to follow orders.

Perhaps, after all, it was just as well, because the sullen atmosphere among the dog owners was really quite depressing. Also, the sensational news of Mrs Fitch being a murderer had produced a myriad of questions, which Sophie and Flora had difficulty answering. They could not reply fully nor air any supposed hypotheses without revealing they knew much more than they told.

During those few intervening days, Mr Clark came home, still heavily strapped and bandaged. He and Sandra Pringle were the most relieved by Cynthia Fitch's arrest. Miss Boddington also returned to St. George's Square. Mrs Murray looked for signs of mental deterioration in her neighbour but, although she could not state there was any marked improvement, she could see that the weight of Miss Boddington's fears had substantially lessened. She was calmer, and that was something, but Miss Boddington never once referred to Cynthia Fitch.

Kuritsyn was his usual affable self, and the revelation of Mrs Fitch being a murderer barely touched him; he soon dismissed the whole affair as something that could have occurred anywhere, but happened to take place in Alexandra Gardens. For good reason, he distanced himself from Sophie and Flora. They understood he and Razov were in contact with the British Government who may already have recruited them. All the young ladies knew was that they were told no more about the matter.

Alan Mellish, on the other hand, turned moody, having found the news extremely distressing. Bristow was visibly upset at first, as though he had had his legs kicked from under him, but he recovered something of his usual manner within a day or so. Miss Villard avoided the square entirely. Of them all, Major Cummings was the most reflective and peaceful over Mrs Fitch's arrest.

During this time, Farhan knocked on the basement door.

"Hello, Farhan," said Ada cheerfully. "Do come in."

"Thank you, memsahib."

She looked at him expectantly.

"Excuse my behaviour," said Farhan. "But I have come to say goodbye."

"Goodbye? Where are you going?" She was astonished.

"It is not I who is leaving. It is you who is leaving. So, I come to say goodbye to my friends. I am not sad, because I will have the memory of you. You will pass my message to the others, please?"

"Er, yes, of course I will. But what makes you think we're leaving?"

"Your hearts are no longer here. I see it in the upstairs memsahibs. There have been comings and goings in this house. You have come, and now you will go."

"Oh, um..."

"You wish it to be kept a secret? I shall not repeat, unless Major Cummings asks me. He will not repeat if I have to tell him. My Sahib will be very sad. He esteems all in this house, and he prizes Memsahib Barker as a precious jewel among women. Tell her this also, please?"

"I'll try," said Ada. "I'm going to miss you, an' all."

"That warms my heart. Goodbye, Memsahib Carmichael."

He bowed his head and put his hands together as if in prayer. So did Ada. Then he was gone, and she shed a tear.

It got even worse for the secret agents just before they left. Detective Sergeant Gowers took Biscuit from them. All the handkerchiefs came out, they were all dampened, and one was even pathetically waved at the car as it drove off. The once lively house became a sombre place without Biscuit and with the suitcases packed and standing in the kitchen. They were all waiting for two Home Office cars to arrive. During the wait, Sophie finished up one little mission. She put the Pitman's Shorthand book through Sandra Pringle's letterbox without an accompanying note.

Gowers dropped off Biscuit at a cubbyhole of an office near the kennels at Scotland Yard. In the office, a burly uniformed policeman sat at his desk. After Gowers had gone, the officer spoke to the dog.

"Well, Biscuit, my boy, did they treat you right?"

Biscuit barked.

"Now, now. Not too loud or we'll get complaints." He reached out a hand. "Put it there." When Biscuit put his paw in the hand, the man shook it. "Well done, my fine boy. Caught a murderer, hmm? That'll look very nice on your record. Now, tell me something. Those ladies didn't ruin you, eh? They didn't make a big fuss or spoil your training, eh…? No? That's good. Now what are these here Biscuit Bones?" He sniffed the contents of the marked bag that the agents had sent via Gowers. "Smell all right. You want one, don't you?"

Biscuit woofed.

"Shh, not so loud. Here you go." He watched as Biscuit crunched the bone. "You liked that plain enough. I wonder where you get them from?" He studied the bag for a moment. "Right, we'll go for a walk, then it's off to the kennels for your grub and to see your mates. They've missed you. Now, for tomorrow, *prepare* yourself. We'll be training all day long." He stroked Biscuit's head. "I'm glad you're back." He got up and went out. Biscuit trotted by his side.

Hamilton's Sheltie, Georgie, never did leave the pub. The regulars spoil him and he certainly doesn't seem to mind the attention. In fact, anyone and everyone can visit him there now, if they wish. Titus, however, fared very differently. Mrs Fitch's brother took care of the dog until he could find a suitable home for him. That home happened to be on a royal estate. The full name of Mrs Fitch's retriever was Wolferton Titus. He joined his brothers of the same litter, Wolferton Ben and Wolferton Dan - dogs belonging to His Majesty, King George V. Together, the three Labrador retrievers were among the prizewinners at Cruft's in 1922. Her brother informed Mrs Fitch that Titus had won.

Dr. Teplov was a busy man, and the demands upon his time were many. However, being an old friend of Lenin, he kept in touch with the leader of the revolution as often as he could. At the end of a letter to the great man, he added a postscript.

'Vova, an interesting hypothetical question has been put to me, and I'm not sure how to answer. Just suppose for a moment, you received a hundred thousand pounds. How much of that sum would you give to the revolution and how much would you keep personally? This is important to be answered, because all the British people want to know what you think.'

After some time, Lenin wrote back in a brief note, "I would give it all to the revolution."

---

After dinner, on the evening following her return to White Lyon Yard, Sophie sat with Aunt Bessie in the drawing room. Her aunt had mentioned earlier that she had important news to relate after dinner, and had been showing signs of repressed excitement ever since. Now that the meal was over, she became serious. Wearing her reading glasses, she consulted a small ledger balanced on her knees.

"This is the book," she announced, peering over the top of her spectacles and fixing Sophie with her gaze.

"The *betting*! You had me wondering what could be the great mystery."

"Good," said Aunt Bessie. "Would you like to hear the results?"

"But we know what the result was. Mrs Fitch murdered Mr Hamilton."

"Try not to be dim-witted, Sophie. I am, of course, referring to the results of having opened a book of betting. Otherwise, why do you think I'm sitting here with a ledger perched on me knees?"

"Go on, then. You deliberately kept me in suspense, and now berate me for a simple and entirely defensible remark."

"Have you finished?"

"Yes."

"Then allow me to continue. All the bets were recorded in this ledger. I cannot divulge individual wagers or the persons placing them because I am duty bound to keep such information in the strictest confidence. Neither can I give you totals, save for one. I have audited Hawkins' work and can pronounce it one hundred percent accurate."

She turned several pages, then looked up. "Betting was brisk and, at times, heavy. When the result came in, it was deemed fair. After reading the account in the newspaper and having been provided with your supplementary report, the adjudicating committee unanimously agreed to the pay out being made at the earliest opportunity rather than waiting for a verdict at the trial. The consensus was that, with Fitch's admission of guilt, there was no need for delay."

"May I ask a question?"

"What is it?"

"If she had denied the charges, and it had proceeded to trial, what would have happened if she were acquitted?"

"The committee was tasked with either authorizing the pay out or returning the bets. It would have waited upon the verdict to decide how to act."

"Are you on the committee?"

"Naturally."

"Is Hawkins?"

"No. That's enough questions or I won't tell you any more."

Sophie put up her hands in mock surrender.

"The winning bettors have already been paid. There were no expenses deducted, and so the Alexandra Gardens Stakes was left with a surplus."

"Good old Hawkins," said Sophie.

"The man excelled himself. So I gave him a hundred out of the balance."

"Good grief, how large is this surplus?"

"In round figures, £870 remains."

"How much!?"

"I'm taking fifty, because it was my idea. I'll give you one hundred and twenty to be distributed among your staff, and the remaining seven hundred is yours."

"Oh, you can't do that, Auntie."

"You're always so difficult. Why not?"

"I don't do this work for money, although some is necessary because of all the expenses. However, I've been paid for all of that. Auntie, it's so generous and lovely of you to think of doing this, and I agree to the money for the staff, but I can't possibly accept seven hundred for myself."

"Just how I thought you would answer." Aunt Bessie smiled. "What shall I do with it, then?"

"I don't know."

"Then how about this? You will take fifty pounds, as I have, and I insist you do so because that's fair. Now the rest... Surely, out of the people you met and who were involved in the case, there is someone who might need assistance."

"There is, actually. Miss Boddington, the woman who was attacked — she needs both medical help and the services of an alienist. Mrs Murray, her neighbour, could help arrange those… Um, there's another matter, but I'm not at liberty to say what it is."

"If you wish to help this person, you'll have to spit it out."

"Should I do so, the matter must be handled most delicately."

"Interestin'… Who is it?"

"Archie."

"In what way?"

"When he marries Victoria, they'll need a house."

"Aha! I am ahead of you there. I have already decided to buy him a house as a wedding gift."

"Have you! What a darling you are!" She ran over and kissed her aunt. "Talk to him soon, though, because he's seen a place, and he's very keen on it. That's all I can really say about that."

"A good job you told me. I'll corner him tomorrow and this conversation *never* took place." She smiled and closed the ledger. "What about the balance?"

"There are a lot of poor people in desperate circumstances."

"Then we know exactly what to do. There are many efficient charities who could use the money."

"Women and children, I think."

"Then that's settled. I'll set aside a hundred pounds for Miss Boddington, and the rest goes to charity for the relief of the poor. Might we have a sherry, now that our consciences are clear?"

At Aunt Bessie's mention of having a clear conscience, Sophie found herself regretting how matters had got out of hand with her friend Inspector Morton. She fervently hoped he would not suffer too much or too long in his disappointment.

It would be some months later, towards the end of a hot and sticky August, that a turning point would come for Inspector Morton. One day he decided he would leave for work earlier than usual. His reasons for doing so were that it would be cooler and he might actually get a seat on the bus for once — upstairs — where he could relax and smoke. It was a short walk to the bus stop, and he was warm by the time he arrived. The queue was short and the bus he wanted arrived two minutes later. Things were looking up.

"Room inside only," said the conductor, his arm barring the stairs because passengers often did not listen to what they were told.

Morton found an aisle seat next to a nurse in her twenties.

"Sorry, is my bag in the way?" asked the nurse. She moved it onto her lap.

"No, no, not at all," said Morton airily, taking his seat. After a few seconds, he said, "You must be going to St. Thomas's."

"I am. My uniform gives me away, of course."

For some reason, and to this very day Morton has not a clue as to what prompted him to speak so to a young lady on a crowded bus, he said, "You'll never guess what I do for a living."

She looked at him. He looked at her.

"Well... I'm probably wrong, but I'd say you were a policeman."

"However did you guess that...? I'm astounded."

They were both amazed and laughed. They continued talking about this and that, but from that day on, Morton always caught the earlier bus, because Annie saved a seat for him.

---

But now it was the morning of Monday 18th of April, 1921, and the excitement of the Fitch case at the beginning of the month was dying down. The agency was busy. In her office, Sophie had just put away what was probably the most singular letter she had ever received. It had arrived that morning and the envelope bore a Whitehall postmark. The note was written in green ink, and simply said,

B,
Well done, and many thanks.

C.

P.S. We will meet some day.

Archie had mentioned once that the head of the Secret Service, Mansfield Cumming-Smith, wrote in green ink and signed his letters 'C'. He was C. and she was B. Now what was it he thanked her for? He did not write because she let the HO agents into number seven. Neither was it for her trailing of Dr. Teplov, because any agent could have done that. She decided it must be because of the two Russians. This meant they had been recruited and were now working for the British Government. She was supremely happy for Kuritsyn and Razov. She smiled to herself and continued to do so while she settled down to work.

Old Fury, as the other typists called her, knocked on Sophie's office door.

"Come in," called Sophie, now working on a newspaper advertisement.

"Sorry to trouble you, Miss King," said Miss Jones. She was called Old Fury because she was the most ferocious stenographer in London, and cranked out sheet after typewritten sheet at a rate that most other typists could only dream about.

"Yes, what is it, Miss Jones?"

"Well, you might think it rather impertinent of me but, unless you can answer a question, I think it could start interfering with my work." The office manageress stood in front of the desk.

"Oh, we don't want that. Your work is invaluable."

"Thank you, Miss Burgoyne."

"What is the question?" As soon as she asked, an alarming thought occurred to her — *She's guessed.*

"I can't help but notice certain things going on in the office."

Sophie stared. *Here it comes.*

"Forgive my rudeness, but do you do police work?"

"Yes,"

"Ahh, I thought as much. Thank you very much, Miss Burgoyne. Sorry to trouble you." Miss Jones gave Sophie one of her extremely rare smiles.

"Oh, it was no trouble. I'm not supposed to tell anyone, otherwise I would have informed you."

"It's none of my business, really, and I shall never breathe a word of it to another soul. I'll get back to work, if I may?"

"Of course... And if anything bothers you in the future, please come and talk to me about it."

"That's very kind."

She left, shutting the door after her.

Sophie decided something miraculous had just occurred. Then she heard a gentleman's voice outside.

"Miss Jones. How wonderful to see you again! Do you know you're an absolute lifesaver?"

"Mr Broadbent-Wicks..., I hardly recognized you."

"Don't let the scruffiness bother you. I'm still the same old johnny underneath it all, don't you know?"

"Oh... What do you mean by lifesaver?" It was hard to say why, but Miss Jones positively liked Douglas Broadbent-Wicks. They were about as polar opposite as two humans can be, and yet, for some reason, they esteemed each other.

"That tip you gave me about digs in Dalston, what? I took your advice. I love Dalston. Couldn't be happier."

"I am so glad for you. You must excuse me, I have work to do."

"Of course, you have, and what a marvellous typist you are, banging out a veritable blizzard of the jolly old pages. And don't forget, if you have any trouble with your machine, send for me and I'll fix it."

"That's too kind of you, Mr Broadbent-Wicks."

"Not at all," he replied.

The next thing Sophie heard was a soft tap on her door. Then he breezed in, dressed in clothes that had seen better days, sporting a rather greasy flat cap pushed far back on his head and a grubby looking small scarf knotted around his throat.

After the initial shock of his appearance and they had concluded the usual preliminaries, Sophie asked,

"Why are you growing a beard?"

"Had to, Miss Burgoyne. Window cleaning with Alfie is mostly conducted in working-class areas. You cannot imagine the trouble I've been getting into."

Sophie did not doubt for a moment that there had been trouble of some description.

"As soon as I opened my mouth, this is on the first day, mind you, they began calling me The Toff. I don't care for that word, it's rather stupid, but I'm stuck with it. Now that I've heard it so often, I've become used to the wretched moniker. Well, matters deteriorated from there. On one round, there are quite a few women customers very close together. One of them, and I refuse to name her, said I had a baby face. From then on, those ladies started calling me Baby Toff. *Well*, I couldn't put up with *that*. Despite my protestations, they insisted on saying it at every opportunity. I was at my wits' end, particularly after the nameless lady pinched my cheek and gave it a familiar shake, saying 'Isn't 'e lovely?' That was *absolutely* the last straw. I had to do *something*, so I decided to grow a beard... Seven days' growth so far. What do you think?"

Talking to Broadbent-Wicks was always the same for Sophie. Nothing went in a straight line and it sometimes felt awkward.

"I think it needs more time," said Sophie. She was far from being against beards, but thought his was awful.

"Yes, it does. But it's already done its job this morning. The nameless lady doesn't like it and kept her hands to herself."

"I'm relieved to hear that. Um, is there a reason for your visit?"

"Right to the point, Miss Burgoyne. That's what I like about you. Now, although I've received a few footman jobs from Burgoyne's beautiful agency, the work seems to have dropped off in the last little while."

"I must give others a chance, you know. And although we are busy, sometimes the temporary work is such that there's no call for a footman. Increasingly, maids are sought to serve at dinners."

"Yes, yes, I thought it was something like that. Totally understandable and I simply have to put up with it."

"Then, let me reassure you. We are about to get busier still, so there will be work for you."

"That's excellent, absolutely super." He paused and became serious for a moment. "I'm also here because what I'm *really* interested in is the *other* work." He nodded significantly. "Window cleaning keeps the wolf from the door, but not much else. I went over my accounts, which took about ten seconds. Ha-ha! Then realized I needed more cash. Therefore, I wondered if you had anything available," he glanced towards the door, then turned back to whisper, "in the spying line."

"Don't say that word again."

"Of course, I won't."

"That work is not under my control. I don't know when the next, um, extraordinary placement will come in."

"You can't just whistle them up then? Oh, that's such a pity."

"All I can say is that if something comes along, I will bear you in mind."

"Miss Burgoyne, you are *wonderful!*"

"Please don't be so effusive."

"Consider it done... I only came to give you the nudge that I'm alive and kicking. I'll get out of your hair now."

"Thank you for coming."

"Don't mention it, Miss Burgoyne. Toodle-oo."

He left, but not without her hearing him say to Elizabeth on his way out, "Let me tell you something, it's always such a real delight to see you."

Sophie could imagine Elizabeth's blush and confusion.

Returning to her work, she found her thoughts wandered elsewhere. A thought had occurred, and she explored it. Sophie imagined that there was an invisible fabric to life wherein haphazard meetings occurred. One type of strand, hers, met another type of strand, the one belonging to Mr Broadbent-Wicks. The consequence of such an intersection was a distortion or a tear in the fabric. She had a foreboding that something was about to happen. Dismissing the notion that his appearance could be a harbinger of anything, she applied herself to the work before her.

An hour later, the telephone on her desk rang, and she jumped ever so slightly. Sophie knew, just knew, before she picked up the receiver, that it would be Archie or Superintendent Penrose.

"Hello, Miss Burgoyne?" She heard the soft Somerset tones of Superintendent Penrose.

"Good morning, Inspector." Everyone called him Inspector, and he preferred it that way.

"Got a pencil handy?"

"Yes," said Sophie.

"Right. Do you remember that family feud business, where one side hosts the annual ball, then t'other does?"

"I do."

"Well, as if it weren't brimful with difficulty enough already, it's been made more complicated"

"Oh, in what way?"

"I'm in a bit of a hurry at present, so I can't explain everything now, but you need to know how it affects you. They've moved the date to May, for one thing. And instead of just the ball and a day-long affair, they've made it three days. Then also there will be a foreign party present."

"Should I expect to hear from someone else?" She referred to Archie Drysdale.

"That's right. Now here's the thing. The family hosting this social event has a lot of young people in it, so bear that in mind when selecting your staff. The requirements are, at present, three maids and a footman. I'm hoping I know who the three maids will be, but the footman should be a youngish chap, active and adaptable, because the situation demands it. Do you have a chap like that?"

Sophie hesitated. A vision of Douglas Broadbent-Wicks materialized in her mind as though he stood before her in the room. She was on the spot, and there was only one person on her books close enough to the type Penrose wanted.

Broadbent-Wicks had produced his effect in the fabric, after all.

"Yes," she said, consciously keeping the uncertainty she felt from her voice.

"Good. In some ways, I mean from a police point of view, this new set of circumstances is better than before. You'll have more time to collect information. But the foreign party? Bless us, that's another headache entirely."

"If you could give me the dates, please, Inspector, I will reserve the appropriate staff for the event." She took her special journal from a drawer. Penrose gave her the dates, and she pencilled them in.

# Also By G J Bellamy

If you have enjoyed this book, please help by leaving a good review. It is greatly appreciated.

### SOPHIE BURGOYNE SERIES
Secret Agency
Lady Holme
Dredemere Castle
Chertsey Park
Primrose Hill
An Old Affair
Amazon US: https://www.amazon.com/dp/B0D3TQPKTG
Amazon UK: https://www.amazon.co.uk/dp/B0D3TQPKTG
An Old Affair

---

### BRENT UMBER SERIES
Death between the Vines
Death in a Restaurant
Death of a Detective
Death at Hill Hall
Death on the Slopes
Death of a Narcissist